While We're Far Apart

WHILE WE'RE FAR APART

LYNN AUSTIN

BETHANYHOUSE
MINNEAPOLIS, MINNESOTA

Cover design by Jennifer Parker
Cover photography by Susan Fox/Trevillion Images

Scripture quotations identified NIV are from the HOLY BIBLE, NEW INTERNATIONAL VERSION.® Copyright © 1973, 1978, 1984 by International Bible Society. Used by permission of Zondervan Publishing House. All rights reserved.

Published by Bethany House Publishers
11400 Hampshire Avenue South
Bloomington, Minnesota 55438

Bethany House Publishers is a division of
Baker Publishing Group, Grand Rapids, Michigan.

Printed in the United States of America

Library of Congress Cataloging-in-Publication Data

Austin, Lynn N.
    While we're far apart / Lynn Austin.
        p.   cm.
    ISBN 978-0-7642-0813-3 (alk. paper) — ISBN 978-0-7642-0497-5 (pbk.)   1. Landlord and tenant—Fiction.   2. Brooklyn (New York, N.Y.)—Fiction.   3. World War, 1939–1945—Fiction.   I. Title.
    PS3551.U839W48   2010
    813'.54—dc22

                                                                      2010015877

In keeping with biblical principles of creation stewardship, Baker Publishing Group advocates the responsible use of our natural resources. As a member of the Green Press Initiative, our company uses recycled paper when possible. The text paper of this book is comprised of 30% post-consumer waste.

green press INITIATIVE

To my mom, Virginia,
a WWII nurse who saved all of her scrapbooks for me.

To my dad, Paul,
who served in the U.S. Navy in the Pacific during WWII.

And to Yaacov and Miriam,
who survived the holocaust in Hungary
and became part of our family.

Thank you for your legacy of courage and faith.

Books by

Lynn Austin

FROM BETHANY HOUSE PUBLISHERS

All She Ever Wanted

Eve's Daughters

Hidden Places

A Proper Pursuit

Though Waters Roar

Until We Reach Home

While We're Far Apart

Wings of Refuge

A Woman's Place

REFINER'S FIRE

Candle in the Darkness

Fire by Night

Light to My Path

CHRONICLES OF THE KINGS

Gods & Kings

Song of Redemption

Strength of His Hand

Faith of My Father

Among the Gods

LYNN AUSTIN is a six-time Christy Award winner for her historical novels *Hidden Places, Candle in the Darkness, Fire by Night, A Proper Pursuit, Until We Reach Home,* and *Though Waters Roar.* In addition to writing, Lynn is a popular speaker at conferences, retreats, and various church and school events. She and her husband have three children and make their home in Illinois.

*May the Lord keep watch between you and
me when we are away from each other.*
Genesis 31:49 NIV

CHAPTER I

BROOKLYN, NEW YORK
SEPTEMBER 1943

ESTHER'S FATHER HALTED the lazy swaying of the porch swing. "Listen," he said. "There's something I need to tell all of you." The darkness in his voice made Esther's skin prickle. He had used the same phrase, the same tone, when he'd told her that Mama had gone to live up in heaven.

"I've been thinking . . ." He paused, kneading his forehead as if his head hurt. He looked so sad. Esther wished she knew how to make him smile again.

They had walked to Grandma Shaffer's house for lunch after church, and Daddy had barely spoken all afternoon. But that wasn't unusual. Grandma had filled the long silences with news about Uncle Steve, who was fighting the Japanese, and Uncle Joe, who was being shipped off to North Africa soon. Grandma's next-door neighbor, Penny Goodrich, had come over to sit on the porch, too, and they had all watched Esther's brother, Peter, chase Grandma's dog around the backyard. It had been such a pleasant afternoon—until now.

Daddy cleared his throat. "I've . . . um . . . I've made a decision."

He paused once again, and the air went still as if the breeze had hushed to listen. Woofer finally stopped barking, and even the traffic on Brooklyn Boulevard a few blocks away seemed to have halted.

"What is it, Eddie?" Grandma asked. "You look so serious. You feeling all right?"

"I'm going to enlist, Ma."

"What?"

"I said, I'm going to enlist in the army." He spoke louder this time because Grandma was hard of hearing, but Esther could tell that she had heard him plain enough the first time.

Esther hugged her skinny arms to her chest, feeling a chill. At age twelve, she was old enough to know exactly what "enlist" meant. She listened to the news reports about the war on the radio every night. She watched the newsreels at Loew's Brooklyn Theater before the Saturday matinee started. Oh yes. She knew it meant that her daddy would go far away like her two uncles had—and that he might never come back. The afternoon felt ten degrees colder, as if the sun had gone behind a cloud.

"Saints above, Eddie!" Grandma shouted. "Are you out of your mind? You can't enlist! You have two children to think about. Who's going to take care of them?"

"Well . . . that's what we need to talk about. I was hoping you would. You said if I ever needed anything . . ."

"Are you crazy? What in the world are you thinking? . . . How on earth . . . ?"

"The war can't last forever. I'll be back."

Grandma gave his shoulder a shove. "And what if you don't come back? Huh? What then? What if you end up at the bottom of the Pacific Ocean like Millie Barker's son? Then what? You want these poor children to be orphans?"

Esther understood the finality of death. She knew she would never see Mama again until she died and went to heaven herself. She also knew that lots of men were being killed in the war. Grandma had hung a little flag in her window with two stars on it, one for Uncle Joe and one for Uncle Steve, and she had explained to Esther why

Mrs. Barker across the street now had a flag in her window with a gold star.

Esther wanted to cry and beg Daddy not to go, but she didn't want to make him angry. The love they shared felt as fragile as spider webs, and Esther was never quite certain that she had his attention, let alone his affection. Sometimes it seemed as though Daddy wasn't home even when he was. She decided to let Grandma argue with him.

"Nothing's going to happen to me, Ma. I'll be in the army, on land."

"You don't think soldiers are dying in the army, too? On land?"

"Listen, I was hoping Esther and Peter could live here with you until I get back."

Grandma stared at Daddy with her mouth open as if she was about to take a bite out of something. Esther tried to imagine living here, and it made her stomach hurt. Grandma had so many rules like "don't leave the door open or the dog will get out," and "don't bother my parakeet," and "don't make noise because it will disturb the next-door neighbors," and "don't touch my stuff"—which lay heaped in piles everywhere. Esther didn't mind visiting on Sunday, but by the time she and Daddy and Peter boarded the crosstown bus for home, she always felt as though she had been holding her breath for three hours.

"How can they live here?" Grandma asked Daddy. "What about school? Did you consider that? They would have to change to a different school if they lived with me. Besides, there's no room for them in this house."

"What do you mean there's no room? You and Pop raised three boys here." But Esther had always wondered how Daddy and her uncles had ever fit. Grandma kept things that most people threw into the trash—piles and piles of things that made it hard to move around from room to room.

"That was years ago, Eddie. Your bunk beds are long gone, and I'm using that room for my own things now. I wouldn't know where to begin to clear everything out. And what would I do with it all?"

"You could always move into our apartment."

"What about my dog, huh? And my bird? They don't allow

pets where you live. Besides, your apartment has too many stairs to climb."

"Ma, listen—"

"No, you listen. I love Peter and Esther, you know I do. . . ." Grandma tossed the comment in Esther's direction like a foul ball at a baseball game. It sounded great when it smacked against the bat, but in the end, it didn't count for anything.

"But saints above, Eddie, I'm too old to raise children! Helping with homework and worrying about measles and chicken pox . . . It's too much! They would be too much for me to handle all day and all night. Let somebody else fight the Nazis. You're thirty-three years old, for heaven's sake. You have responsibilities here at home."

Esther looked up at Daddy to see if Grandma's arguments had convinced him, but the expression she saw on his face sent another chill through her. His lips had turned white and he seemed to be holding his breath. Grandma must have noticed it, too. "What? What's wrong?" she asked him.

"It's too late. I already enlisted."

"You—what!" Grandma exploded like a shaken soda bottle, reaching out to cuff Daddy's ear as if he were a little boy. "Why would you do such a stupid thing? Of all the irresponsible . . . idiotic . . ."

"Listen to me, Ma. I can't go on the way I have been. I just can't." His voice sounded as cold and frosty as a metal ice cube tray, straight out of the freezer. "There are too many reminders of her. Too many things that will never be the same. Rachel is everywhere in that apartment—and yet she isn't."

"Then get another apartment, for crying out loud. You don't have to go off and fight a war if you need a change. Start all over again someplace else. New York is a big city, you know. Brooklyn has plenty of other apartments for rent. Your children need you."

Daddy rubbed his ear where Grandma had cuffed him. "I'm no use to them, Ma. I'm not even a good father, let alone a good mother."

Esther tried to speak, but her chest hurt the way it had after she fell off the monkey bars at school. She couldn't draw a breath. She wanted to tell him he *was* a good father. He fixed their meals and listened to ball games on the radio with them at night. He packed their lunch boxes for school every day and helped them study for spelling tests and took them to church on Sunday. The house did seem much too quiet, and he never sang or played the piano the way Mama used to do. And he didn't tell bedtime stories about people in the Bible, either. They ate a lot of canned soup instead of meat and potatoes, but that didn't matter to Esther. She just wanted Daddy to stay with them in their own apartment, not go away to war and leave them with Grandma.

She put her hand on his arm as she searched for something to say, but when he turned to her and she saw tears in his eyes, she couldn't speak. What if she said the wrong thing and he started crying during the night like he did right after Mama died? Esther remembered the terrible, helpless feeling it gave her to hear her father weeping, especially when she couldn't stop crying herself and there was no one in the whole world to comfort either one of them. Daddy had done his best to console her, but his embraces felt brief and stiff as if he was afraid Esther would break if he hugged her too hard. He was tall and lean, and his callused hands were stained with grease from repairing cars all day. Mama had been soft and warm, and she would hold Esther in her arms for a long, long time.

"Don't do it, Eddie. Please," Grandma begged. "Think of your children. Go down there tomorrow and tell the army you changed your mind."

"I can't. It's too late." He spoke so softly that Esther thought she might have imagined it. For sure Grandma hadn't heard him. But then he cleared his throat and said in a louder voice, "I already resigned from my job. I leave for basic training in two weeks."

His words gave Esther the same empty, floating feeling she'd had after Mama died, as if she were a fluff of dandelion, no longer tethered to the earth. What was going to happen to her? How would she keep from sailing away on the slightest breath of wind?

"Saints above, Eddie! Two weeks? How could you do such a stupid thing?"

Peter must have heard Grandma yelling because he stopped running around the backyard with Woofer and hurried over to the porch. He was three years younger than Esther and as thin as a stick figure—not at all like most rough-and-tumble boys his age. His hair was the same shiny auburn color that Mama's had been. Esther could always look at Peter when she needed to remember. He stumbled up the porch steps, his cheeks flushed, his hair sweaty, and looked from one of them to the next. "What happened?"

Daddy didn't seem to hear him. "I have to do this, Ma. Don't you see?"

"No. I most certainly do not. How can you do this to your children? After everything they've been through? Are you crazy?"

"No . . . but I might go crazy if I stay here much longer."

"I have nothing more to say to you." Grandma struggled out of her rocking chair and stormed into the house, slamming the screen door—something she yelled at Esther and Peter for doing. The chair continued to rock after she abandoned it, and Esther reached across Daddy's lap to make it stop. Mrs. Mendel from the apartment downstairs used to say it was bad luck for a chair to rock with nobody in it—and they didn't need any more bad luck, that's for sure. Again, an eerie silence settled over the backyard. Then Penny Goodrich, Grandma's next-door neighbor, broke the silence.

"Eddie?"

"Yeah?"

"I'll watch them for you."

Esther had forgotten that Penny was even there. Everyone had forgotten her. But that's the way Penny was—so quiet and unimportant that you could look right at her and never see her. Esther had no idea why Penny always showed up at Grandma's house on Sunday afternoons when they came to visit. She was just one of those nosy neighbors with no life of her own, who watched other people's lives as if watching a movie.

Penny was younger than Daddy but looked like she was old enough to get married. Daddy said that she had lived with her parents on the other half of Grandma's duplex since he was a boy and Penny was a baby. Mr. and Mrs. Goodrich must have been very old when Penny was born—like Sarah and Abraham in the Bible—because they were ancient now, even older than Grandma was. They hardly ever came outside to sit on their back porch, and they never used their half of the tiny backyard. Daddy said he used to tease Penny a lot when they were kids because she was such a little pest. Now he turned to look at her as if he, too, had forgotten she was there.

"What did you say, Penny?"

"I'll take care of your kids for you. I mean, I wish you weren't going off to war because it's so dangerous and everything, but I could move into your apartment with them so they wouldn't have to change schools." Daddy stared at her in surprise, but he didn't reply. "I know I've never been a real mother or anything," Penny continued, "but I can cook and take care of a house and everything."

"What about your job? Where do you work again?"

"I sell tickets over at the bus station." She gestured over her shoulder with her thumb. "But you could help me figure out how to get there from your apartment every day, couldn't you? Which bus to take?"

"Don't your parents need you here?"

"Oh, they can manage without me," she said with a wave of her hand. "Mother always says how much I get on her nerves. Besides, I could check on them after work and on the weekends. They'd be okay."

Esther saw the direction this conversation was going, and she didn't like it at all. She had to speak up and put a stop to the idea before she ended up with Daddy far away and Penny Goodrich living in their apartment. Penny was nice enough, always bringing candy and gum and things for her and Peter, but something about her annoyed Esther. She felt in her pocket for the red- and white-striped peppermint that Penny had given her today. Esther had told her, "No, thank you," but Penny had pushed the candy into her hand anyway, saying, "Oh, go on and have one. Your father won't mind."

Grandma said that whenever she tried to give something back to Penny in order to even the score, Penny would do twice as much for her the next time. *If you told her you liked her shoes,* Grandma once said, *"Penny would take them right off, then and there, and shove them into your hands and not take no for an answer."* Esther would never want Penny's clothes. She dressed like an old woman in baggy housedresses and patterned aprons and thick-soled shoes.

"I could still pick up groceries for my folks every week," Penny was saying, "and do their washing and everything while I'm here—and your kids could visit their grandma."

"That sounds like a lot of work for you," Daddy said.

"Oh, it's okay, I don't mind. I get real lonely sometimes, you know? It would be nice to do something different for a change."

"I just don't understand why Ma won't help me."

"Maybe it's because your brothers are already fighting and you're all she has left. She's probably afraid of losing all three of you, and I don't blame her, do you?"

"I probably won't even get to fight. The army needs mechanics to keep their jeeps running. They might teach me how to fix tanks, they said. I'd like to try airplane engines, too."

"That would be nice. And you'd be safe, right?"

"It's just that I need to get away, Penny. There are too many reminders around here and . . . and I just can't take it anymore. Why can't Ma understand that?"

"Poor Eddie. I understand. It must be so hard for you." Penny laid her hand on top of his. He looked down at it in surprise, then up at her. She reminded Esther of Grandma's cocker spaniel with her wide, sad eyes and her head tilted to one side.

"You would really do it?" Daddy asked. "You'd move in and take care of the kids for me while I'm away?"

"Of course I would. I'd love to help you."

Esther watched him consider the idea. She wanted to elbow Daddy in the ribs and say, *Hey! What about me? Why aren't you asking what I think?* But something heavy pushed down on her chest again, making it hard to breathe. "Daddy?" she said softly.

"You probably wouldn't need to live there for very long," he continued. "I'm sure Ma will change her mind and let the kids move in with her once she gets used to the idea."

"Daddy?" Esther spoke louder this time.

"And I know you'd still help Ma out anytime she needed it, wouldn't you? Like if she needed a break?"

"Of course. We'll manage just fine. You'll see."

Panic squeezed Esther's ribs. This arrangement was really going to happen, and she didn't know how to stop it. She didn't want Daddy to go away—and she certainly didn't want boring Penny Goodrich to move in with them and take Mama's place. "Daddy!"

"Yes, doll?" He answered absently, gazing out at the tiny yard, not at her. He took her hand in his and gently caressed it with his thumb, but she knew he wasn't really listening to her. It was as if he were already on board a ship with Uncle Joe or Uncle Steve, sailing miles and miles away.

Esther hesitated to speak her mind, afraid that if she said what she really wanted to say, Daddy would get mad and let go of her hand. And she didn't want to do anything to make him let go.

"Never mind," she mumbled.

Because that was the mistake she had made with Mama. Esther had let go of her hand, thinking she was much too grown-up to hold hands. And now she would never hold Mama's hand again.

CHAPTER 2

PENNY GOODRICH KNEW she had just been given a second chance. Eddie Shaffer's wife had died more than a year ago, and that was a terrible tragedy. But now he needed another wife and a mother for his two children, and Penny wanted the job. Eddie would fall in love with *her* this time. She would make sure of it.

Penny couldn't remember a time in her life when she hadn't been in love with the tall, golden-haired boy next door. Even as a little girl, she had watched him playing baseball in the street with his brothers, and she had loved him. She had wished she could join in those games and hit home runs for him so he would love her in return, but her mother wouldn't allow it. *"You're too clumsy, Penny. You can't play with those big kids. You'll get hurt. Besides, they don't want someone like you on their team."*

On warm summer evenings, Eddie and the other kids would play hide-and-seek or kick the can, and Penny would watch from her front stoop. His blond hair would look yellowish-green beneath the streetlight and he would shout, "Here I come, ready or not," before dashing off to search for the others. She longed to hide in the bushes like the other kids and squeal with excitement when Eddie finally found her. But Mother said it was too dangerous for someone like her to run around after dark. *"You never know who could be hiding in the bushes, waiting to grab you. The world is filled with bad people, whether you have sense enough to realize it or not."*

When she was finally old enough to go to school, Penny wanted to tag along behind Eddie and his brothers as they shuffled through the autumn leaves or tromped through the mounds of snow that the plows left behind, but Penny's mother always walked to school with her instead. *"You wouldn't know enough to pay attention to the traffic. You have no sense at all. You would get run over by a car the first time you tried to cross the street."*

Penny wasn't allowed to go to Eddie's ball games in high school and watch him play, because she wasn't like the other girls. Penny's parents were older than everyone else's parents, and her sister, Hazel, who was seventeen years older, had left home before Penny was old enough to remember her. Penny would sometimes watch Eddie from a distance, and if he dropped a piece of paper or a gum wrapper she would pick it up and put it in the shoebox she kept in her closet. She used to write his name in her notebook while daydreaming in class, filling page after page with *I love Eddie* and *Eddie and Penny* with little hearts drawn around their names.

Penny remembered crying her eyes out when Mrs. Shaffer told her that Eddie was getting married. She and her parents had been invited to his wedding luncheon in the backyard, but Penny had been too heartsick to eat any cake. Instead, she had tucked her piece of cake beneath her pillow that night because it was supposed to make you dream of the man you would marry. And she had dreamed of Eddie, just as she had on so many other nights. But she had thrown the smashed cake into the garbage the next morning, convinced that her dream could never come true.

And now it might.

Eddie needed her help. Penny would be the new Mrs. Edward Shaffer. Of course, she would have to wait until the war ended and he came home again. But she would write long letters to him every single day while he was away, telling him news from home, and by the time the war was over, his apartment would be her home and she already would be like a mother to his two children.

Excitement made her cheeks feel warm as she sat beside him on the back porch, watching him consider her plan. If he agreed, she just might run around the yard for joy the way Woofer did when she chased her ball.

"It's very nice of you to offer," Eddie said. "I'll go inside and talk to Ma about it."

Penny's hand slid off his as he rose to his feet. "Tell your mother that it's really okay if she can't take the kids. Tell her I'll be happy to watch them."

He nodded and disappeared inside where his mother had gone after storming off. To be honest, Penny didn't know how those two kids would ever fit into Mrs. Shaffer's house unless she got rid of the stuff piled everywhere. Penny had never looked inside the two bedrooms, but if they were anything like the front rooms, there wouldn't even be a place for those two kids to sit down, much less go to sleep. Every square inch of space in the living room and kitchen and eating area was jam-packed with towering stacks of newspapers and old magazines and cardboard boxes full of worn-out clothing, leaving only a narrow pathway to walk between. Penny worried sometimes that Mrs. Shaffer's half of the duplex would catch on fire and she and her parents would burn to death, too, living on the other side the way they did. Good thing her parents didn't know what Mrs. Shaffer's half looked like. They worried enough as it was.

The screen door slapped shut as Eddie went inside, leaving Penny alone with the two kids. They were a lot quieter than most kids were, and she wasn't very good at conversation.

"Hey, do you guys like ice cream?" she finally said. "Sometimes the truck comes around on Sunday afternoon. If your father says it's okay, I'll buy you some. Or maybe we could walk to the corner store and get some. I'll treat. Would you like that?"

The girl shook her head and said, "No, thank you." She had hair just like Eddie's, all thick and blond and curly. The boy didn't seem to hear Penny as he continued to stare at the back door, where his grandmother and now his father had disappeared. The kid stood so still that he could have been sleeping with his eyes open.

"What's your very favorite kind of treat?" Penny asked. "I'll bet it's chocolate ice cream, right? Most people say that's their favorite, but I just love a grape Popsicle, don't you? But I'll let you get whatever kind you want—"

"No, thank you," Esther said again.

Penny could have kicked herself for getting off on the wrong foot with Eddie's kids. Sometimes she tried too hard and ended up ruining things for herself. Her mother always said she didn't have the good sense that God gave a green bean. Thankfully, the back door opened again and Eddie came out, his face creased in a frown.

"Can we go home now, Daddy?" Esther asked. She was twelve. The boy was named Aaron Peter but they called him Peter. He was nine. Penny knew everything about them because Mrs. Shaffer had told her every single detail of their lives since the day they'd been born.

"We'll go home in a minute, doll," Eddie replied. "Listen, Penny . . . I think Ma is going to need some more time to get used to the idea. How about if we come over on Friday night so we can talk some more?"

"Sure! I could make dinner for you and—"

"That's not necessary. We'll come by after supper. And if Ma hasn't changed her mind by then . . . well, I may have to take you up on your offer."

"That's okay, Eddie, honest it is. I really meant it when I said I'd take care of them for you."

"It's just that I was so sure Ma would help me out, and so I went ahead and signed up for the army, and now . . ."

"It'll all work out, you'll see."

Penny walked with them to the corner and waited with them until the bus came. Then she hurried home to her half of the duplex to tell her parents the news. They were sitting in their usual chairs in the gloomy front room, listening to a radio program with the curtains drawn. They always kept the curtains closed even in the daytime to make sure that strangers couldn't look inside—not that there was much to see. Penny waited to speak until an advertisement for Lux soap came on. Her father hated it when she interrupted his programs.

"Hey, guess what? I was over next door, talking to Eddie Shaffer, and—"

"You shouldn't hang around over there so much," Mother said. "You'll make a nuisance of yourself. Why can't you stay home where you belong?"

"Mrs. Shaffer doesn't mind. Anyway, Eddie just signed up for the army like his brothers did, and he asked his mother to watch his two kids for him. His mother doesn't think she can take care of them, so I told Eddie that I'd be glad to baby-sit for them while he's away."

"You did what?" Mother stared at Penny as if she had just told her she'd robbed a bank. Penny had seen other mothers gaze at their children with love brimming in their eyes, and she wished, just once, that her mother would look at her that way. Her parents had been old when she was born, and she wondered if they had resented being burdened with a baby at such a late age, especially after they'd already raised a daughter.

"I told Eddie that I would watch his kids—"

"Don't be ridiculous. You don't know the first thing about raising children. Besides, I'm sure he can get a hardship exemption since his children don't have a mother."

"Eddie didn't get drafted; he volunteered to go." Penny understood exactly how he felt. She longed to start a new life in a new place, too, but what could she do? She didn't make enough money at the bus company to afford an apartment of her own. And she didn't have any friends who would share a place with her. If she had become a nurse after high school like she'd wanted to, she could have afforded her own place, but Mother had said she wasn't smart enough to go to nursing school. *You need good grades to be a nurse and your grades are only average.*

Penny knew she was ordinary and average. Eddie's first wife, Rachel, had been pretty and smart and full of life. She had beautiful chestnut-colored hair and the tiniest waist that Penny had ever seen. Eddie could probably wrap his big, strong hands right around her waist with his fingers touching. No wonder he had loved her.

"You should have seen how grateful Eddie was when I said I would help him out."

"In the first place," her father said, joining the conversation, "I think it's a terrible idea for him to leave his children. If anything happens to him, they'll have nobody."

"They'll have me. I'll love them and take care of them."

"And in the second place, what business is it of yours to stick your nose into this? Huh?"

"You don't know the first thing about running your own home or taking care of children," Mother added. "What if something happened to one of them and they got sick? You wouldn't have any idea what to do."

"And what about your job?" Father said. "You can't walk to work from where he lives, you know."

"Eddie's going to show me which bus to take."

"A bus?" Mother repeated the word as if Penny had told her she would be riding to work on an elephant. "All that way? All by yourself? This city isn't safe for a girl like you to be running around on your own. You've never been out in the world, Penny. You can't even take care of yourself, let alone two motherless children."

They were doing it to her again—making her feel stupid. Every time Penny would start to think that maybe she really wasn't so dumb, her parents would convince her that she was.

"And another thing," Father said. "You've never handled money before. How are you going to pay the rent and take care of all the household bills? You'll make a mess of it. You had a panic attack when the grocer gave you the wrong change that time, remember?"

"That was a long time ago, Dad. I was twelve. And I handle money and make change all the time at work." But despite her words, Penny felt her courage dripping away like ice cream on an August afternoon. If she didn't stand up for herself, then her chances of marrying Eddie Shaffer would melt away, too. She couldn't bear to lose him a second time.

"You know that he lives over there in the Jewish part of Brooklyn, don't you?" Father said. "His mother told me there's a synagogue right across the street from his apartment."

"Your father's right. And they're the kind of Jews that have beards and wear those funny black hats. One of them lives in the apartment right downstairs from Ed's family."

Penny felt another trickle of fear. Her parents hated Jewish people and had always talked about them the way other parents talked about the boogey man. Sometimes a Jewish man would come into the bus station to buy a ticket, and just the sight of his black hat and beard and dangling white strings would make Penny shiver. Her heart would race in near panic if she saw a Jew wearing one of those big furry hats that looked like a wild animal had curled up on his head.

"Maybe Ed Shaffer doesn't mind living in that neighborhood," Father said, "but why in the world would you want to live there? Those aren't our kind of people, Penny. You don't belong in that neighborhood. Stay on your own side of Brooklyn."

Penny knew that if she listened to her parents much longer, all would be lost. She rarely stood up to them, but this was one of those times when she needed to. "I-I already told Eddie I would do it. He's counting on me." She wished her voice sounded a little more certain, a little less shaky.

Father smacked the arm of his chair with his palm. "You can't do it. I won't allow it."

Penny cleared the lump from her throat. "Well . . . well, I'm twenty-four years old, Dad. I think I can do whatever I want." She turned and fled to her bedroom, quietly closing the door, but she could hear her mother shouting behind her.

"Penny! . . . Penny Sue Goodrich, you come back here right now!"

She stayed in her room, leaning against the door. She had to admit that she hadn't really considered how hard it might be to take care of two children and run a household. Not to mention living on her own for the first time in her life. In a strange neighborhood. With Jewish people. But as frightening as all of those things were, it would be much, much worse to let Eddie down, much worse to miss this opportunity to win his love. Because that meant she would have to live here for the rest of her life. Alone and unloved.

CHAPTER 3

THE MUSIC OF Beethoven's Third Symphony drifted from the radio as Jacob Mendel tried to compose yet another letter. Maybe this time he would get a response. Or maybe it would lead to another dead end. He had written to all of them: his city councilman, his congressmen, state senators, U.S. senators. He had even written to President Roosevelt. Nobody would help him. Dead ends, every one of them. But he would bury those government officials in a mountain of letters if he had to, until one of them finally helped him find his son, Avraham, his daughter-in-law, Sarah Rivkah, and his little granddaughter, Fredeleh.

Other family members were missing as well—Jacob's brothers Yehuda and Baruch and their families, aunts and uncles and cousins—all of them over in Hungary and not a word from them since America declared war in 1941. His family members should have come to America like he and Miriam had. They should have come when they had the chance. Who knew what had become of them now, with that madman marching across Europe? That was what Jacob was trying to find out: what had become of them. But every avenue he explored had led to a dead end.

Jacob and Miriam had raised their son here in America, in Brooklyn. But five years ago, Avraham had decided that it was the will of *Hashem* that he travel to Hungary to study Torah in the *yeshiva* with a world-famous rebbe. While he was studying over there, Avraham had met Sarah Rivkah. They had married and had a daughter. Now all three of them had vanished.

Jacob had been cutting out newspaper articles about the war ever since Hitler invaded Czechoslovakia, saving maps and news items that told him what was happening. The photographs and clippings now covered the top of his dining room table so he could no longer eat a meal on it. But the table was no longer needed, so what did it matter?

The meager scraps of news from Hungary were always very bad. The Hungarians had formed an alliance with Germany. And the pictures of what Hitler had already done in Germany were horrifying: skeletal remains of synagogues; the devastation of *Kristallnacht*; Jews forced to leave their homes and business, forced to wear yellow stars.

The music ended and a news program came on the radio. The news was certain to be bad. It always was—all of it bad. More U-boats terrorizing the Atlantic. More ships sunk to the bottom of the ocean. Another island in the Pacific lost to the Japanese. What would it be this time? But just as the newscaster began to speak, Jacob's upstairs tenants chose that moment to slam the apartment door and thunder down the stairs—more than one person, from the sound of it—drowning out the announcer's words. Jacob rose from his chair and shuffled across the room to turn up the volume before they slammed the front door on their way out like they always did. But the footsteps halted outside his apartment and a moment later someone knocked on his door. Miriam had been too friendly with their tenants, always inviting those two kids to come inside as if they were her own grandchildren.

Jacob opened the door just a crack and saw that it was the father, Edward Shaffer. The girl stood beside him holding his hand, and the boy clung to his waist like gum on a shoe.

"Hi, Mr. Mendel. Sorry to bother you, but I wanted to give you this month's rent money."

"It is not the end of the month, yet. Only the twenty-fourth." Jacob had just written the date on his letter, so he knew.

"I know, Mr. Mendel, I know. But I'll be going away tomorrow, and—"

"Heh? Going away? For how long?"

Shaffer smiled faintly. "Well . . . until the war ends, I guess, and the Nazis and Japs are licked for good. I've enlisted in the army."

The news stunned Jacob. He couldn't think what to say. Was the government so unfeeling that they would draft a man with two small children and no wife? But no, Shaffer had said that he had enlisted. That made no sense at all, but Jacob would never say so. It was none of his business what the man did.

"You cannot sublet, you know. It is written right into the lease that you are not allowed to sublet the apartment."

"I'm not subletting, Mr. Mendel. A family friend is coming to look after Esther and Peter for me. The army will send her the money every month so she can pay the rent."

Once again, Jacob didn't know what to say.

"I'll be home on leave after I finish basic training," Shaffer continued. "If things aren't working out . . . well, you can let me know then and we'll talk."

"Who did you say would be staying here?"

"Her name is Penny Goodrich. I've known her all my life, and she's very responsible. Doesn't smoke or drink . . . and she's not the sort of woman to live a wild life, if you know what I mean. Believe me, I wouldn't leave my kids with just anyone. Penny's a-okay."

Jacob took the rent money from Shaffer's hand, nodding as if he understood. But he did not. He did not understand at all. Why would this man leave his family if he didn't have to? Little children, no less? Jacob was trying to get his son's family safely home to America. He would never leave his child all alone, not in a million years.

He thanked Shaffer for the money and had almost closed the door again before he thought to say: "Good luck to you. With the war, I mean. Come home safe."

"I will, Mr. Mendel. Thank you."

Come home safe. What a stupid thing to say. Such meaningless words. Jacob felt sorry for Shaffer, no question about it. He knew how Shaffer suffered, losing his wife that way. Jacob had lost his Miriam Shoshanna, too, and he was still angry with Hashem for taking her from him, more than a year later. What kind of a Master of the Universe takes a good woman like Miriam Shoshanna, not to mention those poor children's mother, when there were so many evil people in this world who did not deserve to live? Who runs a universe where automobile brakes can fail and two women can die while buying potatoes for *Shabbat* dinner?

He sat down at his desk again to finish writing his letter, feeling every one of his sixty-five years. When he had licked the envelope and stuck a stamp on the corner, he decided to search the refrigerator for something to eat.

Nothing. Not one thing. On Shabbat, no less. Miriam used to work all day Friday to prepare a feast for Shabbat. She would invite their friends to come celebrate with them, always many friends. Now it was Friday evening and there was nothing to eat.

Oh, he had invitations, plenty of invitations. But Jacob could not bear to watch another woman light the Shabbat candles and recite the blessing. He could not lift a glass of wine in celebration and wish everyone *Shabbat shalom.* He could not pray. He would not pray. His friends still prayed to Hashem, but Jacob Mendel did not.

He closed the refrigerator door and decided to walk to the grocery store and buy a can of soup for his supper. He could drop his letter in the mailbox on the way. He knew the sun had already set and that Shabbat had begun, but he would go shopping anyway. For sixty-five years, Jacob Aaron Mendel had never deliberately broken one of Hashem's commandments. And what difference had it made? Heh?

Jacob put on his jacket and hat and locked the apartment door behind him. He crossed the street and walked past the *shul* where Rebbe Grunfeld and Jacob's other friends would be saying *Kabbalat Shabbat.* He continued down the block and walked past the vegetable market where it had all happened, as if daring Hashem to send another car with no brakes careening onto the sidewalk. Let it plow into him this time.

The market had been restored to normal once again. It had been more than a year, after all, and what did he expect? That they would build a shrine for his Miriam Shoshanna and Rachel Shaffer and the other woman who had died? The owner was a Jew, so the market was closed for Shabbat. That didn't matter to Jacob. He didn't shop there anymore. He used to enjoy going there with Miriam every Friday, talking to Chaim the grocer, who was also from Hungary. He enjoyed picking out strawberries or some other treat for his wife. But Jacob had never gone back there to shop after she had died.

Tonight he went to the shabby Italian grocery store instead, a block away from the market, and bought a can of tomato soup and a box of saltine crackers. The place was crowded, always crowded, and he had to wait a long time just to buy the two items. Afterward, he dropped his letter in the mailbox on the corner, then turned toward home.

He should have taken the long way home, walking all the way around the block to the alley and going in through his back door. He should not have risked walking past the shul again in case the men were just leaving after prayer. But Jacob was not thinking straight. The news that his tenant was going into the army tomorrow had distracted him. Had Shaffer said tomorrow?

Prayers must have ended early—or else Jacob's watch had stopped—because here came all the men, pouring out of the back door of the shul. Jacob whirled around and headed in the opposite direction as fast as he could go, but it was too late. Rebbe Grunfeld spotted him and hurried up the street behind him, calling his name.

"Yaacov! Yaacov, wait!"

He had no choice. He had to stop. This would be a conversation that he did not want to have. "Good evening, Rebbe." Jacob would not wish him Shabbat shalom.

"Shabbat shalom, Yaacov. We have missed you at prayers these many months. You're coming back soon, yes?"

"No."

The rebbe stared at him as if he had uttered blasphemy.

Jacob lost his temper. "Why should I pray? Heh? You tell me why."

"We could simply talk. I would listen . . . perhaps Hashem—"

"I have nothing to say to you or to Hashem. And certainly nothing to thank Him for."

"You don't mean that, Yaacov."

"Yes, I do mean it. I was doing Hashem's work that day, making plans to dedicate His new Torah scroll. That was why I was late. And if I had been on time that day, *I* would have been the one to shop at the grocer's, not my Miriam. Not that young mother from upstairs with two children to raise. She wouldn't have offered to walk with Miriam if I had been home."

"I know, I know. It was a terrible tragedy, but—"

"How could Hashem, who knows everything there is to know, not have known that if I was late, my Miriam Shoshanna would die? Heh?" Jacob was shouting, but he didn't care. "Hashem should have known that Miriam, of all people, would want to finish her shopping before sundown on *Erev Shabbat*. That she would never break a single one of His commandments."

"I don't know what to say, Yaacov, but if you would only come back to us, maybe we could find the answers together."

"Why? What is the use? Hashem has not answered any of my prayers. Nor has He helped me find my son, Avraham. I ask Him questions all the time, and all I ever hear is silence. A silence so loud it is deafening."

"There is no need to shout, Yaacov."

"I will shout if I want to!" He saw people staring at him, even from across the street. The rebbe's cheeks flushed pink beneath his white beard. "Tell me, Rebbe—why would Hashem tell my Avraham to go study in His yeshiva if He knew this madman Hitler was coming? Heh? Didn't He see Adolf Hitler? Were the madman and his plans hidden from Hashem's sight?"

"I don't know, my friend. I don't know . . . But we miss you. The shul isn't the same without you. You did such a wonderful job when you were our *gabbai*, organizing everything for us. Now we are falling apart without you."

"I do not care what happens to the shul! The building can crumble into dust for all I care!" Jacob paused to catch his breath and saw the rebbe glance at the paper bag with the soup and crackers. "Yes, Rebbe Grunfeld, I am carrying a burden on Shabbat. Did everyone hear me? Jacob Aaron Mendel went shopping on Shabbat! Look!" He held the package up high for everyone to see. "This is what happens when Hashem takes a man's wife and son. Hashem should have known this would happen. He should have known!"

Jacob turned and strode away—not toward his apartment, where he would have to walk past all his other black-hatted friends, but back up the street, toward the vegetable stand and the Italian grocery store and the mailbox. Jacob walked past all three places and simply kept going, walking and walking and walking.

Thirty minutes later when his temper had finally cooled, he turned toward home, exhausted and hungry. Everyone would be inside their own houses by now, eating their Shabbat dinners, singing psalms, blessing Hashem. Jacob no longer had to worry about bumping into anyone he knew.

He was a few yards from the back door of the shul when he noticed the smoke. He halted, staring at the familiar brick building as if unable to comprehend what he was seeing. Billowing black smoke poured from beneath the roof. Bright orange flames danced behind the first-floor windows.

"No . . ." he whispered. "No!" Jacob turned and ran back to the cigar store he had just passed, open late on a Friday night. He pushed through the door, out of breath. "Call the fire department! The shul is on fire!"

"The what?"

"The synagogue! The synagogue down the street, on the corner! Congregation Ohel Moshe. Hurry! I saw smoke! And flames inside!"

As soon as the man reached for the telephone, Jacob rushed outside again. Maybe he could find a way to throw some water on the flames until the fire department arrived. He had been gone barely a minute, but when he neared the building again he could see that the flames were already too much for him. He could see them on the second floor, flickering behind the window in the women's section. The fire was rapidly spreading out of control.

It must have started in the *beit midrash*, and with so many books in that study room there was plenty of fuel to burn. All those books, the sacred books! What a terrible tragedy that holy books containing the word of Hashem should burn! That was what that madman Hitler had been doing—burning books. And synagogues. Jacob glanced around frantically. He should hear sirens by now. What was taking the fire department so long?

The Torah scrolls! They were going to burn!

He must not let that happen.

Flames already engulfed the rear of the building by the back door, so Jacob hurried around to the main door, in front. It was locked. Of course it would be locked. Evening prayers had finished. Everyone had gone home. He reached into his pocket for the key, given to him when he served as the gabbai, organizing the prayer times and assigning a *huzzan* to lead them. And there it was, still on the key ring along with his apartment key. A year had passed, and he had never thought to give it back.

People were starting to gather in the streets, pointing to the smoke and flames. As Jacob unlocked the door with shaking hands, he heard someone shout, "Don't go in there! Wait for the firemen!"

He opened the door. A wall of smoke was waiting inside to greet him, rushing out at him. Hot, blinding smoke. He could barely see where he was going, but it didn't matter. He knew every inch of the shul's rooms and hallways by heart. The building faced east, toward Jerusalem, and the *Aron Ha Kodesh,* where the Torah scrolls were kept, was on the easternmost wall.

"You see, Hashem? You see the *mitzvah* I am doing for you?" he said as he groped his way toward the sanctuary. "You did not see fit to save my Miriam, but I am still saving your Torah."

He paused at one of the basins outside the sanctuary and removed his jacket to soak it with water from the sink. The faucet handles were fiery hot to the touch and they burned his hands, but he held the drenched jacket over his nose and mouth as he pushed his way through the second set of doors. Hungry flames were devouring the women's section above him. The thick smoke made him gag and cough, even with the jacket over his face. He could feel the heat on his bare arms as he groped his way up the aisle past the *bimah*. He remembered how proudly his son had stood on that platform to read Torah for the first time. Was Hashem going to allow this shul, and the lifetime of memories it held, to burn to the ground?

Jacob pushed aside the curtains to open the doors to the Ark. He fingered the soft, velvet covers that shielded the scrolls, barely able to see them through the smoke. Then, working quickly, Jacob draped his wet jacket over his arm and carefully . . . carefully . . . removed the Torah scrolls from the Ark and wrapped his jacket around them to protect them. These were sacred objects, not to be grabbed or handled carelessly. With the bundle securely wrapped, he started back down the aisle. Cinders rained down from above him. The heat felt as intense as a furnace.

You know everything, Hashem, and you knew I would save your Torah. You knew I could not let it burn—even if I am not speaking to you anymore.

He tried to hold his breath to keep from inhaling the smoke. It seared his throat, his lungs. His eyes stung so badly he could no longer keep them open to see where he was going. He bumped into the wall where he thought the door should be. He had run out of air, but when he tried to inhale there was no air to breathe.

Is this your punishment? Heh? That I die here? In the very place that I turned my back on?

He finally found the door to the vestibule, then dropped to the floor where there might still be a little air, crawling toward the front door on his knees, the scrolls tucked protectively against his chest, close to his heart. He could see pulsing red lights from the fire trucks through the window on the front door, and he pulled himself to his feet to reach for the doorknob. The metal burned his hand, but he threw all his weight against the door and it finally flew open. He fell forward, collapsing to his knees on the sidewalk, one arm outstretched to stop his fall. Pain shot through his kneecaps and his wrist, and he rolled to the side as his arm gave out. He could not allow Hashem's Torah to touch the ground, even inside its wrappings.

A black-coated fireman ran toward him, grabbing him beneath his arms and dragging him away from the building. "Get an ambulance!" the fireman yelled. "I need an ambulance over here!"

Jacob tried to hand the bundle to him. His throat felt as though he had swallowed a flaming sword as he choked out the words: "Give . . . this . . . to Rebbe Grunfeld."

He couldn't breathe, couldn't see. There was a mound of bricks on his chest. Then the fireman who was bending over him disappeared behind a curtain of blackness.

CHAPTER 4

"WHY CAN'T GRANDMA move in and take care of us while you're away?" Esther asked. "I don't want that other lady to come here." She knew Penny's name but she pretended not to, emphasizing the fact that Penny was practically a stranger.

Daddy's suitcase lay open on his rumpled bed as he packed to leave for boot camp tomorrow. He crisscrossed his narrow bedroom, removing items from his closet, his dresser, his nightstand, checking to make sure he hadn't forgotten anything. He was taller than the sloping sections of the ceiling but so familiar with the layout of the room that he never bumped his head.

"I already explained it a dozen times, Esther. Grandma can't climb stairs. And you know pets aren't allowed. Who would take care of Woofer? And her bird?"

"Penny could take care of them for her."

"Everything is arranged, doll."

"I don't want you to go!" Mama used to scold Esther for using a whiny voice, but she didn't care. She climbed onto Daddy's bed, causing the lid of his suitcase to fall shut. Her stomach ached from crying so hard during the past several days, but even her tears hadn't convinced Daddy to stay home. He wasn't going to change his mind.

"I'll only be gone for six or seven weeks. Then I'll get leave-time after basic training and I'll come home. Maybe by then Grandma will let you move in with her."

"But then you'll have to go away again?"

"Just till the war ends." He reopened the suitcase lid and stuffed in two more pairs of socks. "Look, your friends' fathers are all off fighting, aren't they? And the Hoffmans' father, next door? I have to do my part, doll."

"The other kids still have mothers to take care of them." Esther regretted her words as soon as she spoke them.

Daddy closed his eyes and pinched the bridge of his nose. "I know, doll, I know. But Penny will do a good job taking care of you—"

"I don't want her, I want you!"

Daddy sighed and reached out to caress her hair. His hand felt heavy and warm on the top of her head. "I'm sorry, Esther. There's nothing more I can say." He turned and walked back to the dresser, removing the framed photograph of Mama that always stood on top of it. "I need to take this," he said softly. "You mind?"

Esther shrugged, unsure why he asked for her permission. He blew the dust off the glass and swiped it with his hand before placing the picture frame inside the suitcase and snapping the latches shut. He glanced around the room to see if he had forgotten anything, and as he paused, Esther heard the screen door slam downstairs in the kitchen. A moment later, Peter raced up the steps to the bedroom and burst through the door. He flung himself at their father and clung to his waist, squeezing so hard he wrinkled Daddy's shirt.

"Hey, what's going on?" Daddy asked. "I thought you were play-ing outside?"

Peter pressed his face against Daddy's midsection and didn't reply. He hadn't begged or pleaded with their father the way Esther had, or even asked "why?" over and over again. Instead, he had followed Daddy everywhere for the past few days, hanging on to his pant leg or his shirttails or clinging to his waist. Now he began to cry, a thin, muffled sound like an injured kitten.

"Hey, come on, Peter. Don't make this any harder than it is, okay?"

The bedroom window gaped open, and as Peter continued to whimper softly, Esther heard a different kind of wail in the distance, joining his. She recognized it as sirens, coming from the fire station three blocks away. The sound grew louder and louder until it seemed as though the vehicles were stopping right outside their apartment building. Peter let go of Daddy's waist and put his hands over his ears to drown out the racket. He hated sirens, probably because they reminded him of the ambulances and police cars at the vegetable market on the terrible day that Mama had died. Daddy crossed to the window and jerked out the screen so he could lean outside to look. "Holy cow!" he shouted. "The synagogue is on fire!"

Esther went to her father's side and peered out, too. Thick black smoke churned from the rear of the building, and bright orange flames flashed behind the windows. She saw long fingers of fire reach from one of the windows and grab on to the roof, igniting it. She squeezed her hands into fists, wanting the firemen to hurry and put the fire out, wanting the eerie, unnatural sight to go away and the familiar, tan brick building across the street to look the way it always had. On the street three floors below, firemen in black coats and rubber boots were unfolding ladders and uncoiling long fire hoses that looked like flat, gray snakes. Why didn't they work faster?

She turned away, unable to watch the flames consume the building, and saw Peter standing in the middle of the room, still covering his ears. One of his favorite playthings used to be his toy fire truck, and he used to beg Mama to walk past the firehouse on the way to the park so he could see the big trucks. But that had changed the day Mama died.

"Hey, we'd better shut the windows," Daddy said, "or it'll get too smoky in here. Give me a hand, Esther."

She didn't move, watching as he quickly closed his bedroom windows and stacked the folding screens against the wall. "Is the whole synagogue going to burn down, Daddy?"

"I don't know, doll. I'm sure the firemen will do their best to save it. Run and close your bedroom windows, okay?" Daddy hurried downstairs to check the rest of the apartment.

Esther went into the bedroom that she shared with Peter and wrestled out the screen so that the heavy window could fall closed. Then she followed her father and brother downstairs. Daddy was in the living room with his head and shoulders hanging through the open window, watching the spectacle below.

"Daddy, don't! You'll fall out!"

He pulled his head inside and closed the window. "What's wrong, doll? You're not scared, are you?" Esther nodded and Peter flung himself at their father again, crying as he clung to his waist. "You don't have to worry. It won't spread to our side of the street. Come on, we'll go downstairs and watch."

Esther didn't want to watch. Mama had told her that the synagogue was like a church, except that you had to be Jewish like Mr. and Mrs. Mendel in order to go there. Esther wouldn't want to watch her own church burn down, but Daddy took Peter's hand in his and led them both downstairs. A haze of smoke already fogged the front hallway. Daddy halted to knock on the landlord's door.

"Mr. Mendel? Mr. Mendel, are you home?" No one answered. They went outside and Esther saw dozens of their neighbors perched on their front stoops or crowded along the sidewalk to watch. She didn't see Mr. Mendel standing among them. Mrs. Hoffman from the building next door called to Daddy in a tremulous voice.

"Mr. Shaffer? . . . Oh, Mr. Shaffer? . . . Do you think there's a chance the fire could spread to our side of the street? Should we evacuate our valuables?" Esther had been inside the Hoffmans' apartment and couldn't recall seeing anything valuable.

"Our buildings should be okay," Daddy told her. "There's no wind. What a shame about the synagogue, though."

The Hoffman kids were all out on the sidewalk watching, too. Their son Jack was a year older than Esther and sometimes used swearwords. He got sent to the principal's office a lot in school. Mama had called him and his younger brother, Gary, "ruffians." Now the two brothers stood near the fire hydrant, splashing in the puddles from the leaking hoses and annoying the firemen. The look of glee on their faces made Esther shiver.

Jack's older sister, Lois, was fifteen and boy-crazy. She used to walk to school with Esther, but lately she acted as if she was much too grown up to hang around with her. Lois sat on the front steps of her building, chewing a wad of gum and blowing giant pink bubbles. The neighborhood was much quieter now that Mr. Hoffman had enlisted in the navy. Before that the Hoffmans used to argue all the time, shouting so loudly that Esther could hear them from inside her own building, especially in the summer when the windows were open.

There was no sign of their landlord, Mr. Mendel, but a group of Jewish men with black hats and bushy beards had gathered in front of Esther's apartment building. She saw such horror and loss in their expressions that she had to look away. One of them pushed forward to plead with the firemen. He was as short as Esther was, with a black hat and snowy white beard.

"Please, you must save the Torah scrolls. They must not burn."

"We'll do our best, Rabbi. Now, please step back."

Suddenly the front door of the synagogue flew open and their landlord, Mr. Mendel, staggered out, collapsing onto the sidewalk. He wasn't wearing a coat, and Esther recognized him by the striped suspenders he'd had on when they had visited him earlier this evening. A firemen rushed toward him yelling, "I need an ambulance!"

The white-bearded rabbi pushed forward, skirting around the firemen and fire trucks and stepping over the maze of hoses as he crossed the street. "Yaacov! Yaacov!" he called. "Are you all right?"

Mr. Mendel had been carrying a dark bundle, and the fireman handed it to the rabbi, then motioned for him to go back across the street to wait. Esther could feel the heat of the flames and knew it must be even hotter in front of the synagogue. Daddy released her hand as he hurried over to the rabbi.

"Is that Mr. Mendel?" he asked. "Is he okay?"

The white-bearded man lifted his shoulders as he nodded sadly. "Yes, it is him. We must pray that he will recover. He did a very brave thing to save our Torah."

"I'm Mr. Mendel's tenant," Daddy told him. "Let me know if

there's anything I can do." The man didn't seem to hear Daddy as the others gathered around him to unwrap the bundle, talking in a language Esther couldn't understand.

"Any idea how the fire started?" she heard Daddy ask one of the men.

The man shook his head. "No, but I wonder . . . with so much hatred in the world, it would not surprise me if it was deliberate."

At last the ambulance arrived, the siren howling so loudly that Peter covered his ears again. So did Esther. She watched the men carefully lift their landlord into the back of the vehicle, remembering how they had lifted Mama's limp body the same way. The vehicle drove away again, sirens wailing.

Meanwhile, some of the firemen began climbing their ladders so they could aim their hoses at the roof of the synagogue. More firemen were smashing the lower windows with axes and pouring water into the first floor. Police cars arrived from two different directions and pulled to a stop in the middle of the street, blocking traffic. The patrolmen jumped out, leaving their doors wide open. They began pushing back the crowds, shouting for everyone to stay clear. "Out of the way, folks. Let the firemen do their work."

Esther took Daddy's hand again, and Peter gripped his other one as they moved onto the front porch of their apartment building to escape the smoke and heat. Only the headlights on the fire trucks lit the dark night, along with the eerie glow of the flames. Brooklyn's streetlights had been turned off months ago, and the air-raid warden had ordered everyone to hang blackout curtains in their windows to disguise the city from enemy U-boats and airplanes. If there was a moon out tonight, the sky was too smoky for them to see it.

They watched for a long, long time. The firemen worked until they were exhausted, but they couldn't save the synagogue. Esther's eyes burned and itched from the smoke. She could taste it in the back of her mouth and throat.

"Yeah, my eyes burn, too," Daddy said when he saw her rubbing hers. "Let's go inside." They walked up the stairs together. The excitement had helped Esther forget that Daddy was leaving tomorrow, but now her grief returned in full force.

"Are you still going away, even though there was a fire and Mr. Mendel got hurt?"

Daddy nodded sadly. "There's nothing I can do about either one, doll. Get ready for bed, okay? You too, Peter." Daddy came upstairs to tuck them in after they had washed their faces and brushed their teeth.

Esther had trouble falling asleep. A sheen of smoke hung in the beam of light beneath her door. Her eyes burned whenever she tried to close them, and she didn't know if her tears were from the smoke or her sorrow. Maybe both. This was the last night that Daddy would be home for a long, long time, the last night that he would tuck her into bed and kiss her good-night. She could hear Peter sobbing into his pillow.

She was still awake hours later when Daddy came to bed. He stood in the doorway gazing at them before finally coming inside and bending over Peter's bed to stroke his hair. Esther pretended to be asleep when Daddy turned to her bed. He pulled the sheet over her and touched her hair, too. She longed to say something to him, but she was afraid he would be mad because it was very late and she was still awake. At last he turned away and closed the bedroom door.

The synagogue across the street was one more loss in Esther's life that could never be replaced. Mama was gone. Nice Mrs. Mendel who baked honey cake and cookies was gone, too. Now the synagogue had been destroyed and Mr. Mendel had been rushed away in an ambulance. Esther's world was slowly coming apart, unraveling like the favorite pink sweater she'd once had. It had begun with a small hole after she'd snagged the sleeve on a nail, and as time passed, the broken strand of yarn kept growing longer and longer until the hole was so huge she could no longer wear the sweater. Tomorrow Daddy would leave her, too.

And she couldn't do anything about it.

CHAPTER 5

PENNY AWOKE BEFORE DAWN, too excited to sleep. Today she would move into Eddie Shaffer's apartment! The anticipation was like that moment in the movie theater when the lights dimmed and the music began to play. Music should be playing right now as the sun rose on this wonderful day. A huge banner should stretch across the sky saying, *This Is Chapter One of Penny Goodrich's Brand-New Life.*

She got out of bed, eager to begin, and carefully smoothed the bedspread and fluffed the pillow, making her bed for the last time. The only thing that could dampen her excitement would be another argument with her parents—which was why she had decided to leave home early, before they woke up. Penny had tried as hard as she could to explain to them why she needed to help Eddie, and they had done everything they could to talk her out of it. The arguments had gotten louder and angrier every day for the past two weeks, but nobody's mind had changed—not Penny's, and certainly not her parents'. She had gone to bed early last night to avoid another fight. She wished her mother would hug her good-bye this morning and give Penny her blessing, but that was about as likely to happen as a blizzard in July.

Penny tiptoed into the kitchen with her two bags of belongings and fixed a bowl of cereal instead of toast so the aroma wouldn't awaken her parents. She was putting the milk bottle back into the refrigerator when she heard her mother's voice behind her.

"You're making a big mistake, Penny. It's not too late to change your mind, you know."

"Yes it is. I promised Eddie I would help him. He's counting on me."

"His mother is the one who should be helping him with those children, not you. I told you I would go next door and talk to her for you."

"Please don't. It's all arranged. I promised to stay with them, like I explained."

"And I explained why you shouldn't go. Your father and I are very angry with you for defying our wishes this way."

"I know. I know you're angry." Penny sank down at the table and bowed her head to say grace before gulping down her cereal. She wanted to run out the door right this minute rather than endure any more lectures, but she needed to eat something first.

She glanced up at her mother and saw her standing in the kitchen doorway with her arms folded. She had such an angry expression on her face that it brought tears to Penny's eyes. She knew she was supposed to honor her father and mother—they had quoted that Bible verse to her repeatedly in an effort to convince her to stay—but did that mean that Penny had to live here with them forever? Didn't other daughters grow up and leave home and start lives of their own? Penny wanted so much to be like everyone else, but as her mother constantly reminded her, she wasn't like other girls.

She gulped the last spoonful of cereal and rose to put the bowl in the sink. "I'll stop by in a day or two and let you know how everything is going."

"No, Penny. You will call me as soon as you get there. If you insist on leaving home against our wishes, then the least you can do is call and let us know you made it there safely. I don't think I need to remind you of all the things that could happen to you on the way."

"Okay, okay. I'll call you." She longed to add that she was only traveling across Brooklyn, not to the moon, but Penny had never spoken disrespectfully to her parents in her life. She had felt so courageous when she awoke this morning, but now the cereal she had just eaten churned in her stomach like the agitator on a washing machine. She needed to leave right now, before her mother made her feel any more frightened than she already was.

She slipped her purse strap over her head and across her chest the way her mother had taught her, so that purse-snatchers couldn't grab it, and picked up the two shopping bags that held her belongings. Neither Penny nor her parents owned a suitcase. None of them ever traveled.

"I'm going now. I'll see you in a few days."

"Wait!"

Penny obeyed, turning back to face her mother.

"You're such a scatterbrain, Penny. Stop and think for a minute before you go running off like a fool. Do you have everything you need? Enough money for the bus? The directions to get there? And you'd better put your sweater on; it looks chilly outside."

Tears squeezed Penny's throat. "I'll be fine, Mother. Good-bye."

She closed the door behind her and walked to the bus stop as fast as she could with the heavy shopping bags. Penny didn't own very many clothes and figured she could bring them over a few at a time when she came home to visit on the weekends. Eddie didn't own a car. He had drawn the bus route for her, explaining which one to take and where the stops were.

The first bus that pulled up to the curb was hers. It seemed very crowded for a Saturday morning, and nearly all the passengers were servicemen. A young man in a U.S. Marines uniform sitting near the front jumped up when she boarded and gave her his seat. She thanked him and sat down by the window to watch for street signs and landmarks. Twenty minutes later she reached her stop. According to Eddie's directions, she only had to walk one block to his apartment. She felt proud of herself for not getting lost or being accosted, the two things her mother had fearfully predicted would happen.

The storefronts and signs in Eddie's neighborhood had a lot of

Jewish names and Hebrew lettering on them. She walked past several men with black hats and beards and felt a ripple of fear. Her father had warned her that a lot of Jews lived in this part of Brooklyn. At last she rounded the corner onto Eddie's street, then halted in surprise when she saw the burned-out building in front of her. Part of the roof had caved in, and black soot smudged the tan-colored brick around its broken windows. The air smelled like a bonfire. Was that Eddie's apartment? She hurried forward, searching for his house number, finally finding it on the building across the street from the fire.

The sight of the ravaged building shook Penny. What if Eddie's apartment caught on fire that way? What would she do? How would she and the kids escape from their bedrooms way up on the third floor? Maybe she had been wrong to take on so much responsibility. Maybe her mother had been right.

But no, Eddie was counting on her. Penny hurried up the steps to the narrow front porch and rang the doorbell with *E. Shaffer* printed beside it. A moment later she heard footsteps tromping down the inside stairs. Eddie opened the door. He looked relieved to see her.

"Hi. You found us."

"Yeah, I made it here just fine. Your directions were great."

"Let me take your bags."

He led her inside the small, smoky foyer, and she saw right away that the steps to Eddie's apartment on the second floor were much too steep for his mother to go up and down every day, especially with her rheumatism. Penny herself was puffing by the time she climbed to the top of them.

"Our landlord lives downstairs," Eddie explained as they climbed, "and we have the second and third floors. Make sure the kids don't jump around the living room too much and bother him." Eddie opened a second door at the top of the stairs, where Penny saw his suitcase, packed and ready to go, standing in the small hallway. "Come on in and I'll show you around."

Penny peeked into the black- and white-tiled bathroom first. It could use a good scrubbing with cleanser, but she didn't say so. The kitchen had a small wooden table with four chairs, a corner cupboard for dishes, and one of those nice kitchen hutches that Penny had admired in magazines. It had a porcelain countertop that slid out for rolling pie crusts and a built-in flour bin and spice rack behind the neat cupboard doors. From the window above the sink she glimpsed a second-floor back porch with a roof for shade.

"This kitchen is very nice."

"It's still a little smoky in here from last night's fire." Eddie led her through the dining room and into a living room that overlooked the street below. "You can open the windows later."

"You mean that building just burned down last night? Was it an apartment building?"

"No, a synagogue. Want to see upstairs? Peter and Esther are still asleep."

"Don't worry about it. I can look around later. Was anyone hurt in the fire?"

"Yeah, our landlord, Mr. Mendel. They took him away in an ambulance. That reminds me, could you check on him when he gets home from the hospital? See if he needs anything?"

Penny didn't know how to explain to Eddie that Jewish people frightened her, especially the kind with black hats and beards. Her father had ranted on and on about them for as long as she could remember. She was about to confess her fears when Eddie suddenly added, "Rachel was good friends with our landlord's wife. She would take Mrs. Mendel shopping and things like that. In fact . . ." He paused to clear his throat, which had begun to sound very hoarse. "In fact, Mrs. Mendel and Rachel were both killed in the same accident."

"Oh! I didn't know that."

"Yeah. And one other person, too. The other two died instantly, and Rachel died in the hospital a few hours later. Esther and Peter saw it all. They were with her." Eddie turned and led the way back to the kitchen. "Here are my keys to the apartment. This one is for the back door and these are for the two front doors." A moment later, Penny heard footsteps overhead, then the sound of two children thumping down the stairs. Esther froze in the doorway when she saw Penny, her expression hardening in anger and mistrust. Peter pushed past his sister to grip their father around the waist. Penny couldn't recall ever hugging her own father that way.

"Good morning, sleepyheads," Penny said, desperate to say something. "How are you this morning? Did you have a good sleep with sweet dreams?"

"We're not babies," Esther said.

"I know. I-I'm sorry." Penny didn't know how most mothers greeted their children in the morning, so she had said the words that she wished her mother would say.

"Hey, you be nice to Penny, okay?" Eddie said. "She's doing us a huge favor. And she'll write and tell me if you don't behave. Right, Penny?"

"I'll be glad to write to you, Eddie. Just let me know what your address is."

Esther was still pouting, so Eddie lifted her chin until she had to look up at him. "Promise me you'll be polite, okay?" he asked again. She nodded faintly.

"I can fix you some pancakes or scramble some eggs, if you want," Penny said. "How about it, Esther? You hungry for something special this morning?"

"No, thank you." She crossed the kitchen to remove two bowls from the corner cupboard and poured cornflakes for herself and her brother. Peter clutched his father as if he never intended to let go.

"Sorry about the mess," Eddie said, gesturing to the dirty dishes piled in the sink.

"That's okay. I can wash them later."

"And I didn't have a chance to change the bed sheets. You'll find clean ones in the linen closet. Esther will show you where everything is, won't you, doll?"

"I suppose." There was so much ice in her voice that Penny figured they could keep cool all summer long.

"Washing machine is down in the basement. One of them belongs to the landlord. There's a line to hang the clothes on out back."

"Maybe I'll just do all the washing at my house," Penny said. "I have to go home every Saturday anyway to help my folks. And the kids can see their grandmother at the same time. Would you like that?" Neither of them replied.

"Listen, I don't know how I will ever thank you," Eddie said.

Marry me, she longed to reply. Instead, she said, "I don't mind. Really."

"Well . . . I guess I'd better get going."

"No!" Esther wailed. "Don't go, Daddy!"

"Please don't make this any harder than it already is, doll," he said softly. He gave Peter a long hug and kissed the top of his head, then pried his arms off so he could hug Esther. He even gave Penny a brief, stiff hug—a tantalizing glimpse of what it would be like when the war ended and they could be together forever. She would wake him up with a kiss every morning and give him another kiss before he left for work, just like the wives in the movies did.

Both kids were crying hard, and Eddie silently signaled for Penny to hold them back. Her heart broke for all of them as she watched Eddie hurry away, grabbing his suitcase and closing the door behind him. The children didn't try to follow him. Instead, they twisted out of Penny's grasp and ran upstairs to their room.

Penny couldn't stop crying, either. She went into the kitchen and washed and dried the dishes as tears continued to roll down her cheeks. Nearly every dish in the house seemed to be dirty, so it took a long time. She tried to figure out where everything went in the cupboards and decided that it didn't matter for now. The two bowls of uneaten cereal still sat on the table. Should she carry the kids' breakfast upstairs to them?

No, maybe they needed to be left alone.

Penny wandered into the living room and saw pretty lace curtains on the windows and an upright piano that she hadn't noticed before. She wondered who played it. The apartment was very quiet. She didn't know what else to do, so she sat down in the rocking chair near the window and gazed down at the street below her. A crowd had gathered to gawk at the burned-out building.

A long time later the phone rang. Should she answer it? It seemed wrong to answer someone else's phone, but the kids were still upstairs in their room. Besides, it might be Eddie, checking to see if they were okay. She lifted the receiver.

"Hello? . . . Um . . . Shaffer residence."

"Penny! You were supposed to call me! It's been hours!" Mother sounded furious.

"Oh! I'm sorry . . . I-I had things to do and . . . and Eddie was showing me all around and . . . and then I forgot."

"You forgot? You would forget your head if it wasn't attached to your body. Your father and I have been worried sick. I almost called the police. You didn't give me the phone number so I had to go next door and bother Mrs. Shaffer for it. She's a wreck, by the way, with *three* sons fighting in the war now, thanks to you."

"Well, I arrived here just fine. I'm sorry I forgot to call. But you have the number now, in case you need anything. I have to go. Good-bye."

Penny slammed down the phone, grabbed her shopping bags from the front hallway, and carried them upstairs to Eddie's bedroom. He had emptied a bureau drawer for her to use, and she carefully filled it with her own neatly folded things. The room was messy but she might not straighten it up just yet. These were Eddie's clothes. He had slept in this rumpled bed. His scent was everywhere.

Rachel was everywhere, too, in all of the feminine little touches. The crocheted doilies on the bureau and nightstands, the tatted lace and embroidery on the pillow covers. Penny sat down on the unmade bed. She had made a terrible mistake. What was she doing here? Eddie was gone and his kids hated her. She shouldn't have come. Mother was right, as usual. Penny didn't have the good sense that God gave a green bean.

CHAPTER 6

"I WOULD LIKE you to stay in the hospital for one more night, Mr. Mendel. Just to be sure." The doctor scribbled something on the chart that hung from the end of Jacob's bed as he made his evening rounds. Jacob, however, wasn't in the bed. Why lie around for no good reason? His bruised knees still ached from his fall to the sidewalk, but his legs weren't broken, were they? Only his arm.

"To be sure of what?" Jacob turned away from the window and the uninspiring view. His sore throat made his voice sound hoarse, not at all like his own. His chest hurt every time he drew a wheezing breath.

"Your blood pressure is elevated. And there is always the risk of infection with third-degree burns."

Jacob looked down at his bandaged hands and the cast on his right arm. Like the righteous Job in Scripture, Jacob had lost his family and now his health. But he wanted to go home and sleep in his own bed.

"I am fine. I would like to go home. Kindly give me my clothes."

The sun had set, which meant that Shabbat had ended. He could travel now—not that it mattered. Why should he care about Hashem's rules?

Habit. That was all it was, a lifetime of habit.

"I'll discharge you, Mr. Mendel, but you will be going against my advice if you leave."

"I understand. Thank you."

Jacob could smell the aroma of smoke on his clothes as soon as the nurse brought them into the room. He went into the little bathroom to get dressed, and the sleeve of his shirt barely fit over his cast. It took a very long time to close the buttons and zippers with his useless hands. He had to leave half of his shirt buttons undone. When he came out, he was surprised to see his friend Meir Wolfe and Rebbe Grunfeld standing beside his bed. Naturally, they had waited until after Shabbat to visit him.

"Yaacov! There you are!" His friend wore a wide grin.

"I hope you came by car, Meir, because I am ready to go home. You can drive me there."

"But the nurse said you would be here for one more night."

"The nurse is misinformed. Will you take me home, please?"

Jacob sat in the front seat beside his friend while the rebbe sat in the back, surrounded by casserole dishes and fruit baskets and boxes of food. The aroma of potato kugel made Jacob's mouth water. He had been unable to eat very much in the hospital. His sore throat made it painful to swallow.

The rebbe leaned forward from the back seat. "Several of the women have prepared food for you, Yaacov, as you can see. And I am going to arrange for them to come every day to help you clean, do the dishes, take out the garbage—anything you need."

"Thank you, but that is not necessary."

"You have bandages on your hands, Yaacov, and your arm is broken. Everyone wants to help. It's the least we can do to thank you for saving the scrolls. What a blessing that you were nearby and noticed the fire. Of course, it wasn't so good that you were injured—"

"I will be fine. Did the firemen save the shul?"

"Well, no. It looks very bad. A great deal of damage. Some of us will go through the building and see what we can salvage once the fire department says it's safe, but—"

"Do they know how it started?"

"A fire inspector must come and make that determination. We

won't know until he is finished. But it seems to have started in the beit midrash in the rear of the building. That's where the worst damage was. We have been trying to think what might have been in that room that could have started the fire, something electrical maybe, but nothing comes to mind."

Meir Wolfe grunted angrily. "I cannot help thinking that it was deliberate. In the old country, such vandalism happened all the time, remember? And now the hatred has made its way here to America."

"Let's not think that way, Meir," the rebbe soothed. "We don't know for certain how the fire started."

"But we do know that we are hated here in America, too. Everyone says what a pity it is that Hitler persecutes the Jews, but will anybody help us? No. Nobody wants the Jews to move to their country."

The rebbe shook his head. "I'm sure they'll discover that the fire was an accident. You'll see."

They arrived on Jacob's street a few minutes later, and he saw the damage for himself. And even though he hadn't attended shul in more than a year, the sight of the ravaged building still saddened him. So many milestones in his life had taken place there. He had presented his tiny son for *pidyon ha'ben,* redeeming his firstborn. Six years later, he had held his son's hand as they'd walked across the street for Avraham's first day of Hebrew school in the beit midrash. And he had watched in pride as Avraham put on *tefillin* to pray with the men for the first time when he turned twelve. Now Jacob turned his back on the destruction and a lifetime of memories and walked up the steps to his porch, his friends following him, balancing boxes and baskets of food.

The daily newspaper lay on the porch outside his door. Later, he would go through it and read the latest news about the war, cutting out the photographs and articles he wanted to save. But how could he cut anything if he couldn't use his hands?

"You will have to help me unlock both doors," he said when he reached the first one. He hated his helplessness. "The key is in my pocket, if you don't mind." When he stepped inside he realized he had left a window open and a haze of gauzy smoke lingered inside the apartment.

"Can we talk, Yaacov?" the rebbe asked when he and Meir had finished carrying in the food.

"No one is stopping you."

"I wish to ask you for a favor. We will need a place to meet now that the shul is damaged, and I wondered if we might say prayers here? Your apartment is spacious and very close to the shul."

"What makes you think I want to start praying again?"

Rebbe Grunfeld smiled gently. "You risked your life for the scrolls, Yaacov. Surely that must mean something."

Jacob had no idea what it meant. He had lain awake in the hospital most of the night, his eyes burning, his lungs aching, wondering the same thing.

"We need each other now more than ever before," Meir said. "These are terrible times we are living in, and we must stick together. Our people haven't seen this much persecution since Queen Esther's time, when the wicked Haman ordered our destruction."

"We don't know how long it will be until the shul can be rebuilt," the rebbe added.

"Ask me another day," Jacob said. "I need time to think. . . . But even if I do allow you to meet here, I cannot promise that I will join you."

"Thank you. And one more thing, Yaacov. I know how concerned you've been for your loved ones in Hungary. Many of us have been awaiting news, and now a group of congregations with families in Europe is trying to get an appointment with the State Department. I thought you might like to join us."

"Yes, of course I would." Jacob would spend every dollar he had to find Avraham and his family. He would empty his bank account, sell this apartment building, sell everything he owned. He would look for work in one of the new armament factories to earn even more money if they would hire him at his age. "Tell me where and when."

"Yes, I will let you know the details. Also, a group of some four hundred rabbis are planning a march in Washington in October."

"If only it would do some good," Meir grumbled. "The government knows what is happening. They've known since last November that

Hitler is persecuting Jews. Remember the National Day of Mourning we held? What good did it do? They still won't do anything."

"It's because no one wants to believe it is true," the rebbe said.

"How can they deny it?" Meir asked. "They know that people have hated us for hundreds, maybe thousands, of years. How is that new? It's why we moved here, isn't it?"

"Yes, they know it is true," Jacob said. His throat ached each time he spoke, making his eyes water. "But there are high officials in Washington who hate us, too."

Rebbe Grunfeld held up his hands. "Please, let's not speak ill of our government. We need their help."

"If they wanted to help us," Jacob said, "they could have changed the immigration quotas back when all this madness began so the Jews in Europe would have had a place to go. My son is an American, born here in America, yet he could not get papers for his wife and child who were born in Hungary. And he would not leave them."

"And remember that ship full of refugees that no country wanted?" Meir's voice was growing louder, angrier. "Hitler said, 'Go! Every Jew in Germany can leave! Good riddance to you!' But would our government step forward and allow even one of them to come here? No. More than nine hundred Jewish passengers were left with no place to go except back to Germany. Don't try to tell me our government is eager to help."

"I think we should leave now," Rebbe Grunfeld said. "Yaacov needs peace and rest, Meir, not strife. But you will think about what I asked, Yaacov? About meeting here to pray?"

Jacob nodded and walked with Meir and the rebbe as far as the door. His throat felt raw, so it was good that they left when they did. Afterward, he wandered out to the kitchen to eat a few spoonfuls of kugel, right out of the casserole dish. It tasted wonderful, just like Miriam used to make, but he could only eat a few bites. The potatoes scratched his throat when he swallowed them. He pulled a banana from one of the fruit baskets, struggling to open it with his bandaged hands before finally biting the end off and peeling it with his teeth. At least the banana was easier to swallow.

Later, he sat down at his desk and looked through his collection of old letters from his son. Jacob had put them all in order according to the dates that Avraham had written them, and he allowed himself to reread one each day. He lifted the top letter, gazing at the neat printing, remembering the rainy afternoon that he and Miriam Shoshanna had taken their son to the pier to board the ship for Hungary. He remembered the pride he had felt in his son and in his desire to study Torah—but also his overwhelming dread as he had watched him sail into the maelstrom of another European war. Jacob had come to America to escape pogroms and war and hatred. Why, then, had Hashem led Avraham back there?

Jacob struggled to pull the letter from the envelope, but finally managed by blowing into the envelope and pulling out the letter with his teeth. It was one of Avraham's very first letters. Jacob spread it out on his desktop.

Dear Mama and Abba,

I know it has only been six months, but you will be happy to know that I feel very much at home here already. My studies are still challenging, but I am learning so much—and loving what I am learning. Each layer of text that I peel away reveals even more of Hashem's treasures, and I have come to see that I can never mine all the richness of these jewels, even after a lifetime of study.

I also have news of another jewel that I have discovered. Samuel, my study partner, invited me to celebrate Shabbat with his family last weekend, and I met the most wonderful woman—his younger sister, Sarah Rivkah. I know this will sound unbelievable, but the moment I saw her, I understood how our ancestor Jacob felt when he saw his Rachel for the first time. Not only is Sarah beautiful, but she is sweet-tempered and righteous, as well. I would gladly serve her father for seven years to win her hand!

I know that I came here to study, and I am working very

diligently at that. But I have never met a woman who has capti-
vated me the way that Sarah Rivkah has. . . .

The doorbell rang, interrupting Jacob's reading. He shuffled to
the door, then out to the foyer, and finally managed to fumble open
the outside lock. A gray-haired man in an odd-looking uniform stood
on his doorstep. Experience in the old country had given Jacob an
instinctive distrust of men in uniform. He opened the door a mere
crack. "Yes?"

"Jacob Mendel?" the man asked. He looked too old to be in military service, and besides, the uniform was not the right color for any
of the usual branches.

"Who is asking, please?"

"I'm Inspector Dalton from the fire marshal's office." He produced
an identification badge and held it up to the crack. "I'm conducting the
investigation into the fire at the synagogue across the street. I'm told
that you went inside the building to rescue some scrolls, and I wondered
if you would be willing to answer a few questions for me."

"Yes, I suppose." Jacob widened the crack a few more inches, letting in a swirl of cool night air. He would not invite the man to come
inside. He wanted to be left alone.

"Could you tell me what you remember from last night—in your
own words?"

Jacob frowned. Whose words would he use, if not his own? "I
went for a walk—"

"Do you recall what time you left home?"

"No, but it was after sunset. On my way back—"

"How long were you gone?"

"I don't know. I paid no attention to the time."

"Okay, go on."

"On my way back I saw smoke and flames in the rear of the shul,
in the beit midrash and—"

"Excuse me, I'm not familiar with those words."

"The shul. You would call it the synagogue. And the beit midrash
is the room in the back where we study. Where all the books are
kept."

"Thank you. Go on, please."

"I was walking down the street, approaching the shul from the rear when I noticed the fire. I had just passed a cigar store a little ways back, and so I ran in there and told the clerk to call the fire department."

Jacob paused. The man was writing everything down in a little notebook, and Jacob worried that he was talking too fast. But the inspector nodded without looking up and said, "Yes, continue please."

"I looked around to see if there was a way I could throw water on the fire while I waited for the trucks to arrive, but there was nothing I could do. It was spreading too quickly. Then I realized the sacred Torah scrolls were going to burn and I could not allow that to happen. So I ran around to the front door—"

"Why did you go to the front?"

"Why? Because the fire looked worse in the back, and besides, it is easier to get to the Aron Ha Kodesh—the place where the scrolls are kept—from the front door."

"Weren't you concerned for your own safety, entering a burning building?"

"I did not think; I simply reacted. It had to be done."

"I understand that you were able to save the scrolls, Mr. Mendel. But you were injured in the process?"

"Yes." He opened the door a scant inch wider and lifted his broken arm. "Some burns on my hands, I inhaled smoke, and I broke my arm when I fell."

"How did you burn your hands?"

"How? . . . I don't know how, exactly," he said with a shrug. "I must have touched something hot. Everything happened very quickly."

"I see. Is there anything else you can tell me about the fire? Anything else that you recall?"

Jacob shook his head. "No. That is all I know." He wanted the man to leave. He didn't want to remember the fire or think about the devastation to the shul he had once loved.

"Well, if you think of anything else, Mr. Mendel, please contact the fire marshal's office."

"Do they know how the fire began?"

"I couldn't say. It's still under investigation."

Jacob pondered the inspector's answer as he closed the door. Did it mean that they still weren't sure or that he wasn't allowed to tell? What if the fire had been deliberate, as his friend Meir seemed to think? Everyone knew that the Nazis had set fire to synagogues and Jewish businesses in Germany. And his son had described the hatred he'd experienced in Hungary—before his letters had stopped coming, that is. And while Jacob knew there were anti-Semites in America, surely they wouldn't burn down a synagogue in Brooklyn or make every Jew wear a yellow star, would they?

He didn't know the answers to these questions. Nor did he know how to push away his disquieting thoughts.

CHAPTER 7

ESTHER DIDN'T HEAR a word that the Sunday school teacher said. She used to love answering Mrs. Nevin's questions and would be the first person with her hand in the air, but none of it seemed important anymore. Who cared what a bunch of people who lived a long time ago in a faraway land did and said? The stories had nothing to do with Esther. They couldn't explain why everything in her life was swerving out of control like the car that had killed her mother. And as far as Esther could see, nothing in the Bible could tell her how to get her old life back again.

One week had passed since Daddy went away. It seemed like a year. They had skipped church last Sunday because it was the day after he'd left. During the week, Esther and Peter had stayed in their room every evening after school, avoiding Penny Goodrich. Esther hadn't wanted to get dressed and come to church this week, either, but Penny had insisted.

"I promised your daddy that I would take you to church . . . and I know you don't want to disappoint your daddy, do you? And besides, your grandma is expecting you for Sunday dinner afterward."

So here they sat in Sunday school. Esther glanced at Peter and saw him staring vacantly into space, showing no more interest in the lesson than she did. He was supposed to be in a class with kids his own age, but ever since he had been old enough to attend Sunday school he had insisted on staying with Esther, refusing to leave her side. "Either he stays with me or we both go home," she had told the superintendent that first day. Peter had been in her classes ever since.

"Well, our time is nearly up," Mrs. Nevin was saying. "Does anyone have a question? Something to share?"

Esther raised her hand for the first time. "Our father went away to fight in the war last week."

"My dad is fighting, too," someone said.

"Yeah, so is mine."

Esther raised her hand again. "Why do there have to be wars?"

The teacher removed her eyeglasses and cleaned them on a corner of her sweater. The tiny, prim woman had tightly curled hair that was so gray it looked blue. "Well, I'm sorry to say, Esther, that it's because there are evil people in the world, and they have to be stopped."

"Why doesn't God just kill all the evil people himself? Why do our fathers have to do it?"

Mrs. Nevin's pleasant smile faded. She wiped her glasses so vigorously, Esther thought the lens might pop out. "We don't really have time today to—"

A year's worth of unanswered questions suddenly spilled over like boiling soup. Esther was sick and tired of holding them all inside and no longer cared what Mrs. Nevin or anyone else thought of her. "I want to know why people who never did anything wrong have to die, and meanwhile the bad people get to keep on living?"

The room went very still. Even the rowdy boys who usually whispered and snickered throughout the lesson sat as still as mannequins. "I'm not really sure," Mrs. Nevin finally said, "but I think we should take a moment to pray for our loved ones who are off fighting."

"Why?" Esther asked. "What good will prayers do? Everyone prayed that my mother would live after the car accident, but she died in the hospital." Mrs. Nevin didn't seem able to reply. "Even if we pray and pray," Esther continued, "God doesn't stop people from dying, so what good does it do?"

"Everyone dies, Esther. But God promised that those of us who know Him will go to heaven to live with Him after we die."

"Why does He need more people up in heaven? Didn't you tell us that God owns the whole universe and all the stars and planets and things? Aren't there already a bunch of angels up in heaven with Him?"

Mrs. Nevin walked over to Esther's side and laid her hand on her shoulder. "I can't answer your questions, dear. I'm so sorry—"

"Well, who can?"

"Would you like me to ask Reverend McClure to visit you at home?"

Esther's anger fizzled into the familiar darkness once again like the last dying burst of fireworks. "Never mind. It doesn't matter."

"Yes it does, dear. I'll speak with the pastor right after the worship service, okay?"

"Don't bother."

Penny Goodrich was waiting for Esther and Peter in the church lobby, smiling and talking with everyone in her mile-a-minute way as if she had attended Esther's church all her life. She hadn't. Penny had never set foot in this church before. She didn't belong here. "Why can't you go to your own church?" Esther had asked her this morning as they boarded the bus.

Penny's smile had wavered like a birthday candle in the wind. "Well . . . because your father wants you to keep going to your regular church. And I'm taking care of you now."

The sight of Penny making herself at home here in church the same way she had made herself at home in the apartment made Esther furious. She hurried ahead into the sanctuary and plopped down in the pew so that Peter would have to sit in the middle beside Penny. Esther lowered her chin and stared at her shoes. The familiar sanctuary seemed like a different place for some reason.

She tried to remember what it had been like when she and Peter and Mama and Daddy used to come to church together. On the Sundays when it was Mama's turn to play the piano they would sit up front in the very first pew, right behind Mama. Esther loved to watch her mother's strong fingers dance across the keyboard. Mama had begun to teach Esther how to play, but now all the music had faded into silence.

The service lasted forever. Afterward, they walked over to Grandma Shaffer's house for Sunday dinner. Penny said good-bye and went next door to eat dinner with her own parents. Grandma greeted Esther and Peter in her housecoat and slippers.

"There was no sense in fixing a big meal now that your father isn't here to eat it," she said. "I made beans and franks. You like that, don't you?"

Esther shrugged. "I guess so." She didn't feel hungry.

It seemed very quiet without Penny's endless, cheerful chatter. Grandma put the pot of food on the table and sat down with Esther and Peter, but she didn't eat anything. She didn't even have a plate or silverware in front of her. She seemed very sad. "What's wrong?" Esther asked her.

"What do you think is wrong? All three of my boys are fighting in this terrible war, and I don't know what in the world I'll do if anything happens to them."

Esther didn't know what to say. She poked holes in her hot dog with her fork as Grandma's parakeet chirped noisily in the background. "We got a letter from Daddy this week," she finally said. "He told us that he has to sleep in a big room with lots of other men."

"Yeah, he sent me a letter, too. It's here somewhere, if you want to read it." Grandma braced her hands on the table and got up to search through the endless piles of papers on her countertops.

"Never mind," Esther said. "It's probably the same as ours."

Peter didn't play his usual game of fetch with Woofer after lunch, even though the dog begged and begged, dropping her slimy ball at Peter's feet and gazing up at him with her happy doggy smile and lolling tongue. Instead, they all sat in the crammed living room, listening to *The Old Fashioned Revival Hour* on the radio. Grandma's house smelled stuffy and stale, like a closet full of old clothes that no one ever wore.

"Knock, knock," Penny finally called through the back screen door. "Lunch all finished?"

Esther wove through the piles of junk to get to the door, relieved to see Penny. "Can we go home now?" she whispered.

Penny had filled two more shopping bags full of her things, and she lugged them to the bus stop. When the bus arrived, she set them down for a minute to help an elderly woman board the bus—then nearly left the bags behind. "I'm such a scatterbrain," she fussed when they were safely on board.

The woman reached across the aisle to pat Penny's hand. "Thank you for your kindness, dear. You don't find very many young people who are kind these days, especially a pretty young lady like you."

Esther made a face. Did the woman need glasses? Penny wasn't pretty at all.

As soon as Esther stepped off the bus, she took off at a run, sprinting ahead of Penny and Peter all the way home and clambering up the stairs to their apartment. She had her own keys. Daddy had given them to her so she and Peter could let themselves into the apartment after school.

That evening after supper, Esther was reading a book in the living room when she heard Penny's raised voice coming from the kitchen. "You're not being very nice, Peter. When someone asks you a question, you're supposed to answer it."

Esther had never heard their mousy caretaker raise her voice before. She had spoken to them in a sickeningly sweet voice all week as if they were babies. Had Penny only pretended to be shy and nice all this time? Esther stuck a marker in her book and hurried to rescue her brother.

Penny gripped Peter's arm as he struggled to get away. "No, wait. I want to know why you won't talk to me. You've been ignoring my questions all week. I don't want to write to your father, but—"

"Don't you dare touch my brother!" Esther grabbed Peter's other arm, winning the tug-of-war as she yanked him away from Penny. He looked pale and frightened, but he didn't cry out or make a sound. "Come on, Peter." Esther pulled him upstairs to the bedroom they shared and slammed the door.

"Are you okay?" she asked. He nodded.

"What was Penny so mad about?" He stared at her, not blinking.

"Come on, you can tell me. I'm on your side." She waited, trying to be patient, but he still said nothing. "Are you mad at me or something?"

He shook his head as tears pooled in his eyes. "Then why won't you tell me what's wrong?" Peter's face turned red as he continued to stare at her, his mouth slightly open as if he was trying to speak—but nothing came out.

"What's the matter with you?" she asked, giving him a shove. Esther wouldn't hurt her brother for anything in the world, but there was something unnatural about the mute way he stood there, as if he couldn't breathe or was choking on something. Her heart sped up. "Say something! If this is a game, then it isn't very funny."

Peter lowered his gaze and lifted his bony shoulders as if trying to make his head disappear down the collar of his shirt. He never had been a chatterbox like Esther was, and when he did speak it had always been in a soft mumble. People would have to lean real close to hear what he was saying, and Grandma Shaffer, who was hard of hearing, couldn't hear him at all. Everyone always said that Esther did enough talking for the both of them.

"Now, listen to me, Peter. I'm mad about the way things are around here, too, but it's going to get a whole lot worse if we make Penny mad. So come on, talk to me. Tell me what's wrong. I promise I won't tell anybody." She waited for almost a minute, but Peter still didn't reply. "Are you mad at me?" she asked again.

He shook his head and a tear slipped down his cheek. He wiped it with the heel of his hand. Esther sighed and sank down on her own bed across from his, listening to the traffic noise on the street below as they stared silently at each other.

That was when it dawned on Esther that Peter hadn't spoken a single word since Daddy left a week ago. Peter had walked to school in silence, eaten his meals in silence, done his homework, read comic books, and gone to bed in silence. Her heart began to race as if she had just run up two flights of stairs to their bedroom. She jumped up in a panic and rummaged through their toy box in search of Peter's small, square blackboard and a piece of chalk. When she found them, she pushed them into Peter's hands. "If you won't talk to me, then at least tell me why not."

He held the slate against his chest for a moment before lowering it to his lap and writing: *I can't.*

"You can tell me, Peter. I promise not to tell."

He shook his head from side to side, as if trying to shake off water, and rapped his knuckles against the board. When he had her attention he added one word to what he'd already written.

I can't talk.

"Don't be stupid. You talked fine a week ago—and the week before that. Is your throat sore or something?"

He shook his head again, erased the words with his fist, and wrote: *The words won't come out.*

Dread rolled through Esther. She didn't know what to say. Peter erased again and wrote: *Please don't make me.*

"Okay," she said softly. "Okay. Everything will be okay." But she wasn't at all certain that it was true. What would she do if something happened to Peter? He was the only person she had left.

She heard a knock on their bedroom door. Penny. "Please go away," Esther said. There was a long pause, but she could tell that Penny hadn't left. Esther could picture her biting her lip and twisting her fingers in that annoying way she did.

"Um . . . Esther?" Penny's voice sounded shaky. "I'm sorry I yelled. What happened was . . . I mean . . . all I did was ask Peter if he would dry the supper dishes because it's his turn, and . . . and he wouldn't answer me. So then I was trying to see if he was okay because he seemed real quiet all week, and . . . and he still wouldn't answer me. You know I would never hurt either one of you, don't you?"

Esther felt a small measure of power. Penny was probably afraid that she would write to Daddy and give him a bad report. "I'll be out in a minute," she said. "And I'll dry the dishes for him." She turned to her brother and pointed to the chalkboard. "If you won't talk, then at least explain to me what's going on, okay?" Peter nodded in reply.

Penny was standing right outside the door when Esther opened it. "Listen, is Peter okay?" she asked.

"He's fine." Esther squeezed past her and went downstairs to the kitchen. Penny had already washed the dishes and piled them on the drainboard, so Esther pulled a dish towel off the hook to wipe them. Daddy had never made them dry the dishes when he'd been in charge. Sometimes they hadn't washed the dishes for days and days, and when they finally did get around to it, they would let them air-dry. But Penny had given them chores to do, making them clean up and help with supper and wash the dishes. Esther resented it, even though Mama had given them chores to do around the house, too. But Penny wasn't their mother. She would never take Mama's place.

Esther had just put away the last dish when the doorbell rang. Penny got there first, but Esther arrived in time to hear the man say, "Good evening, Mrs. Shaffer."

"She's *not* Mrs. Shaffer," Esther shouted before Penny could reply. "She just takes care of us."

"I see. Well, I'm Inspector Dalton from the fire marshal's office." He held up a silver badge. "I'm canvassing the neighborhood, looking for witnesses to last week's fire at the synagogue across the street. I'd like to ask you a few questions, if I may."

"I'm sorry," Penny said, "but I wasn't here that night. I came the day after the fire."

"Is Mr. Shaffer home, then?"

"No, I'm sorry," Penny began. "He—"

"He left to fight in the army," Esther finished.

"What's your name, young lady?"

"Esther Shaffer."

"Were you home on the night of the fire?"

"Yes."

"Would you please tell me, in your own words, what you remember?" He pulled a small notebook and a pen from his pocket and wrote everything down while Esther talked.

"We were upstairs when we heard the sirens. Daddy was packing to go away. He made us close the windows because of the smoke, and then we went outside to watch. That's when we saw our landlord, Mr. Mendel, come out of the burning building. He must have been hurt because an ambulance came and took him away."

"How did you know it was Mr. Mendel?"

"Because he had on striped suspenders. We talked to him a little while before the fire and he was wearing them then."

"How did he seem to you earlier that evening?"

Esther shrugged, not quite understanding the question. "Crabby. But he's always in a bad mood. His wife used to be nice, but she—" Esther halted, remembering the horrible sound the runaway car made as it crashed into the fruit stand. "His wife died."

"But you were sure it was Mr. Mendel who came out of the synagogue?"

"Daddy asked one of the other men if it was him, and he said yes."

"Do you recall anything else?"

She shrugged and shook her head. She didn't want to remember. Watching the fire had been a terrible way to spend the last night with her father. She never would forget the feeling of the heat on her face, the smoke and cinders that stung her eyes and throat. Or the feeling of Daddy's hand in hers as they watched the building burn. A year ago, Esther had let go of Mama's hand, insisting that she was old enough to cross the street without holding hands like a baby. She had left Mama's side to wander around the vegetable market on her own. This time it was Daddy who had let go of her hand first.

After the inspector left, Penny pulled Esther aside. "Listen, I hope you're not going to stop talking to me, too. We need to try to get along for your father's sake. I don't want to have to give a bad report when I write to him."

"Go ahead and tell him whatever you want—I don't care. Maybe then he'll come back home and take care of us himself."

Penny shook her head. "He signed up for the army, Esther. He can't just quit and come home. He made a promise to them."

"He *has* to quit! They *have* to let him come home!"

"The army doesn't work that way. If you don't believe me, ask your schoolteacher. Ask anyone."

Esther tried to wiggle away, but Penny stopped her. "Listen, would you be happier staying with your grandmother? I can talk to her, if you want. I can see if she'll change her mind about taking care of you."

Esther shook her head. "I don't want to stay at Grandma's house."

"I'm doing my best, Esther. I just want to help your father out. I'm sure he's worried about you."

"Daddy doesn't care about us, or he never would have left us!" Again she tried to leave, and again Penny stopped her.

"I just want you and Peter to be happy. What would make you happy?"

"If everything was back the way it was!"

Penny finally let her go, and Esther ran upstairs to her room. Peter was lying facedown on the bed, his favorite Captain Marvel comic books abandoned, his sobs muffled by the pillow. He had left the slate on Esther's bed, and she picked it up to see what he had written.

> *I don't know what's wrong.*
> *I try to talk and nothing comes out.*
> *Help me!*

CHAPTER 8

OCTOBER 1943

PENNY SNAPPED THE LATCHES shut on the children's lunch boxes and stood them on the porcelain countertop. "Okay, your lunches are all packed," she said. "Don't be late for school."

"We've been going to school by ourselves for more than a year," Esther mumbled into her cereal bowl. "Daddy always left for work before us."

"Oh. Sorry." Penny could have kicked herself. Why did she always say the wrong thing? "Well, I guess I'll see you after school, then. Bye." Penny grabbed her own lunch box and waved to the kids, but they didn't even look up at her.

Winning their affection was proving to be harder than she'd expected. She had lived with them for nearly three weeks now, but Esther remained cool and distant, and Peter hadn't spoken a single word to her since she arrived. Eddie sent short notes to her every week—along with much longer letters to his kids—asking Penny how everything was going. How could she tell him that everything was awful? Instead, she wrote long letters back to him, pretending that things were fine. Maybe everything would be fine in another week or so. She didn't want Eddie to worry—or to find another woman to take her place.

Penny hurried to the corner bus stop and waited with the crowd of black-clothed Jewish men. They made her feel like a sparrow among a flock of crows. Her father would demand that she move home immediately if he knew that she mingled with so many Jewish people every day. That's why she never mentioned Eddie's neighborhood when she visited her parents on Sundays. As it was, they would spend the entire afternoon trying to convince Penny to give up this foolish idea and come home. She would never do that. Returning home would mean giving up her dream of marrying Eddie.

When the bus finally arrived, Penny didn't see any empty seats. Swaying passengers filled the aisle, gripping the leather straps above their heads. She didn't like to be jammed inside with so many strangers, but if she waited for the next bus she would be late for work. As she hesitated, halting with one foot on the step, a marine in one of the front seats stood up.

"Here, miss. Take my seat."

"Are . . . are you sure? That's very kind of you." He smiled, and Penny thought he might be the same soldier who had sacrificed his seat for her once before. Who could tell with so many men in uniform these days?

"Are you on your way to work, miss?" he asked as they maneuvered to trade places. Penny nodded. Mother had warned her repeatedly not to talk to strangers. The stranger's smile widened into a grin.

"Don't tell me," he said, "let me guess. I'll bet you're a . . . what do they call them nowadays? The gals who build ships for the war effort? . . . Rosie the Riveter!" He had such a friendly manner that she couldn't help smiling in return. He reminded her of Mickey Rooney with his round, youthful face and pug nose—and Penny loved Mickey Rooney's films. Mickey wasn't tall and handsome like other movie stars, just plain and ordinary—like she was. He made her believe that ordinary people could live happily ever after, too.

"No, I work at the bus station," she replied. The marine had gallantly forfeited his seat for her. The least she could do was be polite.

"The bus station is close to the Navy Yard, isn't it?" he asked. "I'm assigned to the Navy Yard—that's where I'm headed, in fact."

Penny's curiosity momentarily outweighed her fear. Or maybe it was loneliness that caused her to look up at him again and continue the conversation. With her parents mad at her and the children barely speaking to her, she hadn't had a friendly conversation in days. "What does a soldier like you do at the Navy Yard?"

"Security work—making sure nobody sneaks inside the shipyard who isn't supposed to be there. It's no secret that they're building ships for the war effort, so it's the Marines' job to keep out spies and saboteurs. Remember the German spies who came ashore on Long Island a few years ago?"

"I do! There haven't been more since then, have there?"

"No, and there won't be if I'm doing my job right," he said with a laugh. He let go of the strap for a moment when the bus halted at the next stop and offered her his hand. "My name is Roy Fuller."

Penny found it hard to break through years of fear. She had been frightened enough just boarding a bus every day instead of walking to work. But what could it hurt to be nice? She offered her hand for a quick shake. "Penny Goodrich."

"Nice to meet you, Miss Goodrich." The conversation ended as more people boarded the bus, pushing Roy farther down the aisle. Penny wasn't sure if she felt relieved or disappointed. It had felt good to talk to someone and extend a hand of friendship, so when she arrived at the bus station and saw a panhandler begging for food, Penny opened her lunch box and gave him her sandwich. Everyone needed a little love now and then.

She sat at her cashier's window all morning as bus after bus pulled into the station, disgorging passengers and then filling up again, like a scene from a cartoon. When the morning rush finally dwindled down to a trickle, her thoughts returned to handsome Eddie Shaffer and how he would be coming home on leave in a few weeks. What would he think of the job she was doing for him? Yes, his house was clean and his children were washed and fed, but Peter refused to talk to her, and Esther hated her guts. Penny didn't know how to win them over. If she wrote to Eddie and complained, he would take his children's

side. Right now he obviously loved them more than he loved her. . . .
Loved her? Ha! He barely knew she existed!

Think, Penny, think. She wished she were smarter and could figure
things out better. Should she buy them ice cream and other treats?
Take them to the movies next Saturday?

"Miss Goodrich . . . Excuse me, Miss Goodrich?" She turned to
see her boss standing behind her in the doorway of her ticket booth.
How long had he been there?

"Yes, Mr. Whitney?"

"Would you come into my office, please? I need to talk to you."

"But . . . my ticket window?"

"You can close it. Miss Napoli can cover things now that the
rush is over."

"Yes, sir." Penny pulled the shield down over her window and
locked the cash drawer, then slid off her stool and followed him to
his office. Was she in trouble? Had something terrible happened? Her
cash drawer had balanced to the penny yesterday, so it couldn't be a
shortage. Had she accepted a counterfeit bill by mistake?

"Sit down, please, Miss Goodrich." He motioned to a chair as he
sat down behind his desk. Penny obeyed, but worry kept her on the
very edge of it, as if she might have to leap up and run.

"Miss Goodrich, I understand that you've worked here for more
than five years now?"

"Yes, sir. Ever since I finished high school."

"And you've been one of our best workers—smart, honest, and
very reliable. How would you like a promotion?"

It took a moment before she could speak. "Me? . . . A promotion?"

"Yes," he said, smiling. "And it would include a pay raise, too. I
understand you help out your elderly parents, don't you?"

She nodded, too stunned to speak.

"The thing is, I need bus drivers right now more than I need
cashiers. A lot of our drivers are either enlisting or leaving us for
higher-paying work in the armament industry. And we need to add
more buses to destinations like the Navy Yard and the military bases,

with so many servicemen stationed around here. I'm sure you've noticed how crowded the buses are these days."

"I-I don't even know how to drive a car, Mr. Whitney."

"That doesn't matter. We're starting a training program for new drivers. The company will train you for free, help you get your license, the whole works. I appreciate the fact that you haven't already left us for a munitions job."

"That kind of work isn't for me, Mr. Whitney. I would hate being cooped up in a noisy factory all day. Besides, I hear they make you work long hours, seven days a week at the Navy Yard, and I can't do that because I'm taking care of two children for a friend of mine who went into the army."

"Well, this will be perfect for you, then. We can assign you to a bus route right here in Brooklyn, Monday through Friday only. You'll have seniority since you already work for us. You can do it, Miss Goodrich, I'm certain of it."

No one had ever shown confidence in Penny before, and she longed to prove Mr. Whitney right. But driving a bus? That wasn't a job for someone like her, Mother would say. Besides, hadn't Penny already tackled more changes than she could handle?

"Did I mention that your pay would increase by more than fifteen dollars a week?"

Penny could only stare at him. It seemed like a huge amount of money.

"So how about it, Miss Goodrich? What do you say?"

She didn't know what to say. "Could . . . could I think about it?"

"Sure, but you'll have to let me know shortly. The drivers' training program begins soon. Oh, and if you do decide to sign up for it, you'll need some form of identification to start the licensing process. A birth certificate will do."

Penny felt as though she was sleepwalking as she made her way back to her ticket booth and slid open her window. "What was that all about?" the other cashier asked. Penny wasn't sure if she should tell her . . . then decided that it didn't matter since she probably wouldn't accept the job.

"Mr. Whitney asked me if I wanted to learn to drive a bus."

"Wow! You gonna do it?"

"I don't know. I'm such a Dumb Dora . . . and I don't even know how to drive a car."

"You? Dumb? Are you kidding? Your cash drawer always balances right to the penny, every single day. Mine never does. Boy, if I could get out of this crummy booth I'd do it in a minute!"

"But I don't think . . . I mean . . . I can't drive a great big bus."

"You should do it. I'll bet you'll meet a lot of servicemen. The buses are full of them these days. You're so lucky!"

"I don't care about meeting servicemen," Penny said with a little laugh. "I already have a boyfriend."

By the end of the workday, Penny still hadn't made up her mind about the promotion, teetering back and forth between taking it and not taking it like a kid on a seesaw. On a whim she decided to run home to her parents' house on her way to the apartment and pick up her birth certificate just in case. Her mother had the ironing board set up in the kitchen and was listening to the radio as she pressed Father's shirts. The sweet smell of steaming cotton filled the room.

"Your birth certificate!" she said when Penny told her what she wanted. "What do you need that for?" She made it sound as though Penny had asked her for the moon. Too late, Penny realized her mistake.

First of all, Mother would have a conniption fit if she found out that Penny wanted to learn to drive a bus. And after she recovered, she would nag Penny day and night until she finally talked her out of it. She didn't think Penny was capable of riding a bicycle, much less driving a huge bus filled with people—and all of them strangers!

"Well, you see . . ." Penny started backing out of the kitchen and into the living room as she talked. "My boss at work says I might be getting a promotion soon, but he needs to see my birth certificate. So if you just tell me where to look, I'll find it myself. You don't have to bother. Is it here in the desk with Father's important papers?"

Mother set down the iron with a thump and hurried after Penny, leaving the appliance plugged in—something she repeatedly warned Penny never to do. "Don't go digging through the desk. It isn't in there."

"Well, where is it, then?"

"You don't have one."

Penny stared at her. "Everybody has a birth certificate."

"Well, you don't. It got lost years ago . . . when we moved into this house. I never replaced it."

"Lost? But . . . but I need it. I won't get the promotion unless—"

"What kind of promotion is this? Who ever heard of such a thing? You didn't need a birth certificate when you started working for the bus company. Why would you need one now?"

Penny didn't dare tell her the truth—nor did she want to lie. She knew Mother was still furious with her for moving into Eddie's apartment, and she wasn't likely to help her now, no matter how much Penny begged.

"Never mind. I need to get back to the apartment. I don't like to leave the kids alone for too long after school."

"Those children should be living next door with their grandmother, not with you. When are you going to give up this ridiculous notion of playing house and come back home where you belong? And why in the world would you want a promotion when you already have more responsibility than you can handle?"

Penny slouched toward the door. "I'll see you and Dad next Sunday. Bye."

Mother's reaction made Penny fume all the way across town. Long before she arrived home, she reached the conclusion that no matter what happened, she would never move back home with her parents. Never. If Eddie fired her and hired someone else to watch his kids, she would find a little apartment of her own. She could do it with a pay increase of fifteen dollars a week. If Mr. Whitney thought she could drive a bus, then maybe she could.

Penny had found a seat close to the front of the bus, and she watched the driver at work, imagining herself doing his job. He had a lot to look out for with so many cars and pedestrians and buses filling the streets. But other than that, all he did was stop and go, and take people's tickets, and hand out transfers, and make sure passengers dropped enough change into the little metal slots to cover their fares.

Penny had endured the same boring, day-to-day existence her entire life—living at home, selling tickets at the bus station, listening to her mother's criticism—and suddenly, she couldn't stand the thought of living that way for the rest of her life. *Fifteen extra dollars a week.* She would be rich. She would sign up for drivers' training tomorrow.

She smiled at the driver as she got off the bus. She practically skipped all the way upstairs to Eddie's apartment. She had her confidence back and was growing more and more excited about the new job when the ringing telephone interrupted her thoughts.

"Shaffer residence, Penny Goodrich speaking."

"Hello, this is Mrs. Cole from Waring Elementary School. I'm Peter's teacher. I wondered if you could meet with me tomorrow afternoon after school."

"Well . . . I'm not a relative, Mrs. Cole. I'm just taking care of Peter and Esther while—"

"I know. Mr. Shaffer came to the school and explained the arrangement before he left for the army. Would this time tomorrow work for you, Miss Goodrich?"

"I guess so. I could come right after work."

"Thank you. I'm in Room 5. I'll see you tomorrow."

Now what? Did Peter need extra help with his homework? Was he causing trouble? Penny hoped not, because she didn't know how to handle discipline problems. She couldn't even get Peter to talk to her. Now Eddie would realize for certain that she didn't know anything about kids. She was in over her head and dumber than a green bean to have volunteered for this job in the first place. She would be an even bigger fool to think she could drive a bus.

Penny barely slept that night for worrying. She was groggy-eyed the next morning when Mr. Whitney came to her cashier's booth again. "I don't want to rush you, Miss Goodrich, but I will need to know your decision soon."

"I'm sorry, Mr. Whitney, but I don't have a birth certificate. My mother said she lost it years ago and—"

"Where were you born?"

"Here in Brooklyn, I guess."

"Well, the New York State Vital Records Office can issue you a new one. You'll probably have to pay a few dollars, but it shouldn't be a problem."

She was about to explain that she had made up her mind not to take the job when Mr. Whitney added, "In fact, I'll give you an extra half hour for lunch today so you can go over and apply for a new one. That's how badly I need drivers, Miss Goodrich."

Penny did as she was told. She always did. As soon as she finished filling out all the papers at the records' office, she shoved the job decision to the back of her mind as she continued to worry about this afternoon's meeting with Peter's teacher. Her knees shook as she walked through the doors of his elementary school.

"I'll come right to the point," Mrs. Cole said after the introductions. "Peter hasn't spoken a word to me or anyone else in school in weeks."

The news astonished Penny. She would have fallen over if she hadn't been sitting on a chair. "You either? He hasn't talked to me since the day I arrived and his daddy left for boot camp. I thought he was mad at me for some reason. I had no idea he wasn't talking to anyone."

"His sister, Esther, came to me a few days after their father left and said that Peter had laryngitis and couldn't talk. I sent him to the school nurse, but he didn't have a fever and his throat didn't seem swollen. I decided to wait and see if he was going through a phase, but when nothing changed I thought you and I should talk. He has been doing fine with his schoolwork, and he doesn't cause any trouble. He simply communicates by writing, not speaking."

"What should I do? I-I don't know what to do. I don't have any experience with children, Mrs. Cole. I just wanted to help Eddie out."

"I'm aware that Peter's mother passed away over a year ago and that his father has recently left home. I've heard of cases like this before where a child becomes so traumatized that he simply shuts down. For a boy as sensitive as Peter, I can see how losing both of his parents in such a short time might have that effect."

"Do you think I should take him to a doctor?"

"Not yet. You seem like a kind, capable woman, Miss Goodrich, and I have a feeling that once you and the children settle into a new routine, Peter will be okay."

It was the second time in two days that someone had told Penny that she seemed capable. She felt like a fraud.

"Will Peter's father be coming home anytime soon?" Mrs. Cole asked.

"He'll get a furlough when he finishes basic training."

"Then I think the best thing to do is to simply wait and see. Don't pressure Peter. If the problem doesn't resolve on its own, we can all meet to talk about the situation when Mr. Shaffer comes home."

Penny thanked Mrs. Cole and walked back to the apartment. For some reason her tears would not stop falling the entire way. She didn't want to raise two difficult children. She didn't know how. All she wanted to do was marry Eddie Shaffer. Was that asking for so much?

CHAPTER 9

A BASEBALL GAME blared from Jacob's radio. It had done so for the past hour, but he could only stare at the machine in frustration. He wanted to change the station or at least lower the volume, but every time he tried to manipulate the tiny knobs with his useless hands he made matters worse. That was how he had ended up with the baseball game in the first place instead of the musical program he usually listened to.

He was tired of wearing bandages on his hands, tired of being helpless. The dressings should have come off a week ago, but the doctor had detected a problem. The burns were not healing right. There was a slight infection, and Jacob would not only have to keep the dressings on for another week but the doctor had made the bandages even thicker. The bulky cast on his right arm added to his frustration.

A stack of newspapers cluttered his dining room table. They contained articles he wanted to save, the latest maps showing where the battle lines were drawn, and photographs of the Nazi bombings in London. But Jacob could not hold a pair of scissors, much less cut with them.

Women from the congregation continued to come by every few

days to drop off casserole dishes and quarts of soup. They offered to come inside and help Jacob, but he chased them all away. Let the dirty dishes pile up—what did it matter? Rebbe Grunfeld still coaxed him to let the men from the shul come here to pray. The deluge of food must be part of the enticement as they tried to persuade him to join them again. Jacob continued to refuse.

"It's a line drive into center field . . . the runner heads toward second base. . . . The center fielder scrambles for the ball . . . and he fumbles!"

Would the baseball game never end? Jacob wanted to hear the latest news about the war and the Allied invasion of Italy. The news should come on soon. It usually did around suppertime—and suppertime meant more frustration as he tried to heat up another meal with these mittens on his hands. The doctor should try working with these clumsy things. See how he liked it.

He sighed and sat down at his desk, fumbling for his son's letters. Jacob had waited all day to reread one. After much practice these past few weeks, he had finally figured out how to blow into the opened envelope and remove the letters with his teeth, then smooth them out on his desk with his mittened hands.

When Avraham had first begun writing, it had been easy for Jacob to picture his son through these letters and visualize the life he led in Hungary. He could imagine Avi's excitement when he saw the old country for the first time and when he met his relatives and their families. Later, Avi's letters had given details of his studies and told how much he valued the rebbe's wisdom and insights. Then Sarah Rivkah had entered the picture, and Avraham had spoken of little else as his love for her blossomed.

Jacob had read the letters so many times that he had their contents memorized. He already knew what today's letter would say. He knew both the joy and the pain it contained.

Dear Mama and Abba,

I have wonderful news. Sarah Rivkah and I have decided to marry. I love her and she loves me. I don't want to live another day of my life without her. She is a precious gift to me from Hashem, blessed be He.

I know the news of our engagement may upset you, and I am so sorry for that. You will say that I am too impetuous, that I am moving forward too quickly. You will advise me to wait a year before marrying her. I can almost see your face, Abba, and hear the concern in your voice as you say these things. But Uncle Yehuda knows Sarah's family very well, and he has agreed to act in your place for our betrothal and marriage. Mama, I am so sorry that you will not be here with us to celebrate this joyous day, but I know that you will love Sarah Rivkah the moment you meet her. She is the daughter you have always wished for. Please rejoice with us.

I received your most recent letter, Abba, and I understand why you are begging me to come home. I am as concerned as you are, now that the Nazis have invaded neighboring Poland. You are probably right in believing the war will eventually spread to America, too. But if another worldwide war truly is coming, then Sarah and I want our chance at happiness before it does. Right now it is very difficult to emigrate to the U.S. from Hungary because of all the quotas. Nobody wants to take in more Jews, it seems. But since I am an American citizen, I've been told that it will be easier for Sarah Rivkah to immigrate if we are already married. It might make it easier for her parents and the rest of our family to come, as well.

Jacob stopped reading. He knew the rest. The mail took so long to travel across an ocean filled with U-boats and warships that by the time Avraham's next letter arrived, the wedding had taken place. Eleven months and dozens of letters later—after Belgium, the Netherlands, and France had all fallen to the Nazis—Hashem had blessed Avi and Sarah with a little daughter.

Jacob didn't even try to stuff the letter back into the envelope. It couldn't be done. The bandages must come off. Now. If he couldn't cut them off himself, he would swallow his pride and go upstairs and ask his tenant for help. Jacob started toward the door, then stopped. Ed Shaffer wouldn't be there. In the aftermath of the fire, Jacob had forgotten that his tenant had left to join the army. Well, maybe one of the children could help him cut off the dressings. He gripped the doorknob between both hands and turned it. The door opened—and the boy from upstairs tumbled into Jacob's living room as if he had been sitting on the floor with his back against the door.

"What in the world . . . ?"

The boy scrambled to his feet, ready to run.

"Wait. Don't run away, please." Jacob tried to corral him with his cumbersome hands. "I would like to ask a favor of you."

The child turned to him, and the fear Jacob saw in his eyes made him feel like an ogre in a fairy tale. He hadn't meant to frighten him. The boy had never run from Miriam that way. But then Miriam Shoshanna had spoiled both of those children, passing out caramel drops and slices of honey cake. Surely they knew she was gone, didn't they?

Jacob shook his head to clear his thoughts. "Could you come inside please and help me with the radio? I cannot do it so well with these." He held up his hands. He tried to smile to put the boy at ease, but his smile felt so forced that Jacob wondered if he had forgotten how. "Come, come. The radio is right here." He rested his hand on the child's shoulder to herd him through the door. "Tell me your name again?"

Instead of replying, the boy dug into his pocket and pulled out a piece of lined notebook paper, folded many times, and the stub of a pencil. Smudged writing filled the paper on both sides, but he found a blank place and printed: *Peter.*

Odd. Very odd. But perhaps Peter thought Jacob was odd, as well.

"I am sorry if I frightened you, but I was not expecting anyone to be leaning against my door. I never heard you knock because my radio is too loud . . . Was there something you wanted?" Maybe he had come to ask him to turn it down—something Jacob had tried in vain to do.

Peter nodded shyly and pointed to the radio.

"Heh? My radio? You would like me to turn it down, yes?" Peter shook his head vigorously—no—and made a motion like a ball player swinging a bat. He managed a flicker of a smile as he pointed to the radio again.

"Ah. You were listening to the game." A nod. Jacob wondered why the pantomime? Why not simply speak up? He had no patience with guessing games.

"And so as the seventh inning comes to an end," the announcer said, "the Brooklyn Dodgers lead by three runs."

Peter's smile widened, and he held up three fingers in triumph.

"Is that the team you like?" Again, a shy nod. Jacob didn't have the heart to make him change the station. He would do it later himself, after the boy helped him cut off the bandages.

Just then the door to the apartment upstairs rattled open and the sister shouted down the stairs. "Peter? Peter, where are you?"

The boy went to the open doorway and looked up, silently waving his arms at her. Apparently he was playing his little game with everyone, not just Jacob.

"What are you doing?" she called down to him. "You know we're not supposed to bother Mr. Mendel."

Jacob was going to lose his assistant. He hurried over to the door. "Please, he is not a bother. I asked him to come inside. I need a favor."

She stared at Jacob for a moment, then descended the stairs silently and gracefully. She was a lovely girl, blond like her father, and she carried herself like a princess. He recalled that her name was Esther, like the queen in Scripture. She would be a beauty like her mother, no doubt. The brief memory of the children's mother—so tightly entwined with the memory of Miriam Shoshanna—stuck him like a knife in his ribs.

"How are you doing, Mr. Mendel?" Esther asked politely. "We haven't seen much of you since the night of the fire. Are you okay now?"

"Yes. I am fine. But I would like someone to cut off these bandages for me. As you can see, I am quite helpless with them on."

She took a small step backward. "Shouldn't a doctor or . . . or a nurse do it? I've never done anything like that before. I wouldn't want to hurt you."

"You cannot hurt me. Just cut them off, please. You will find a pair of scissors in that desk drawer."

"Why do you need them off?"

"Because I cannot do anything for myself with them on. I cannot turn on the stove to heat up my dinner or turn down the radio—I can barely feed myself, and I am growing tired of it."

"I can turn on the stove for you. And fix the radio."

"Are you going to feed me, too? Heh?" He saw that he had frightened her a bit, and he hadn't meant to. Why vent his frustration on her? "I am sorry. I should not have said that."

"That's okay. I can help you in the kitchen, if you want."

Jacob glanced at Peter. He was sitting cross-legged on the floor in front of the radio, listening intently.

"It's another base hit for the Dodgers . . . Looks like it's going to be a double . . . Yes! He's safe on second . . ."

"Do you have a radio of your own upstairs?" Jacob asked her.

"We do, but we're not supposed to listen to it until after our homework is done."

"Ah. I see." He would let the boy listen a while longer. "Come into the kitchen then, if you don't mind, and we will see about some food." He opened the crammed refrigerator for Esther and showed her what he wanted to eat. "Do you know the best way to warm it up? I am tired of eating everything cold, but as you can see, all my pots are dirty and I am unable to wash them."

"I'll wash them for you."

"It would be less work for you to simply cut these off." He felt a smile tugging his mouth as he held up his hands again. "Then I could wash them myself."

She caught the joke and smiled in return. "I don't know anything about bandages, Mr. Mendel, but I do know how to wash dishes."

"Fine. Whichever you prefer."

He watched her choose a pot from the pile and scrub it clean with soap and water. "It's really sad about the synagogue burning down, isn't it?" she asked as she worked.

"Yes. Yes it is. I suppose they will rebuild it. But even so, it will never be the same."

She scooped several spoonfuls of the casserole he had chosen into the clean pot and put it on the stove to warm. It had been a long time since Jacob had watched his wife work in the kitchen. Miriam Shoshanna had loved to cook. Watching her knead the dough and braid the *challah* for Shabbat had been like watching a sculptor at work. He wondered about the daughter-in-law he had never met, Sarah Rivkah. Did she bake challah for Avraham and light the Shabbat candles and recite the blessing? And his granddaughter, little Fredeleh—

"Can I ask you a question?" Esther interrupted his thoughts.

"Yes?"

"Everyone says that my mama and Mrs. Mendel are up in heaven now, but I don't understand why God wanted them, do you? Couldn't He see that we need them down here a lot more?"

Jacob felt tears burning his eyes. He looked at his cluttered kitchen, the stack of dirty dishes, then at the child waiting for his reply, and he realized her need was every bit as great as his was, even if her graceful hands were not covered in bandages.

"I am sorry. But I do not know the answer to your question."

"Sometimes . . ." she said softly, "sometimes I feel really, really mad at God."

He could hardly speak. "Yes. Yes, so do I."

She looked up at him, and he saw her tears through his own. And before Jacob realized what was happening, Esther flung herself at him, clinging tightly to him, sobbing against his chest. He wrapped his arms around her, hugging her in return—the first embrace he had felt for a very long time.

CHAPTER 10

ESTHER HURRIED TO FINISH drying the supper dishes for Penny, swiping the towel across a plate and shoving it into the corner cupboard. She didn't want to stay in the kitchen with Penny Goodrich a minute longer than she had to. She wished she could go downstairs and help Mr. Mendel with his dishes again. She had felt a kinship with him last evening that she didn't quite understand except that he seemed as sad and as lonely as she was. But Mr. Mendel had insisted that the dishes were too many for her to do all at once, and so when Peter's ball game had ended, she and her brother had returned to their own apartment.

Penny seemed to be taking her sweet time washing the dishes tonight, as if her mind wasn't really on her work. She still had all the pots and pans to finish, but she suddenly pulled her hands out of the soapy water and wiped them on the front of her apron as she turned to face Esther. "Can I ask you something?"

"What?"

"Does Peter talk to you?" Penny kept her voice low, as if she didn't want Peter to overhear them, even though he was all the way upstairs in the bedroom.

Esther shrugged and turned away. She had been taught to tell the truth and to respect her elders, but she didn't want to reply. She busied herself by straightening the dishes in the corner cupboard, nesting a stack of smaller bowls inside the larger ones.

"I met with Peter's teacher the other day," Penny continued above the rattle of glassware. "His teacher said that he doesn't talk at all in school. Not one word. And he never talks to me. . . . So I was wondering if he talks to you when the two of you are by yourselves."

Esther slowly turned around and looked up at Penny. She could only shake her head as tears squeezed her throat. Worry and fear for Peter had weighed Esther down like a sack of rocks, and even though she resented Penny's interference, she was tired of carrying the burden of her brother's silence all alone.

"He writes everything down," Esther finally managed to say. "Even to me."

"Did he tell you why? Or what's bothering him?"

Again, Esther could only shake her head as she struggled not to cry. Penny would treat her like a baby if she did. She took a moment to control her tears. "Peter says he wants to talk, but he can't make the words come out. I thought he was playing a game at first, and that he'd get tired of it in a day or two. But I think he's scared now."

"So he isn't doing it on purpose?"

"No. . . . Do you think there's something wrong with him?"

"I don't know. His teacher says he just needs time to get used to all the changes around here. I asked her if I should take him to see a doctor, but she said to wait until your father comes home."

Esther nodded and turned away again. She was trying to be strong, trying not to let Penny see how scared she was.

"I know you want to help him, Esther, and so do I. Do you think we could work together and help each other?" She waited for a reply. Esther didn't offer one. "Your father will be home for a visit after basic training, and I'd hate to get him all worried about Peter. He has enough on his mind now that he might be going off to war soon. Wouldn't it be better if we tried to help Peter before he comes home?"

Esther didn't know what to do as fear for her brother battled the resentment she felt toward Penny. She didn't want to cooperate with her. She wanted everything to be the way it used to be, with Penny gone and Daddy home again.

"Talk to me, Esther."

She whirled to face Penny, spilling her anger instead of her tears. "Daddy will see how much we need him here. He'll see that he can't go away again—he can't! Peter needs him!" She threw down her dish towel and hurried from the kitchen. Then, worried that Penny would follow her and keep trying to wear her down, she bolted upstairs to the safety of her bedroom.

Peter looked up at her in surprise as she rushed inside and slammed the door behind her. But he didn't speak, didn't ask what was the matter, even though he must see Esther's tears. He was the only family member she had left, yet he lived in his own silent world, reading Captain Marvel and Superman comics and shutting Esther out. She scooped up the slate from the dresser and threw it at him.

"Everybody's worried about you, you know. Your teacher and Penny both know that you're not talking to anybody. And things are going to get a lot worse if you don't start talking. They're going to take you to see a doctor. You have to tell me what's wrong!"

Peter looked angry as he climbed off the bed to retrieve a piece of chalk. He began to write, his lips pressed together in a tight line, leaning so hard on the chalk that it snapped in two. When he finished, he held up the slate to show Esther.

I don't know what's wrong!

"Can't you try to say something?"

I do try!

"Well, do you want them to take you to the doctor?" He shook his head vehemently, then wrote, *Just leave me alone.*

"Fine! I'll leave you alone!"

She hated the word *alone*. Thousands of people lived here in Brooklyn with her, yet Esther had never felt more alone in her life. This was all her fault. If she had stayed beside her mother that day in the market instead of stomping off, maybe she could have protected Mama from that runaway car. Mama would still be alive, Daddy would still be living here with them, and Peter would still be able to talk. In that one defiant act of letting go, Esther had caused everything to go wrong, and now she had to figure out a way to make everything right again.

She rummaged in her school bag for a pad of paper and a pencil and flopped down on her bed to start a list for her father, scrawling across the top: *Reasons why you have to leave the army and come home.*

1. *We miss you.*
2. *We're all alone.*
3. *It's not the same here without you.*
4. *Grandma Shaffer is sad, too.*
5. *Something is wrong with Peter and you have to help him.*
6. *Penny is—*

Esther tapped the pencil against the pad as she searched for the right word. To be honest, everything Penny did around the house was okay: cooking, cleaning, washing their clothes. She was never mean to them, never yelled at them, and she tried really hard to be cheerful and friendly—too hard, in fact. Esther didn't want to be Penny's friend. When it came right down to it, Esther couldn't think of a single bad thing to say about Penny except that she wasn't Mama and she never would be. No one could take Mama's place. Ever. Esther closed her eyes, trying to picture her mother's face. Panic squeezed her chest when she realized that she couldn't do it.

She threw down the pad and jumped up, hurrying into Daddy's bedroom to look at the photograph he kept on his dresser—except that the framed picture wasn't there anymore. Esther had forgotten that her father had taken it with him. A jumble of Penny Goodrich's things stood in its place on the dresser top: a jar of cold cream, a hairbrush and bobby pins, a handkerchief, and a pile of loose change for the bus. Esther gazed around the room in dismay. Nothing looked the same or even smelled the same now that Penny lived here. Daddy had rarely opened the shades to let in the sunlight after Mama died, but Penny rolled them wide open every morning.

Esther went to the window to look down on the street and saw the ugly, blackened shell of the synagogue. She hated the sight of it, all closed off with barricades to keep people away. In the distance, she saw Mr. Mendel coming slowly up the street toward the apartment, walking with his head down, his eyes focused on his feet as if he didn't have the strength to lift his head and look up. Maybe he couldn't bear to see the synagogue, either. Esther felt drawn to him for reasons she couldn't explain, and without knowing why she hurried all the way down both flights of stairs from the third floor and went outside. She sank down on the top step of the porch, out of breath. A moment later, Mr. Mendel came up the sidewalk and turned toward the building.

"Hi, Mr. Mendel. Do you need any help today? Is there something you want me to do for you?"

He gazed at her with a look of confusion before managing a faint smile. "It is very nice of you to offer—but see?" He held up his hands, which were no longer bandaged, even though he still wore the plaster cast on his right arm. "My fingers are free at last. But thank you just the same." He squeezed past her and climbed the porch steps, gripping the railing with his left hand.

"Do you know when they're going to start fixing the synagogue?" she asked him.

"I imagine they must wait for the insurance company. Such things take time."

Esther sprang to her feet and followed him to the door. "What did people do inside there? Before it burned down, I mean."

He paused, jingling his keys in his hand. "It was a place to study Torah and to pray . . ."

Esther's anger returned at the mention of prayer, remembering all of her unanswered ones. She needed to know what she was doing wrong. "Does God answer people's prayers if they pray inside a synagogue?"

He shifted his gaze away from Esther, staring into the distance with a look of such deep sadness that she was sorry she had asked. "No," he said softly. "No, not everyone's prayers. Not always."

"That's what I don't understand, Mr. Mendel. Why should people bother to pray if God doesn't answer? What's the use?"

He turned toward the door, slowly shaking his head as he stuck his key into the lock. "That is a question for men who are much wiser than I am."

Esther stayed on the front porch after he went inside. The night air was cool for mid-October and she wasn't wearing a jacket, but she didn't want to go back upstairs to her lonely apartment yet. She wrapped her arms around herself and sat down on Mrs. Mendel's porch glider. It squealed when she rocked on it, unused for more than a year. She rocked harder, letting the motion soothe her anger.

A few minutes later she saw Jacky Hoffman from next door pedaling his bicycle up the street, heading in her direction. She stopped rocking so the noise wouldn't draw his attention and slouched down on the seat. But he spotted her anyway and halted on the sidewalk in front of the porch.

"Whatcha doing, beautiful?"

"Go away, Jacky."

He planted a hand on his hip, gripping his bike with the other. "That's a fine way to pay a fella back for a compliment."

"You didn't mean it."

"Wanna bet?"

"No. I don't want to bet." She stared past him at the synagogue again. It looked sinister in the growing dusk. He turned around to see where she was looking.

"It's a mess over there, isn't it?" he asked. "A real eyesore. I wonder when the stupid black-hats are going to tear it down." She remembered how gleefully Jacky had played in the water on the night of the fire, leaping over the hoses and splashing in the puddles. But he looked very different tonight, almost respectable with his shirttail tucked into his pants and his dark hair neatly combed. No one would ever guess he could be such a troublemaker in school.

"How come you're all dressed up?" she asked him.

"I have a job after school delivering groceries. You should see all the money I make in tips." He grinned, and Esther was surprised to realize how cute he was, like a younger version of the movie star Gary Cooper. She shook her head to erase the absurd idea.

"What are you going to do with all the money you make?"

"Well, I'm going to the matinee at Loew's Theater on Saturday after work. Wanna come with me? My treat."

Esther's face suddenly felt warm, as if the synagogue across the street were burning again. Jacky had invited her to go to the movies with him. She had felt so lonely only a moment ago, with no one in the world to talk to. And now Jacky Hoffman, dressed up and looking respectable, was offering to be her friend, inviting her to the movies. He had called her beautiful.

"Thanks," she said, "but my brother and I have to do chores on Saturday."

"Hey, what's wrong with your brother, anyway? I heard some of the kids making fun of him, calling him a moron and saying he doesn't know how to talk."

Anger made Esther sit up straight. She lied without a second thought. "For your information, there's something wrong with his throat, and it keeps him from talking. People shouldn't make fun of him, because he can't help it!"

"Is that right." Jacky flashed his handsome grin again. "Well, from now on, I'll stick up for him when the other kids pick on him, okay? All those little kids are afraid of me."

Her anger vanished as quickly as it had flared. "Thanks. That would be very nice of you to stick up for him." She couldn't imagine why Jacky was being so nice for once, offering to defend her brother. She recalled his reputation for schoolyard brawls and added, "Just don't hurt anybody."

He laughed. "Nah, I never pick on anyone littler than me. You and your brother can walk home from school with me anytime you want to from now on."

Ever since Peter stopped talking, Esther had felt so isolated at school. She would time their arrival in the morning so they'd get there just as the bell rang, avoiding the other kids. Then she would rush out the door with him after school and hurry home without talking to anyone. It was the only way to protect her brother from the other kids' questions and jeers. She smiled up at Jacky now, seeing him in a whole new light. The kids wouldn't dare make fun of Peter with Jacky around. "Okay," she said with a smile. "Thanks for the offer."

"See you tomorrow, then." He waved and continued walking his bicycle toward his apartment building next door. Halfway there he turned around again to shout, "And I meant what I said, Esther, even though you don't believe me. You're the prettiest girl in school."

Esther didn't know how to feel about the compliment, especially when it came from someone like Jack Hoffman. She jumped off the glider and unlocked the front door, shaking her head as she bounded up the steps to her apartment. Of all the many changes in Esther's life these past few months, the change she had just seen in Jacky Hoffman was one of the strangest.

The next morning, Esther and Peter carried their dirty clothes down to the basement so Penny could wash them. For the first two weeks that Penny had lived here, she had dragged their laundry to her parents' house every Saturday, but she had quickly decided that was too much work. Now she used Mama's washing machine in the basement, letting Peter shave the soap into the tub and giving Esther the job of feeding the clothes through the wringer. When all the laundry was hung outside on the clothesline, Penny let Esther and Peter choose from a list of other chores that needed to be done—things like running the carpet sweeper, dusting the furniture, emptying the wastebaskets, and scrubbing the bathroom sink with cleanser.

"The work will go much faster if everybody pitches in," she said in that cheery voice Esther hated. Esther still resented Penny, of course, but she really didn't mind the work. Her mother used to give them chores to do, too. And Esther had hated the way Daddy let the apartment get so messy after Mama died.

Today, as Esther dusted the furniture, she recalled how Mama had sometimes chased her with the feather duster and tickled her beneath the chin with it as they worked together. She wondered if Peter remembered things like that. He was pushing the Bissell sweeper across the living room rug, putting all his nine-year-old muscle into the job. Penny was rubbing furniture polish onto the piano bench when it accidentally tipped and some of the sheet music spilled onto the floor.

"Hey, I didn't know this lid opened up. Look at all this music."

"Don't touch it! Those are Mama's!"

But Penny ignored her, paging through the music as she picked up each sheet from the floor. "So this was your mother's piano." Penny's voice was soft, as if she were inside a church. "Did she play a lot?"

Esther gave a quick nod. It felt wrong to talk about her mother with Penny Goodrich.

"Do either of you know how to play?" Penny looked from one of them to the other until Peter—the traitor—pointed his finger at Esther. "You can play the piano, Esther?"

"Our mother was teaching both of us," she said, shooting an angry glance at Peter, "but then she died."

"I wish I could play," Penny said. "I think it would be so much fun to be able to sit down at a get-together or a birthday party and play songs to cheer everyone up." She studied the cover of one of the books. "This has your name on it, Peter. Come on, sit down and play something for me." He shook his head. "Please?" He shook it again. Penny held the book up in front of him and smiled. "I'll make you a deal. If you play one song for me, I'll finish sweeping the carpet for you." Another shake of his head. "And I'll empty all the wastebaskets for you, too. What do you say?"

Once again, Peter turned traitor. He smiled mischievously as he swapped the carpet sweeper for the piano book and sat down at the keyboard. No one had played Mama's piano since she'd died, and as Peter slowly picked his way through one of his beginner's pieces Esther remembered how music had once filled the apartment like perfume. Everywhere Esther went, whether upstairs in her bedroom or on the back porch, she used to hear her mother practicing. It had always made her smile. That was one of the things that was wrong with their apartment now—the silence.

Penny applauded when Peter finished, even though he hadn't played very well. "We haven't practiced in a long time," Esther said. "Nobody felt like it." She needed to explain, defending her mother's reputation as a teacher.

"Well, he plays a lot better than I ever could. I can't even read music. Now let's hear you play something, Esther."

Again she felt a stubborn unwillingness to cooperate with Penny. She shook her head.

"I'll scrub the bathroom sink for you, if you do," Penny said, winking at Peter. Esther still refused.

Peter slid off the bench and pulled the feather duster out of Esther's hand, tugging her toward the keyboard, his big eyes pleading with her to play. She wondered if it would help him start talking again—if his silence had anything to do with the piano that had stood mute for so long. She decided to try it and see, performing for her brother, not Penny.

Esther dug through the collection of lesson books until she found the one she had been using a year ago. She thought she could smell her mother's cologne as she riffled through the pages. Her mother had written notes at the top of the pages, recording the date of each lesson and making a check mark when Esther had completed it to her satisfaction. Esther chose an easy piece near the beginning of the book and began to play—and for those few, brief moments it seemed as though Mama sat right there on the bench beside her. She remembered how her mother used to run her hand through her hair as she watched Esther play, hair that had been the same rich mahogany brown color as the piano.

Esther played the next piece, and the next, lost in the music and in the memories of her mother. When she glanced at Peter she saw him sitting cross-legged on the rug, listening with his eyes closed. Esther felt tears stinging her eyes as she finished the song. Would she ever stop missing her mother?

She lifted her hands from the keyboard and closed the lid.

Chapter 11

It was Sunday morning and Penny couldn't get Esther out of bed for church. "Why do we have to go? It's a waste of time," she complained. "Why can't we sleep in, instead?"

Penny did everything but yell and utter threats to make her get up. "You aren't doing this for me, Esther. I promised your father that I would take you and Peter to church, every week. You don't want to disappoint your father, do you?" Esther finally gave in, but she moved so slowly that they barely made it to the church on time.

Afterward, the three of them walked in silence to the duplex that Eddie's mother shared with Penny's parents. Penny had grown to dread spending Sunday afternoons with her parents, but today she had a different concern. She was desperate to get Peter talking again before Eddie came home on leave, and she needed Grandma Shaffer's help and advice to do it. Mrs. Shaffer stood waiting on her back porch as Penny and the children arrived.

"Can I talk to you alone?" Penny whispered while the kids galloped off after the dog.

"Don't get your Sunday clothes all dirty," Mrs. Shaffer called to them before turning to Penny. "What's the matter?"

"I'm worried about Peter. He hasn't spoken to me or anyone else since his father went away, including his teacher and his school friends. He doesn't even talk to Esther. It's probably my fault, but I don't know what to do about it. I need your advice. Do you think I should take him to see a doctor?"

"I told Eddie this would happen. I told him! This is exactly why I didn't want to take care of those kids myself." Mrs. Shaffer suddenly sounded breathless, as if she had been running around the yard with the children. "I don't know what to do about him. How am I supposed to know what to do?"

Penny knew she had made a terrible mistake. "I'm sorry, Mrs. Shaffer. I didn't mean to upset you or worry you. His teacher thinks he'll be okay, and he is fine except for not talking. I just thought I should let you know—"

"I'm not well, you know. My husband is gone, all three of my sons are in harm's way, and now this?"

"I know, I know. I'm sorry, Mrs. Shaffer." Penny took the older woman's arm to lead her toward a chair so she could sit down. "I shouldn't have mentioned it. I just thought—"

"Did you write and tell Eddie? Did you ask him what to do?"

"Not yet. I didn't want him to worry. I keep hoping that Peter will get over it before Eddie comes home."

Mrs. Shaffer pulled her arm from Penny's grasp, refusing to sit. "You want me to talk to Peter? Is that it?"

"I . . . I don't know. To be honest, I don't know what to do. I just thought that I should tell you about the problem since you're his grandma. You don't have to say anything to him . . . and please don't worry."

"Tell the children their lunch is ready." Grandma Shaffer turned and stomped into her house. Penny sighed. She had made a mess of things again. She called to the kids, telling them to go inside with their grandmother, then trudged over to her side of the duplex. Her mother stood watching from the kitchen window.

"I certainly hope you were able to talk some sense into Mrs. Shaffer this week," she said as Penny came through the door. "It's time she fulfilled her responsibilities toward those children."

"She can't take care of them by herself, Mother. Her health isn't very good. Besides, she would have trouble managing all the stairs in Eddie's apartment."

"How much longer are you going to run yourself ragged this way? You look terrible, Penny. For no earthly reason. Why in the world did you get involved in all this nonsense in the first place? I warned you that it was a foolish idea. Why couldn't you be happy with the way things were?"

"I promised Eddie I would help him. He didn't have anyone else." She had repeated the same refrain for weeks, yet Mother never seemed to hear it. Nor was she listening now. Penny wished she could turn to her mother for advice, not only about the children but about whether or not to sign up for drivers' training at the bus company. She had been trying to make up her mind ever since Mr. Whitney first mentioned it, but she still wasn't convinced that she could do it. Her mother was the last person Penny could go to for the boost of self-confidence she needed.

"Would you like me to set the table?" Penny asked when she saw it hadn't been set.

"We don't sit at the table anymore, now that you've left us. It's too much bother. We can eat from trays in the living room just as well. Your father likes to listen to the news about the war."

Penny turned and saw nothing cooking on the stove. Mother hadn't prepared any food. "Do you need help making lunch?"

"What do you think? Of course I need help! How am I supposed to fix a big meal now that you've gone running off? I can barely do the shopping every week with all the nonsense they put us through with those ration coupons. Sure, you gladly help the neighbors out, but how about helping your own parents?"

"I'm sorry. I didn't know you were having trouble shopping." She hurried to the pantry and opened the door. "What shall I fix? I could peel some potatoes. Father likes potatoes, doesn't he?"

Suddenly the Shaffers' back door slammed shut with a mighty *bang* that rattled the windows. A moment later, someone pounded on Penny's kitchen door. She dropped the sack of potatoes and ran to answer it, fearing a catastrophe. Esther stood on the doorstep. She didn't look frightened or injured; she looked furious.

"I want to go home. Take us home right now please."

Penny went outside to talk to her, closing the door so Mother wouldn't overhear them. "We can't go home yet, Esther. You haven't even had time to eat your lunch or visit with your grandma."

"I don't want to visit with her."

"What's wrong?"

"Grandma started yelling at Peter because he won't talk, telling him to stop being naughty. She said she would spank him with the paddle if he doesn't stop playing games. I tried to tell her that Peter can't help it, but she won't listen to me."

"Come on." Penny grabbed Esther's hand as they hurried next door. Peter sat slumped at the table with his head buried in his arms. His shoulders heaved with silent sobs. Mrs. Shaffer looked red in the face as she paced back and forth in the tiny space between piles of old newspapers. "I'm so sorry, Mrs. Shaffer," Penny said. "I never meant to cause all this trouble. What can I do? How can I help?"

"Take us home," Esther said from behind Penny.

"You want to leave?" Grandma Shaffer asked. "Fine! Go home! . . . Go on, get out!" Peter leaped up at her words and scurried out the door.

"Mrs. Shaffer, please . . . I'm so sorry . . ."

"You too, Penny. Go home!" Mrs. Shaffer stalked away, weaving through her living room and slamming her bedroom door.

Penny felt sick. What a mess she had made. She didn't know whom to comfort first, but since Mrs. Shaffer had kicked her out, she hurried after Esther and Peter. They were off the porch and walking toward the back gate before Penny could shut the kitchen door. "Wait!" she called, running to catch up with them. "I'll take you home, if that's what you want. But I need to tell my parents first. Wait right here."

She ran up her own porch steps and into the kitchen to retrieve her purse. "I'm sorry, Mother. Something has come up, and we need to go back to the apartment right away."

"What did you do now?"

Tears filled Penny's eyes. Her mother was right, of course. This mess was all Penny's fault. It was always her fault. She never should have told Mrs. Shaffer about Peter. Now it was too late. "I'll call and explain it to you later. Tell Dad I said good-bye."

"You haven't eaten anything! What about—?"

"I'm sorry." She closed the door on her mother's protests and hurried back to the children.

They were gone.

Penny opened the gate and ran around to the front of the house in time to see Esther and Peter jogging up the street, half a block ahead of her, heading toward the bus stop. "Wait up," she hollered. "Wait for me!" She saw a bus coming and ran faster, but the children never stopped. When the bus halted at the corner, they boarded it without her. She saw the door close as the bus pulled away from the curb.

"No, wait!" Penny ran as fast as she could, waving her arms frantically, but the driver must not have seen her. Why didn't the kids tell him to wait? She sprinted down the street behind the bus, wild with fear. Just when she thought she couldn't run anymore, the bus halted and the door opened. She staggered toward it and climbed aboard, gasping for breath. "Thank you . . . thank you for stopping . . ."

The children sat in the back of the bus, ignoring her as she fed coins into the slots with shaking fingers. She would have liked to take a paddle to both of them, but she didn't have the strength.

"Hey—Miss Penny Goodrich, right?"

She looked up at the sound of her name and saw a familiar marine sitting by the window near the front. Roy Fuller greeted her with a grin. She had seen him several times in the past few weeks, riding on the same bus that she took to and from work, but they hadn't been close enough to talk to each other since the time he'd given up his seat for her. She was surprised that he remembered her name, but then she had remembered his.

"Yeah. Hi," she said weakly. She fell into the seat beside him as the bus lurched forward.

"I saw someone running to catch the bus, but I didn't realize it was you. I told the driver to hold up."

"Thank you. Those kids scared me half to death getting on the bus without me that way."

"Are they with you?" he asked, tilting his head in their direction. Penny nodded, embarrassed to admit that she was responsible for such rude, ill-behaved children. Anyone with a pair of eyes could see that the kids were defying her authority, ignoring her, running away from her.

"I don't know what got into them, running off on their own like that. I never dreamed they would get on the bus and ride away without me. Thank you for telling the driver to stop. It would have been another twenty minutes before the next bus came along, and who knows what would have happened to them, riding around Brooklyn on their own."

"I'm happy to help. You okay?"

"Yeah . . ." She exhaled. Then, as her tears began to fall, she shook her head. "No. I'm having a terrible day."

"Aw, it'll be okay," he soothed, patting her arm. "It must be hard raising two kids all alone with your husband in the service."

"They're not mine. I'm taking care of them for . . ." She turned to make sure they were out of earshot, then said softly, "For the man I hope to marry. Their mother died, and they aren't used to me trying to take her place yet."

"Which branch of the service is he in?"

She pulled out a handkerchief and dried her eyes, grateful to Roy for distracting her with conversation. "The army. He's a mechanic. In his last letter he said that he would probably be shipped to England to work in the motor pool after he finishes basic training."

"I wish the Marines would ship me someplace exciting. I thought I'd get to see the world when I joined up. Instead, they assigned me to the Brooklyn Navy Yard."

"I hear the Marines are fighting really hard on all those little islands in the Pacific. You wouldn't want to be there, would you? Wouldn't your family worry about you?"

"Yeah, I guess so. My girlfriend worries about me all the time as it is, and I'm only stationed in Brooklyn. She thinks it's dangerous here."

"Where are you from?"

"I grew up in a small town near Scranton, Pennsylvania, called Moosic."

"*Music?* That's a funny name for a town."

"No, it's spelled M-o-o-s-i-c. Moosic. You want to see my girl's picture? Her name's Sally." He leaned against Penny for a moment as he reached into his back pocket for his wallet. He showed her two photographs: a close-up of Sally that might have been a graduation picture, and one of her and Roy with their arms around each other. She looked very young, and Roy looked very happy.

"She's beautiful," Penny said, handing them back.

"I know! She's the prettiest girl in Pennsylvania. I can't believe she chose me." He leaned into her again as he maneuvered his wallet back into his pocket. "I hope to marry her after the war."

And after the war maybe Eddie would marry her. Penny drew a calming breath as she remembered why she had volunteered for this job in the first place. She needed to keep that bigger goal in mind in order to get through the bad days. That was what the newspapers kept saying about this endless war they were fighting. If people kept the bigger goal of defeating the enemy in mind, they could face all the daily difficulties like rationing, long lines, and shortages, not to mention the worry and fear for their loved ones' safety.

"Tell me about your girlfriend, Roy." She listened as Roy described how he had known Sally for a while but they finally had started dating after meeting up at a mutual friend's picnic. Sally wanted to be a beautician and hoped to own her own beauty parlor someday. Talking with Roy helped Penny to calm down and forget her own troubles for a while.

"This is our stop," she said when they reached Eddie's neighborhood. "It was nice talking to you, Roy. And thanks again for stopping the bus for me."

Penny made sandwiches for the kids when they got home, then called her mother to try to explain why they had left in such a hurry. She didn't mention that Peter couldn't talk. Why make things worse?

She spent the afternoon writing a long, chatty letter to Eddie, leaving out her problems with Peter and Esther and his mother. Penny could well imagine the horrible stories that Esther and Peter wrote about her, but she never read the letters they sent to their father or the ones that he sent to them.

The long Sunday afternoon seemed as though it would never end. The terrible scene with Grandma Shaffer and the incident with the bus had upset all of them. Penny went to bed early, determined to take a deep breath and start all over again with a brand-new week.

It was a relief to go to work on Monday and take her place on her familiar stool behind her usual window at the bus terminal. This job used to seem hectic to Penny, but it was simple compared to raising children. The pace had just slowed down after the morning rush when Mr. Whitney stopped by to see her.

"You all set to start drivers' training, Miss Goodrich? Got your birth certificate?"

Penny struck her forehead in dismay. What a scatterbrain! She not only hadn't decided about the job, but she had never returned to the records' office for her birth certificate. "I'm really sorry, Mr. Whitney, but I haven't had time to go back to the records' office—"

"Why didn't you say so? I'll give you an extra half hour for lunch today if you want. You can have more time, if you need it."

Penny ate her lunch on the bus on her way to the records' office. She trudged up the steps of the building, wishing she knew how to say no to people and to stand up for herself. How could she turn down Mr. Whitney's offer now after he'd been so nice and encouraging to her, giving her time off like this—twice? He needed drivers and he was counting on her.

She might as well try the drivers' training classes, she decided as she waited in line for her birth certificate. The instructor would prob-ably realize right away that Penny couldn't drive—hopefully before she crashed one of their buses or ran over somebody—and then she could go back to being a cashier again. Of course that meant no pay increase and no apartment of her own. If Eddie didn't marry her, she would have to move back home with her parents. The thought depressed her.

She handed the clerk the receipt when it was finally her turn.

"I ordered a copy of my birth certificate? My name is Penny Sue Goodrich?"

The clerk paged through a stack of papers before finding it. "Here it is. We had a lot of trouble with this, Miss Goodrich. You could have saved us a great deal of bother if you would have mentioned that you were adopted."

Penny shook her head. "You must have me confused with someone else. I'm not adopted."

The clerk frowned and studied the paper again. "Your name is Penny Sue Goodrich, right?"

"Yes, but—"

"We found a birth registration with your name, your birthday, and your parents' names, but it's a certificate of adoption. They are listed as your adoptive parents, not your birth parents."

Penny's smile turned into a frown. "Well . . . that can't be the right one. I'm not adopted."

"Look." The clerk turned the piece of paper around so Penny could read it. "This is your certificate of adoption. Albert and Gwendolyn Goodrich applied for it on the day of your birth, and it has been officially registered with the state of New York. That means they adopted you."

Penny stared and stared at the certificate, but it still made no sense to her. Was someone playing a joke? "This . . . this can't be mine. I think somebody must have made a mistake."

The clerk slapped the counter. "Look. What do you think are the chances that there are two people in New York state named Penny Sue Goodrich, both born on the exact same day and in the exact same year, in Brooklyn, with parents named Albert and Gwendolyn Goodrich? Huh? I would say that it's highly improbable, wouldn't you? This has to be yours."

"But . . . but if it's true and my parents did adopt me, why didn't they ever tell me?"

"You'll have to ask them that question, Miss Goodrich, not me." The clerk leaned to one side to look around Penny as if to see how long the line was. Penny didn't move, couldn't move.

"Then who are my real parents?"

"The state doesn't list that information on an adoption certificate."

"Can you find out for me?"

The clerk's irritation smoothed to a look of pity. "Maybe. First we would have to find out if your adoption record was sealed or not."

"What does that mean?"

"Many times the birth mother doesn't want her identity to be known, so she asks for the records to be officially sealed. In that case, even your adoptive parents may not know who your real parents are."

"How do I find out if it was sealed?"

"We could do another search for you. It would take at least a week and cost an additional fee. If the record has been sealed, then your birth parents' identities would remain a secret at their request. And I have to warn you, Miss Goodrich, in nearly all of the adoptions I've seen over the years, the records are always sealed."

Penny hung on to the edge of the counter. The world had been knocked sideways, and she feared she might topple over if she let go.

"Would you like to pursue the search, Miss Goodrich?"

"I guess so. I mean . . . yes." Her hands shook as she dug into her wallet for more money. The clerk handed Penny a new form.

"Here you go, Miss Goodrich. You can return it to me after you've finished filling it out. Who's next?"

Penny stumbled toward a row of chairs in the waiting area, needing to sit down. No wonder Mother had been so upset when Penny had asked for her birth certificate. She had left the iron plugged in while she'd hurried into the living room to stop Penny from searching the desk. She hadn't wanted her to know the truth.

But why not? If she really was adopted—and Penny still didn't quite believe that it was true—why hadn't her parents ever told her?

Somehow Penny managed to return to the bus station and do her job. She was so distracted as she took in money and handed people their change and their tickets that it surprised her when her cash drawer added up to the exact penny at the end of the day, as usual.

"So, all set to start training?" her boss asked as he checked her receipts.

"I-I'm adopted. I have my adoption certificate but not a birth certificate."

"I'm sure that will be fine. Any legal identification will do. You just have to prove who you are."

But who was she?

Penny still clung to the belief that someone had made a mistake. She would find out the next time she returned to the records' office that this was all a huge misunderstanding or an elaborate joke. Except who would play a joke on her? Her parents had no sense of humor. And the joke wasn't funny at all.

CHAPTER 12

JACOB READ THE DATE on the calendar. Today was his son's thirtieth birthday. He looked down at the letter he held in his hands, the last one he had ever received from Avraham, and saw it was nearly two years old. The unending silence during all that time had been torture. Surely the truth, no matter how bad, would be better than this terrible silence.

Today he would reread Avraham's final letter. Tomorrow Jacob would start reading through the pile of letters all over again, one each day, beginning with Avi's descriptions of his first days in Hungary. He had been there only a short time when the government passed the first anti-Jewish laws, banning Jews from working in the professions and owning their own land. Avi should have come home right away. Everyone should have known it would only get worse. Later, Avi would tell all about his studies in the yeshiva and how much he was learning, along with news that Hungary had joined with Germany to invade Czechoslovakia.

Avraham's letters would get longer and more exuberant as he described how he had met Sarah Rivkah and had fallen in love with her. They had decided to marry, he would write. Then he would tell how thousands of Polish Jews had fled across the border into Hungary for refuge after Hitler invaded Poland. Avi's joy had multiplied when little Fredeleh had been born—as did Jacob's fears. Couldn't Avraham see that Hitler was intent on conquering the world? Hungarian troops had marched off to fight alongside German ones against the Soviet Union, and Jacob had begged Avraham not to stay in a land that was allied with a madman. Jacob had written letters to every government official he could think of, pleading for help in rescuing his family. But there had been no rescue, no visas, no way out for Avraham and Sarah Rivkah. Even Jacob's prayers had met with silence.

Dear Mama and Abba,

We have just heard the shocking news that the Japanese have attacked the Americans in Pearl Harbor. They are saying the U.S. will now join the war against the Axis powers. That means America and Hungary may soon be at war with each other, and mail will no longer be allowed to pass between our countries. And so I am writing this quick letter to let you know we are all fine. For now, we are being left alone to live our lives as usual. I'm not so certain the same is true for Jews in other lands. Some of the Polish Jews who have escaped across our borders tell horrible stories about massacres in their country. But so far Hungary is still a safe place for us.

We've heard rumors that able-bodied Jewish men might be drafted into labor companies soon, and I'm not sure if I should admit I am an American or not. No one knows if it will make matters better or worse for me now that America and Hungary are enemies. Either way, I pray that Hashem will guide me and that I won't have to leave Sarah and Fredeleh behind.

If there had been any way that we could have left Hungary and come home by now, we surely would have. But I am still unable to get the necessary immigration papers for my wife and daughter, and now the American Embassy in Budapest will close.

We are all saddened that our beloved Hungary would ally itself with a man like Adolf Hitler and the hatred he embraces. Our government officials did it for the promise of land, to increase our territory to its proper borders and to regain the land that was stolen from Hungary after the first war. Our soldiers may fight for Germany's cause, but I don't think our leaders believe in what Hitler does. Let's hope it ends soon. And that by the time it does, the immigration papers that I filled out for Sarah and the baby will finally be processed.

Sarah Rivkah and Fredeleh send their love. We are all praying for this madness to end so Fredeleh can finally meet her American grandparents. Stay well and don't worry.

All my love,

Avraham

This last letter had arrived a few months before Miriam died. She would never meet her daughter-in-law or hold her little granddaughter. And unless Jacob's last few letters had somehow gotten through to Avraham, he did not know that his mother was gone. But maybe it was better that Miriam Shoshanna had been spared the agony of silence and waiting. Especially if something had happened to their only son and his family. Miriam's tender soul never could have handled such terrible news about the persecution of Jews in Europe—atrocities that no one wanted to believe were true, massacres and starvation in the Jewish ghettos. Who knew what other horrors would take place if the war continued to drag on? Were the Jews in Hungary still safe? How could they be when their nation was allied with a monster?

But was that any reason for Hashem to take Miriam's life? Why not stop the atrocities instead? Why not let Miriam live and let Adolf Hitler die?

Jacob sifted through the photographs he had cut from the newspaper, including the latest picture, smuggled to the press from Warsaw,

Poland. It showed "death carts" gathering up corpses. The caption read: "Jews starve to death under the Nazis' new order which severely restricts food rations for Jews." Another picture from April of 1941 showed the burnt remains of a synagogue in Bucharest, Romania, with the caption, "Hundreds of Jews burned to death." Aside from the date, it was indistinguishable from pictures of the synagogues that had burned in Germany five years ago on Kristallnacht, "the night of broken glass." And whenever Jacob looked out his front window, the remains of the shul across the street looked eerily similar to the photographs from Europe.

The doorbell rang, interrupting Jacob's thoughts. He could maneuver doorknobs easily now that his bandages had finally come off. Only the plaster cast on his arm remained. When he opened the door, Jacob was surprised to find the gray-haired fire marshal standing there. What did he want now?

"Good evening, Mr. Mendel. I'm Inspector Dalton from—"

"Yes. I remember. The fire marshal's office."

"I have a few more questions about the fire in the synagogue. Do you have a moment?"

"I already told you everything I know."

"I understand. But I need to confirm a few things now that I've interviewed other witnesses."

Jacob leaned against the doorframe in resignation. "What would you like to know?"

"May I come inside, please? This shouldn't take long."

Jacob's wife would have chided him for his lack of manners. She would have offered Mr. Dalton coffee and a slice of honey cake. But Jacob did not feel very sociable. "Have they determined how the fire started?" he asked as he led the man into his living room.

"Yes, Mr. Mendel. It was set deliberately. Arson. That's why we are continuing to investigate."

A small shudder traveled through Jacob. He needed to sit down. Deliberate? Who would do such a thing? His friend Meir had warned that the fire was likely motivated by hatred.

The inspector glanced all around the room as if memorizing its contents, pausing as he glanced at Jacob's desk. "May I?" he asked.

He reached to pick up the clipping of the destroyed synagogue in Romania, then laid it down again. "I thought for a moment that this was the synagogue across the street. They are quite similar, don't you think?"

"Everywhere, people hate us." Jacob motioned to the sofa. "Have a seat, Mr. Dalton."

The inspector removed the small notebook from his pocket and took a moment to page through his notes before asking, "What is your relationship with Congregation Ohel Moshe?"

"My relationship? I have no relationship, at the moment."

"But you do know the rabbi and all of the other leaders, correct?"

"Yes, they are my friends."

"I'm told that for several years you held an honored position among the men. You were called the gabbai?"

"Yes."

"How long ago did you resign your position?"

"A year. Maybe a little more than that."

"Why do you no longer attend the congregation?"

Inspector Dalton had been firing questions one right after the other without giving Jacob time to think. This time Jacob drew a breath before answering. "I don't understand what that has to do with the fire."

"I'm just getting some background information, Mr. Mendel."

"It is nobody's business but mine if I attend or not."

"But you are very familiar with the synagogue's layout, the use of the rooms, and so forth?"

"Yes."

"And you have a key to the building, is that correct?"

"Yes."

"Did you use your key to let yourself into the building on the night of the fire?"

"Of course I used it. The front door of the building was locked."

"So you unlocked it and went inside?"

"Yes. I saw the flames and I went inside to save the Torah scrolls."

Inspector Dalton nodded, then consulted his notebook once again. "I understand you had a conversation with Rabbi Grunfeld shortly before the fire began. Is that correct?"

Jacob had to think back to that night. It seemed like a very long time ago. He recalled that he had bumped into the rebbe on his way home from the store that evening, just as the men were coming out of the shul. "We had a short conversation that night, yes."

"May I ask what you discussed?"

"How should I know what I said so many weeks ago? Do you remember the conversations you had in the past?" He was losing patience with these idiotic questions.

"Perhaps I can help jog your memory." Inspector Dalton leafed through the pages of his notebook. "Ah, here it is. Several witnesses overheard you shouting that night. Arguing with Rabbi Grunfeld. They said you sounded very angry. You said something to the effect that you didn't care what happened to the synagogue, that the building could fall down for all you cared. Do you recall saying that?"

For the first time Jacob felt real fear. These weren't innocent questions that the man was asking. He was trying to lead Jacob down a path chosen well in advance. And Jacob had the feeling that something terrible awaited him at the end of it. "Why do you ask me questions if you already know the answers?"

"I'm just trying to confirm that the information is true, Mr. Mendel. Did you raise your voice that night?"

"I suppose I did."

"I'm told that you were carrying a paper bag in your hand. May I ask what it contained?"

"My supper. I bought a can of soup and some crackers at the store. That was why I left the apartment in the first place."

"Isn't it against your Jewish beliefs to make purchases between sundown on Friday and sundown on Saturday?"

"My beliefs are my own business. They have nothing to do with the fire."

"What happened to the bag that evening?"

"To the bag? What do you mean?"

"I'm told that you were carrying the scrolls, wrapped in a bundle, when you came out of the burning synagogue. You no longer had a bag at that time, nor is there any mention of a bag or a can of soup among your effects when they admitted you to the hospital."

Jacob stared at the man, shocked by the information he seemed to possess. Again he thought back to the night of the fire, remembering how he had let himself into the synagogue, then dampened his jacket in the sink. He had no idea what had become of the soup. "I suppose I must have set the bag down inside somewhere. I don't remember."

"After your argument with Rabbi Grunfeld, what did you do next?"

"I went for a walk."

"To any destination in particular?"

"No. I just walked."

"Is there anyone who saw you and can verify where you went on your stroll?" Jacob's stomach rolled with another wave of fear. He shook his head. "And at the time that you went for this walk, Mr. Mendel, the synagogue would have been empty? You saw all of the men leaving, correct?"

"No. I saw Rabbi Grunfeld and a few others leaving. I have no idea who remained inside."

Inspector Dalton nodded, then flipped back a few more pages in his notebook. "The owner of the cigar store gave a description of the man who reported the fire and asked him to call for help. He said that he was Jewish, with a black beard and hat, wearing a black suit and striped suspenders. Was that you, Mr. Mendel?"

"Yes. I noticed the flames as I was completing my walk and returning home."

"Then what happened?"

"I saw that it was taking too long for the fire trucks to arrive. The Torah scrolls were going to burn. So I went inside to save them."

"Using your key?"

"Yes. Of course using my key."

Dalton fell silent for a moment, as if thinking. He reminded Jacob of a hunter carefully setting a trap in the stillness of the woods. "Mr.

Mendel, I understand that Rabbi Grunfeld and the others are very grateful to you for what you did."

"Ask them, not me."

"And so, after being angry with the other members of Congregation Ohel Moshe for more than a year—"

"I never said I was angry with the congregation or anyone else."

"Let me rephrase that . . . after being *estranged* from the others for more than a year, you are once again in their good graces, is that right?"

Good graces? The phrase made Jacob angry. He stood abruptly. "I would like you to leave now. I have told you everything I know about the fire. I saw the flames as I was returning home. I asked the store clerk to call the fire department. I went inside to save the Torah. That is all there is to it."

Mr. Dalton smiled faintly. "Thank you for your help, Mr. Mendel." He seemed to take his time rising from the sofa and crossing to the door, pausing beside a bookshelf to examine Miriam's small glass kerosene lamp.

"This belongs to you?"

"It was my wife's." Miriam used to use it as a night-light on Shabbat. Jacob hadn't touched it in more than a year.

"This burns kerosene?" Mr. Dalton bent to sniff it.

"Yes. Good day, Mr. Dalton."

By the time the inspector left, Jacob's entire body trembled with fury. He remembered feeling this same impotent rage as a young man in Hungary when he'd seen how his people were treated, but he hadn't experienced it in a long, long time. Not here in America. He stuffed his hat on his head and walked the two blocks to Rebbe Grunfeld's apartment on the ground floor of a six-story brick building.

"You need to tell me what is going on," he said the moment the rebbe opened the door.

"Yaacov? What—?"

"A man from the fire department just interrogated me as if I were a criminal. What did you tell him about me?"

"About you? Nothing, Yaacov. I never said anything—"

"Do you know how the fire started? Did they tell you that?"

"Please, come inside and sit down. The hallway is no place to talk." He put his hand on Jacob's shoulder and guided him through the door. "Let me tell my wife that you're here. She'll make coffee."

The rebbe's living room glowed with gentle light, warmed by softly whistling radiators. The aroma of home filled the apartment; the smell of roasted meat and spicy potatoes, of bread baking and soup simmering, the scent of cinnamon and fresh coffee. Jacob's house had once smelled just the same. He should not have come.

"I do not want coffee," he said, refusing to sit. "I want to talk about the fire. Do you know how it started?"

"They said it was arson, that the fire had been deliberately set. They found a burned kerosene can in the beit midrash."

Kerosene. Jacob closed his eyes. "Were there signs of a break-in?"

"No. . . . Yaacov, please. Sit down and tell me what's wrong."

"Don't you see? They think I set the fire!"

"You? That's ridiculous. Who thinks that?"

"The inspector who just interrogated me. The questions he asked all led to that conclusion. I have a key to the building. I have not attended shul in a year. I argued with you after evening prayers on the night of the fire. . . . I am telling you, he thinks that I started the fire!"

"That's absurd. I already told him how grateful we all are that you risked your life to save the scrolls that night. How valuable they are to us, and—"

"And he thinks that was why I did it, to get back into your 'good graces.' That is exactly what he said."

"No. No, that can't be. I'll tell him he's wrong, Yaacov. I'll tell him you would never do such a terrible thing."

"Then you had better be ready to tell him who did set the fire. Because nobody broke in, Rebbe, and I happen to be one of the few men who has a key."

"How can I tell him who set the fire? We don't know who set the fire. Or why."

"Of course a Jew must be to blame. A Jew is always to blame, yes?" Jacob turned to leave, but Rebbe Grunfeld grabbed his sleeve.

"Listen, Yaacov. I'm certain that you are worried for nothing. I'll talk to the inspector. I'll convince him that you are innocent. Please believe me. You have nothing to worry about."

But as Jacob walked home through the rustling leaves, he worried nonetheless.

CHAPTER 13

ESTHER DIDN'T UNDERSTAND why some of the boys in school like Jacky Hoffman always acted rowdy in music class. She loved going down to the music room once a week and listening to the recordings the teacher played for them on her phonograph. Esther excelled in class, of course, because she already knew how to read music. And Miss Miller was one of her favorite teachers. Esther wished the combined class of seventh and eight graders met more often, and that the boys would behave so Miss Miller wouldn't have to yell.

The hour-long music lesson had sped by much too quickly, as usual. But as Esther and the others began lining up to return to their classroom, Miss Miller pulled her aside.

"Could I speak with you for a moment, Esther?"

She turned to her classroom teacher, who nodded her approval. Esther waited behind while the other students shuffled out.

"Your caretaker, Miss Goodrich, came to see me the other day," Miss Miller began.

"Penny did?"

"Yes. Miss Goodrich and I had a very nice conversation."

Miss Miller's words made Esther angry. This school, this music class, was her territory, and Penny Goodrich had no right invading it. Penny didn't belong here or in the apartment or any other part of Esther's life, for that matter. She would tolerate Penny until Daddy came home if she had to, but—

"Miss Goodrich told me how well you play the piano, and she asked me if I knew anyone who could give you lessons. I told her that I would be happy to teach you."

Why did Penny always make Esther feel pulled in two directions at once? She wanted nothing to do with piano lessons if they were Penny's idea. Who did she think she was? But at the same time, Esther liked Miss Miller a lot. And she had missed playing the piano, missed the sound of music in their apartment. Esther used to love studying the tiny black notes on a sheet of music, discovering the magic they contained and bringing them to life. She loved to create a story from the notes, making them say something happy or sad or playful or majestic.

Miss Miller rested her hand on Esther's shoulder. "So . . . would you like to take piano lessons with me?"

Esther tried not to cry as she struggled to make up her mind. Should she do it? Then she remembered how Mama had seemed to come back to life the other day when she had played the piano for Peter. Esther nodded. "Yes. Yes, I would."

"Good. I told Miss Goodrich that Peter may take lessons as well, if he would like to. Would you ask him for me?"

"Yes, ma'am. I'll ask him." She wondered if Miss Miller knew that Peter couldn't talk. The entire school probably knew.

"How about if we start your lessons tomorrow after school? You can bring some of the books you were working on, and we'll go from there."

Esther nodded again as happiness battled with anger. And guilt. Was she being disloyal to her mother to study with another teacher? "How much does it cost?" Esther thought to ask. Daddy always worried about money.

"Miss Goodrich and I already worked everything out. I'll see you tomorrow right after school. I'm looking forward to it, Esther."

"Yes. Me too."

As Esther helped with the supper dishes that night she wondered if Penny would mention the piano lessons. Esther knew she should thank Penny—it was rude not to—but she couldn't make herself do it. If she opened the door just the tiniest crack, Penny would elbow her way inside.

When the last pot was dry, Esther escaped downstairs to the front porch. The apartment seemed stuffy and confining with Peter silently inhabiting their bedroom and Penny in the kitchen and the piano looming in the living room, tugging Esther in opposite directions between guilt and anticipation.

The fall weather was too chilly for sitting outside, the wind damp and blustery, but Esther sat down on Mrs. Mendel's glider just the same. She wished she could talk to Mr. Mendel again, but she didn't have the courage to knock on his door. She knew he was home because she could hear music pouring from his radio, filling the vestibule and drifting faintly outside past his living room window. He liked orchestra music, the kind Miss Miller played in music class. Esther sat very still on the rusty glider, listening.

The music ended a few minutes later and the announcer began to speak. She had been listening with her eyes closed, scarcely daring to breathe. When she opened them she saw Jacky Hoffman pedaling toward the apartment on his bicycle. He had made good on his offer and had walked home from school with her and Peter a couple of times, but now she scrunched down, hoping that he wouldn't see her. He pulled to a stop in front of the porch, brakes squealing.

"Hey, beautiful!"

"Go away, Jacky. I'm mad at you."

"Why? What'd I do?"

"You and the other boys always act up in music class. You always spoil it for everyone else."

His forehead creased in a scowl. "You like music class?"

"Yes! Miss Miller is one of the nicest teachers in the whole school."

He grinned like a movie star. "Well, from now on I'll be on my very best behavior. Just for you. And I'll clobber anyone else who acts up, okay?"

He was being nice again, but Esther didn't know whether to forgive him or not. She felt as wary of letting him in the door as she did Penny Goodrich, even though she longed to have a friend to talk to.

"Okay," she finally said. "Thanks. And I noticed that the other kids haven't been teasing my brother as much. You have anything to do with that?"

"Yep. I told them that they'd have to answer to me if they give him a hard time." He made two fists and punched the air like a prizefighter.

"Well . . . thank you for that."

"What did you say was wrong with your brother?"

"The doctors don't know yet. His throat doesn't work right." She knew better than to lie, but Peter was the only family she had left and she had to protect him.

Esther's earliest memory was of the day that Peter had been born, and she'd seen him for the first time, lying in their mother's arms, only a few hours old. Mama said that Esther had glared at him as if she wished he had never been born. He had taken Esther's place in Mama's arms, which was reason enough to hate him.

But then Mama had let Esther hold Peter, and Daddy took a photograph of the three of them together. Whenever Esther and her mother came to that picture in the photograph album, Mama would say, "See how tiny your baby brother was? But you helped me take such good care of him." Nine years after Aaron Peter Shaffer had come into Esther's life, she knew that she would lie, cheat, and probably steal in order to continue taking care of him for Mama.

"Hey, you missed a great movie last Saturday." Jacky said, interrupting her thoughts. "We watched *Andy Hardy's Double Life*. You like Mickey Rooney?"

"He's the best. My dad used to take us to see all his movies—before Daddy went off to war, that is."

"I'll take you anytime you want to go. I have spending money now that I'm working."

"Thanks. It's nice of you to offer . . . but I don't know if I can."

Penny would probably agree to anything Esther asked in order to get on her good side. Penny had arranged piano lessons for her, hadn't she? But Esther wasn't sure if she really wanted to go to the movies with Jacky Hoffman. Once again she felt pulled in opposite directions. "Could Peter come, too?"

"Sure, if he has money. I'm only paying for your ticket." He grinned, and he looked just like Clark Gable with his rogue's smile and a lock of hair hanging over one eye.

"Okay. Maybe Peter and I will go with you this Saturday."

"I have to deliver groceries in the morning, but meet me right here in time for the matinee."

He started to leave and Esther found she didn't want him to go quite yet. "How's your dad doing?" she asked. "Do you get letters from him?"

"Yeah. Sometimes we go a few weeks without hearing anything, and then a whole pile of letters will come all at once."

"Where is he stationed now?"

"He's on a battleship in the Pacific Ocean somewhere. He isn't allowed to tell us where or the censors will cut up his letters like Swiss cheese."

"Do you miss him?" she asked, thinking of her own father.

"Yeah, sure." But Jacky looked away when he spoke, and Esther could tell that he was lying. Too late, she recalled how Jacky's father used to yell at his kids and chase after them with his belt. Mr. and Mrs. Hoffman used to argue all the time, and the neighborhood had been a lot quieter since he had enlisted. Their home probably was quieter, too.

"My father says I have to be the man of the house while he's away," Jacky said. "That's why I took this job delivering groceries."

"Do you like it?"

"Yeah. I make real good money in tips. Lots of women are working at the Navy Yard all day now, and they don't have time to stand in line for groceries when they get home. They're real grateful when I deliver them right to their houses."

Esther wondered if the new job and the responsibility of being the man of the house had caused the changes she saw in Jacky. And she also wondered if they were permanent. Maybe he was like Mickey Rooney's character in the new movie, only this time it was Jacky Hoffman's Double Life.

"Hey, I'd better get home and eat supper," he said. "Ma is keeping it warm for me. See you Saturday." He waved and steered his bike into the narrow passage between their two apartment buildings.

The evening seemed to turn colder after Jacky left, and Esther decided to go inside. She got as far as the vestibule and she could hear the music so clearly that she stood there for several minutes, listening. When the piece ended she summoned all her courage and knocked on Mr. Mendel's door. He opened it a mere crack.

"Yes?"

"Hi, Mr. Mendel. I really like the music that was playing on your radio just now. Could you please tell me which radio station that was?"

"Heh? The station? I cannot recall. But I suppose you could come inside and look on the dial for yourself. The numbers are hard for me to read without my glasses."

"Thanks." She slipped through the door as he opened it wider and knelt down on the carpet in front of the radio console to read the tiny numbers.

"Here is some paper," Mr. Mendel said. "You can write the numbers down."

"Thanks. I always fight with Peter over which station to play," she said as she copied the numbers. "He likes to listen to ball games. The Dodgers are his favorite team."

"Yes. So he has told me."

Esther nearly lost her balance. "He talks to you?"

"Well . . . he used his hands as I recall, not words. I thought he was playing a game."

"No, it isn't a game. Peter can't talk. There's something wrong with his throat, I think." Esther stood again and handed back his pencil. "Is there something I can do to help you today, Mr. Mendel?" The music had started playing again, and she wanted to stay and hear it. And to talk to him. "It must be hard to wash dishes with only one good arm."

"Thank you, but I cannot take advantage of your kindness again."

"I don't mind, honest. And I could listen to the music while I worked."

He studied her in silence for what seemed like a very long time. Esther could tell that he was struggling to make up his mind, as if he felt pulled in two directions at the same time just like she sometimes did. But she didn't understand why it was such a hard decision.

"How would it be if I paid you to help me?" he finally said.

"You don't have to pay me. I'll do it for nothing."

"No, I insist. My dishes do need to be washed, and I am afraid there are a good many of them."

He led the way into the kitchen, and as they passed the dining room table she saw it was covered with photographs and clippings and maps cut from the newspaper. She wanted to stop and look at the pictures more closely, but instead she followed him through the kitchen door. Esther saw right away that he was right about the mess. Plates and bowls and pots filled the sink, the way they used to pile up in her own kitchen before Daddy joined the army and Penny had come to live with them. More dishes covered the tabletop.

"See what I mean?" he asked. "Would you like to change your mind?"

Esther thought of what she could do with the money and shook her head. "Our dishes used to pile up like this, too, after Mama died." She took off her jacket and began rolling up her sleeves.

"I should warn you that you will have to wash these two piles separately. The dishes and silverware by the sink cannot be mixed with the ones on the table."

"Okay . . . but why?"

"That is our law," he said with a shrug. "One set of dishware and pots are for serving meat, the other for dairy. The meat utensils go in this cupboard and in these drawers, and the dishes for dairy go over there. The pots must be separated, as well. Meat goes here, dairy there."

Esther turned on the faucet and waited for the water to get hot. She feared making a mistake now that she knew there was a wrong way to do it. "Mr. Mendel? I'll try to be really careful, but what happens if I make a mistake and accidentally mix them up?"

Once again he looked at her for a long moment before replying. She wondered if he would change his mind and send her away. But he finally shrugged and said, "Nothing. Nothing will happen. I do not even know why I bother, now that Miriam is gone. She was always so careful about her kitchen, making sure to follow all the laws of *kashrut*. I suppose I am doing it for her sake. She would be very upset with me if she were here and saw how I lived. But what does it matter? She is not here."

"I liked Mrs. Mendel," Esther said softly. "She was so nice. I'll be careful for her sake, too." She put the plug into the drain and sprinkled in Ivory Snow powder as the sink filled with water. "I really miss her. I'll bet you miss her, too."

"Yes." She saw his Adam's apple move up and down as he swallowed. "Yes."

Esther felt sorry for him, living all alone. She was about to ask if he had any children when she remembered Mrs. Mendel telling Mama about her son who was a grown man like Daddy. Esther couldn't remember if he was fighting in the war or not, but she seemed to recall that he was far away somewhere.

"Mrs. Mendel showed us pictures of your son, once, and said that he lived far away from here. Is he fighting in the war?"

Mr. Mendel pulled out a kitchen chair and sank onto it. His cast clunked against the porcelain tabletop as he rested his arm. "No. No, our son went away to a small town in Hungary to study Torah, and now he cannot get home. The United States is at war with Hungary, you see."

"Is that why you're cutting out all those pictures and maps from the newspaper?"

"I have not found any newspaper pictures from Hungary, but I am trying to gather what little news I can about my people."

"You mean your relatives?"

"In a sense. I meant the Jewish people."

"Oh. I'll bet you wish this war would end so your son could come home."

"Yes. He has a wife and little girl now. I have never met them."

Esther suddenly understood the tie she felt with Mr. Mendel. He must miss his family the same way she missed Mama . . . and now Daddy, who was far away, too. But at least she still had Peter, even if he couldn't talk to her. Peter could keep her company at night and walk to school beside her and sit beside her at the table as they ate their meals. And she still had Grandma Shaffer, too, even if she had been mean to Peter the last time they had visited her. How awful it must be to live all alone like Mr. Mendel.

"Do you have any other children, besides your son?"

"No, he is the only one."

"Do you have any other relatives? Sisters and brothers?"

"Yes, I have two brothers, but they did not come to America when I did. They are still in Hungary, where Avraham is. I am trying to find out what has happened to all of them, but there is no longer any mail service."

"Is that your son's name? Avraham?" Mr. Mendel nodded. "Peter and I don't have any family close by, either. That's why Penny Goodrich had to move in with us. Grandma Shaffer can't take care of us because she's too old and doesn't have any room in her house. We have an aunt named Gloria—she's Uncle Steve's wife—but nobody likes her because she's Italian."

The drainboard had become too full to hold any more dishes, so Esther pulled a dish towel from the hook and began drying them. "They go up here? In this cupboard?" she asked.

"Yes, please. What about your mother's family?"

Esther stopped drying to look at him in surprise. "Mama's family?"

"Yes. Do your mother's relatives live here in Brooklyn?"

Of course Mama must have relatives. Everybody had a family, didn't they? But no one had ever talked about Mama's family, and Esther couldn't recall ever meeting them. Moisture from the wet plate soaked through her blouse as she held it against her chest, chilling her. "I don't know anything about Mama's family," she murmured. But why didn't she? Why was it such a mystery?

"If you are tired of doing dishes you may stop anytime," Mr. Mendel said. "There is no need to do all of them tonight."

His words jarred Esther from her thoughts, and she resumed her task. "No, I don't mind. I like helping you."

"I have thought of hiring a housekeeper, but my broken arm will be healed in a few more weeks and I will be able to do things for myself again."

"You can hire me until then. I know how to do all kinds of things around the house besides dishes. I can dust and sweep, clean sinks. And I could use the money to buy war bond stamps and take Peter to the movies once in a while. And to pay for my piano lessons." The idea of paying for her own lessons had just occurred to Esther, but she thought it was a good one. "Penny Goodrich is paying for my lessons right now, but I don't want her to. She's not my mother." Her words came out more harshly than she intended.

Mr. Mendel frowned. "I see," he said, nodding slowly. "Then perhaps this arrangement will work well for both of us."

CHAPTER 14

PENNY'S STOMACH CHURNED as she stood at the stove, scrambling eggs for breakfast. She divided them between two plates instead of three when they were cooked, feeling much too queasy to eat. Today she would start training to be a bus driver. She couldn't recall ever being so nervous.

"I might be a little late coming home from work today," she told Esther and Peter when they joined her in the kitchen. "I start training for a new job today." She waited, wondering if they would show an interest and maybe ask her about it. Neither of them did.

"Okay . . . well, your lunches are all packed. I guess I'll see you tonight." Penny grabbed her own lunch pail and hurried downstairs to the bus stop, not wanting to be late on the first day. She didn't know if she would be able to eat a bite of food at noontime, either.

She waited on the corner, and when the bus arrived, she was relieved to see her marine friend, Roy Fuller, sitting in his usual place in the front. He greeted her with a grin. "Here you go, Penny. I saved you a seat. But you'll be on your own for the next few days. I'm going home tomorrow on a three-day leave."

"That's wonderful, Roy. I'll bet you can hardly wait."

"I'm counting the hours until I can kiss my girlfriend."

"How long has it been since you've seen her?"

"Three and a half months. How about you and your soldier boy?"

"Eddie's been gone nearly a month already, but he should be coming home on leave pretty soon." The reminder sent Penny's stomach rolling like a barrel down a steep hill. "It'll be the first time I've seen him since he left for basic training."

"You going to do something special for the occasion? Maybe buy a new dress to wear?"

"A new dress? You mean for me?"

Roy laughed out loud. "Well, I hope your boyfriend doesn't wear dresses." Penny smiled for the first time all morning.

"I can't remember the last time I bought a new dress," she said. "Long before the war started, that's for sure."

"The first time I came home on leave, Sally got all dolled up for me. New dress, new hairstyle. Boy, she looked pretty. I asked her to marry me right then and there."

Penny caught her breath. "You really asked her to marry you?"

"You bet! It showed me how much she cared, going to all that trouble for me and everything. You have to remember that I'd been around a bunch of men for weeks and weeks, so Sally was a sight for sore eyes. I'll bet your boyfriend will be happy to see a pretty gal like you, too, after living in an army barracks all this time."

For a moment Penny couldn't speak. No one had ever told her she was pretty—least of all a man. When she finally found her voice again she asked, "So when are you and Sally getting married?"

"We're not engaged yet. She had to turn me down. Her father said she was too young. I wanted to elope, but I only had a three-day pass and Sally deserves a nice, big wedding."

"I'll bet she's sorry she said no, now that you're so far away."

"I'm not sure what she thinks. I'm trying to woo her but it's hard to say all the things I want to say in a letter. I never was very good at writing, and I've never been good with girls, either. I was too shy around them in high school. I guess that's why I'm twenty-six years old and still not married. I never had any sisters, so I don't know how girls think or what they like men to say to them."

"You should watch some romantic movies like *Gone With the Wind* or *Robin Hood*. Errol Flynn and Clark Gable seem to know all the right things to say to a girl. You could get some ideas from them."

"What does your beau say in his letters?"

Eddie's letters were brief and not at all romantic: Were his army payroll checks arriving? Did she have enough money for food and to pay the bills? Were the kids doing all right in school? "He's not very good at writing letters, either," Penny finally said.

"Hey, I have an idea. Maybe you could write down a few things for me that you wish your beau would say to you and I could say them to Sally."

"Shouldn't your letters to her be in your own words?"

"I don't think she'll care as long as I sound romantic. Please, Penny? I sure would hate to lose her because my letters are too dull. She might decide that I'm dull, too."

"You're not dull at all, Roy. You always help me get my mind off . . . everything. And you make me smile." Mother would have a conniption fit if she knew that Penny was being this friendly with a stranger. But Roy didn't seem like a stranger anymore. He seemed like a friend. And she wanted to help him.

"Okay, let me think of something romantic you could say . . ." She pictured Eddie in her mind and thought of the much-too-brief moments she used to spend with him when he came to the duplex to visit his mother. She thought of how she longed to be held in his arms, to rest her head against his shoulder and feel his arms around her, to feel his embrace, his lips touching hers. She held back a sigh. "You could say something like, 'I wish I could capture time in a bottle when we're together and throw it into the deepest ocean. Then I would have forever to spend with you. I wouldn't need air to breathe or food to eat. Holding you in my arms would be all the food I would need. Having your love would be the only air I would need to breathe.'"

"Wow!" Roy murmured when she finished. "That's great! Could I use that with Sally?"

"Sure." She gave a little laugh. "It's just a bunch of words."

"Do you have a pencil I could borrow?" He pulled an envelope from his breast pocket. It looked like a letter from Sally. Penny gave him a pencil from her purse and watched Roy chew his lip in concentration as he scribbled her words on the back of the envelope. "If you think of anything else, will you write it down for me?" he asked when he finished.

"Sure. And thanks for your advice, Roy. Maybe I will buy a new dress to wear for Eddie."

"And don't forget, men like to see their sweethearts wearing a pretty new hairstyle, too. And perfume—wear lots of nice perfume."

"Okay. Thanks." Maybe Eddie would notice her if she took Roy's advice. And maybe he wouldn't notice that his kids hated her. "Now tell me what else you and Sally have planned for your trip home," she said.

Penny listened intently as Roy described the supper club where he wanted to take Sally and how they would dance until morning, then watch the sun come up at Lake Scranton. Penny imagined an evening like that with Eddie and sighed. "See, Roy? You're very romantic. And if I don't see you again before you go home, I wish you luck with Sally."

"Thanks. And good luck with Eddie. I hope you knock him dead when he comes home on leave."

"Me too. Bye." The bus rolled into the station where Penny worked, and as she stood to get off, she remembered that she was starting drivers' training today. Roy had distracted her for a short time, but now her insides squirmed once again. She turned back to him and said, "Hey, Roy, say a little prayer for me, okay? I'm trying out for a new job today." He folded his hands and closed his eyes for a second as if in prayer, then looked up at her again with a wide grin. He pointed his finger toward heaven.

Penny's knees felt weak as she walked into the depot. Her boss, Mr. Whitney, directed her to a vacant office next to his that had been converted into a classroom. She was relieved to see that the seven other people who would be learning to drive along with her were all women. Penny took a seat beside a young dark-haired woman about her age.

"Hi. Are you as nervous as I am?" Penny whispered to her.

The girl nodded. "I don't know whether to run from the building or throw up."

"Me either. I think I might do both." Penny managed a smile and the girl smiled in return. "My name's Penny Goodrich. And I can't even drive a car, let alone a bus."

"I'm glad I'm not the only one. I'm Sheila Napolitano. Nice to meet you."

Penny's nerves calmed considerably when the teacher entered and told them that for the first few days, all their instruction would take place in this room. "You will have to pass a written test and qualify for a learner's permit before we put you behind the wheel of a bus. Then you'll have to pass another written test, an eye test, and a road test before you qualify for a license."

That seemed like a lot of hurdles to jump over. Penny listened intently all morning, taking notes in the margins of the instruction manual they had given her. "There's so much to learn!" she told Sheila as they ate lunch together. "I'll have to study at night with the kids when they do their homework."

"You're married?" Sheila asked.

"No, I'm taking care of two children for a friend of mine while he's away in the army. Well, actually . . . I hope he's going to be more than a friend someday. I hope he marries me after the war. His first wife died, and he needed somebody to take care of his two children and I said I would do it and so . . . Oh, boy. I'm doing it again. I always babble on and on whenever I'm nervous, and believe me, learning to drive a bus makes me very nervous. How about you, Sheila. Are you married?"

"Yeah." She held out her left hand to show a wedding band and tiny diamond ring. "Tony and I got married one year ago last August, but we've only been together for a few weeks since. We met at Coney Island in July, got married in August, and he got shipped off to California two months later."

"Gosh, you must be lonely without him."

"Yeah. I was hoping I would get pregnant right away so I'd have

Tony's baby to keep me company while he's gone, but it didn't happen. That's why I applied for this job."

Penny could feel herself blushing at the mention of getting pregnant. The few conversations she could remember having about "the birds and the bees" had frightened her half to death. Her parents had never liked to talk about such things.

Her parents.

Penny's stomach made a sickening flip inside her. Ever since the clerk in the records' office had told Penny the news, she hadn't stopped thinking about the fact that she was adopted. *Adopted.* Her parents weren't really her parents. Unless of course someone in the records' office had made a mistake, which was what Penny still wanted to believe. It just didn't make sense. Why hadn't they ever told her? Penny hadn't been home to see her parents since discovering the truth a few days ago, but she probably wouldn't have the nerve to ask them about it even when she did go home on Sunday. She really didn't want to know the truth.

"I just love babies," Sheila continued. "I want to have a houseful of them someday, don't you?"

"Yes . . . I mean, who wouldn't love to have a little baby?" According to her birth certificate she had been adopted on the same day she'd been born. Was it possible that her real mother hadn't wanted her and had given her to strangers to raise? Penny didn't want to think about it anymore.

She watched as Sheila pulled out a compact and used the mirror to apply bright red lipstick after she finished eating. "It's called *Victory Red*," Sheila said when she saw Penny watching her. "Don't ask me why. I mean, how can a lipstick help win the war?" She snapped her compact shut again. Sheila was pretty and stylish with wavy black hair, just the right amount of makeup on her dark brown eyes, and a flowered dress that showed off her tiny waist.

Penny was desperate to get her mind off her parents. Maybe she wouldn't go home at all this weekend. "Can I ask you something, Sheila?"

"Sure."

"Do you know of a good place where I could get my hair done? I really like the way yours looks, and I want to get dolled up a little bit for when my boyfriend comes home on leave. Can you recommend a place?"

"Sure, the beauty parlor where I go isn't too far from here. I can give you the address. They stay open later on Fridays and Saturdays since so many women are working. You could probably make an appointment for this Saturday." She reached out to feel Penny's ponytail. "Your hair is nice and thick, not all kinky like mine. I'll bet you would look pretty if you got it cut in a bob instead of wearing it pulled back like that."

Penny feared she might cry. Sheila was the second person today who had told her she was pretty. Did she dare to believe it? She felt a shiver of excitement at the thought that Eddie might think so, too. "And where's a good place to go shopping? I want to buy something new to wear that isn't too expensive. Do you know of a store where they could give a girl like me some good advice?"

"I'd be glad to go with you. I love to shop."

"Really? You would help me?"

"Sure. I don't have much to do on Saturdays now that Tony is away. It would be fun. And you look like you could use some modern clothes. Yours are a little old-fashioned—no offense."

"That's okay. No one ever helped me shop before, except my mother. And she's seventy years old."

"Let's have a look at you." Sheila gestured for Penny to stand up and then gave her a once-over, from her hair to her feet. "We'll have to do something about your shoes, too."

"My shoes? What about them?"

"How old are you?"

"Twenty-four."

"No offense, but you're too young to wear shoes like that all the time."

"My mother says they're sensible shoes. She would have a conniption fit if she ever saw me wearing high-heeled pumps. She says they're a waste of money and calls them 'floozy shoes.' "

"Well, your shoes are sensible, I suppose, if you're seventy years old. We need to buy you some new shoes, too. You can afford them once we get this new job, huh?"

"We'll be rich!"

By the end of the day, Penny's head felt stuffed full of all the new information she had to learn. The teacher was about to dismiss the class when Mr. Whitney arrived and issued rumpled, dark gray uniforms to everyone.

"I'm sorry, but for now all we have are men's uniforms," he said. "And they are secondhand uniforms, at that. You ladies will have to do a little sewing to make them fit, but I'm sure you can handle it."

Men's uniforms? That meant Penny would have to wear pants, and she had never worn them in her life. Again, Mother would have a conniption fit.

It was much later than usual by the time Penny left the bus station to head home. She felt disappointed when her bus arrived and Roy wasn't on it. She would have liked to share her day with him. Rush hour was in full swing by now and the buses were all very crowded. They moved like slugs in the thickening traffic. Penny checked her watch repeatedly, worried about the children. She had never left them alone for this long after school.

She finally reached her stop nearly an hour late and raced home to the apartment. It seemed very quiet inside. No one was listening to the radio or practicing the piano or sitting at the dining room table doing homework.

"Esther?" she called. "Peter? Where are you?" She felt tired from the long day and from lugging the bundle of uniforms all the way home. She dumped them on a dining room chair so she would remember to alter them after supper and went upstairs to look for the kids. Their bedroom was empty. Penny felt a flicker of panic. She hurried down from the third floor and checked the back porch, the yard, the basement where the washing machines were, even the garage and the alley behind it, calling their names. There was no sign of them.

They knew they weren't supposed to leave the apartment after school until she came home. Where could they be? She went around the building to the front and looked up and down the avenue. Maybe she should go back inside and telephone somebody, but who could she call? The police? Grandma Shaffer? No, the last time Penny had asked Mrs. Shaffer for help, she had made a gigantic mess of things. Penny went in through the front door and got as far as the vestibule when the Jewish landlord's door suddenly opened, and there he stood with his bushy black beard and little black beanie, just three feet away from her. She jumped back, scared half to death, her hand on her heart.

"I am sorry for startling you," he said. "But if you are looking for the children, they are in here with me."

Penny sagged onto the bottom step in relief. "Thanks. I know I was very late today, and I'm so sorry if they've been a bother—"

"No bother. They are a help to me since I am burdened with this." He held up his arm to show her a white plaster cast. Eddie had asked her to check on their landlord weeks ago, telling her that he'd been hurt in the fire across the street, but she hadn't done it.

"We have not met," he said. "I am Jacob Mendel. Mr. Shaffer told me you were a friend of his, coming to care for the children."

"Yes. Penny Goodrich. Nice to meet you." She was relieved that he didn't offer his hand to shake. "I didn't know where they could be. I'm sorry I was late, but I don't think it will happen again. Today was my first day on a brand-new job and . . . well, it isn't really a new job, not yet. They're teaching me how to drive a bus, but I didn't actually drive anywhere yet, and I won't get to drive unless I pass a bunch of tests first—" She stopped, aware that she was babbling. She always talked too much when she was frightened, and right now her heart was pounding like an African drum. Whether it was from the scare the children had given her or from talking face-to-face with a Jewish man, she couldn't tell. Maybe both.

"You look shaken, Miss Goodrich. Would you like to come inside and sit down for a moment?" He opened the door wider and beckoned to her.

Penny nearly shouted, *No!* Her father said that Jews were not to be trusted. They lured Christian children into their homes and performed strange, evil rituals. Had Mr. Mendel already lured Esther and Peter inside? Was this a trick to lure her, too?

But surely Eddie would have warned her to stay away from their landlord if he were dangerous. Instead, he had asked Penny to check up on him. Then she remembered something else that Eddie had told her: Mr. Mendel's wife and his wife had been friends. They had died in the same accident.

"Come in, please," he said again.

It would be rude not to accept his offer. Besides, Penny was responsible for Esther and Peter's safety. She needed to see what they were doing in there. Her heart pounded faster as she stepped through his door.

The first thing she noticed were the books, shelves and shelves of them. They reminded her of encyclopedias, lined up in sets of the same size, with leather bindings and gold lettering. There were no paintings on the walls, just a few framed documents with Jewish writing on them. She saw several candlesticks of various sizes, the Jewish kind that held more than one candle at a time. And every doorway had a small rectangular box with Jewish lettering on it, hung at an odd angle. The foreignness of the apartment made her want to run upstairs and slam the door, even though nothing had happened to frighten her.

"I hope it is all right with you, Miss Goodrich, but I have been paying the children to help me. I am not supposed to get this plaster cast wet, and that makes it very hard to wash dishes. The children are a help to me."

She followed him past a dining room table littered with newspaper clippings and into his spacious kitchen. Esther stood at the stove, keeping watch over two bubbling pots. Whatever she was cooking smelled wonderful. She looked happy and content. But when she turned around and saw Penny, she looked as though she wanted to point to the door and order Penny to leave. A moment later, Peter came in through the back door with an empty garbage pail in his hand. He took a step back when he saw Penny, like a dog expecting a beating. Penny couldn't imagine why they would react this way except that their father had told them not to bother Mr. Mendel, and here they were in his kitchen.

Mr. Mendel cleared his throat as if he had noticed the tension between the three of them. "You are all welcome to stay and eat dinner with me," he said. "I have plenty. The women from the shul continue to bring me more than I can possibly eat."

Before Penny could graciously refuse, Esther spoke. "Peter and I want to stay. I helped heat everything up and it's all ready. May we?" She was asking for Penny's permission, but it was very clear that Esther didn't want Penny to stay. Nor was Penny courageous enough to sit at a Jewish man's table and eat his food.

"Thank you for asking, Mr. Mendel. The kids may stay, but . . . but I'm not feeling very well. I had a hard day at work today."

"Perhaps another time."

"Yes . . . Well . . . don't stay too long," she told the kids as she backed out of the kitchen. "You have school tomorrow."

Mr. Mendel walked Penny to the front door. "I will send them upstairs as soon as we finish eating. I hope you feel better soon, Miss Goodrich."

"Thank you." She looked at the kindly man and wondered if he was being sneaky and deceptive or if her father could have been wrong about Jewish people all these years. Either her father was mistaken or Eddie was a fool to live here. They couldn't both be right.

She trudged upstairs, too weary to think about it. What a day this had been—starting a new job, getting advice from Roy, and meeting Sheila and asking for her help with a new hairstyle and new clothes. Penny sank down at the kitchen table and kicked off her shoes. The sensible shoes that her mother had made her buy.

Her mother. If the adoption certificate was correct, she wasn't Penny's real mother at all. Nor was her father really her father.

How had this whole mixed-up chain of events ever gotten started? How had Penny changed so quickly from the quiet, dutiful daughter who sold tickets at the bus station and lived with her elderly parents into a girl who was about to cut her hair and learn to drive a bus? A girl who talked to strangers and to Jewish people. A girl who was responsible for two children and who might buy a pair of "floozy" shoes next Saturday. A girl who no longer knew who her real parents were. Was this really the only way to win Eddie Shaffer's love?

Tears filled Penny's eyes when she recalled her mother's words: *I warned you that this was a foolish idea. Why couldn't you be happy with the way things were?*

CHAPTER 15

ALL OF JACOB'S INSTINCTS had warned him not to let those two children into his apartment, much less his life, but he had ignored the warnings. The girl seemed lonely and forlorn, missing her parents. The boy would no longer talk. And so Jacob had been unable to turn them away, inviting them inside just as Miriam Shoshanna had done. He soon discovered that his need for companionship was every bit as great as theirs.

How many times could he read Avraham's letters, trying to imagine his face, his voice, before the memories of his son faded and lost their power? How many meals could he eat alone in Miriam Shoshanna's orderly, kosher kitchen before loneliness shrank his starved soul into a bitter kernel? "It is not good that man be alone," Hashem had declared at Creation. Had He forgotten His own words? Is that why He had taken Jacob's family? And the children's family?

And so Jacob had opened his door to them. And now? Now he caught himself glancing at the clock to see if it was nearly time for them to return from school. Now he listened for the sound of music from upstairs as Esther practiced the piano. The sound brought back memories of the children's mother and of Miriam Shoshanna. *"Listen,"* Miriam used to say, pointing to the ceiling. *"Rachel is playing again. Isn't it beautiful, Jacob? Doesn't it take you to Paradise?"* That was one of the reasons why he had begun to play the radio all day after the two women had died—to drown out the silence.

His doorbell rang. It could not be the children; they would knock on the downstairs door, not ring the bell. Might it be Inspector Dalton again? Jacob shuddered at the thought. He would pretend not to be home, let it go unanswered. But when he peered cautiously through his front window and saw that it was Rebbe Grunfeld, he went out to open the door.

"Good day, Rebbe. What can I do for you?"

"Good day, Yaacov. My wife baked a honey cake for you, to celebrate the New Year and Yom Kippur." He held out the plate, wrapped in waxed paper, like an offering. Of course Jacob must offer hospitality in return.

"Would you like to come in, Rebbe?"

The traditional honey cake meant best wishes for a sweet year, but Jacob wanted to ask how there could possibly be a sweet year? He wanted to show the rebbe the photos he had cut from the newspaper, which chronicled the warfare and destruction and starvation. But he kept silent as he ushered Rebbe Grunfeld inside.

"My wife also insisted that I invite you to celebrate *Sukkot* with us this year. Will you come please, Yaacov?"

"Kindly tell the *rebbetzin* thank you, but no thank you."

"I will tell her that you are thinking about it. Who knows? Tomorrow you may change your mind. May I sit down? There is something else I must ask you."

Jacob set the plate of honey cake on his desk as he gestured to the sofa. He turned his desk chair around and sat facing the rebbe, waiting.

"I need to ask for your forgiveness."

"My forgiveness? For what?"

"I fear that I have offended you in some way. I fear that we didn't do enough for you after Miriam Shoshanna died, and that is why you are harboring resentment toward us."

"I am not harboring anything. I wanted to be left alone after Miriam died, and so I closed the door on everyone, not just you. I am not angry at you or anyone else."

"Are you certain, Yaacov? Not even the driver of the car?"

Jacob looked at him in confusion. Why was he bringing this up now, a year and a half later? Then he remembered that it was the high holy days and he realized why the rebbe had come. On Yom Kippur, Jacob was supposed to search his soul and to ask for forgiveness—from others and from Hashem. He was supposed to confess all his sins and transgressions. And Jacob knew that he had transgressed the Torah's commands many times over, breaking the kosher laws, breaking the Sabbath, neglecting prayer, straying from the path.

"No. I am not angry with the man who drove the car," he said with a sigh. "It was an accident, a matter of faulty brakes. It was not intentional."

"Yes, an accident. So who can you blame except Hashem, am I right, Yaacov?"

The rebbe knew Jacob was angry with Hashem. Jacob had told him so when he had lost his temper on the night of the fire. Did the rebbe want him to admit it?

"I have been a rabbi for a long time now," he continued. "And many times I have seen people direct their anger at me or at our synagogue or people in the congregation when the true target of their anger is Hashem, not those of us who serve Him."

"Very well. I admit I am angry. I am angry with the immigration officials for not allowing Avraham's wife and daughter to come home. And with the lawmakers who made such heartless quota laws. I am angry with the people who hate us just because we are Jewish and who want to keep more of us from coming to America where we will be safe."

"That's a lot of anger to hold inside, Yaacov. And you know that during these holy days we offer *selichot,* the prayers for forgiveness—"

"But none of these people have asked me to forgive them, so how can I? Nor can they ever make restitution for their crimes if something has happened to my son and his family. President Roosevelt and the others in our government—they have not asked for our forgiveness, either. It has been nearly a year since we went to them with evidence of Hitler's crimes, two million of our people already dead in Poland. Has our government done anything? No. We fasted and prayed—a day of mourning for the Jews of Europe. Remember that, Rebbe?"

"Yes, of course. Rabbi Stephen Wise and the American Jewish Congress are doing their best to—"

"Never mind the Jewish Congress. Has Hashem answered our prayers?" Jacob stood and scooped up a handful of newspaper clippings from his desk, then dropped them on the rebbe's lap. "Look at these. Families left with nothing but rubble, lives destroyed. There are not even enough graves for all of the dead. And why? Ask *Herr* Hitler why. Then tell me how anyone can forgive Hitler. How can Hashem stand by and allow it?"

The rebbe took a moment to study each of the pictures that Jacob had thrown at him, examining them all before replying. "The prophet Habakkuk lived in a time that was much like ours. He, too, asked Hashem, 'Why do you tolerate the treacherous? Why are you silent while the wicked swallow up those more righteous than themselves?' And you know Hashem's reply as well as I do: 'The righteous shall live by his faith.' We may never understand Hashem's plans and purposes, or see the fulfillment of all that He is doing. But He asks us to live our lives in humble faith, trusting Him even when we cannot see."

Jacob looked away from Rebbe Grunfeld's sorrowful eyes. "I remember a time when I could read the Scriptures and find comfort in them, too. But not now, Rebbe. Not anymore." The weight of his unanswered prayers was too heavy, his anguish too deep for consolation.

He heard the outside apartment door open and close, then footsteps on the stairs to the second floor. The children were home from school. He hoped that they wouldn't knock on his door today. He hoped that Esther wouldn't play the piano. He could not bear it if she did.

"I read the papers, Yaacov," the rebbe said. "I, too, have my doubts. But two days from now, on the most solemn day of the year, I will ask Hashem to forgive me for those doubts and to renew my trust.

We know that Hashem is good and just and holy. All of these terrible things—" he held the clippings aloft— "these must somehow fulfill His purposes. If only we had eyes to see it."

"But I cannot see it, Rebbe Grunfeld. I cannot see it at all. And my eyes have grown weary from looking."

CHAPTER 16

October 1943

Dear Mama and Abba,

It has been so long since I've received a letter from you, and I know that the silence must be just as hard for you to bear in America as it is for me here in Hungary. Every time I look at my little daughter and I try to imagine being separated from her, not knowing if she is well or if she is suffering, I understand how you must feel. And so after much prayer, I have decided that I must write this letter to you and trust that Hashem will allow you to receive it in America someday.

I have made friends with the minister of the Christian church here in our village. He is a very kind man, and I plan to give him this letter and ask him to mail it to you after the war ends. The rumors that we hear about this war and what the Nazis are doing to our people are terrifying. And if anything should happen to us—Hashem forbid—you will at least know something of our story.

When Germany invaded Poland five years ago, many

Jewish refugees fled here to Hungary and to our village to escape from the Nazis. We crowded as many as we could into the Yeshiva and into our homes. These survivors told us that the Nazis are trying to kill all of the Jewish people—not thousands of us, but millions. Hitler is a modern-day version of Haman, Queen Esther's enemy from the Scriptures. He wants every last one of us dead. I'm not sure if the world knows this truth yet, but if they do, it seems as though no one is doing anything about it.

In July of 1941, the Germans began to put pressure on the Hungarian government to arrest all of their enemies, which included the Jews. To appease their ally, Hungary rounded up all the Polish Jews who had sought refuge here and deported them. In a village as small as ours, there was no place to hide and not enough time to escape. They were taken back to Poland, and we fear the worst for them.

I have asked the rabbi why our people are experiencing this great suffering. Was it for some great sin we have committed? What have we done to bring this upon ourselves? He believes that it is not because of sin that we are persecuted but because of the Torah. The Hamans of this world want to wipe out all memory of our people and of our covenant with Hashem, as well as all memory of His Law so that evil can flourish unfettered. In the time of Queen Esther, Haman sought to destroy our people because we would bow only to Hashem, not to him. In Daniel's time, the three faithful Jews were thrown into the fiery furnace because they would not bow to a golden statue. But like Joseph, who was sold into slavery in Egypt, we must trust and believe that what our enemies intend for evil, Hashem will turn into good. As the prophet Habakkuk has written: "Though the fig tree does not bud and there are no grapes on the vines, though the olive crop fails and the fields produce no food, though there are no sheep in the pen and no cattle in the stalls, yet I will rejoice in the Lord, I will be joyful in Hashem my Savior."

After our Polish friends were taken away, we were left to live in peace for a time. But two weeks ago, suddenly and unexpectedly, the soldiers burst into our shul on Shabbat and took all of the able-bodied men away to work in forced labor gangs. The only reason I am able to write this is because I was at home in bed when they came, struck ill with a terrible fever and pneumonia. In fact, I nearly died. I didn't understand at the time why Hashem had allowed me to suffer such a serious illness, but now I see that it was His way of sparing me when all the other men, including Sarah Rivkah's father and brothers, were taken away.

Two years ago when the first wave of forced labor conscription took place, we had no idea what it meant. Now we do. The "lucky" ones will be put to work inside factories all day— factories that are the targets of Allied bombs. Others will be forced to mine the raw materials needed for the war or to work in gangs repairing and building roads and railroads. In other words, they are slaves. No one has returned home except to die. The government won't feed men who have become too weak or too sick to work, and so they are sent home to die.

Now that I am no longer ill, I live in fear that they will come back to conscript me. After much prayer, I have decided that Sarah Rivkah, Fredeleh, and I must leave the village. It's too difficult for me to hide here, and except for my Christian friend and his wife, I don't know which of our Hungarian neighbors I can trust. I have tried to convince our families to join us—Abba's brother Yehuda, Mama's family, Sarah's family. I

*have begged them all to come to Budapest with us. It is easier
to hide in a big city, I tell them. But they all say, "What about
food? How will we live? The whole country is suffering from
shortages and famine. At least we can grow our own food, raise
our own chickens in the country."*

*Everyone believes they are safer here in the provinces. No
one will listen to me except for Sarah's mother. And so tomorrow I will take her and my wife and daughter to Budapest to
stay with Abba's brother Baruch, if he will have us.*

*I love you, Mama and Abba. And I am hoping that even
if the worst happens to us, you will receive this letter one day.
I place all of my trust in Hashem, who is able to keep us in His
care.*

Love always,
Avraham

CHAPTER 17

THE PIANO BENCH felt very hard to Esther as she tried to concentrate on the piece she was supposed to learn for her next lesson. She wanted to get it right so she could play it for her father as a surprise, but tonight she felt much too restless to practice the piano. Daddy was coming home in only three more days, and she wished she knew how to make the long, endless weekend pass more quickly. He would make everything right again when he got home. Well, almost everything. Mama would still be gone. But Daddy would see how much they needed him and he would quit the army. Then Peter would start talking again and Penny would go back home where she belonged. And maybe, just maybe, Esther would feel happy again.

Esther glanced over her shoulder at Penny. She was sitting beneath the living room lamp, sewing the hem on an ugly gray uniform with a needle and thread. Penny never used to wear a uniform to work, and these ugly ones had pants—something Penny never wore at all, even at home.

Esther tried once again to concentrate on the music and couldn't. She pounded the keyboard with a discordant crash and whirled around to face Penny, who had a startled look on her face. "May Peter and I go to the movies on Saturday?"

"Tomorrow? Well . . . I was planning to go shopping with a friend from work. I thought you might want to come with us and do girly things."

"No, thank you. I'd rather go to the movies." She hoped Penny wouldn't ask which film was playing because Esther didn't know. The idea of going with Jacky Hoffman—the new, nicer Jacky Hoffman—made her heart jump around inside her chest like a game of Double Dutch skip rope. He walked home from school with her nearly every day, and she liked talking to him.

"What time does the movie start?" Penny asked. "I don't know how long it will take me to shop, but I could try to get back in time to take you."

"You don't have to. Peter and I can go to the movies by ourselves. I'm almost thirteen. And the theater is only a few blocks away."

"I don't know, Esther . . ."

"Besides, some friends from school are coming with us."

"Which kids? Does your father know them?"

"Sure. They live right next door. We walk home from school with them sometimes."

Penny didn't reply. Esther wished she knew what Penny was thinking, but since Esther wasn't being completely honest with Penny, she feared looking her in the eye. Mama had always been able to detect a fib.

"I think I should ask your father first," Penny said. "Can you wait and go to the movies another Saturday? I'll ask him when he comes home. It's just a few more days."

"He won't mind if we go. We used to go to the Saturday matinee all the time when he was home." Esther didn't mention the fact that he had gone with them. "And if you're worried about money, Peter and I can pay our own way. We have money from doing chores for Mr. Mendel."

"I don't know . . ."

Esther was losing her temper but thought it might work against her to throw a tantrum. Grandma Shaffer had once told her, "*You can catch more flies with honey than you can with vinegar."* Esther hadn't known what that meant until Grandma had explained it. She would try the "honey" approach now. "Please, Penny? You shouldn't have to change your plans just for us. The theater is even closer than the school is, and we walk to school without you every day. Please?"

"Well . . ."

"Thanks, Penny. We'll work extra hard and get all of our chores done tomorrow morning."

"But I—"

"And I promise that we won't even complain while we do them." She blew Penny a kiss before she could protest and sprinted up the stairs to tell Peter the good news. He sat hunched on his bed like a little old man, thin and looking worried.

"Hey, Peter, guess what! Penny said we can go see a matinee tomorrow afternoon."

Peter seemed to shrivel even more, as if he wanted to crawl under the blankets and hide. She felt a jolt of fear and wanted to shake him until he was all right again.

"I'll pay your way, don't worry. It'll be fun."

He found the little slate he sometimes used and wrote: *By ourselves? Without Daddy?*

"Jacky Hoffman says he'll go with us." She felt herself blush as she said his name out loud, remembering how cute he was. "He has to deliver groceries in the morning, but he'll be done in time for the matinee. His brother, Gary, might come, too." At the mention of the Hoffman brothers, Peter started shaking his head vigorously from side to side. "What's wrong? Why are you shaking your head like that?"

Peter wrote on the slate: *not with them.*

"Why not? Jacky's been sticking up for you at school, you know. That's why the other kids don't make fun of you anymore for not talking. He's been acting nice lately, hasn't he? Walking home from school with us and everything?"

Peter continued to shake his head as he pointed to the slate, *not with them.*

"You make me so mad sometimes! I went to all that trouble to talk Penny into it and now you don't want to go? She won't let you stay home alone, and I don't think you want to go shopping with her, do you?"

Peter slouched lower, still shaking his head in defiance.

"Stop that! You can't sit around this room reading your stupid comic books for the rest of your life. I want to go to the movies, and you're coming with me whether you like it or not!"

He turned his head away and lifted his comic book to hide his face. Once again Esther remembered the honey and vinegar approach. "Please, Petey? Won't you please do this for me? I'm so tired of being cooped up in this apartment every Saturday, aren't you? Don't you want to get out of here and go to the movies like we used to do with Daddy?" She waited, but Peter didn't respond. "Please? I'll do the dishes for you all week . . . and I'll let you listen to any radio program that you want."

He finally lowered his comic book again and wrote: *OK, but just us.*

Esther could have agreed to go by themselves, only she didn't want to. She was surprised to discover how much she wanted to go with Jacky. It felt like such a grown-up thing to do. And it felt nice to be a grown-up. Exciting. He had called her "beautiful."

"I promised Penny that we would go with the other kids. She won't let us go alone. Besides, Jacky is different now that he has a job after school. You'll see. Please, Peter? . . . Pretty please?" When he finally nodded his head, she felt like kissing him.

Esther worked extra hard on Saturday morning to finish her chores. Penny had added a few extra ones, saying she wanted to make the apartment especially nice for their father's homecoming on Monday. As the time to leave for the movie theater approached, Esther worried that Peter would change his mind. She saw his reluctance in every move he made as he slowly put on his jacket and followed her downstairs to the front porch, where Jacky and Gary were waiting for them. Esther's heart thumped so hard as they walked the one block to the cinema that she barely had enough breath to talk.

A teenaged couple waiting in the ticket line in front of them was holding hands. Esther knew that the pair would probably sit upstairs in the balcony and smooch. Would Jacky consider this a date if she let him pay her way? Would he try to hold her hand or steal a kiss, too? It made her feel very grown-up to imagine that he was her boyfriend. But Esther wasn't sure she wanted to be that grown-up yet.

"Peter and I can pay our own way," she said when they reached the ticket window. She quickly shoved enough nickels through the slot to pay for both of them.

"Suit yourself," Jacky said with a shrug. But when they got inside, he sat down right beside her and shared his box of Jujubes with her. Peter sat on Esther's other side, acting mad. Too bad. She was glad for once that he couldn't talk. She could ignore him easier this way. Even if Peter tried to write her a note, she wouldn't be able to read it in the darkened theater.

The newsreel played first, showing tanks rolling across a desert, airplanes flying low, and a huge ship with hundreds and hundreds of soldiers aboard, waving as they sailed away. The film brought tears to Esther's eyes. Her father might soon be one of those men, sailing away into danger.

After seeing all those soldiers going off to war, Esther didn't think the cartoons were very funny at all. They were all about the war, too, and even Donald Duck was marching off to fight. The weekly *Masked Marvel* serial was next, then the first movie began to play. Jacky tossed his empty candy box on the floor and draped his arm around the back of Esther's seat. Once again her heart thumped like Double Dutch skip rope, even though he wasn't really hugging her or anything.

The double feature—one film with Judy Garland and another with Abbott and Costello—distracted Esther for a little while, but the afternoon ended much too quickly. The lights came on, the fantasy faded, and she was back in a movie theater with sticky floors and worn velvet seats, stale popcorn crunching underfoot. Happily-ever-after was only an illusion.

They emerged from the theater, squinting in the bright afternoon sunlight. Jacky brushed up against Esther a few times as they walked home together, their shoulders bumping. She suspected that he'd done it on purpose, and it made her feel excited. As they neared home, Peter hurried on ahead, disappearing around the corner. Let him go. She didn't know why he acted so weird, almost as if he was jealous that Esther had another friend besides him. Too bad. He would have to get used to the fact that she was growing up and wasn't going to do everything with him all of the time.

They rounded the corner and the burned-out synagogue came into view, a dreary pile of burned bricks and twisted beams. Esther still couldn't get used to the ugly sight, and even though the cleanup work had begun, it reminded her of the bombed-out ruins in Mr. Mendel's newspaper pictures. And of Daddy's last night at home.

"Do you think the synagogue will ever look the way it did before the fire?" she asked.

"Are you kidding? I hope they tear it down and turn the vacant lot into a ball field."

"Where would the Jewish people go to pray?"

"Who cares? This neighborhood could use a nice park—and fewer Jews."

His harsh words startled her. He seemed like the old Jacky Hoffman all of a sudden.

Then he smiled his roguish grin and punched her lightly on the arm. "Just kidding."

They halted on the front steps of her apartment building. They were alone. Peter had gone inside, and Jacky's brother had gone home. Esther usually had no trouble thinking of things to talk about, but today she felt tongue-tied. For a long moment neither of them spoke. Esther could hear the rush of traffic on the next block. Why couldn't she think of something to say?

"Um . . . what did you think of the movies?" she finally asked.

"They were okay. The newsreel was my favorite. Boy, I sure would love to fly an airplane and drop a few bombs on some yellow-faced Japs." He gripped imaginary airplane controls as he imitated the sounds of planes diving and bombs exploding. He was still making bombing noises when Mr. Mendel came around the corner and walked up the sidewalk toward them. Esther waved when she saw him coming.

"Hi, Mr. Mendel."

"Good afternoon, Esther."

Jacky's expression hardened as Mr. Mendel went past them. "You always talk to kikes?" Jacky asked after Mr. Mendel had gone inside.

Esther wasn't sure what *kikes* were, but the ugly face Jacky had made as he'd spat out the word told her that it wasn't good. "Mr. Mendel is our landlord."

"He's just another dirty little kike, if you ask me."

The popcorn and candy Esther had eaten churned uncomfortably in her stomach. Once again she felt pulled in opposite directions. Mr. Mendel was her friend and she wanted to defend him, but Jacky Hoffman was her friend, too. The day suddenly seemed tired and faded, like threadbare clothes that had been washed too many times.

"Well, I should go inside," she said. "Thanks for going to the movies with me."

"We should go again sometime."

Esther hesitated. Would she be betraying Mr. Mendel if she did? But the excitement of having a friend like handsome Jacky Hoffman was too strong to resist.

"Yeah, we should."

"See you later, then." Jacky gave a little salute and sauntered away as if the pavement rested on box springs.

The apartment was very quiet when Esther went inside. Penny still wasn't home, and Peter had probably crawled back into a hole somewhere. Esther trudged up the stairs to the third floor, then stopped outside Penny's bedroom. No, she wouldn't call it Penny's bedroom; it was Daddy and Mama's bedroom. The door stood open, and she went inside to rummage through Daddy's closet, searching for Mama's photograph album. Esther felt like a snoop, but she didn't care. She found the album on the closet shelf beside the hat Daddy used to wear to church every Sunday. Esther sat cross-legged on the bedroom floor to page through it. Tears blurred her vision as she studied her mother's face. She missed her so much. The black-and-white photographs couldn't capture the rich brown color of Mama's hair or her hazel eyes. She recalled how Mr. Mendel had asked about Mama's family the other day, and suddenly Esther wanted to know all about them.

The album began with pictures of Mama and Daddy, looking very young and happy. In nearly every picture her parents were holding hands or standing with their arms around each other, belonging to each other. In several photos they stood in Grandma Shaffer's backyard beside a table filled with food. Mama had said that those photographs had been taken on the day she and Daddy got married.

Esther saw pictures of her parents on a beach wearing swimsuits and pictures of herself as a little baby. It made her tears fall faster to see how happy Mama looked as she held Esther in her arms. She turned the page and saw Mama standing on the sidewalk in front of their apartment building, holding Esther's hand. She could see part of the synagogue across the street, and that made her sad, too. Why did everything have to change?

She turned the page and saw pictures of Peter, including one of Esther holding him in her arms. Mama sat right beside them, smiling and happy. Always happy. In another picture, Mama smiled as she sat at her piano keyboard. Esther remembered the day Daddy had taken that picture. He had brought the piano home as a surprise for Mama's birthday. Uncle Steve and Uncle Joe had helped him wrestle the heavy instrument up the stairs.

"I guess we'll have to live in this apartment forever," Daddy had joked, *"because I'm not moving that blasted piano again."* Daddy was smiling in all of the pictures, too. Esther had nearly forgotten what his smile looked like.

There were pictures of some of the trips they'd taken together— a day at Coney Island, a ferry ride across the river, an afternoon at Luna Park. There were pictures of Grandma Shaffer and Daddy's two brothers, Uncle Joe and Uncle Steve. Pictures of Uncle Steve and Aunt Gloria when they got married. But among all the photographs, Esther couldn't find a single one of Mama's family. Didn't everyone have a family? Was Mama an orphan?

The apartment door downstairs banged shut. "I'm home," Penny called out. "Esther? Peter?"

Esther scrambled to her feet. She felt guilty for snooping, even though it was Daddy's bedroom and Mama's album. She quickly shut the book and put it back on the shelf in Daddy's closet.

"We're up here," she called before running into her own room and flopping onto her bed. Peter sat on his bed reading a comic book and eating the last of his candy from the movies. Esther heard Penny climbing the stairs and quickly grabbed a book and pretended to read.

"How was the movie?" Penny asked from the bedroom doorway.

The voice sounded like Penny's, but when Esther looked up at the person standing there, it wasn't Penny Goodrich at all! The hair that she always wore pulled back had been cut to shoulder length and curled in a pretty wave around her face. There was something different about her eyebrows, too. They used to remind Esther of caterpillars, but now they were thin and arched like Betty Grable's eyebrows. Penny was wearing lipstick. And a new dress. And she had real shoes on her feet instead of grandma-shoes. She looked like a completely different person, as if she finally had taken off the Halloween costume of a dowdy old maid, revealing a much younger person underneath—years younger. You would almost say she was pretty if you didn't know Penny very well.

"What did you do to your hair?" Esther asked. Her question didn't come out the way she had meant it to. Penny seemed to shrink away like melting butter. And there she was again, the old Penny Goodrich, not the new one.

"I-I just wanted a change. I thought it was time to try something new. My friend Sheila said that since I might be getting a new job soon, why not get a new haircut, too? Try something new for a change, you know?" She paused, her smile wavering as she patted her hair. "Do . . . do you like it?"

"It's okay." Esther shrugged and went back to reading her book. She didn't know why, but the change in Penny made her furious. Maybe because it was yet another change in Esther's life and she didn't like it. She didn't like it at all. How would she ever get her old life back again if everything kept on changing?

CHAPTER 18

PENNY MADE UP HER MIND not to let Esther's reaction to her new hairstyle discourage her. Shopping with her friend Sheila had been fun. Getting her hair cut had been fun, too. When the hairdresser had spun the chair around at the beauty parlor and Penny had looked in the mirror for the first time, she hadn't recognized herself. She had wobbled home in her new shoes feeling giddy, like a brand-new person. Then she had made the mistake of asking Esther's opinion. Penny felt as though she had blown the biggest chewing gum bubble ever, only to have it burst, leaving a sticky mess all over her face.

She carried her purchases into Eddie's bedroom—her bedroom— to unpack them. She had worn her new dress home. Maybe she would wear it to church tomorrow, too. She had used up all her ration coupons to buy the new shoes, but they had been worth it. The heels weren't as high as the ones Sheila wore, but they were still very stylish. Penny had also purchased a new gray suit and a pale blue blouse to wear to the train station when Eddie came home on Monday.

And Sheila had talked Penny into having her eyebrows plucked at the beauty salon. The pain had made her eyes water, but what a difference! Her brows didn't resemble her father's bold, glaring ones anymore. After the beauty salon, Penny had gone with Sheila to Woolworth's five-and-dime store to buy just a teeny bit of makeup—Tangee rouge to brighten her cheeks, Maybelline mascara for her eyelashes, and a tube of Max Factor coral lipstick for her lips. For the first time that Penny could ever remember, she had felt like a woman.

"You should come with me to volunteer at the USO sometime," Sheila told her. They had stopped at a diner on the way home to buy Cokes and slices of cherry pie. "It's fun. They have dances on the weekends, and you get to meet a lot of nice people. The servicemen come from all over America."

"But you're married. Doesn't your husband mind if you go to a dance without him?"

"He can't expect me to become a hermit while he's away. Besides, all I do is serve coffee and talk to people, maybe dance with one or two of them, that's all. These poor guys are so far away from home, and they're lonely and scared. They're about to be shipped who knows where. Dancing with a pretty girl helps boost their morale. Wouldn't you be happy to know that somebody's keeping your boyfriend's mind off the war while he's far from home?"

"No," Penny said, taking a sip of soda. "I think I would be a little jealous."

"Oh, it's not like that at all." Sheila's diamond sparkled as she waved her hand. "Come with me sometime, and you'll see. Most of the men have wives or girlfriends back home. There's nothing to it."

Penny watched her friend scoop up a bite of pie and pop it daintily into her mouth. She wished she were as feminine as Sheila. Penny felt awkward in comparison, like a plodding mule beside a graceful deer. "I don't know how to dance," she said with a sigh.

"You don't have to. The USO always needs volunteers to pass out coffee and doughnuts. Or just talk to the fellas for a while."

"I'm real good at talking."

"You sure are," Sheila laughed. "It's a lot of fun, Penny. You'd be doing something for the good of our country. And if you decide you want to try dancing, I could teach you how. I mean, look at you!

You're already a brand-new person with your new dress and hairstyle and shoes—why not take up dancing, too?"

Penny smiled to herself, happy with the thought of doing something for the war effort. But talking to a group of strangers? Mother would have a conniption fit. "I guess I could think about it," she told Sheila.

"Good. We could go together. And if I teach you to dance, you'll be able to dance with your boyfriend when he comes home. He'd like that, I'll bet."

Penny had no idea if Eddie liked to dance or not.

She'd had so much fun on their shopping trip, only to return to the apartment and Esther's indifferent reaction. Penny changed out of her new dress and shoes and put them away in her closet. She hung up her new suit and blouse and put on her old dress and her sensible shoes again. She sat down at the dressing table that had once belonged to Eddie's wife and arranged her new makeup on top of it. She had remembered what Roy had advised and had bought a small bottle of perfume, too.

Penny looked at herself in the mirror and it seemed scary to see a different person gazing back. But Penny couldn't help smiling at her reflection. She liked what she saw.

On Sunday morning Penny woke up early, too excited to sleep. Only one more day and Eddie would be home. She got the children up and dressed for Sunday school, and when they boarded the bus for the ride to church, Penny was overjoyed to see her friend Roy Fuller riding up front. At first he didn't seem to recognize her, then his eyes grew wide, as if they might pop right out of his head. He broke into a grin as he looked her up and down.

"Wow, you did it! Your hair is different and . . . and everything's different. You look great, Penny. Just like a movie star." She could see the admiration in his eyes and hoped Eddie would react the same way.

"Thanks. I took your advice, Roy." She sat down beside him as the kids found seats in the rear of the bus where they liked to ride. "I splurged and bought this dress and a new suit, too. From now on

I'll be wearing a uniform to work—a man's uniform, no less—so I wanted to treat myself to something new and girly."

"Does that mean you got the job you were hoping for?"

"Not yet, but I'm partway there. I'm learning how to drive, and if I pass all the tests, I'll be driving a bus just like this one."

"No kidding? A pretty little gal like you, driving a bus?"

She nodded. His compliment brought tears to her eyes, and she bit her lip to fight them back.

"Good for you, Penny! I've driven a truck before, but never a bus."

"I already passed the first written test and got my learner's permit. Now we're practicing outside in the back parking lot on an older bus, going through the gears and getting used to shifting and the clutch. You have to do it just right or the bus starts hopping around like a bucking bronco."

Roy laughed. "I've been on a few bus rides that were like that."

"Me too. The instructor says you have to be patient and let the clutch out slowly. He says most young people are in too big a hurry and driving a bus requires patience. But I've got plenty of patience, believe me. I've spent a lifetime with parents who are the same age as most people's grandparents, and they're never in a hurry. It takes them forever to do anything. Besides, I'm too scared to press the gas pedal all the way to the floor and see how fast the bus will take off."

"I wish I could see you driving," he said, laughing. "I'll bet you look cute behind that great big steering wheel." Penny blushed, but she couldn't help laughing, too. Roy was so easy to talk to, just like her friend Sheila.

"Speaking of steering," she continued, "our teacher set up a row of barrels for us to steer around, like an obstacle course. My friend Sheila knocked over three of them so far, but I haven't hit a single one. They told us we have to think ahead of the bus and steer into the turn before we get there, because it takes a while to get something that big and slow to turn. But like I said, it's a lot like helping my parents. It takes a lot of planning ahead of time to get them to go in a different direction."

"You're a comedienne, Penny. And it sounds like you're really learning a lot."

"The instructor told me I was doing great. He said with a little more practice I would be ready to take the road test soon."

"Your boyfriend must be real proud of you."

Her smile faded. "I haven't told Eddie about the training."

"Why not?"

"I was afraid I might fail the test and I'd have to go back to selling tickets again. I didn't want him to know that I failed."

"Well, when you do get your license, make sure you go someplace special to celebrate."

"It will have to be Nathan's hot-dog stand," she laughed. "I spent all my money on my hair and clothes and shoes."

"It was worth every cent. You look terrific."

She felt her cheeks getting warmer and warmer. If Roy kept on complimenting her, she wouldn't need her new rouge. She decided to change the subject. "Hey, here I've been babbling on and on, and I haven't asked you about your visit home to see Sally. How did it go?"

Roy looked away. "Well . . . not exactly as I planned. Sally's father nixed the idea of us dancing all night, not to mention going to Lake Scranton to watch the sun come up. She lives at home and still has a curfew."

"My father would be the same way. He's very strict, too. But that doesn't mean Sally doesn't love you."

"I know. We had a great time when we were together, but the furlough went by much too fast. Now I miss her more than ever . . . Say, isn't your boyfriend coming home soon?"

"Tomorrow." The thought made Penny shiver with excitement. "I already know the time will go by much too fast for Eddie and me."

"Can I ask your advice about something, Penny?"

"Sure."

"Sally told me that she writes letters to three other servicemen she knows besides me. She said not to worry; they're only friends and not boyfriends. She says she feels sorry for them and that she's just doing it so they'll get some mail from home to keep up their morale. I hate to sound like a jealous boyfriend, but . . . but I guess I am one."

"Listen, my friend Sheila from work is married to a sailor, but she goes to the USO dances every weekend to cheer up the servicemen and boost morale. She says there's nothing to it at all."

"Really? And she's married?"

Penny nodded. "Listen, you and I are friends, right? We talk all the time and it doesn't mean anything. Maybe that's all Sally is doing in her letters—just talking with her friends who happen to be men, like you and I do."

"I guess you're right." He was quiet for a moment as he played with a button on his uniform. "What really bothers me is the fact that these friends she writes to are all stationed overseas. I'm worried that Sally might decide they're braver than I am because they're seeing action and I'm stuck here in Brooklyn."

"Your job is an important one, too. Imagine what would happen if saboteurs got into the shipyard. I feel a lot safer knowing not all of the soldiers are overseas. We need somebody to stay here and protect us on the home front, right?"

"I guess so. . . . Thanks." Once again she saw the admiration in his eyes as he looked at her. "You look real nice, Penny. I didn't recognize you at first. Is Eddie taking you someplace special when he gets home?"

"I don't think so." She glanced over her shoulder to make sure the kids were out of earshot. "We'll have the kids to think about. He won't want to leave them after being away for so long. And they're not going to let him out of their sight for a single minute, especially to go out on a date with me."

"Are they still giving you a hard time?"

"Yeah. I wish I knew how to get them to like me. I let them go to the movies with their friends last Saturday, but it didn't seem to help. I guess it's only natural that they don't want anyone taking their mother's place."

"Hey, I know! Why not cook Eddie a real nice supper at home? After weeks and weeks of army chow, I'll bet he'd love a home-cooked meal. What's his favorite dish?"

"Um . . . I'm not sure. But I'm going over to his mother's house after church today, so maybe I can ask her." She leaned close to whisper. "I don't dare ask the kids what he likes because they'll sabotage me, telling me how much he loves calves' liver when it really makes him gag."

"They'd do that?" Roy asked with a laugh.

"I wouldn't put it past them. Hey, I have to go. This is our stop. But listen, Roy. Don't worry about Sally writing to those other guys. She would be crazy to two-time a nice guy like you."

"Thanks. I hope you and Eddie have a great time together."

"I hope so, too."

Penny took Esther and Peter to their grandmother's house after church. While the kids ran around the yard with the dog, she asked Mrs. Shaffer if she wanted to come with them to the train station tomorrow to welcome Eddie home. "I could come here and get you right after work and you could ride with the kids and me to meet him. I already found out which buses and subways to take to get to Grand Central Station."

"All the way to Manhattan?" Mrs. Shaffer shook her head, just like Peter always did. "No, that's too much for me. Too much walking, too many buses. A trip like that would be the end of me."

This would be Penny's first trip to Manhattan by herself, too. She hoped Mrs. Shaffer wouldn't tell her parents about it. Mother would have a conniption fit.

Penny suddenly remembered Roy's suggestion. "Listen, I want to cook a special dinner for Eddie tomorrow to welcome him home. What are some of his favorite meals?"

"He likes chicken and dumplings. And pork chops with sauerkraut. Roast beef with mashed potatoes and gravy. But good luck getting a nice roast unless you can steal some extra ration coupons."

"I know. Well, thanks for your advice. I'll see you later." Penny waved good-bye and crossed the tiny yard to her parents' half of the duplex. In all the excitement surrounding Eddie's homecoming she had forgotten how different she looked until she saw her reflection in the window of the back door. Mrs. Shaffer hadn't seemed to notice a difference, but Penny's parents certainly would. She paused to rub off any remaining lipstick and rouge before going inside, nervous about their reaction.

"Hi, I'm home."

Mother sat at the kitchen table, pasting War Bond stamps in a booklet. She looked up, and from the expression on her face, Penny might have been wearing a hideous Halloween mask.

"What did you do to your hair? And those clothes! Are you turning into a hussy?"

"This is the way all the girls look nowadays."

"Well, you have to be more careful. You're not like other girls."

Penny had heard those words all her life, but now she wondered what they really meant. Was she different because she was adopted? Did Mother know a terrible secret about her real parents? "How am I different from other girls?" she asked.

"And those shoes! What did you do with your real shoes?"

"Nothing. I'll still wear them to work. But it's Sunday. I wanted to dress up for church. How am I different from other girls, Mother?"

"You wore that dress to church? You look like a floozy."

"I'm not a floozy." Whatever that was. Penny had only a vague idea. If Mother wasn't going to answer her question, then Penny decided to change the subject. "Eddie is coming home on leave tomorrow."

"Good. Tell him you're done. It's time for his mother to take over with those children. We need your help here at home. Sure, you're willing to help the whole world—strangers even. Why not help your own parents?"

Penny wished she had the courage to get angry and say, *Why should I want to come home? So you can yell at me and tell me I'm as dumb as a green bean and call me a floozy?* But she already knew how Mother would reply. She would accuse Penny of being ungrateful and remind her of all the sacrifices they had made for her over the years.

She watched her mother get up from the table and hobble over to the stove to stir the pot of soup, and she seemed like a stranger to Penny. She had managed to forget about her adoption certificate during the week as she kept busy with her drivers' training and the kids. But the questions came racing back as she sat here in their house.

It couldn't be true, could it? Could the reason she had felt unloved all her life be because she wasn't their daughter? Maybe Mother had never gazed at her the way other mothers did because she wasn't really her mother.

"The soup is ready," Mother said after tasting it. "Go get your father. We'll eat here in the kitchen today. "

Penny did as she was told. She found her father dozing in his chair in the living room while the Andrews Sisters harmonized on the radio. He looked older than she remembered. She watched his chest rise and fall as he snored. How could her parents have lied to her all these years? Part of her wanted to confront them and demand to know the truth, but another part of her was afraid to know. Who was she if not their daughter?

In the end, Penny's fear won the argument. She couldn't confront them. First she would return to the records' office and find out if her birth record was sealed. That's when someone in the office would finally discover that it had all been a huge mistake. Her real papers had been filed in the wrong place or accidentally exchanged with someone else's. There was no sense in angering her parents for nothing.

"Hey, Dad," she said, gently shaking his shoulder. "Lunch is ready."

He opened his eyes and looked up at her, blinking. "Penny? . . . What in the world have you done to yourself?"

Chapter 19

Jacob sat at his desk, cutting articles from the paper and listening to the news headlines on the radio. He heard footsteps descending the stairs to the foyer, and a moment later someone knocked on his door. He rose to open it, expecting to see one of the children, but instead it was the woman who took care of them. She wore such a worried look on her face that he feared something terrible must have happened.

"I'm so sorry to bother you," she said, "but I'm in kind of a jam and I don't know what to do. Eddie—the children's father—is coming home tonight, and I wanted to cook a real nice dinner for him because he's been away for so long, so I went shopping all over town on my lunch hour looking for a nice roast to fix. But then I was at work all afternoon and now it's time to leave for the train station and the roast isn't finished cooking yet, and—"

Jacob held up his hand to stop her. He was relieved to know nothing had happened to the children, but she talked so fast he could barely keep up. "Please, you will have to speak more slowly, Miss . . . I am sorry, but I have forgotten your name."

"Goodrich. Penny Goodrich. Sorry. I always babble on and on when I'm nervous. Sorry."

"That's all right. How can I help?"

"Well, I was just wondering if you thought it would be all right to leave our oven turned on upstairs while we go to the train station to pick up Eddie. He's coming home on leave tonight. The roast needs to cook a little longer, but I don't want to burn the building down by leaving the oven on."

"You may bring it down here and leave it in my oven, if you would like."

"Are you sure?"

"Yes. I am sure."

"Thanks. I guess that's better than leaving it in the oven with no one home, isn't it? And you're welcome to join us for dinner in repayment. There's plenty of food."

"I need no repayment. Besides, I cannot eat meat unless it comes from a kosher butcher shop."

"Oh." She looked so hurt that Jacob regretted mentioning it. Even if the meat was kosher he would not feel comfortable intruding on their reunion that way. "Please, Miss Goodrich. Bring your roast down here and I will watch it for you."

"Okay, thanks. I'll be right back." She smiled for the first time and there was something different about her that he couldn't quite place. Maybe he hadn't gotten such a good look at her the last time they had met, but tonight she looked very pretty. Was it for Ed Shaffer that she wanted to look so special?

Jacob didn't know his tenant very well, but the man couldn't be much older than Avraham was. How long would a military leave last? A week, perhaps? The children would want to spend all of that time with their father, and by the time he went away again, the cast would be off Jacob's arm. He wouldn't need the children's help anymore. From now on he would begin to put more distance between himself and his tenants. He never should have become so attached to them in the first place. And now this—baby-sitting their roast in his oven? Who knew what he would be doing for them next?

Miss Goodrich returned a minute later, carrying a hot roasting pan swaddled in kitchen towels. The aroma made Jacob's mouth water. He led the way into his kitchen and set the oven temperature for her.

"Thanks so much, Mr. Mendel. If we're not home by seven o'clock, you'd better take it out of the oven."

"I will do that."

He heard the family leave a few minutes later and was happy for them. The children had missed their father. He sat down at his desk again to finish listening to the news. Every night he compared the battle reports on the radio with the maps he'd cut from the newspaper. He seldom heard news of Hungary, but since the war was now worldwide, a battle in one nation affected all the others. He spread out everything on his desk, tracing the Allies' path since the invasion of Italy a month ago. Their progress seemed slow. How long would it take to rescue all of Europe from those madmen?

Jacob had lost all track of time when the doorbell rang, interrupting him. Were his tenants home? Had they forgotten their key? He went out to the foyer and opened it to find two middle-aged men in hats and suits and ties standing on his porch. He glimpsed a police car parked out front and felt as though someone had punched him in the stomach. The last time the police had come to his door, it was to tell him that Miriam Shoshanna had been killed in an accident.

"Mr. Jacob Mendel?"

"Yes." His heart thumped so violently he could hardly breathe.

"I'm Detective O'Hara and this is Detective Flynn. We would like you to come down to the police station with us and answer a few questions. We have a car waiting to drive you there."

"To the police station? Why? For what purpose?"

"We need to ask you a few questions about the fire across the street. Inspector Dalton from the fire marshal's office has turned the case over to us."

"Am I being arrested?"

"Should you be? Have you broken the law, Mr. Mendel?"

"Of course not. I am merely asking what is the purpose of taking me to the police station. If it is simply to talk, I can answer any questions you have right here."

"We would prefer it if you came with us. We'll discuss the details once we're down there."

Jacob's anger boiled, but he knew he must control his temper or they would use it as evidence against him. As he tried to think what to do, he suddenly remembered that he had his neighbor's roast in the oven.

"I cannot go anywhere with you, I am sorry. I have food cooking in the kitchen and I cannot leave the oven turned on. If I turn the gas off, the meal will be ruined. You will have to return another day."

The men looked at each other. "In that case," Detective O'Hara said, "may we come inside and discuss this?"

Did Jacob have a choice? If he refused, they would come back another day. Why prolong this? Why not get it over with, find out what they wanted? "Very well. Come in." They would smell the roasting meat inside his apartment. At least they would know he was telling the truth.

Detective Flynn gestured to Jacob's sofa. "Have a seat, Mr. Mendel."

"You are telling me to sit down in my own apartment?"

"Sorry. Force of habit." Flynn sat down instead, but O'Hara remained standing, as if guarding the door. Both men scanned the living room, while Jacob turned off the radio and sat down in his desk chair, turning it to face the detective.

"So, this is about the fire?"

"Yes. I'll be frank with you," Flynn said. "We think you got into an argument with the rabbi, went home and got a can of kerosene, put it inside a paper bag, then came back and set the place on fire. We think you decided to save the scrolls so your friends would think you were a hero—which is exactly what they do think, by the way."

"That makes no sense. I was carrying the paper bag when I talked to Rebbe Grunfeld. It contained my dinner—a can of soup and some crackers. Ask him."

"We have asked him. He claims that he saw you carrying a bag, but he can't identify the contents. We know you keep kerosene in your apartment."

"So do hundreds of other people in Brooklyn. Why harass me? Why would I start the fire?"

The two men exchanged glances as if they knew a secret that Jacob did not. They reminded him of schoolyard bullies, closing in on their prey. "Inspector Dalton from the fire marshal's office has uncovered several possible motives," Detective O'Hara said. "We know that you were estranged from the congregation, so he thinks you did it to regain their favor."

"That is ridiculous. Rebbe Grunfeld has asked me repeatedly to return and say prayers with him. I have many friends there. I am always welcome."

"If that's true, why haven't you attended in more than a year?"

Jacob wanted to tell them that it was none of their business. He hated sharing his personal life with anyone, much less these arrogant detectives. But he feared they would continue to harass him unless he answered their questions. He cleared his throat. "My wife was killed in an accident more than a year ago. I have not gone to the shul since then because I have not felt very much like praying."

"So you admit that you're mad at God? What better way to get even with Him than to burn down His synagogue?"

Jacob stifled a groan. He had made things much, much worse by telling the truth. He should not have said anything at all. He cleared the lump from his throat again and tried to answer calmly. "I would never do a thing like that. To deliberately burn all of those holy books would be unforgivable."

"Look. Just tell us the truth so we can settle the insurance claim and your people can get on with rebuilding the place."

"I am telling you the truth. I did not start the fire."

"Can you prove to us that you didn't?"

"Can you prove that I did?"

"Not yet, Mr. Mendel, but we will. We will."

Jacob was thoroughly angry now. He had thought he would be free in America, that Jews would no longer be falsely accused of causing every misfortune. Why leave your family and travel thousands of miles and struggle to start a new life in America if things were no different here?

Jacob rose to his feet. "I have nothing else to say. You have called me a liar to my face and accused me of committing a terrible crime. I think you should leave now."

Detective Flynn stood and took a step closer to Jacob. "We know you're guilty, Mr. Mendel."

"How dare you!"

"It's only a matter of time until we find the proof we need or a witness comes forward. You will pay for your crime."

"Kindly leave my home."

Jacob closed both doors behind them, trembling with fury. He must talk to Rebbe Grunfeld immediately and straighten this out. He grabbed his hat and coat from the front closet and got as far as the foyer when he remembered the roast in his oven. He came back inside, threw his hat and coat onto a chair, and sat down to wait. He didn't have to wait long. The family from upstairs arrived home a few minutes later, and Miss Goodrich knocked on his door.

"Is everything all right?" she asked. "When our taxi pulled up there was a police car out front. We were worried."

"Everything is fine. I hope your dinner is fine, as well." He led her out to the kitchen so she could retrieve her roast from the oven.

"Are you sure you don't want to join us?" she asked.

"Thank you, but I need to pay a visit to someone this evening."

"Oh. I hope we didn't keep you from going out. Have you been waiting a long time for us?"

"Not at all." But Jacob put on his hat and coat and hurried out the front door before she reached the top of the stairs. He need not have bothered with his coat. The fall evening was warm, Rabbi Grunfeld's apartment only a short walk away. Jacob's hands still trembled with rage as he knocked on the door.

The moment the rebbe opened it and Jacob heard the laughter and saw all the people gathered inside, he remembered what day it was. Of course. The rebbe and his family were celebrating Sukkot. Once again the warmth of home and the aroma of food overwhelmed Jacob, reminding him of all that he'd lost. He slowly backed away.

"I am sorry for disturbing you. I will return another time."

"Oh no, you won't." Rebbe Grunfeld draped his arm around Jacob's shoulder and drew him inside. "Look, my dear," he called to his wife. "Yaakov Mendel is here. He has changed his mind and has accepted our invitation after all."

There was nothing Jacob could do but join them. He needed the rebbe's help with the police and he couldn't risk offending him by refusing his hospitality. He started to remove his hat and coat, but the rebbe stopped him. "You might want to leave your coat on. We have built our booth outside, and we are just about to sit down and eat."

Jacob followed him to the back courtyard, where a festive table had been set beneath a canopy of branches. The rebbe's family members gathered around, taking their seats. "See? We have just put the food on the table. Please sit down, Yaacov."

The rebbe's son and daughter-in-law hurried to add an extra chair and another place setting. Jacob noticed that they used kerosene lamps outside for light. Why hadn't the fire marshal accused Rebbe Grunfeld of starting the fire?

Jacob's anger and fear had time to cool during the meal. In their place, sorrow and grief began to seep into his heart once again. Sukkot was a feast of joy, celebrated with laughter and singing and sumptuous food. The familiar traditions made him long for the past and ache for his own family. Would it be asking too much of Hashem to bring Avraham and his family safely home? He was so weary of being alone.

Jacob tried to forget about the policemen's accusations and join in the celebration, but worry prevented him from eating much. It was late when the meal and the blessings ended, and Rebbe Grunfeld led him inside to his study to talk. Jacob told him about the visit from the police detectives.

"No, no, no. That cannot be true," the rebbe said. "The fire inspector never spoke a word of these suspicions to me. Are you sure you aren't reading more into their visit than you should?"

"You think I am making this up? The police came into my home, Rebbe. Two detectives. They wanted to take me to the police station to question me, but I refused to go with them. They looked me right in the eye and said, 'We know you are guilty. You will pay for your crime.' They accused me in my own house!"

"That is unbelievable."

171

"Go down there and ask them yourself."

"Tell me their names and I will do that."

"Detectives Flynn and O'Hara. The fire inspector has turned the case over to them."

"I will talk to them first thing tomorrow and straighten this out. No, wait. Tomorrow is *Simchas Torah*. It will have to be the next day. But you must come back tomorrow and celebrate with us. When we dance and rejoice over the Torah this year, we will have you to thank for saving our scrolls."

Jacob simply shook his head. No. He could not rejoice.

"Listen, Yaacov, I'm sorry for not keeping up with the fire investigation, but I have been so busy with my meetings with the American Jewish Congress. I never dreamed the police would accuse you. But I will go there and tell them how wrong they are."

"Thank you. I will leave you to your celebrations now. I am sorry for interrupting. Thank you again for the dinner."

"No, don't leave yet. Please, sit down. I want to tell you what has been going on in Washington behind the scenes. You will keep it confidential, yes?"

"Of course." Jacob sat down on the edge of the chair, unwilling to get too comfortable.

"It seems that several highly respected men in the Roosevelt administration have drafted a plan to help rescue European Jews. The plan was first proposed in June, and now they are very close to creating a new government agency with funding to specifically help Jewish refugees."

"That is wonderful news." Yet even as he said the words, Jacob was afraid to believe it. "What can I do?"

"They will need money from Jewish organizations and individuals in America to help fund this new agency. Of course our congregation is planning to help. Please, Yaacov, come to the meeting with me after Sukkot and learn more for yourself. You were always so much better than any of us at organizing things and raising funds."

Jacob closed his eyes. Did he dare to believe that something was finally going to be done for the Jews who were trapped in Europe? He felt a sliver of hope for the first time in four years.

"I will help any way that I can. Tell me where and when." He stood to leave, but again the rebbe stopped him.

"There is so much I want to say to you, Yaacov . . . and I don't know how to put it into words. I know how much you are suffering— losing Miriam Shoshanna, worrying about Avraham, and now this terrible business with the police. I understand how difficult it must be to rejoice with such a heavy heart. . . . But I pray that you will allow Hashem to speak to you through our celebration of Sukkot tonight. The flimsy booths that we live in and eat in during this time remind us once again that our lives here on earth are a journey and not our permanent resting place. Our protection and security don't come from what we build on our own, but from Hashem." He paused, but Jacob didn't reply. "I worry about you, my friend. I fear that the walls you are building to shelter yourself from hurt may end up walling you off from life."

Jacob looked down at his feet, not at the rebbe, recognizing the truth of his words.

"Hashem is with you on your journey through this wilderness, just as He was with Moses and our ancestors. If you cry out to Him, my friend, He'll provide protection and the strength to persevere, just as He did long ago. We sang the words tonight: 'O house of Israel, trust in Hashem—He is their help and shield.' And 'Hashem is with me; I will not be afraid . . . I will look in triumph on my enemies.' He longs to show you mercy, Yaacov. He longs to comfort you beneath His shelter."

Jacob couldn't speak. He turned and walked to the front door, determined to leave this time. Rebbe Grunfeld walked the traditional three steps outside with him to see him on his way. "Good night, my friend."

"Good night, Rebbe. And thank you."

Jacob wanted to believe the rebbe's words, wanted to believe that Hashem had not truly abandoned him. But as he walked home to his apartment, remembering the policemen's threats, Hashem felt very far away.

CHAPTER 20

So many soldiers poured from the trains and crowded into Grand Central Station that Esther wondered how she would ever recognize her father. The soldiers all looked alike in their green army uniforms and flat-topped caps. The huge, echoing station was a maze of hallways and tunnels, jam-packed with people. Peter clung to Esther's coat sleeve, wide-eyed. Penny had hovered very close to both of them for the entire trip, but whether she feared losing track of them or getting lost herself, Esther couldn't tell. After wandering around for several minutes, they finally found the right platform just as a train lumbered into the station.

"I think this is your father's train," Penny yelled above the clang of bells and rumble of locomotive engines. "Let's wait right here where he can see us."

They could hardly move on the crowded platform. Esther wanted to jump up and down with excitement. Soldiers hung out of the train windows, waving their hats, blowing kisses. And suddenly she saw Daddy standing in the doorway of one of the cars. He jumped off before the train even came to a halt and ran toward them. He dropped his duffel bag as Esther flew into his arms, and he lifted her off her feet in a bear hug. Then he crouched on one knee to hug Peter. He gazed at them with love and tears in his eyes.

Esther couldn't stop crying. "We missed you so much, Daddy!"

"I've missed you, too, doll." He stroked Esther's cheek and ruffled Peter's hair. "What do you say we go home?" He stood, wiping his tears on his sleeve. Then he noticed Penny Goodrich for the first time. She had been standing in the background, giving them space. Esther wished she would leave altogether now that Daddy was here.

"Penny . . . you look different. I almost didn't recognize you."

"You look pretty nice yourself in that uniform. Welcome home, Eddie." Penny looked as though she wanted to hug him, but Esther clung tightly to her father, refusing to let go.

"Thanks for bringing the kids down to meet me."

"I'm glad I did. I haven't seen them this happy in weeks."

Esther didn't like the way Daddy and Penny smiled at each other. She nudged her father in the ribs. "Can we go home, Daddy?"

"Sure. But let's not wait for the bus. Let's splurge and take a cab home." He hefted his duffel bag onto his shoulder and grabbed Peter's hand. Esther clung to his arm as Penny led the way out of the bustling station.

Daddy hailed a cab outside. Esther and Peter climbed into the back seat with him while Penny rode up front with the driver. Esther had stored up a million things to tell her father and now, in her excitement, she couldn't remember a single one. The taxi sped out of the glittering city and across the Brooklyn Bridge.

"How was your trip?" Penny asked.

"Long! Time slows down when you're anxious to get home. But you should have seen the reception we got along the way. In many of the small towns we passed through, people would come out to meet the train and serve coffee and sandwiches and homemade cookies to all the soldiers."

"Why'd they do that?" Esther asked.

"Just to be patriotic. To show the soldiers they wished us well."

"I'll bet it's because you're going off to fight in the war and might never come back," Esther said, remembering Mr. Mendel's newspaper photos.

"Don't talk that way, doll. I think it's because nearly every family has someone in uniform, so they treat all of the soldiers nice, for their loved ones' sakes."

They arrived home in no time, and Penny retrieved the roast from Mr. Mendel's oven. "I had to borrow meat coupons from my parents," she said as she carried the platter to the dinner table. "I hope it tastes good."

"It looks wonderful, Penny. Thanks."

Esther brought in the bowl of mashed potatoes, and when she saw the way Daddy was smiling at Penny again, she set down the potatoes and distracted her father with another big hug. "I helped make supper, too, Daddy. And I set the table."

"That's great, doll. I'm sure Penny appreciates your help."

They all sat down, and after Daddy said grace, they passed around the food and began to eat. They seemed like a happy family again, except that Penny Goodrich sat across from Daddy instead of Mama. And Peter still hadn't spoken a word, not even to greet him or to tell him how much he missed him.

"We're so glad you're back home with us again, Daddy," she said to make up for Peter's silence.

"It's good to be home."

"How long will you be able to stay?" Penny asked.

"I'll be on furlough for a week. Then I have to report to an army base in Virginia and prepare for deployment."

"Virginia isn't too far away. Will we get to see you more often?"

"I don't think so, Penny. I'll be sent over to England on the next troop ship. Very soon, in fact. Ordinarily the army would want me to have more training before being deployed, but since I'm already a licensed mechanic and I'm needed overseas, they want to get me over there as quickly as possible. Have to keep those jeeps running, you know."

"Why England? I thought the army was fighting in Italy now?"

"We are. But there's a big build-up of troops going on in England,

and a lot of people think it's because the invasion of Europe is coming next spring."

"I don't want you to go to England," Esther said. "The Nazis are dropping bombs on London. I've seen pictures of it in the newspaper."

"We're giving it right back to them, doll. We're bombing German targets now."

"Will you have to fight when the invasion comes?" Penny asked.

"I don't know. The U.S. government is keeping very quiet about it all. 'Loose lips sink ships' and all that. They never tell you more than you need to know. But I probably won't be fighting—although they issued me a weapon and taught me how to use it. But once the invasion force is on the ground over there, the generals will need jeeps to get around in, and it's my job to keep the vehicles running. Ambulances too."

Tears filled Esther's eyes at the mention of ambulances. "Please don't go, Daddy. We need you here at home."

"Come on, doll. Don't start all that again. I want us to enjoy our time together, not spend it arguing. I've already explained that I have to do my part and help win this war, remember?"

She nodded, even though she didn't agree. Everyone else ate heartily, and Penny passed the dishes around for second helpings. But Esther had no appetite. As she wiped her tears on her sleeve she saw Daddy give Peter's shoulder a gentle punch. "Hey, buddy. You haven't said a word all evening."

Esther squeezed her hands into fists beneath the table, afraid to breathe. She had worried that Penny would tell Daddy about Peter's silence in her letters, but it appeared that she hadn't. Esther had been afraid to tell him, hoping that Peter would start talking again once Daddy came home.

"Hey, it's too bad about the Dodgers, huh, Pete?" Daddy said. "No pennant this year, I guess. And to think they made it all the way to the World Series two years ago."

Esther could see how badly Peter wanted to reply. His face turned very red, as if choking on the words he was trying to say. He finally gave up and sagged back in his chair with his shoulders hunched, staring at his lap.

"Don't take it so hard, son. There's always next season, right? . . . Come on, say something."

Peter looked as though he wanted to shrink away and disappear.

"He doesn't talk very much, Daddy," Esther said.

He reached out to ruffle Peter's hair. "You don't need to be shy around me. I haven't been gone that long, have I?"

Esther glanced at Penny, wondering what to do. Penny pushed back her chair and stood. "I made chocolate cake for dessert. Who wants some?" She quickly collected the dinner plates and disappeared into the kitchen, returning with the cake on Mama's fancy cake stand. No one said a word as Penny made two more trips, carrying away the serving bowls and fetching dessert plates and forks.

"I used up an entire month of sugar rations, just so it would taste good," Penny said. "They print recipes in the newspaper telling you how to make cakes and desserts without using sugar or shortening, but they just don't taste the same. So I figured I would make the cake the regular way and never mind what that old Ration Board says." She sliced into the cake and served a big piece to each of them.

"Thanks," Daddy said. "It looks delicious." Esther thought the crisis had passed, but Daddy turned to Peter again. "I want to know why you won't talk to me, Peter."

For a long moment, everyone was silent. Penny cleared her throat. "He doesn't talk at all, Eddie. He hasn't said a word to anyone since you left."

"What do you mean? What's wrong, Peter? You can tell me." Peter lowered his head and covered his face. "This isn't funny, Peter. You have to stop fooling around. You're worrying me."

Penny touched Daddy's arm. "He can't help it, Eddie. He's not doing it on purpose."

"Is that right, Peter?" He looked up at his father and nodded. "Do you need to see a doctor? Would that help?" Peter shook his head from side to side. "Well, what then?"

Peter pulled a folded piece of notebook paper from his shirt pocket and wrote something on it, then pushed it to his father.

"*Stay home.* Is that what this is? A tantrum to get me to stay home?"

"He hasn't thrown any tantrums," Penny said. "He's been good as gold and does whatever he's told. He just doesn't talk. His teacher said we should just give him time. I'm sorry I didn't tell you, but I thought for sure he'd start talking again when you got home."

"What do you think I should do?" he asked Penny.

"Go see his teacher. She knows more about kids than I do."

Daddy was no longer smiling. He looked angry and worried. He finished his cake in a few quick bites, then pushed back his chair to get up from the table. Penny sprang to her feet. "You and the kids go on in the living room and visit. I'll clear the table and take care of the dishes."

"Okay. Thanks again for the food. I haven't eaten this well in a long time."

Daddy sank onto the couch and put his arms around Esther and Peter as they sat down on either side of him. Esther had retrieved Peter's little chalkboard, and she handed it to him. "He uses this to talk to us," she told their father. "It's easier."

Daddy frowned. "I think it would be easier just to talk."

"Not for him. Go on, Peter. Tell Daddy what you want to say."

I missed you, he wrote.

"I missed you, too." Daddy's voice sounded soft and very sad.

Please don't go away again.

"I can't stay, Peter. Don't you understand?"

"No, we don't understand," Esther said, joining the battle. "Tell the army people that Peter can't talk. Tell them you have to come back home and take care of him."

"The army doesn't care. They'll send Peter to doctors and psychiatrists. Is that what you want?"

"You could explain everything to the Hardship Board," Esther said. "I read all about it in the newspaper."

"Since when do you read the newspaper, doll?"

Esther shrugged. She didn't want to tell him that she had been

179

looking at Mr. Mendel's collection of articles and photographs. Daddy would tell her to stop bothering Mr. Mendel, like he always used to do.

"There are lots of other men who can go and fight the war, but you're all we have."

His arm tightened around her in a hug. "I don't want to spend our time together arguing, doll. Besides, I'm not all you have. You have Penny and Grandma Shaffer and the rest of our family."

Esther saw her chance to ask him about her mother's family. "What about our grandparents from Mama's side?"

"What do you mean?"

"Mama must have had parents. Everybody does. And sisters and brothers? How come we never visit them—or even talk about her side of the family?"

"I don't know much about them. Your mother and her family were estranged."

"What does that mean?"

"It means there were hard feelings between them. They disagreed about certain things, and so they went their separate ways."

"I don't believe it. Everyone loved Mama. She was always nice to everybody."

"You're right, she was. But the hard feelings were on your grand-parents' side, not hers. Your mother tried to patch things up, but . . . both sides have to agree to forgive and forget or it doesn't work."

"What did they fight about?"

"Look, there's no point in talking about it. It doesn't matter anymore. Your mother is gone, and digging up the past won't bring her back. And believe me, her family wants nothing to do with us."

"I don't think I would like people who didn't like Mama."

"Me either. Forget about them, doll."

She snuggled up close to her father and sighed. It felt wonderful to have Daddy home again, to feel him beside her, strong and warm. She listened as he described the train trip and the scenery along the way. "I've never traveled very far before," he said, "but I think we should all take a train trip out West when the war is over. Would you like that?"

"Yeah!" Esther said. Peter smiled, too. He looked happier than he had in a long time. Then Penny interrupted.

"Um . . . Excuse me?" She stood in the living room doorway. "I'm done with the dishes and . . . and I guess I'll head home now."

Good. Daddy needed his bedroom back, so Penny would have to go home now. Esther wiggled out of Daddy's arms. "I'll go get your coat." She jumped up to fetch it from the coat tree before Daddy could invite her to stay a little longer.

"Thanks again for the great dinner," she heard Daddy say when she returned with it.

"You're welcome . . . Um . . . When do you want me to come back?" Esther crossed her fingers, hoping Daddy wouldn't invite her back at all while he was home on leave.

"Well . . . we need to talk about that." Daddy struggled up from the sofa and led Penny into the dining room, out of earshot. They talked for only a minute before he returned and Penny went upstairs to pack. She had her coat on when she came down again and her clothes in two shopping bags.

"You want me to walk you to the bus stop?" Daddy asked. "It's dark outside."

"No, that's okay. I'll be fine. Well . . . good-bye."

Esther held her breath until she heard the front door close, then she sagged in relief onto the sofa beside her father again.

"Penny looks different," Daddy said. "Is it her hair?"

"She got it cut." Esther didn't want to talk about Penny, nor did she like it that Daddy had noticed the changes in her.

"Does she have a new boyfriend or something?"

Esther made a face. "A boyfriend? I don't think so."

Peter rapped his knuckles on the slate to get Esther's attention, then held it up to show her what he'd written: *The man on the bus.*

"What man?" It took Esther a moment to figure out what Peter meant. "Oh yeah. She talks to a soldier on the bus all the time. They seem very friendly."

Peter held up the slate again. *He's a marine.*

"Good for Penny. That's great, isn't it?" Daddy asked. "She deserves to meet a nice fellow. Listen, I've been writing to Grandma

Shaffer and telling her how unhappy you are, and she finally agreed to let you move in with her until I come home. Our apartment lease is up soon and—"

"No!" Esther shouted.

"What's wrong, doll?"

"I don't want to move. This is our home." If they moved, Esther couldn't visit Mr. Mendel or take piano lessons with Miss Miller anymore. And Grandma's house had no room for Mama's piano. In fact, if they moved out of this apartment, all traces of Mama would be lost forever. The memories made Esther sad sometimes, but they were all she had left.

Daddy frowned at Esther. "I don't understand. From the sound of your letters, I got the impression that you weren't happy living here with Penny."

"She's okay. We want to live here, right, Peter?" He nodded his head vigorously.

"Then why are you always complaining about Penny in your letters?"

"I don't know. But she's not so bad. We want to stay here."

"Listen, you need to make up your mind, Esther. Grandma is finally willing to help us out. And she says that Penny's parents need help. They're getting pretty old."

"Why can't Grandma come here? Then we wouldn't have to go to a different school."

"We've been through all of this before. There are too many stairs in our apartment. And Grandma can't leave her pets. I wish you kids would make up your minds and not make this so hard for me. I'm doing my best to make you happy—and don't tell me to quit the army. That's not going to happen."

"We don't mind living with Penny. Right, Peter?"

He nodded in agreement.

Daddy sighed and tried to run his fingers through his hair, but it had been cut very short. "How about if you stayed with Grandma on the weekends from now on? It would give you and Penny a break from each other, and she would have time to help her parents or go to the movies with her boyfriend if she wanted to."

At the mention of movies, Esther thought of Jacky Hoffman. She wouldn't be able to go to a matinee with him again if she stayed with her grandmother every Saturday. "We don't want to stay there every weekend. Just once in a while, okay?"

"Are you sure this time? Because once I make the arrangements, they can't be undone. You can't write and tell me you've changed your mind when I'm on the other side of the Atlantic, you know."

"I know."

"And it looks to me like Penny is doing a good job. The apartment looks great. You both look well fed. Are you happy with the way things are, Peter?"

He hesitated for a moment before nodding.

"Well, if you're sure you want to stay here, I'll talk to Mr. Mendel about renewing the lease. But you'll have to stop complaining about Penny and learn to get along with her, understand?"

"We will." Esther felt guilty for complaining about her, especially when she remembered how Penny had arranged for piano lessons. She wondered if her father knew about them.

"I have a surprise, Daddy," she said, squirming to her feet again. "Sit right there and close your eyes. No peeking."

"A surprise?" He smiled as Peter reached up to help cover his eyes. "Okay. They're closed."

Esther tiptoed to the piano and sat down, quietly lifting the lid. She found the piece she had been practicing for Miss Miller and began to play it, making the notes say everything she felt, the way Mama used to do—sad in the slow, mournful parts, and happy in the dancing, joyful parts. She ended with a soft *pianissimo*, then turned around, expecting to see Daddy smiling proudly. Instead, he looked stunned, white-faced.

"When did you start playing again?" he asked.

"A few weeks ago. I've been taking lessons."

"Lessons?"

"From Miss Miller, the music teacher at school. Peter is taking them, too. Didn't Penny tell you about it in her letters?"

"She never mentioned it."

"I guess she wanted it to be a surprise. Want me to play another song for you?"

Daddy got up and crossed the room. He wrapped his arms around Esther and held her tightly for a long moment, then he let go and closed the lid to the keyboard. "I'm sorry, doll." His voice sounded hoarse. "You played very well . . . but I . . . I'm just not ready to hear Mama's piano yet."

CHAPTER 21

PENNY STUMBLED DOWN THE STAIRS from Eddie's apartment and ran to the bus stop as fast as she could in her wobbly new shoes. Her feet ached from wearing them all afternoon, walking to bus stops and along subway platforms and all over Grand Central Station in them. But the pain in her feet couldn't compare with the hurt and disappointment in her heart. She needed to get as far away from Eddie's apartment as possible.

When the bus arrived, she was glad that her friend Roy wasn't on it. If she tried to speak, all of her sorrow and tears would spill out, and she wasn't certain that she could ever stop them again.

Eddie had barely noticed her all evening. She had hoped that he would invite her to sit down with the family and visit for a while after she finished the dishes, but instead he had led her into the dining room away from the kids. Her heart had hopped around in her chest like a jumping bean at the nearness of him, the touch of his hand on her back. Was he going to ask her out on a real date?

"Listen," he'd said softly. "I don't want to put the kids through a big scene when it's time for me to leave in a week. I'll take them to my mother's house next Sunday, and then I'd like to leave from there, by myself, if you don't mind. Could you pick up the kids at my mother's after I leave and bring them back here?"

"Sure, Eddie. Anything you want." She had waited for him to say more, but he hadn't. "Well, then . . ." she said, "I guess I'll see you on Sunday?"

"Right. Thanks, Penny."

Esther had been so eager to get rid of Penny that she had fetched her coat. Penny had hurried upstairs, grabbed a few of her clothes and toiletries, and fled to the bus stop. Eddie would be home for an entire week, and she wouldn't even get to see him.

Penny used the mirror in her compact before arriving at her parents' duplex to make sure her tears hadn't left black trails down her face. She wiped off her rouge and the remnants of her lipstick, too.

"Hi, it's me . . . I'm home," she called as she let herself in through the kitchen door.

"More new clothes?" Mother asked the moment Penny walked into the living room. She had left Eddie's apartment in such a hurry that she still wore the new suit and blouse she had bought for his homecoming. All for nothing. Fresh tears burned in her eyes, but she didn't dare let them fall. Mother would ask too many questions.

"My old clothes looked pretty worn out," she mumbled.

"What are you doing here on a weeknight?" Father asked.

"Eddie's home on leave. He's giving me a break from the kids for a week."

"It's about time." He returned to his newspaper.

"How did you get here?" Mother asked.

"On the bus."

"All alone? At night? It's dark outside. What were you thinking?"

"It isn't very far."

Mother stared at Penny as if waiting for her to go back and undo her error. What would she say if she knew that Penny had gone all the way to Manhattan on the subway this afternoon? Or that she was learning to drive a bus?

"Listen, I'm really tired," Penny said. "I think I'll go straight to bed."

But she didn't sleep. After tossing around on her mattress until long after her parents had gone to bed, Penny got up and turned on her desk lamp. She found an old notebook left over from her high school years in one of the desk drawers and decided to use it like a diary, pouring out all of her heartache. An hour passed as she filled page after page with everything she longed to tell Eddie, declaring her love for him and her dreams for their future together. When she stopped to reread what she had written, she realized that Roy Fuller probably could use some of this to declare his feelings for Sally. Penny had been trying to help Roy, giving him ideas from time to time. One thing was certain, she would never say these words to Eddie, so her friend may as well make use of them.

Penny wouldn't see Roy for an entire week because she could walk to work from her parents' house. She would miss her morning conversations with him, but it was just as well. Roy would ask about her reunion with Eddie, and she probably would burst into tears.

After a short, sleepless night, Penny left for work the next day, carrying her uniform hidden in a paper bag. She would change into it in the ladies' room so her parents wouldn't have a conniption fit when they saw her in pants.

Her parents. They were another source of anxiety in her life, but she forced herself not to think about the adoption papers. She simply couldn't worry about one more thing right now, especially something as upsetting as wondering who she really was and who her real parents might be. No, most of the time she was able to convince herself that one of the clerks in the records' office must have made a mistake.

At least one thing in her life was going well these days—the drivers' training. This morning Penny and the other students took turns maneuvering the bus through real traffic on real city streets, just as they had been doing for the past few days. Then after their lunch break, the instructor got behind the wheel and surprised them all by driving them to the Motor Vehicle Bureau.

"You're here to take the test and get your drivers' licenses," he announced. "Right now. Today." Penny felt her knees go weak.

"Now?" someone asked. "Why didn't you warn us?"

"Because I knew you'd start fussing about it and get all worked up and you'd probably flunk. But you can all pass the test. You're ready."

Penny glanced at her friend Sheila. "I sure don't feel ready," she whispered.

"Besides," the instructor continued, "don't you girls know there's a gasoline shortage in this country? How much longer do you want to drive around wasting gas? There's a war on!"

His words made everyone laugh as they filed off the bus and into the building to take the written test. When all eight of them passed it, they lined up in alphabetical order to take the road test. Penny was so weary from tossing in bed all night and crying herself to sleep that she felt as if she were sleepwalking as she climbed behind the wheel. She did whatever the examiner told her to do—turning left and right, changing lanes, dodging cars, and slowing for pedestrians—while he sat in the seat behind her, taking notes on a clipboard.

"You passed, Miss Goodrich," he told her when they returned to the Motor Vehicle Bureau. "Congratulations."

Penny hugged her friend Sheila, who had also passed her driving test. They laughed and cried at the same time. All of the students returned to the bus station with their new licenses in hand, and the teacher herded them into their makeshift classroom for the last time.

"You'll each be assigned to a training route for the remainder of the week with a licensed driver riding with you. Beginning on Monday, you'll be assigned to a route of your own."

Penny felt a little shiver of fear but also excitement. She couldn't wait to tell Eddie about her accomplishment—although she would probably have to write to him and tell him in one of her letters. And she should probably tell her parents, too—but not yet. She didn't know why she was afraid to tell them, but she was.

"Before you're dismissed," the instructor continued, "I would like to honor our top driving student, Miss Penny Goodrich."

Penny stopped breathing, stunned by his words.

"Miss Goodrich didn't miss a single question on any of her tests. And even more important, she was the only student who never hit a barrel during practice out back."

She heard laughter and applause. Sheila patted her on the back. Penny opened her mouth but, like Peter, she couldn't speak a single word.

"Great job," the teacher told her, shaking her hand. "For a reward, you will get the first pick of the new bus routes. Once again, congratulations to all of you. Take the rest of the afternoon off, ladies. Class dismissed."

Everyone except Penny jumped from their seats, laughing, congratulating each other, saying good-bye. She couldn't move. She had passed the course. She was a bus driver now. Roy said she should celebrate, but who could she celebrate with?

"Congratulations, Penny," Sheila said. "I hope we'll still see each other once in a while." She already had her coat on and was preparing to leave.

"Yeah. I hope so, too."

"Call me if you decide to volunteer with me at the USO sometime."

"Okay. Thanks."

Penny finally found the strength to stand and put on her jacket, but she didn't know what to do with the remainder of the afternoon. She didn't want to go home to her parents' duplex and have them drain all of the joy and pride from her accomplishment. They wouldn't be happy for her at all. Instead, they would overwhelm her with worry and fear, listing all of the terrible things that might happen to her.

Penny went to the ladies' room and changed out of her uniform, then wandered out to the front of the bus station. She was trying to decide where to go for a few hours when she remembered her adoption certificate. She had been so busy taking care of Eddie's kids and learning to drive a bus that she hadn't had time to return to the records' office to find out if her birth record was sealed. She had already paid the money. Why not follow through with it?

She got on a bus before she could change her mind and rode to the records' office. Part of her was afraid to learn the truth. It would be so final. If a clerk somewhere hadn't made a mistake, then she would have to accept the truth that she really was adopted. But how much longer could she push the whole mess to the back of her mind, trying not to think about it a hundred times a day? She would find out the truth now, while she was still feeling brave, while she carried her brand-new bus driver's license in her pocket.

The records' office was crowded, as usual. It looked like a joyless place to work with its colorless walls and drab, functional furniture. Penny glanced around for the clerk who had helped her the last time but didn't see her. She would have to explain her embarrassing situation all over again. She waited in line for her turn, then laid down the mangled-looking receipt she had carried in her purse all this time.

"Hi. My name is Penny Goodrich, and I—"

"Let's see that." The clerk snatched up the receipt and looked it over before Penny could finish explaining. "One moment." She hopped off her stool and sifted through the ranks of file drawers in the rear of the office. She returned a minute later with Penny's receipt and an official-looking piece of paper.

"You requested to see your original birth documents, Miss Goodrich?"

"Yes." Penny crossed her fingers and held her breath, prepared to hear the clerk tell her it had all been a huge mistake, that she hadn't been adopted after all.

"I'm sorry, Miss Goodrich, but the record was sealed at your birth mother's request." She handed Penny the paper and motioned for her to move aside. "Next, please."

Penny didn't bother to look at the document. She folded it in half and then in half again, and by the time she reached the bus stop she had folded it into a very small square. She shoved it into her purse and went home.

Mother had made meatloaf for dinner, one of Penny's favorites, and they sat at the kitchen table to eat it. "You seem quiet tonight," Mother said. "What's wrong with you?"

Penny didn't know how to reply. So many things were wrong. She had a new job, she had passed all her tests, she had finished at the top of the class—and no one cared. She had learned today that she truly was adopted, that it hadn't been a mistake, which meant that the two people closest to her in the whole world had deceived her for twenty-four years. And not only had her real parents gotten rid of her, they had sealed the record, as well, making sure they would never have to hear from her again. But the worst tragedy of all was that Eddie would be shipped overseas to England soon, to fight in a war that seemed as though it would never end. He would be in danger, he might even be killed, and he had barely noticed her.

"Nothing's wrong," she replied. "I'm just tired, that's all."

"You're not getting sick, are you?" Mother reached over to feel Penny's forehead, and the motherly gesture nearly brought tears to Penny's eyes.

"No, I'm fine." She had to change the subject. "So I guess Thanksgiving is coming soon. If we all start saving our ration stamps, we should be able to plan a real nice dinner. I'll have the children to care for, and I thought I would invite their grandmother to share it with us—and I'm inviting the two of you, of course."

"Inviting us where?" Father asked.

"Well, I thought we could all gather at Eddie's apartment. There's plenty of room."

"I'm not eating Thanksgiving dinner in a Jew neighborhood," Father said. He pointed to the bowl of mashed potatoes and gestured for Penny to pass them.

Penny thought of Mr. Mendel and how kind he seemed. "How can you feel that way, Dad? Especially when we keep hearing about the awful way the Nazis treat Jewish people over in Europe?"

"You're naive, Penny. You don't know much about the real world."

"But the newspapers say that the Nazis may have killed thousands of Jews in Poland—"

"The papers are making up all those things. Nobody could kill that many people. And for what reason? It doesn't make sense."

"I think you should cook Thanksgiving here," Mother said. "We could all eat here."

"But we don't have a dining room, and this kitchen is so small. It would be very crowded with all of us here." Penny also knew that Esther and Peter would die of boredom in this dreary, overheated house.

"Do whatever you want," Father said, "but I'm eating Thanksgiving right here in my own house."

Penny drove her apprentice bus route all week, returning to her parents' home every evening, sleeping in her childhood bedroom. The house felt as if all of the joy had been sucked out of it and that the walls were ten feet thick and made of cement. She couldn't bear the thought of moving back after the war ended. She longed to ask her parents who she really was and why they had adopted her in the first place, but every time she tried to ask, fear choked off her words before she could say them. She thought she understood how Peter must feel, unable to speak his thoughts.

On Sunday, Eddie's last day at home, Penny put on her new gray suit and went to the worship service at Eddie's church. She had gone there with the children for the past few months and had gotten to know many of the people. It felt like home to her. She sat with Eddie and the kids during the hour-long service, ignoring Esther's glares of disapproval, and afterward they walked back to the duplex together.

"You kids go on inside and help your grandmother with lunch," Eddie told them. "I'll be right in. I want to talk to Penny alone."

Her heart started jumping around inside her chest again as she stood beside him in the backyard, waiting for the kids to disappear. She knew it was impolite to stare, but she couldn't take her eyes off of him. Eddie looked so handsome in his dress uniform, even if the army had cut off his beautiful blond curls.

"Listen, Penny. The kids say they're happy living with you and they want you to keep on taking care of them—if you're still willing, that is." His words surprised her. She had expected Esther to complain so bitterly about her that Eddie would find someone else to watch them.

"Of course I'm willing, Eddie. I'm happy to do it."

"Good. I've been talking to my mother about the situation, and she has agreed to let the kids stay here on the weekends from now on so you can get a break. I helped Ma clear a place for them to sleep."

"That was nice of you to think of me."

"I also went to see Peter's teacher like you suggested. She says he seems fine and that he hasn't caused any problems. She thinks we should just give him more time and that he'll start talking again. I don't know, though. Should I be worried?"

Penny didn't know what to say. She could hardly concentrate on his words, standing so close to him. She longed to touch his face and smooth away the worried creases. "His teacher seems to know a lot about kids," she finally said. "I think you can trust her judgment. Besides, what good will worrying do?"

"You're right. . . . But promise me you'll let me know what's happening from now on, okay?"

"I'm sorry I didn't tell you about Peter. I didn't want you to worry. Sorry."

"That's okay. And I really appreciate your letters, Penny. I hope you'll keep writing to me. I feel like I'm right back home when I read them, and I can picture everything you're describing."

She couldn't help smiling at his compliment. "I enjoy your letters, too."

The back door suddenly opened, and Esther stuck her head out. "Lunch is ready, Daddy."

"I'll be right there, doll. . . . Well, I guess I'll say good-bye for now. I'll be leaving right after lunch. You can take the kids home after I'm gone. Thanks again for everything, Penny. I don't know how I can ever thank you."

"You can come home safe and sound, that's how." Penny didn't wait for Eddie to hug her first. She moved forward and threw her arms around him, hugging him tightly, pressing her cheek against the front of his wool uniform. After a moment, she felt him embrace her in return.

"I won't say good-bye, Eddie, because I hate good-byes."

"Yeah, me too."

The embrace ended much too quickly. Eddie released her and

went inside. Penny watched until the door closed behind him. She started toward her own back door but couldn't bear to go inside just yet. Instead, she leaned against the rear wall of the duplex where no one could see her crying.

Penny's first thought when she woke up on Monday morning was: *This is it—the first day of my very own bus route.* She felt nervous and excited at the same time. She said good-bye to the kids and left the apartment a few minutes early so she wouldn't be late on her first day. When the bus arrived at her stop, she was happy to see her friend Roy on board. He moved over to make room for her.

"Hi, Penny. It seems like ages since I've seen you. How did everything go with Eddie?" Penny thought she had run out of tears long ago, but her eyes quickly filled with them. She didn't want to tell him the truth.

"He's being shipped to England," she said, her voice faltering.

"Oh no. That's got to be tough on you and the kids. No wonder you're upset."

She nodded and pulled out a handkerchief to wipe her eyes. "Listen," she said when she could speak. "I wrote down a bunch of things you can tell Sally when you write to her . . . if you still want them."

"Yes, of course I want them."

She opened her purse and handed him the copy she had made for him, watching his face as he unfolded the page and scanned the words she had written. His eyes got moist. "Hey, this is great. Thanks, Penny."

"Glad to help." She took a deep breath, then exhaled. "Now, I have some good news that I've been dying to tell you. I passed the driving test. I got my bus driver's license."

"That's terrific! Congratulations!" He offered her his hand. It felt strong and warm as she shook it.

"Thanks. I drove as an apprentice all last week, and today I'm going to start my very own bus route."

Roy frowned. "Does that mean I won't get to see you anymore?"

"No, you'll still see me. My new route will start out from the bus station. I'll probably be riding this bus every day, same as usual. Hey, how are things with Sally?"

"Great. I'll get a one-day leave for Thanksgiving, and I think I'm going to propose to her again."

"That's wonderful, Roy. I hope she says yes this time."

"Me too. How's it going with the kids? Are they being any nicer to you now that their father has been home?"

"A little bit. They told him that they still want me to take care of them while he's away, so I suppose that's something."

"I've been thinking about your situation, Penny. Maybe if you did some fun things with them, you could win them over, you know what I mean? I hear Coney Island is fun. Haven't been there myself. Have you?"

"No, never!"

"Why did you say it like that?" he asked, laughing. "It was as if I asked if you'd been to the moon."

Penny couldn't help laughing, too. "My parents have always been very protective of me—and wary of *strangers*. I'm sure they would think the moon was much safer than Coney Island. At least there aren't any *strangers* on the moon. Believe me, they filled me with all kinds of fears when it comes to Coney Island. It's the devil's playground, according to them. I would be lucky to come out of there alive. And the amusement park that's there—Luna Park? Well, that's the very pit of hell itself."

Roy grinned. "Wow. The devil's playground? Now I have to go there for sure! We don't have a devil's playground back home in Moosic, Pennsylvania."

"You're so funny, Roy. But if you do decide to go there, you should probably wait until summer. The beach isn't much fun this time of year."

"So Coney Island is out for now. Hmm. Where else could you take those kids? I know, how about one of the War Bond rallies in Times Square? I hear that famous movie stars come to those things and singing groups like the Andrews Sisters."

"I would love that. But I had enough trouble getting Esther and Peter to Grand Central Station to meet their father's train, let alone handling them in a place like Times Square with so many *strangers*."

"Well, if I'm not being too forward . . . I'd be glad to go with you and help you out."

"Oh, Roy . . . really?"

"Sure, I'd love to. You could hang on to one kid and I'll hang on to the other. Hey, we're at your bus stop already," he said as the bus slowed to pull into the station. "I'll find out when they're having the next War Bond rally, okay? And if that doesn't work out, there's always the Bronx Zoo. Ever been there?"

Penny smiled and shook her head. "Never. Don't you know there are thousands of *strangers* at the zoo? . . . See you tomorrow, Roy." She was almost off the bus when she heard Roy calling to her.

"Hey, Penny! Have fun with your new job today."

"I will." Penny hadn't thought about her job being fun. But it would be, in a way. Up until a month ago, she had been trapped in a stuffy old ticket booth, and now she would get to drive all around Brooklyn, meeting new people—nice people like Roy. She walked into the bus station smiling. And thinking that Sally was a very lucky girl to have a guy like Roy for a sweetheart.

CHAPTER 22

Budapest, Hungary
November 1943

Dear Mama and Abba,

Once again I am writing this letter to you so that when the war finally ends, you will know what has become of us. Everything is changing so rapidly, and I am preparing for the very worst.

We left the village a few months ago and arrived safely at Uncle Baruch's home here in the city. He and Aunt Hannah were kind enough to take us into their home, even though they already have taken in three of Aunt Hannah's relatives. But that's the way it is here in the Jewish section of Budapest. With food and heating fuel so difficult to come by, many families have been forced to crowd together into one apartment.

Uncle Baruch and I and some of the other men from our building go out every day to forage for food and firewood and to work at whatever jobs we can find to earn money. This is difficult to do since I must also hide from any authorities who may try to conscript me for a labor gang. I know that I speak Hungarian with an accent since it isn't my first language, so I must be extra cautious not to speak unless I am forced to. In spite of all my precautions, I fear that it is only a matter of time before we are conscripted into a work gang. Age doesn't matter to the government officials. With so many of the young men fighting in the military, the Hungarian government needs laborers to keep the factories and railroads running and the roads repaired.

What little news that we hear about the war is very bleak. All of Europe is under the shadow of the Nazis. We are told that England is barely hanging on and that the Russians are suffering, as well. I fear that the Americans may have joined this war too late and that they were not fully prepared to fight when they did join. Everyone is worried that the American forces will be spread too thinly as they try to help the allies here in Europe while fighting the Japanese in the Pacific at the same time.

When Sarah and I first arrived in Budapest we felt relatively safe, but now the Nazis have begun making demands on their Hungarian allies. Everyone fears that Jews may soon be persecuted here the way they have been in Germany and Poland. Lately, the rumors have become so frightening that I decided to search for a better way to keep Sarah and Fredeleh safe. I learned that a group of Catholic nuns in a convent here in Budapest are hiding Jewish children in their orphanage. I went to speak with them last week, and they agreed to keep Fredeleh there. They will change her name to a Christian one and hide her and the other Jewish children among the war orphans. They told me to prepare a letter with all of the important information about my family in America and about Sarah's family here in Hungary. That way, if anything should happen to Sarah and me—Hashem forbid—the Christian nuns will be able to contact Fredeleh's relatives after this terrible war finally ends.

I told Sarah about this plan, but she can't bear to let Fredeleh go. Our sad news is that Sarah had been expecting our second child, but with so little food to eat, she miscarried the baby. I didn't have the heart to take Fredeleh away from her, too. And so we have decided to stay together for now and pray and trust Hashem to tell us when the time is right. If the Germans come to Hungary and force us to wear the yellow stars, we'll know it is time to ask the Christians for help. I will put this letter with Fredeleh's identification papers at the convent so they can send it to you in America after the war.

I continue to worship Hashem and ask Him for the meaning in all of this hardship our people are suffering. He has reminded me that our people once suffered as slaves in Egypt and that as part of our deliverance, all of Egypt was destroyed just as Europe is now being destroyed. But deliverance did come at last for us, and the Promised Land of Israel became our home. Perhaps it is too much to believe that all this suffering will bring us to the Promised Land again one day, and that Israel will be our Jewish homeland after nearly two thousand years of exile. But I believe that Hashem is able to perform miracles, and I would gladly give my life so that Fredeleh could be free one day. Imagine it, Mama and Abba, our own land where we would be free from pogroms and persecution, free to serve Hashem.

I love you both,
Avraham

CHAPTER 23

DECEMBER 1943

THE COLD DECEMBER WIND blew straight off the East River and right through Jacob's coat as he hurried home to his apartment. He had to hold his hat firmly on his head to keep from losing it. Snowflakes drifted from the sky, dusting the sidewalks and the meager patches of grass along the streets. Miriam Shoshanna would have said the snow looked lovely, like a sprinkling of powdered sugar.

Jacob stomped the snow off his shoes before coming inside, wiping his feet on the mat. In spite of the bitter weather, he felt more hopeful than he had in many months after he and Rebbe Grunfeld met with the American Jewish Congress. One month from now, President Roosevelt would announce the creation of a new government agency to help rescue refugees. The state department would send any money Jacob helped raise to Europe to rescue innocent victims of enemy persecution, most of whom were Jewish.

"What about Hungary?" he had asked. "Are there plans to help the Jews who are trapped in Hungary?"

The answer had given him hope. The new agency would work with neutral nations such as Switzerland and Sweden, which still had embassies in Axis-controlled countries like Hungary. Food and other aid would be distributed through them.

Jacob had just sat down and opened the newspaper when he heard Esther and Peter arrive home from school. They had fallen into the habit of coming down to his apartment after discarding their coats and boots, bringing their schoolbooks with them and staying until Miss Goodrich arrived home from work. They would sit at his kitchen table to do their homework, listening to classical music on the radio, and Jacob would help young Peter with his arithmetic. He unlocked his apartment door in anticipation, but they didn't come downstairs right away. When they finally did, tears streaked Esther's face.

"What's wrong?" he asked as they came inside.

"We got a letter from Daddy." She waved it in the air. "He said that by the time we read this he'll be on his way to England!" She rushed into Jacob's arms, clinging to him, sobbing. He didn't know what to say or what to do except to hold her in return. He saw Peter's silent tears and reached to draw him close, as well. The boy didn't make a sound, yet his thin body trembled with silent grief.

"I don't want Daddy to fight in the war!" Esther wept.

"I am so sorry," Jacob murmured. "So sorry." He understood the children's helpless anger and grief, but he had no idea how to console them. So he simply held them, saying nothing until Esther's tears finally subsided.

"It's so unfair!" she sniffed, wiping her nose and eyes with her handkerchief. "We need him here!"

"When your father was home on leave he told me that his job is to take care of the vehicles. He did not think he would be doing any fighting."

"But he's going to England! That's where all the bombs are falling on people. You have pictures of it." She went to the collection of newspaper clippings on his dining room table and began picking out photos and holding them up. He knew what they showed without looking at them: piles of bricks and burnt wood, buildings destroyed, homeless families huddled in the street, gazing at the remnants of their homes, air-raid wardens searching the rubble for survivors. Every afternoon Esther looked through his collection of pictures, as obsessed with them as he was. Now Jacob regretted that she had ever seen them. He took the clippings from her and laid them back down on the table.

"Come, we will go into the kitchen and have tea."

For the first time he saw the photos the way she must see them. While he had been documenting the world at war, Esther had seen the world as a frightening, capricious place where bombs could fall out of the sky on a whim of the Almighty, crushing her father, just as the car had crushed her mother. And what could Jacob say to Esther? Did he believe, as Rebbe Grunfeld had insisted, that Hashem was his help and his shield, his canopy of protection? Could he promise these children that Hashem would keep their father safe? No, he could not.

When Esther went home today, Jacob decided, he would put the clippings out of sight. They had fueled his own anger and fear as well as hers.

"Here, I bought some cookies the other day," he said. "Tell me what you think of them." He pried open the tin and put it in the middle of the table as Esther and Peter sat down. The cookies weren't nearly as good as Miriam Shoshanna's homemade ones, but they were the best he could do. He remembered how he used to chide his wife for spoiling these children with treats—and here he was buying cookies for them.

"No one can promise that your father will be kept safe," he said as he took down three teacups. "But worry and fear will do nothing to help, either."

Esther sat with her elbows propped on the table, her chin resting on her hands. Peter had begun nibbling on a cookie. "Is it good?" Jacob asked him. He nodded.

"It's going to be a terrible Christmas," Esther said.

"I do not know very much about your Christian holidays—only what I see in the department store windows and what I hear about Santa Claus. But why will this holiday be such a terrible one?"

"Because Daddy is so far away! We won't be able to do any of the things we used to do, like put up a Christmas tree and open presents. It won't be the same."

"Traditions are good. They give order and stability to our lives. But change is part of life, too. The secret is to find the balance between the two."

"I don't want everything to change."

"I understand. When our son Avraham went away, his mother and I sometimes found it very difficult to celebrate our holy days. They did not seem the same without him. But Avraham is a grown man, and it would have been wrong for us to keep him a little boy forever. He has his own life to live, just as you will one day grow up and move away from your father."

"But weren't your holidays sad without him?"

"Yes, at first. But Miriam said we must learn to celebrate the true meaning of the holiday, with gratitude. She said that happiness is something that comes from our own hearts, not from other people."

Jacob felt like a hypocrite saying these things. He hadn't heeded Miriam's advice. Jacob hadn't celebrated anything since Miriam died until he'd eaten the Sukkot meal with the rebbe a couple of months ago.

"I miss my son, of course," he continued. "But when I was a young man, I also left my family and moved far away from home. I am sure that my parents were very sad, but they wanted me to have a better life here in America."

The water boiled, and he rose to make the tea. He knew just how the children liked theirs—not too strong, with more milk in the cup than tea.

"Thanksgiving Day was terrible, too," Esther told him. "We had to eat it at Penny's house, and her parents are old and grumpy. Our grandma came over to eat with us, but she's sad all the time because all her sons are fighting in the war. Penny tried to get everyone around the table to say what we were thankful for, but I didn't have any reason to be thankful."

Peter reached into his pocket and pulled out the piece of paper he always carried. He wrote something on it, then held it out for Esther and Jacob to read: *Penny tried to make it nice.*

Esther lifted her shoulders in a shrug. "I guess."

I felt sorry for Penny, he added. Jacob laid his hand on Peter's shoulder for a moment. He was such a gentle, sensitive boy. Avraham had been that way, too, always thinking of someone else.

"Yeah, I felt a little sorry for Penny, too," Esther admitted. "She worked so hard in that hot little kitchen, and everyone complained—except you, Peter." She reached to take a cookie from the tin and then slumped back on her chair. She had calmed down since first coming into Jacob's apartment.

Peter wiped the cookie crumbs from his mouth with the back of his hand and wrote on his piece of paper again: *Does your son live near England?*

"No. Hungary is quite a distance away. Here, I will show you on a map." He went into the dining room and retrieved one of the maps he'd cut from the newspaper that showed the movements of invading troops and locations of battles. He glanced at the picture beneath it and shuddered. The caption read, "Death Cart in Warsaw Ghetto," and the picture showed the shriveled corpses of Jews who had starved to death in Poland. He had cut that photo from the newspaper one year ago and never should have kept it. He would put all of these pictures away after the children left.

"See, Peter?" he said when he returned to the kitchen with the map. "Here is England, where your father will be . . . and here is Hungary, down here. These arrows show which way the troops are marching . . . and for now, England is far away from the fighting."

"But the Nazis are dropping bombs on London."

"Yes, Esther. They are. But the British have air-raid warning sirens and bomb shelters for safety."

"Our minister prays every Sunday for all the men in our church who are fighting in the war, but I don't even close my eyes. Why bother? God didn't answer my prayers for Mama."

Jacob suddenly felt weary. He had to sit down. He pulled his mug of tea closer and took a sip, but didn't reply.

"Do you think it does any good to pray, Mr. Mendel?"

The truth was that he was still too angry with Hashem to pray. But just as his newspaper photos had fueled Esther's fear, he saw that his lack of faith would have an influence on her, too. It would be very wrong to lead these children into the dark, hopeless world where he lived. Should he tell them not to come anymore? No, Jacob had grown very fond of them. They were the only bright spot in his life right now. He groped for a reply.

"Sometimes, Esther, it is wrong to judge the effectiveness of prayer by looking at the immediate results. Do you know the story of Joseph from the Bible?"

She looked thoughtful for a moment. "You mean the boy with the coat of many colors?"

"Yes. Exactly so. In the story, everything looked very bad for Joseph—sold as a slave by his own brothers, living far from home. He was even locked in prison for a while, falsely accused of a crime he did not commit. His father feared he was dead." Jacob had to pause as grief strangled him. He closed his eyes, thinking of his son and the cart full of Jewish corpses, thinking of the detectives who had come to his apartment making false accusations. The police wanted to put Jacob into prison, too, for a crime he did not commit.

"All that time," he said when he could speak, "all that time Joseph prayed, and it must have seemed like Hashem wasn't listening."

"Is that God's name, Hashem?"

"No, Hashem means 'The Name.' One of the Ten Commandments says it is wrong to take His name in vain. We believe that His name is so holy that we must never speak it. Instead, we say Hashem—The Name."

"So, Joseph prayed to Hashem?" Esther asked.

"Yes. I am sure that he prayed something like, 'Get me out of this prison! Get me back home to my family!' Hashem may not have answered Joseph's prayers the way that Joseph wanted Him to, but it turned out that Hashem had a very good reason for keeping him in Egypt. Of course, Joseph could not see how it was good until many years had passed. But Hashem was at work all that time, raising Joseph up to become a leader in Egypt. And when famine came to the land of Israel, Joseph's family came to him there and were rescued."

Peter wrote something on his piece of paper and pushed it across the table for Jacob to read: *Mama used to tell us that story.* Jacob thought of Rachel Shaffer and his own Miriam Shoshanna, and several moments passed before he could speak.

205

"Hashem may not answer our prayers the way we want Him to," he said, clearing his throat. "He did not deliver Joseph from prison right away. But Hashem was there with Joseph, even in the silence."

"Is that true, Mr. Mendel? Does God—Hashem—really hear our prayers?"

Esther and Peter were looking to him for answers. And for hope. He felt none. Why had he ever opened his door to them? Should he lie?

"'The righteous shall live by faith,'" Jacob finally said, remembering the rebbe's words. "Faith is believing, even when you cannot see it. Like Joseph did. He never stopped believing in Hashem. And in time, his prayers were answered in ways he never could have foreseen."

Jacob wondered if his son, Avraham, still believed, even though he was surrounded by evil on all sides, even though his prayers for his family's immigration visas had gone unanswered and deliverance had not come.

"I didn't know that you had the same Bible stories we do," Esther said.

"Yes, many of them are the same. I believe that your Jesus was a Jewish man, like me, yes?"

"Are you going to get a Christmas tree, Mr. Mendel? Oh, wait . . . I guess you don't believe in Christmas, do you?"

"No. We do not celebrate Christmas."

"What do you celebrate, then?"

"Jewish people celebrate Hanukkah in December by lighting special candles to remember the miracle Hashem performed."

"What miracle?"

Jacob saw the children watching him, waiting for him to explain. Why had he ever opened his mouth? "A long time ago, our enemies tried to destroy our faith and our traditions. They desecrated our temple and allowed the holy lamps to go out." Jacob thought of the burned-out shul across the street and paused to clear his throat again. "But Hashem gave us victory over our enemies, and we were able to rededicate our temple to Him and light the lamps once again. The problem was, the priests had only enough sacred oil for one night. But they lit them in faith, and by a miracle of Hashem, the lamps burned for eight full days on only a tiny amount of oil. And so we light candles every night during Hanukkah for eight nights. We put the candles in the window as a sign of hope for everyone to see."

"Why doesn't God do miracles like that all the time?"

"If we could understand Him, Esther, then that would make Him just like us, yes? Or make us just like Him. He would not be the Almighty One. As He has said, 'My thoughts are not your thoughts, neither are your ways my ways.' "

Peter bent to write something: *Are you going to light candles?*

What could Jacob say—that he no longer had any hope? That he no longer believed in miracles? He couldn't drag these children down any further than he already had. "I have no one to celebrate with," he said.

Esther jumped to her feet. "We'll light them with you." Peter nodded in agreement.

What was the harm in lighting the candles, letting the children hope for a miracle? He rose and went to the kitchen drawer where Miriam had kept the Shabbat candles and the menorah candles and the special *havdalah* candle. In a way, he hoped the drawer would be empty so he would have an excuse. But it held a plentiful supply, along with some matches. Miriam would have made certain not to run out, and Jacob had not lit any candles since she died.

"Tonight is the second night of Hanukkah," he said, closing the drawer again, "so we must light two candles, along with the *shammus*, the servant candle."

He led the way into the living room and lifted the *Hanukkiah* from the top of the bookshelf, wiping the dust from it with his hand. Miriam would be disgusted with him if she could see such dust.

"We always used to put it in front of the window on this table," he explained, "for everyone to see." He pulled the little end table into place and parted the curtains, then set down the menorah and put the first two candles in their holders. "We add a candle each night for eight nights, lighting them with the servant candle, which will go here, in the middle. Tomorrow we will light three candles, then four, and so on, to remember the miracle of the oil."

"May I light them?" Esther asked.

The boy couldn't speak, but he stood by Jacob's side, eager to help. Avraham had always loved lighting them, too. "Tonight we will have ladies first. Tomorrow it will be your turn, Peter. They must not be lit until after sundown, but the sun sets very early in the winter months, after four o'clock, I believe."

"It's twenty minutes past four," Esther said, glancing at the clock on his shelf.

"Very well, then." What did it matter if they lit the candles a few minutes early or late? He handed the shammus candle and matches to Esther. "First we must recite the special blessings." Jacob closed his eyes and recited the Hebrew blessings by heart. How long had it been since he had blessed Hashem? How long since he had spoken to Him at all? When he opened his eyes again, tears blurred his vision. "You may light them now, Esther," he said softly.

"What were those words you said?" she asked when all three candles were burning.

"They were words of praise to Hashem, the King of the universe, blessing Him and thanking Him for His commandments . . . and for life . . . and for His miracles."

"Do you still believe in God . . . even though . . . ?"

She didn't finish, but Jacob knew what she meant: even though the universe seemed to be spinning out of His control with senseless automobile crashes and wars that filled the entire earth. Jacob was very angry with Him, but he nodded just the same. "Yes," he replied. "I believe."

But did he believe everything that he had told the children tonight? That Hashem was always at work, even when we could see no proof? That we could trust Him, even when we didn't understand what He was doing? That Hashem was good and loving, able to perform miracles for His children?

He watched as Esther and Peter gazed at the flickering candles in fascination—symbols of hope that would shine in his front window for everyone to see—and Jacob knew that the answer was yes.

Yes. He still believed all of those things.

Later, when the children were gone and the candles had burned out in wisps of smoke, Jacob whispered a silent prayer for the first time in many, many months. He asked Hashem for a miracle, asking Him to protect Avraham and Sarah Rivkah and Fredeleh wherever they were tonight. And he prayed for protection for Edward Shaffer, too, so he could return safely home to his children.

It wasn't much. But it was a beginning.

Chapter 24

The holiday song "White Christmas" played on the radio as Esther made a bed for herself on Grandma Shaffer's sofa. The Bing Crosby tune was very popular this time of year and played so often that Esther had grown tired of hearing it. She dropped the blanket she was tucking in and wove her way through the narrow aisles of junk to turn the radio off.

"What did you do that for?" Grandma asked.

"I hate that song. It makes me sad. I don't want to hear it anymore."

"Well, I suppose it is time for bed."

Esther pulled cushions off Grandma's chairs to make a bed on the floor for Peter. Daddy had helped Grandma clear a spot in her living room before he went away so Esther and Peter would have a place to sleep on the weekends. He had tried to convince Grandma to throw away some of the useless stuff she collected, but she had refused. In the end, Daddy had no choice but to push everything against the walls and in front of the window in order to make a space on the floor where Peter could sleep. Once Grandma turned out the lights, Esther always felt like she was sleeping in a storage closet.

"Did Daddy tell you about the places where he has to sleep?" she asked as Grandma fluffed a pillow for Peter.

"No. Where does he sleep?"

"Well, on the troop ship he slept in a bunk bed that was like a hammock. There were rows and rows of them hanging on top of each other from the floor all the way to the ceiling, and he didn't even have enough space to sit up. Then, when he first got to his army base in England, there were too many men and not enough beds, so everybody had to share. Half of the men had to stay awake while the other half slept, then they traded places. He said the sheets would still be warm when he climbed in between them."

"I wouldn't like that very much," Grandma said. She spread a blanket over Peter, then made her way to her birdcage and draped a cover over it for the night. "The two of you can change places, you know, if the floor gets too uncomfortable for Peter."

"We will."

Esther didn't like staying at Grandma Shaffer's house, but she had decided to use the time this weekend to find out more about Mama's side of the family. Esther had tried to forget about them after Daddy said they had argued with Mama and wanted nothing to do with her. But everyone Esther knew had dozens of relatives—aunts and uncles and cousins and grandparents—and she barely had any. Maybe if she found Mama's family, she wouldn't feel all alone. And so ever since Penny had dropped them off earlier tonight, Esther had tried to summon her courage, waiting for the right moment to ask. As Grandma wove her way toward the light switch, Esther knew she'd better ask now or miss her chance.

"Grandma . . . where was Mama from?"

"Here in Brooklyn, I think."

"Does she still have relatives here? Brothers and sisters?"

"I don't know."

"Did you ever meet any of them?"

"No."

"Well, how did Mama and Daddy meet each other?"

Grandma seemed to shrink back, as if Esther was hurling the questions at her like a game of dodge ball. "You need to ask your father these things, not me."

"But he's so far away, and it takes so long to send letters back and forth. Can't you just tell me?"

"I don't remember the story."

Esther had the feeling that Grandma did know the story but didn't want to tell it. "Why did Mama's family get mad at her?" Esther asked.

"Because they were—" Grandma stopped. "Who said they were mad at her?"

"Daddy did. He said that they were 'estranged' and that it meant there were hard feelings between them. How could anyone get mad at Mama? Especially her own family?"

"It was a long time ago, Esther. It doesn't really matter anymore." Grandma turned off the light and began inching her way through the living room, heading toward her bedroom. "Good night, you two."

"Wait!"

Grandma halted and turned to Esther. "What now?"

"I've looked all through Mama's photo album, but she doesn't have any pictures of her family. Didn't they come to Mama and Daddy's wedding?"

"No."

"Why not?"

"I was told that they didn't want her to marry Eddie and give up her chance to study music."

"Where was she going to study music?"

"Look, that's all I'm going to say. It isn't my place to talk about your mother or her family. You need to ask your father these questions. Now, good night."

"Grandma? Did Mama's family come to her funeral?"

"No," she said softly. "No, they didn't."

"Why not? . . . Didn't they know about Peter and me?"

"Good night, Esther."

"Good night," she said with a sigh. She might have to give up for now, but she was determined to try again in the morning.

She lay down, waiting for her eyes to get used to the darkness. Grandma's piles looked spooky in the shadowy room, like rubble from the bombed-out buildings in Mr. Mendel's newspaper pictures. Esther wished she and Peter were back home in their own bedroom. Jacky Hoffman had invited her to go to the movies with him tomorrow, but she'd had to turn him down. He was still walking home from school with her and protecting Peter from the other kids. She didn't know why Jacky had called Mr. Mendel names that time, but she liked talking to Jacky on the way home from school and then visiting Mr. Mendel afterward. Both of them were her friends—the only friends she had.

Esther rolled over onto her side and looked down at Peter. A shaft of light from the streetlamp filtered past Grandma's sagging drapes, making it bright enough to see him. He had the dog beside him, holding her like a teddy bear.

"Peter?" she whispered. "I don't want to stay here for Christmas, do you?" He looked up at her and shook his head. "Remember how Penny said her friend Roy would take us to Times Square if we wanted him to? I know I told Penny that I didn't want to go—but maybe I do now. And maybe we could stay at our own house next weekend. You want to?"

Peter nodded. Esther gazed down at her brother, clinging to the dog on his makeshift bed, with stacks of newspapers and cardboard boxes towering over him, and he looked so forlorn that it brought tears to her eyes. Mama would cry, too, if she could see what had become of them. Grandma's threadbare blanket looked much too thin to keep Peter warm and safe, so Esther pulled the crocheted afghan off the back of the couch and draped it over him.

"Peter?" she whispered. "Do you think you'll ever start talking to me again?" He lifted his palms in a helpless gesture. Esther lay back down and sighed. "I miss you, Petey."

Esther had never seen a crowd as huge as the one that jammed Times Square for the War Bond rally. Thousands of people stood in front of the stage to listen to the musicians and singers perform. Famous movie stars told jokes and urged people to buy war bonds, while beyond the stage, a gigantic cash register kept track of all the money they'd raised for the war effort. Penny had linked arms with Esther as they'd shuffled on and off the jam-packed subway, and for once Esther didn't mind having Penny right beside her. Her friend Roy, the marine, watched out for Peter, carrying him piggyback when he got tired of walking and hoisting him onto his shoulders so he could see the stage over everyone's head.

"I've never seen a real live movie star in person before, have you?" Penny asked.

Esther shook her head. "We should have come earlier so we could get closer."

"Next year," Roy said with a wink. But Esther hoped with all her heart that Daddy would be home by next Christmas and that the war would be over and nobody would need to buy war bonds.

They listened to Judy Garland perform, and they sang along with her on some of the Christmas carols. They laughed and cheered with the rest of the crowd at Abbott and Costello's antics. All the while, the numbers on the giant cash register kept going higher and higher. The show was fun and exciting, but for Esther it seemed to end much too soon.

"What do you say we go over to Macy's department store and look at the window decorations?" Roy suggested. Peter hopped up and down with excitement. He'd been so happy all day that Esther thought for sure the words would burst out of his mouth any minute. He really liked Roy and his corny jokes. She hadn't seen Peter this happy in a long, long time.

"Okay, let's go," Esther said. Penny looked surprised and pleased when Esther linked arms with her again. But Esther only did it so that she wouldn't get lost in the vast crowd.

Everything looked glittery and pretty as they walked around the outside of the department store, admiring the decorations in the windows. The joy of Christmas began to bubble up inside Esther like the fizz in a soda bottle. She began to wish the day would never end.

"Where to next?" Roy asked when they'd completed their circuit. Peter pointed to a five-and-dime store across the street, then pulled off his mittens and wrote on his piece of paper: *I want to buy some presents.*

Esther had a quick discussion with him, whispering and writing notes, and they decided to buy Penny a new lipstick and Grandma a box of her favorite talcum powder. "We'll meet back here in half an hour," Roy decided. He and Peter went in one direction to get the lipstick, and Esther went the opposite way with Penny to buy the powder and also a present for Peter. She began to believe that this Christmas might be a good one after all. What was it Mr. Mendel had said? *"Happiness is something that comes from our own hearts, not from other people."*

Late that afternoon they took the subway back to Brooklyn, then rode a bus to their own neighborhood. As they walked the last few blocks toward home, Peter halted in front of a shop with Jewish writing on the windows. Inside were things like Mr. Mendel had in his apartment: leather-bound books and silver cups and brass candlesticks. Peter took out his paper and pencil and wrote: *I want to buy something for Mr. Mendel.*

"He doesn't celebrate Christmas, remember?" Esther said.

More candles. We used his all up.

"Okay, come on." They went into the store and picked out a box of candles that looked as though they would fit in his candleholder. Mr. Mendel had told them that it was called a *menorah*. She and Peter paid for the candles with their own money.

"It's starting to feel like Christmas," Esther said as they came out of the shop again.

"You know what we really need?" Roy asked, halting in the middle of the sidewalk. "A Christmas tree. What do you say we buy one? There's a vacant lot about three blocks away where they're selling them. Remember, Penny? We pass it every day on our bus route."

"How in the world would we get it all the way home?" Penny asked. "I don't think they allow Christmas trees on city buses."

"We'll just have to use some good old-fashioned manpower, I guess." Roy held up one arm to show his muscles. "I'll bet Peter will help me out. Right, buddy?" Peter nodded and struck a muscleman pose like Roy's. Esther couldn't help laughing.

"You have any decorations at your house?" Roy asked.

Esther hesitated. "We do, but . . ." She knew they had two boxes full of decorations in the hall closet upstairs. Daddy hadn't bought a tree last year because it had been too soon after Mama died and everyone still felt sad, but now Esther felt pulled in two directions again. Peter looked so happy and excited about the idea—and she was, too. Yet it seemed wrong to be happy when Mama was gone and Daddy was so far away. She felt like a traitor celebrating Christmas without them or being happy with Penny taking Mama's place, doing all of the things that Mama used to do for them.

Peter tapped Esther's shoulder, then folded his hands as if in prayer, silently pleading with her. "Oh, okay," she said with a sigh. "Let's get a tree."

They hopped on another bus and rode the short distance to the Christmas tree lot, looking at about a dozen trees before Roy and Peter finally picked out one. Everyone helped carry it home. Esther's mittens got sticky with sap, but the tree smelled wonderful, like pine and happy memories. She smiled all the way home, watching Peter trying to show off his muscles and listening to Roy do his imitation of Abbott and Costello.

Let's put it in the front window where everybody can see it, Peter wrote when they finished hauling it up the apartment stairs. That was where Daddy had always put their Christmas trees. Esther remembered how Mr. Mendel had placed his menorah in the front window, telling them how it symbolized Hashem's miracle. And hope. Wasn't Christmas about a miracle, too? God sending His son?

While Peter and Roy wrestled the tree into place, Esther pulled the boxes of decorations from the upstairs closet. Penny helped her carry them down to the living room, and as Esther opened the first box, the memories fluttered out like moths. Each ornament she hung reminded her of Mama and Daddy and how much fun they used to have as the four of them decorated the tree. There were fragile ornaments that had to be handled carefully, along with colorful, gaudy ones that Esther and Peter had made in school out of construction paper and glue and plaster of Paris. Mama said she treasured the homemade ones most of all. Esther glanced at Peter and wondered if he remembered, too.

Penny went out to the kitchen and made popcorn for them to string into a garland, but they ended up eating most of it rather than stringing it together. Esther ate an entire bowl of popcorn herself, while Peter and Roy had a contest, trying to toss the popcorn into each other's open mouth. Later, Peter sat on the sofa next to Roy, writing notes to him, and it seemed wonderful to see Peter smiling and "talking" instead of slouching in his room, reading his comic books over and over. She was glad that he felt comfortable with Roy. She sat down beside them to see what Peter was saying.

Is it fun being a soldier?

"I can't say that it's fun," Roy replied, "but it certainly is an honor. I keep thinking of all the brave men who fought in wars before me, making sure our country remained free. And now it's my turn."

Our daddy is in the army.

"So I've heard. You should be very proud of him. He was very brave to sign up when he didn't have to. You read in the paper all the time about the cowards who pretend they're sick or shoot themselves in the foot so they won't have to fight. But your dad stepped right up to do his part."

I didn't want him to go.

"I know. But he must have decided that this was something he had to do. Imagine how he would feel if he didn't go, knowing all the other men were fighting to keep our country free and he didn't help out. That would be very hard to live with."

So our daddy is brave? Like Superman?

"Yes. Braver than Superman. And now it's your turn to be brave and keep things going here at home while he's far away. He wouldn't want you to be sad, would he? He's going to want a happy family to come home to."

Penny began gathering up the empty cartons and tissue paper, and when Esther got up to help her, she found the little wooden stable and the figurines from the Christmas story in the bottom of one of the boxes. Every year Daddy would read the Bible story out loud while Peter and Esther put the wise men and shepherds and the holy family in their places. But this was one tradition that Esther didn't want Roy or Penny to do in Daddy's place. She quickly unpacked the stable and set it on the top of the piano, then put all of the figures in their places herself. As she laid baby Jesus in the manger she recalled what Mama had always told them every year: *"Jesus is God's Christmas present to us. We're His children and He loves us."*

Suddenly Esther needed to get away. "I'm going outside for some air," she said. She grabbed her coat and mittens and hurried down the front stairs. It was so hard to believe that God loved her when so many terrible things had happened to her. Yet Mama wouldn't lie. If she said that God loved her, then He must.

She knocked on Mr. Mendel's door, needing to ask him what he thought. He didn't celebrate Christmas, but maybe he could tell her if it was really true—that God or Hashem, or whatever He was called, really did love her, even though it didn't look that way. She knocked again, but there was still no answer. Mr. Mendel had said he would be very busy from now on, attending meetings and raising money to help people like his son and granddaughter, who were trapped in the middle of the war.

At last Esther gave up and went outside to sit on the front porch, brushing a light dusting of snow off the glider so she could sit down. The metal felt wet and cold beneath her, and the swing gave a harsh metallic squeal as she glided back and forth on it. The evening grew dark and cold. She wouldn't be able to wait for Mr. Mendel for very long.

Esther finally got up to go back inside. But before she did, she decided to cross the street to see what their Christmas tree looked like in their upstairs window. As she stood looking up at it, Jacky Hoffman sauntered up the street toward her with his jacket hanging open and no hat or mittens on, as if the weather were balmy, not so cold you could see your breath.

"Hey, beautiful," he called to her. He raked his unruly hair from his eyes like a pirate. "What are you doing out here all by yourself?"

"I wanted to see what our Christmas tree looked like." She pointed to the window across the street. Jacky glanced up at it, then looked back at her.

"You gonna be around while we're off from school for Christmas vacation?" he asked.

Esther's heart thumped wildly. "Most of the time. We have to go to our grandmother's house for dinner on Christmas Day."

"You want to go to the movies sometime?"

"Yeah," she said with a smile. "I would like that."

She would like that very much.

Chapter 25

December 31, 1943

"Oh my. This isn't at all what I expected." Penny stood in the doorway of the USO lounge on New Year's Eve, staring into a room jam-packed with soldiers and sailors and marines in uniform. She had agreed to volunteer at the dance with Sheila while Esther and Peter stayed overnight with their grandmother. Now she regretted her decision.

Lively music played somewhere inside, but the rumble of conversation and laughter nearly drowned it out. Through the haze of cigarette smoke that hung in the room like fog, she glimpsed a crowded dance floor filled with swaying couples. Several pretty girls stood behind a counter on one side of the room, serving coffee and punch. But the majority of people who had crammed into the room were servicemen from all branches of the military, outnumbering the women by at least three to one.

"Come on, follow me," Sheila said. She grabbed Penny's arm and towed her into the melee. There wasn't an empty table or chair in sight and barely enough room to stand, let alone walk. Penny saw men eyeing them up and down as they inched across the room. She heard wolf whistles from some of the soldiers they passed and calls of "Hey, baby" and "Hubba hubba."

"I don't like this," she told Sheila. "It's scary being ogled this way."

"It's just a dance, Penny. You make it sound like such an ordeal."

"I never went to dances in school like all the other girls."

"You'll be fine. All you have to do is talk to these fellas. They just want a few laughs." Sheila halted for a moment, leaned closer to Penny, and whispered, "Some of them won't live to see next New Year's Eve, you know."

Her words made Penny shudder. *Not Eddie,* she prayed. *Please, not Eddie.* He was stationed in England now, on a military base near the sea. He wasn't allowed to say where exactly, and Esther worried constantly that he might be near London, where German bombs might fall on him. Penny worried, too. His letters all came by V-mail, which meant they weren't his original copies at all but photographs of them, shrunk down and reproduced on special paper. Sometimes the censors blacked out words or sentences that contained restricted information. But she treasured every letter he sent her, no matter how brief or marked up it was.

Penny stood with Sheila behind the serving counter for a while, passing out coffee and doughnuts and punch. The men she served were so friendly and nice, and many of them reminded her of Roy with their easy way of talking to strangers. Penny started asking them where they were from as she filled their coffee cups and discovered that they enjoyed talking about their homes and families. She was amazed to hear that they came from cities and towns all over the country.

An hour or so later, new volunteers arrived to take Penny's and Sheila's places. "Go dance for a while," they said. "Have some fun!"

"I just want to sit down and rest my weary feet," Sheila replied.

Penny followed her friend out into the crowded room again, looking for a place to sit. As they squeezed past a tableful of men, someone snagged Penny's arm. "Hey, ladies. How about joining us?"

"We saved you a couple of seats." One of the sailors slid back his chair and gestured to his lap. Penny blushed. Did he really think she would sit on a stranger's lap?

"Sure, we'll join you," Sheila said, "but you'll have to give us a couple of real chairs. We're not sitting on anyone's lap."

"Aw, c'mon." The men all laughed as they made room for them around the table. Sheila did all the talking as they introduced themselves, making it clear right from the start that she was a married woman. "But my friend Penny is single," she added.

"I-I do have a boyfriend, though."

"A pretty girl like you? I'd be surprised if you didn't have one."

"We could steal you away from him, don't you think, fellas?"

"Anyone ever tell you that you've got a pair of legs like Betty Grable's?"

Penny didn't know how to reply. Would saying thank-you sound flirtatious? "Um . . . my legs get me where I need to go," she finally said. Everyone laughed.

The men bantered back and forth, teasing each other, showing off for her and Sheila. Penny finally got up enough courage to join the conversation and told them about her job as a bus driver and how she was taking care of Eddie's two children while he served over in England. Then she asked them about their girlfriends and what part of the world they would be shipped off to in the New Year. She had just started to relax a little when Sheila got up to dance with one of the sailors, leaving her alone with the tableful of men. A soldier named Hank invited Penny to dance.

"No, thanks," she replied. "I don't know how to dance."

"I could teach you." Hank draped his arm around the back of her chair. He sat much too close, with his face right in front of hers. She smelled alcohol on his breath. Sheila said the soldiers weren't allowed to drink at USO dances, but one of the men at their table took a little flask from inside his jacket, and Penny saw him pouring from it into everyone's glass of punch. Hank offered her a sip of his drink.

"Come on, try a little. It'll help you relax."

"You have to celebrate the New Year, you know," the man with the flask told her.

"In fact, why don't we go someplace really fun," Hank decided.

"I know a nice little nightclub nearby where we can ring in the New Year in style."

"Yeah, let's get out of here," the others agreed.

Before Penny could protest, the men at her table all pushed back their chairs and stood up. Hank took her arm and helped her to her feet. "No, thank you . . . I don't want to go someplace else . . . I mean—"

"Give me your hatcheck ticket, Penny, and I'll get your coat."

The room was so crowded that as Hank and the other men moved toward the door, they pulled Penny right along with them. She didn't want to make a scene, but she didn't know how else to break free. Besides, she didn't think anyone would hear her above the noise, even if she shouted. Just as she started to panic, she saw Sheila hurrying toward her.

"Hey! Where do you fellas think you're going?"

"We decided to find a livelier place. You should come with us, Sheila."

"No thanks. My husband wouldn't like that very much. Penny and I are staying right here for the evening." Penny felt like she had narrowly escaped a disaster as Sheila pulled her from Hank's grasp.

"Suit yourself, ladies." They left the dance without her.

Penny nearly collapsed with relief. Sheila could fend off unwanted advances with ease, and the men didn't try to pressure her the way they had Penny. They must have seen how inexperienced she was and that she didn't know how to handle their unwanted attention.

"Come on, Penny. Let's go powder our noses." Penny followed Sheila, even though she had no idea what that meant. "It means we're going to the ladies' room," Sheila said when Penny asked her. "I think it's time to find a different group. Those fellas have been hitting the hooch."

The lights seemed very bright in the ladies' room after leaving the hazy dance floor. Penny squinted at her reflection in the mirror and barely recognized herself. The girl in the mirror wasn't her, not the real Penny Goodrich. Men might think she was pretty, but she had only wanted to look nice for Eddie, no one else. She hated it here at the USO dance. She wanted to go home, far away from all of these strangers.

She waited for Sheila to come out of the stall, then gathered up her remaining courage. "Thanks for inviting me, Sheila, but I'm not comfortable here. I'd hate to ruin your fun just because I'm not having any, so I think I'll go home."

"You just got here. Give it another chance. Not all of the men are like that last bunch." She pulled a makeup case out of her purse and touched up her lipstick.

"I'm sorry, but I want to go home. There's too much cigarette smoke, and it's making me feel sick. You can stay, though."

Sheila planted her hands on her hips, scowling as she looked at Penny. "I thought you wanted to help boost morale?"

"I changed my mind. I'm sorry. I'll see you at work." She hurried away as quickly as she could in the overcrowded room and retrieved her coat from the hatcheck girl. Sheila probably wouldn't invite Penny to go with her ever again, and that was too bad. But coming here had been a mistake. Penny never wanted to come back.

She stood outside for a moment, breathing fresh air, trying to decide whether to go back to Eddie's apartment or to her parents' duplex, where Esther and Peter were. She decided on the apartment. Her mother would smell the cigarette smoke on her clothes and have a conniption fit if she knew Penny had gone to a USO dance wearing makeup and floozy shoes.

She thought of Roy as she boarded the bus back to Eddie's neighborhood, wondering how his New Year's Eve with Sally was turning out. He had given Sally a ring for Christmas. They were officially engaged now, and Roy had been walking on air ever since.

"I only have a twenty-four hour pass for New Year's Eve," he had told Penny, "and I'm not sure if I can get a bus ticket with all the holiday crowds, but I'm going home to see Sally if I have to walk all the way to Pennsylvania."

"Don't the buses and trains give special preference to servicemen?" she had asked. "You won't really have to walk, will you?"

"I don't know—but I'm not even going to sleep the entire time

224

I'm home. I want to get the most out of my pass." Penny had laughed and wished him well.

Now she got off the bus at her usual stop and picked her way carefully along the icy sidewalks in her high heels. As she came up the front walk to Eddie's apartment building, she noticed the outside door to the building was open and a set of keys dangled from the door lock. She hurried up the porch steps and found Mr. Mendel collapsed on the stairs in the foyer as if he could go no farther. His face looked very pale against his dark beard and clothing, with blue hollows beneath his eyes.

"Mr. Mendel, are you okay?"

"I think so . . . in a minute . . ." He wheezed whenever he exhaled, as if he had run all the way home. "I felt a little dizzy when I came in from my walk. I needed to sit down."

Penny removed his keys and closed the front door to keep out the cold air. "Should I call a doctor?"

"No, thank you. I will be fine."

"Are you sure? You want me to help you into your apartment?"

"Yes. That would be good."

She used his keys to unlock his apartment door, then offered him her arm. "Here, let me help you up. Move slowly, though, and don't try to stand up too fast. You can lean on me."

He shuffled across the foyer, leaning against Penny. When he reached the doorway he paused for a moment to touch his fingers to his lips, then touched a little metal box on the doorpost. Penny helped him take off his coat and lower himself into the nearest chair. "Can I get you some water or maybe a cup of tea?"

"You need not bother. I will be fine in a moment."

"It's no bother, really."

"Well . . . maybe a little water."

She went into his kitchen, found a glass, and filled it with water. When she spotted a kettle sitting on the stove she decided to fill it with water and light the gas burner before returning to the living room. "Here," she said, handing him the water. "I'm heating water for tea in case you change your mind. It might help you warm up."

He sipped the water, pausing to cough a few times. He had taken off his hat but wore a small, round skullcap beneath it. "Are you sure you're feeling better?" she asked after a moment. "I would be glad to call a doctor."

"I will be fine."

Penny didn't believe him. He still looked very pale, and even though his breathing had slowed, he wheezed with every breath. She decided to stay with him for a few minutes. "It sounds like you caught a cold. It's freezing outside tonight."

"Yes, it is cold out. But ever since I breathed too much smoke on the night of the fire, I've had trouble with my chest." He paused to cough again.

"You should stay inside in weather like this." Penny sounded more like her mother than she cared to admit. "If you ever need anything from the store, the kids and I would be happy to get it for you."

"It is not only the weather, I am sorry to say. I got upset tonight and lost my temper. My heart began to race and I am sure that my blood pressure went up, making everything worse."

Penny sat down on the sofa, waiting for him to explain. Maybe it would help if he had someone to talk to. And she wanted to make sure he was all right, still thinking he needed a doctor.

"I have been doing a bit of detective work," he said. "I have not told the children because I do not want to worry them, but the police suspect me of starting the fire in the shul."

"Wait a minute . . . didn't you go inside that night and try to save something?"

"Yes, the Torah scrolls. Nevertheless, they believe that I started the fire. I often see the two detectives who accused me hanging around outside, watching me for no reason. They do it to let me know that they still think I am guilty. I must clear my name, so tonight I went to the Italian grocery store on the next block to talk to the clerk, to see if she remembered that I bought groceries there that night. She said the store is always very busy, so many customers, and she did not recall seeing me. I became upset with her. How many Jewish men, looking as I do, have come into the shop on a Friday night, our Sabbath? Surely she must remember. When I raised my voice, the manager came." Mr. Mendel looked down at the floor, shaking his head. "Now she will tell the two detectives that I have a bad temper."

Penny's heart went out to him. She didn't know what to say. He looked up at her again after a moment and said, "I think the water is boiling in the kitchen."

Penny heard it, too. She stood. "Tell me where you keep the tea, and I'll make some for us."

"You should not bother. I should not keep you here, listening to a tired old man. You look so pretty, all dressed up. Are you going out somewhere special tonight? It is New Year's Eve, yes?"

"I've already been out. I was coming home for the night when I saw you in the foyer."

"So early? It is not yet nine o'clock."

"I know. It's a long story, but the evening didn't go very well. I was about to go upstairs and have a cup of tea and go to bed. The year will change to 1944 whether I stay up until midnight or not."

Mr. Mendel braced his hands on the arms of his chair and stood. He was no longer as pale as he had been. "Come, then," he said. "We will have our tea together."

He led the way into the kitchen, spooned leaves into a teapot, and poured in the boiling water. Penny sat down on one of the kitchen chairs and slipped her arms from the sleeves of her coat, letting it hang from the back of her chair.

"Tea leaves are hard to come by these days, yes?" he asked.

"I can hardly find them anymore. But it's such a treat to have a cup now and then."

"I suppose they must come from a part of the world where there is fighting—and which part of the world is not fighting? Then there is the problem of getting the tea here to America when all of the ships are needed for the war. And so a simple cup of tea becomes a luxury."

He sat down at the table across from her, waiting for the tea to steep. After everything Penny's father had told her about Jewish people, she knew she shouldn't be here in this apartment, sipping tea with this man, but she didn't feel at all afraid of Mr. Mendel. He seemed very kind and trustworthy, certainly not a horrid "bogeyman" as her father believed all Jews to be. Perhaps it was her father who shouldn't be trusted—the man who had lied to her all these years, never telling her that she was adopted.

"I suppose I will not be welcome in the Italian grocery store anymore," Mr. Mendel said with a small smile. "Not after creating such a fuss."

"No one can blame you for being upset, especially with the police suspecting you like that. Isn't there any other way to prove you didn't start the fire?"

"There was another witness from that night who I have been trying to find. A young man saw me going in through the front door that evening to save the scrolls, after the fire was already burning. As I unlocked the door, he called to me from across the street and said not to go in but to wait for the fire department. If I could find that person, he could tell the police that I had the bag in my hand at the time, after the fire was already burning. The bag could not contain a can of kerosene, as they insist. Every evening I take a walk through the neighborhood and look for the man who called out to me. I remember that he was about your age, very tall and thin, with thick, wavy black hair and a square chin. He could help to clear my name."

Penny hesitated as she watched him pour the tea into two cups, then decided to say what she was thinking. "Most men who are my age are in the military, Mr. Mendel."

He looked up at her in surprise, then closed his eyes. "Yes, of course. I did not think of that. He surely must be gone by now." Mr. Mendel looked so discouraged that Penny regretted mentioning it.

"I can help you keep an eye out for him. I ride the bus through this neighborhood every day going to and from work. You shouldn't go out walking in such cold weather."

"Thank you. But as you say, the young man is probably long gone. Where are the children, by the way? Your apartment looked dark when I came home."

"They're with their grandmother until Sunday. Eddie arranged it so that I would have some weekends off once in a while. I was supposed go out and have fun tonight since New Year's Eve fell on a Friday, but it didn't work out."

"It seems we are both having a bad night, yes?" He smiled faintly.

"Would you like to tell me about your sad evening? You were kind enough to listen to mine."

"I went with a friend to a USO dance. I don't have any experience with dances and things like that, much less with men. My parents were very strict and never allowed me out on my own. But I went tonight because a friend talked me into it, and the dance hall was filled with servicemen from all over the country. There were so many men there, and a couple of them were trying to dance with me and flirt with me, but I just wanted to get out of there. Besides, I'm not interested in having a boyfriend, because I'm in love with—" She stopped, wondering if she should tell him. Would he let the cat out of the bag and tell Esther and Peter?

But Mr. Mendel didn't wait for her to decide. "You are in love with the children's father, yes?"

"How did you know?"

"Because there is no other reason why a pretty young woman like yourself would sacrifice all of her free time to care for two rather ungrateful children unless love was involved somewhere in the equation. I have noticed how Esther treats you—like a servant rather than a friend—and so it cannot be because of your love for her. I also noticed how nice you looked on the night that Ed Shaffer came home, and how you fussed over the dinner you were making. I cooked your roast in my oven, remember?"

Penny smiled in spite of herself. "You make a very good detective, Mr. Mendel."

"I admire you for taking on the task of caring for a home and children who are not your own. That is very unselfish of you. I hope that their father comes home safely from the war, for everyone's sake."

"Me too." She had finished her tea and Mr. Mendel appeared to be well again. There was no reason to stay. "I guess I should go," she said, rising to her feet.

"Thank you for helping me." He stood, and as he walked with her to the door, she noticed the little brass box again.

"What is that for?" she asked.

"It is a reminder of Hashem's commands. In His Torah it says that we must write His law on our doorposts so we will remember to obey them when we go out into the world and when we come into our homes again. There is a little scroll inside each box with words from His Law on them."

She thought of the soldiers she had met tonight, drinking too much and pressuring her to go with them. She remembered how her married friend had danced and flirted with other men. "We could all use a little reminder of God's laws," she said. "Happy New Year, Mr. Mendel."

"Yes. Let us hope it is a happy one—for the world's sake."

CHAPTER 26

Budapest, Hungary

Dear Mother and Father Mendel,

This is your daughter-in-law, Sarah Rivkah, writing this letter to you. Avraham asked me to keep writing to you the way he used to do so that after the war you will know what has become of us.

I am sorry to tell you that something terrible has happened. Avraham has been taken away. We were celebrating Shabbat two nights ago and Aunt Hannah had just said the blessing over the candles when a troop of Hungarian policemen burst into our apartment building. They went door to door to every household and gathered up every man they could find. No one had a chance to escape or hide. They took Avraham and Uncle Baruch and all but the very weakest men from our Jewish neighborhood for their slave labor force.

Of course we pleaded with them not to take our men. How will we survive? Some of the wives even offered the police a bribe if they would allow their husbands to stay. The police took

the bribes—and the husbands, as well. They assured us that
the men will be allowed to rejoin their families after Hungary is
victorious in the war, but it seems more and more that the war
will never end.

Avraham and Uncle Baruch barely had time to gather their
coats and a few belongings and kiss us good-bye before they
were marched away. Avi gave me instructions to write this letter
to you so you would know what happened. His last words were
"Good-bye, Sarah. I love you. May Hashem protect you and
Fredeleh."

We hear such terrible stories of what these forced labor
camps are like and so it is hard not to worry. The men who
are assigned to work outdoors, repairing roads or digging in the
mines, suffer from the cold. Many of them lack warm coats and
proper shoes, not to mention enough food to eat. Most of those
basic supplies are being sent to the soldiers fighting on the front
lines. Some men will end up working in factories in Germany,
and we are told that the Allies have begun to bomb those factories. I despair of ever seeing Avraham again.

We are left with only women now in our apartment in
Budapest—Aunt Hannah and her sister, two of her cousins,
my mother, Fredeleh, and me. We often go hungry because it is
so hard to get enough food to eat, and we often huddle beneath
blankets in front of the fireplace when that is the only heat we
have. It breaks my heart to hear Fredeleh crying because she is
hungry or cold, but at least we are still safe. When I think of
what poor Avraham must be suffering in a forced labor camp, I
know that I should not complain.

It has been a long time since we received a letter from anyone in our family back home in the village, so we have no idea
how they are doing. Before the police came, I asked Avraham if

we should try to go back to the countryside and stay with them. Maybe we would be safer there, maybe we would have more food to eat. But even as they were taking Avi away, he told me that it is better for Fredeleh and me to remain here in the city.

Avi has shown me the Christian orphanage where we can hide Fredeleh, and also the packet of papers that I must leave with her. But now that my husband is gone, I cannot bear to be separated from my daughter, as well. She is all that I have left. Avi says Hashem will show me when it is time to hide her with the Christians. He told me to trust Hashem, but I confess that I sometimes find that very difficult to do, especially after all the suffering I have seen during this war, all the unanswered prayers. Avi's faith is much stronger than mine, and now that we are separated, I don't know how I will be able to stay strong. He told me that it is fine to yell and plead and cry out to Hashem whenever I need to. He said I can talk to Him about everything that I fear. Avi also said I should recite from the book of Tehillim whenever I am afraid, and so that is what I try to do. I think that the authors must have suffered as we do, because the words they wrote are so close to my own thoughts:

"I cried out to Hashem for help; I cried out to Hashem to hear me . . . Has His unfailing love vanished forever? Has His promise failed for all time? . . .

Then I thought . . . I will remember the deeds of Hashem; yes, I will remember your miracles of long ago . . ."

I hope that you are praying for us, Mother and Father Mendel. May Hashem bring us all together one day in joy.

> Love,
> your daughter-in-law, Sarah Rivkah,
> and granddaughter, Fredeleh

CHAPTER 27

FEBRUARY 1944

THE OVERHEATED STUDY ROOM where Jacob sat reminded him of the beit midrash in his own shul in Brooklyn—before the fire destroyed it, that is. Black-clothed men of various ages and ethnic backgrounds, rabbis and laymen like himself, sat at wooden tables and in straight-backed chairs usually occupied by young Torah students.

Jacob had traveled to Manhattan by bus and subway through the cold and snow of a dreary February day to attend this meeting with Rebbe Grunfeld. And as he'd listened to the mixture of good and discouraging news, Jacob thought of the candles he and the children had lit for Hanukkah and the prayers he had dared to utter for the first time in more than a year. He had been afraid to believe for a miracle as he'd commuted here from Brooklyn, but the fact that officials from the State Department finally had agreed to meet with Jewish leaders and work with them seemed like a small miracle in itself.

Jacob listened as one of the men from Washington read a copy of the personal report that President Roosevelt's advisors had submitted to him in early January: "'One of the greatest crimes in history, the slaughter of the Jewish people in Europe, is continuing unabated,'" the report began. It detailed examples of procrastination, misrepresentation, and the suppression of facts on the part of U.S. government officials. And it accused some people in the State Department of deliberately interfering with rescue efforts, fueled by anti-Semitism. The report had called for immediate action on the president's part to remedy the situation. And President Roosevelt had done so.

"As a direct result of this report," the speaker concluded, "the president issued an executive order on January 22, 1944, to establish a War Refugee Board, as you no doubt already know from the news briefing. He has promised that our government will 'take all measures within its powers to rescue victims of enemy oppression in imminent danger of death' and to provide 'relief and assistance.' That's why all of you are here. To assist President Roosevelt with raising support for this new board."

Silence filled the room when he finished. Jacob could hear the hiss of the radiators, the distant *swish* and *honk* of traffic outside. He looked around and saw that many of the rabbis had closed their eyes. Their lips moved silently as they swayed in prayer.

Jacob felt a mixture of cautious hope and terrible fear—hope that something would finally be done; fear that help would arrive too late. The reports that trickled in from Nazi-occupied countries made the situation clear: The Nazis had sentenced the European Jews—his son, his family—to death.

The next speaker explained how the War Refugee Board would send aid to refugees through the embassies of neutral nations such as Sweden. Some of this aid, Jacob wanted to believe, would go to help his family in Hungary. He tried to tally in his head the number of people in his extended family. Besides Avraham, Sarah, and Fredeleh, Jacob counted his two brothers, their wives, children, and grandchildren; Jacob's cousins, their wives and families, Miriam Shoshanna's brother and his family, and . . . he couldn't count them all. More children and grandchildren surely would have been born since Jacob had last received a letter from any of them.

When the meeting ended, he and Rebbe Grunfeld waited to speak with one of the Washington officials. "We would like to know if you have any reports from Hungary," the rebbe said. "We have family there, and we have heard nothing since America declared war with the Axis powers."

"I'm not sure. Let me ask Ben Cohen."

The man named Cohen, who was Jewish but not observant, drew Jacob and Rebbe Grunfeld aside. "You didn't hear this from me," he said in a quiet voice, "but there have been a few tentative peace overtures from Hungarian leaders. They are disillusioned with Hitler, it seems, and are trying to make a separate peace with the Allies."

"Hashem be praised," the rebbe murmured.

"Nothing is definite, mind you. There have only been a few feelers within the diplomatic community."

"But that is still good news, yes?" the rebbe asked Jacob.

"Yes," Jacob agreed. "Yes."

He left the meeting feeling more encouraged than he had in many months. "From now on," the rebbe said, "we must devote every moment of our time, every ounce of our energy to writing letters, contacting Jewish donors in America, pleading for funds."

"It will be a relief to be able to do something useful besides worry," Jacob said. The work would keep him moving forward through the long, silent days of waiting. But as he walked home from the last bus stop to his apartment at the end of the afternoon in a biting February wind, he couldn't help wondering if Avraham and his family were keeping warm. Did they have enough to eat? Or would help from the new Refugee Board arrive too late?

Jacob unlocked the front door and went inside his warm apartment, stomping the snow from his shoes. Since it was so late in the day, the children would have already arrived home from school. He could hear Esther practicing the piano upstairs. He stood in the living room for a moment with his coat on, listening. She played beautifully for a girl so young, every phrase full of expression. She and Peter would have heard him come home. They would be down soon.

And they were. By the time he'd hung his hat and overcoat in the closet and changed into his house slippers, they already were knocking on his door.

"Come in, come in . . . How was your day in school? And the spelling test you were dreading, Peter? You passed it, yes?" Peter gave

Jacob a shy grin and a nod. "Good, good. I believe the tin of cookies is on the kitchen table. Go and see if there are any left."

"What happened to all your pictures, Mr. Mendel?" Esther had come into his apartment and gone straight to his dining room table, as usual, to look at his newspaper clippings. But ever since Jacob had realized how they fueled Esther's fears—and his own—he had known that he must get rid of them. Late last night he finally cleared them from his tabletop for the first time since Hitler had invaded Czechoslovakia.

"I have decided not to collect them any longer," he told her.

"What? . . . Why not?"

"They were too discouraging. I need to turn my thoughts to other things." He didn't want her to know that he had removed them for her sake, but now that they were gone, he found that his fear had diminished, as well. Listening to radio broadcasts, reading the newspaper would be enough. He didn't need to dwell on the horrors of war in his own dining room.

"What did you do with them?" Esther asked. "Can I have them?"

"I threw everything away."

Esther stuck her lip out in a pout. She looked like a very small child, but only for a moment. Today as Jacob studied her, he could see how much taller she had grown these past months, how mature she was becoming. She was no longer the little girl who used to sit in the kitchen with Miriam Shoshanna, eating honey cake. Esther was becoming a young woman before his eyes.

"I wish you hadn't thrown them away, Mr. Mendel. Why didn't you give them to me? I could make a scrapbook."

"If they are no good for me, then they are no good for you, either. Besides, Esther, we cannot trust what we see in those pictures to tell us the entire story. We cannot know all of the things that are going on behind the scenes that we see in the photographs. They do not show us how Hashem is at work."

"What do you mean? What do you think Hashem is doing?"

Jacob paused. Did he believe what he had just told her or were they only words? Was it wrong to talk to her of faith when his own faith was so tentative? Jacob was angry with Hashem, yes, but he still believed in Him. And he did trust that Hashem was at work, even though he sometimes wanted to tell the Master of the Universe that He wasn't running it very well.

"Today I attended a meeting to talk about a new organization the president has created to help war refugees in Europe like my son. The work they do will be invisible, behind the scenes. You and I certainly cannot see it. But I will raise money to send over there because I believe in what I cannot see."

"Does this mean Hashem is answering your prayers?"

"Perhaps." Jacob hadn't thought of it that way, but she was right, of course.

"I still wish you hadn't destroyed the pictures," Esther said. "Especially the ones from England, where Daddy is. I heard on the radio that two hundred German airplanes dropped bombs on London the other night, and I want to see what's going on."

"Even though you can do nothing about it?"

She gave a loose shrug, her arms folded across her chest, and he saw by her pout that she was cross with him. "Do you know the story of Queen Esther, from the Bible?" he asked.

"A little. Not much."

Jacob put his hands on his hips in mock dismay. "Now, how can that be . . . when you are named after her?"

"Will you tell it to me?"

Peter must have been listening to the conversation from the kitchen, because he suddenly appeared in the dining room doorway with a cookie in his hand. He looked up at Jacob like a puppy pleading for a bone. "You want to hear the story, too, I suppose?" Peter nodded.

"Hmm . . . Let me see something . . ." He went to his desk in the living room and checked his calendar. "Esther's feast, which is called Purim, will be coming soon, in March. Even better than telling you the story, I think we should celebrate it. As part of that celebration it is our tradition to read the story together. Everyone will take a different part—and Esther must be Queen Esther." He turned to Peter and laid his hand on the boy's head. "And you will play the part of Hashem."

Esther frowned at Jacob. "How can he do that? You know he doesn't talk."

"You will see. It will be the perfect part for him."

Peter tugged Jacob's sleeve and showed him what he had written. *Do we light candles?*

"I am afraid there are no candles to light during Purim, but there will be other good things. You must bring noisemakers with you—bells, whistles, tin pots, and wooden spoons—anything that makes a noise."

"Who gets to make the noise?"

Jacob couldn't help smiling at the children's growing excitement. "We all do. Purim is the only time when it is a mitzvah for children to make noise. Another tradition is to dress up in costumes."

"Like Halloween?"

"Perhaps a little bit like that. You must wear a crown like Queen Esther. And we must invite Penny, of course."

"What else? What else?"

Jacob was surprised to discover that he felt excited, too. "Let me think . . . My wife used to make *Hamantaschen*. They are cookies. But I do not know how to bake cookies."

Peter hopped up and down, pointing to Esther and himself. "You will help me bake them?" Jacob asked. When Peter nodded and hugged Jacob's arm, it brought tears to his eyes.

"We used to help Mama bake all the time," Esther said. "Penny can help us, too. All we need is the recipe."

"Very well. Let me see if I can find it." He went into the kitchen with Peter still holding tightly to his arm and looked through the file box where Miriam Shoshanna kept her recipes. Her handwriting, so flowing and elegant, reminded Jacob of dark lace. He found the well-used cookie recipe, smudged and speckled with stains.

"Well, here is the recipe, but I am afraid it is written in our Hungarian language. I will have to translate it for you."

"Can we make them today?"

"I do not have all of the ingredients. Besides, we still have plenty of time to prepare for the feast."

Jacob's mind raced with plans. What else must he do to prepare? He would go shopping. They could bake the cookies the day before Purim. And he would make bags of treats for everyone. It was a tradition to give away candy and other goodies. As he tallied all the things he must do to get ready, Jacob felt different and couldn't quite think why. Then he realized why. He was happy.

He was very glad that he had gotten rid of the newspaper clippings. It would be much better for everyone this way.

After the children went home to eat their dinner, Jacob called Rebbe Grunfeld on the telephone. "I have invited company for Purim, but I am not a very good cook. Is there a woman from the congregation who might be willing to cook for me if I pay her? Tell her that I will buy all of the ingredients and she can fix them in her own kitchen—something simple that I can warm up in my oven."

"I know just the person, Yaacov. I will ask her to call you for the details. I am so happy to hear you sounding so well. And celebrating Purim! Wonderful, wonderful."

"The work with the Refugee Board has lifted my spirits. From now on I will have something to do besides sit and worry. Who knows, we might even make a difference."

Miriam Shoshanna would be pleased, Jacob thought as he spread a cloth on the dining room table and set it with her good china plates and glassware. Tonight was the first time the dishes had been out of the cupboard since she had died, the first time he had invited guests for dinner. The woman he had hired to cook the meal had outdone herself, preparing cabbage rolls and potato *latkes* and a small brisket of beef. She had offered to bake Hamantaschen and seemed surprised when Jacob told her that he had baked them himself—with help from Miss Goodrich and the children, of course.

Esther arrived dressed as a princess, with a crown on her head made of tinfoil and cardboard. Peter had pinned a bath towel to his shoulders and taped the letter *S* to the front of his shirt. Jacob wasn't sure why until Esther explained that he was supposed to be Superman.

They sat down to eat, and as Jacob broke the bread, he recited the blessing over the meal for the first time in nearly two years. Everyone relaxed as they passed the food around the table and ate their fill, even Miss Goodrich. Laughter hadn't filled his apartment in a long, long time.

"Mama used to fix potatoes this way," Esther told him as she helped herself to more latkes.

"Did she? I am glad you like them."

They dined like royalty, and although Jacob had worried that the children might not like the unfamiliar food, there were very few leftovers.

"Just leave the dishes on the table," he insisted when the meal ended. "I will clean them up later. Come, it is time to read the *Megillah*—the scroll of Esther. Did you bring noisemakers? Let me hear what they sound like."

He pretended to cover his ears as the children blew the whistles and rang the bells they had brought with them. Miss Goodrich banged on an old tin pot with a spoon. "Very good. Now, as we read the story, each time the wicked Haman's name is spoken, everyone must stamp his feet and boo and make noise to drown out his name, yes?"

They all sat down in the living room, Penny and Esther on the sofa, Peter on the floor in front of them. They had brought their own Bibles to follow along as Jacob read the narration. He took his copy of the Megillah from the bookshelf and sat in his desk chair, facing them. "Penny can take the part of Mordecai," he told them. "Esther will be Queen Esther, and Peter will be Hashem. Are you ready?"

They read the story together, stomping and booing whenever Haman's name was mentioned, laughing at all the noise they were making. Jacob couldn't help but think of Avraham, remembering how much fun he used to have making noise, just as the children and Penny were doing. Excitement flushed Peter's face as if he was overjoyed to finally have a way to express himself after all these months of silence.

"Now we must talk about what we have learned," Jacob said when they finished reading. "That is how my people have passed on our faith from generation to generation, talking about it in our homes as we celebrate Hashem's feasts and His weekly Sabbaths." It seemed strange to celebrate with Christian children, but they were looking to him, waiting.

"Queen Esther's tragic past is told in just a few words, did you notice? 'She had neither father nor mother,' it says. She was an orphan. There had been a war in her time, too, and her country had been defeated. She and her cousin Mordecai were taken away to a distant country. She must have thought Hashem had abandoned her when all of those terrible things happened, yes? But even though Hashem did not prevent bad things from happening, He made sure that Mordecai was there to adopt Esther and take care of her."

Jacob saw Peter writing something and waited for him to hold up his slate: *Penny takes care of us. Since Daddy left.*

"Yes. Very good." Jacob glanced at Miss Goodrich and saw her biting her lip, trying not to cry. Jacob was glad that Peter was finally accepting her, treating her like more than a servant. Even Esther looked comfortable sitting beside Penny, a pleasant change from a few months ago.

"And once again," Jacob continued, "when Esther was taken from Mordecai's home to become part of the king's harem, a servant named Hegai watched over her and took care of her. She wasn't alone."

"We have you, Mr. Mendel," Esther said quietly.

Jacob could only nod, unable to speak for a moment. "Do you think Queen Esther wanted to be taken to the palace?" he asked, clearing his throat. "Would she choose to leave Mordecai and live in the harem, a place she could never leave? Remember, she did not know if she and the king would grow to love each other or not."

"I don't think so," Penny said. "I think she would want to choose her own husband, not be part of a beauty contest."

"I agree. Now, suppose Hashem had answered Queen Esther's prayers the way she probably wanted Him to. . . . Suppose her country had not lost the war, and her parents had not died, and she had never been taken away to a foreign land. Suppose the king's soldiers had not chosen her for the harem. How would our story have been different?"

Esther looked thoughtful, and for a moment Jacob glimpsed the lovely young woman she would soon become. "She never would have been the queen," she said.

"Yes, that is right, Esther. What else?"

"When Haman—" Esther had started to speak, but Peter interrupted her by making noise at the mention of Haman's name. She swatted him playfully before continuing. "When Haman made his law to kill all of the Jews, there wouldn't have been anybody to stop him if Esther wasn't the queen."

"Yes. Exactly so. Esther and her parents might have been spared for a time, but Haman would have destroyed every last one of Esther's people in the end. What else do you see?"

"I think Esther was very brave to come forward and approach the king," Penny said. "She must have been a special woman to be chosen above all the others. I think she had beauty on the inside as well as on the outside."

"It takes courage to speak up when a wrong has been done," Jacob said. "I think you all know that the Nazis are now persecuting the Jewish people, yet no one is speaking up, no one is helping them."

"But maybe people are helping," Esther said, "and we just don't know about it."

Her words stopped Jacob short. Hadn't this story just shown that Hashem was at work behind the scenes? Jacob wanted so badly to believe it was true for Avraham and his family, as well.

"You are right, of course. The help that the Refugee Board is sending will be used in ways we cannot see. . . . Now, I asked Peter to be Hashem. Did you notice why?"

Esther grinned. "He didn't have any words to say."

"Yes. In fact, Hashem is never once mentioned in this story—yet could you see Him working just the same? Arranging things between the pages?" Jacob saw Peter nodding his head, looking pleased. "Hashem was with Queen Esther all of that time, just as surely as Peter was here with us, even though neither Hashem nor Peter spoke a word."

"I get it!" Esther said. Her smile was the brightest Jacob had ever seen.

And as angry as Jacob still was with Hashem, he was forced to acknowledge the truth of his own words. Hashem would always be with His people, even when silence and hardship made it seem as though He had forsaken them. If only Jacob could look past his grief and confusion and wait for Hashem, trusting in His goodness.

Jacob stood, needing to escape for a moment as he battled his tears. "I will get the cookies we made," he said. "And fix some tea."

By the time the water boiled and he had arranged the Haman-taschen on a plate, Jacob was in control again. He carried them into the living room on a tray and heard Penny saying, "I never noticed before that Esther was adopted. Maybe that's because I just found out that I'm adopted."

"What happened to your real parents?" Esther asked.

"I don't know. I guess my real mother didn't love me so she gave me away."

"Just a minute," Jacob said. "How do you know that she did not love you?"

Penny looked taken aback. "It says on the adoption certificate that she gave me away when I was one day old and then she had the record sealed so I could never find her again."

"There are many reasons why parents must leave their children with someone else," Jacob said. "Ed Shaffer left his children with you so he could fight in the war, yes?"

"But their father loves them."

"And that must have made his decision even more difficult. How do you know that it was not just as difficult for your mother? Where is the proof that she did not love you?"

Tears welled in Penny's eyes. "She gave me up, didn't she?"

"That is not proof. I suggest that you seek out the reason for her decision before you conclude that she did not love you. Sometimes a mother might love her child very much, but she is unable to take care of her. Or she wants a better life for her child, so she does the unselfish thing and lets her go."

"How do you know all of this?" Penny asked.

"Life in Hungary where I was born was very difficult for Jews. I was only seventeen years old when I came to America. My mother was very sad to see me leave, but she wanted me to have a better life."

"Maybe Penny's mother got sick," Esther said, "and couldn't take care of a little baby."

Maybe she died, Peter wrote. Jacob looked at him, aching for him.

"I'll never know the reason," Penny said, "because the birth record is sealed. I don't even know my real mother's name."

"Have you tried searching for her?" Jacob asked.

"I don't know how. I'm not a very good detective like you."

"Perhaps your adoptive parents might know the story of how you became theirs," Jacob said.

Penny shook her head. "I can't ask them. They've never even told me I was adopted. I found out by accident when I needed my birth certificate. They still don't know that I found out the truth."

"Are there other family members who might know?" he asked.

"I have an older sister."

"Is she adopted, as well?"

"I have no idea. Hazel got married and moved away when I was a baby. She lives in New Jersey somewhere."

"Doesn't she ever come to visit you?" Esther asked. "Not even for Christmas and Thanksgiving?"

"She visited once or twice when I was younger, but she has children of her own now, so it's hard for her to travel. And my parents are old and don't like to travel, either, so we never visit Hazel." Penny was growing tearful. Jacob could see that the subject was very painful for her.

"Mr. Mendel is trying to find his son, Avraham, and his family," Esther told Penny. "They're over in Hungary, and he hasn't heard from them in more than two years. But you're going to keep searching for them, right, Mr. Mendel?"

"Yes. And for my brothers and cousins and their families, as well. I will search the world to find the people I love. I will never give up."

"I wish I could find Mama's family," Esther said, "but I don't know any of their names or where they live or how to find them."

"Have you asked other family members about them?" Jacob asked, trying to shift the conversation away from Penny.

"I asked Daddy, but he wouldn't tell me very much. Grandma Shaffer said Mama's parents didn't want her to marry Daddy because then she couldn't study music."

"If you found your mother's birth certificate," Penny said, "it would have her parents' names on it."

"Really? Will you help me find it?" Esther asked.

"Sure. And if we need to go to the records' office, I know where it is."

"A marriage license might also have her maiden name on it," Jacob added.

Penny jumped to her feet as if she wanted to run down to the records' office this very minute. Instead, she said, "Come on, let's help Mr. Mendel with the dishes."

"No, no. Leave them. I will clean up. I have nothing else to do."

"Are you sure? It will go faster if we all help."

"You have to go to work tomorrow, yes? And the children have school? I do not mind doing them."

It took a lot of effort to convince Penny to leave the dishes, but she finally gave in. The children thanked him for the dinner and hugged him good-bye. His kitchen might be a mess, but Jacob felt happy. The evening had been a good one. He turned on the radio so he could listen to it while he cleared the table and carried plates and cups into the kitchen. He had been so busy getting ready for the feast that he hadn't listened to the news all afternoon.

At first the station played music and advertisements. But as Jacob collected the tray from the living room with the cookies and teacups, a news bulletin aired. He paused in the middle of the room to listen to it.

"Nazi troops marched into Hungary today and now occupy that country. Analysts believe that Hitler wanted to forestall attempts by the Hungarian government to sign a separate peace agreement with the Allies. These Nazi forces now occupy Budapest. . . ."

"No . . ." Jacob murmured. "No, that cannot be . . ."

The Nazis are in Hungary.

As the truth began to penetrate his soul, Jacob cried out, "NO!"

His body went weak and the tray slipped from his hands. The dishes crashed to the floor—splintering, like his hope, into a million pieces.

Jacob doubled over as pain spiked through his chest. He couldn't draw a breath. He tried to reach the sofa, but the room spun and his legs gave way and he fell, bringing a floor lamp crashing down with him.

Then darkness.

CHAPTER 28

ESTHER COULDN'T STOP THINKING about the story of Queen Esther that they had read tonight. Penny was trying to hurry her and Peter along because it was past their usual bedtime, but Esther didn't want to rush off to bed. She knew she wouldn't be able to fall asleep right away. While Peter brushed his teeth in the bathroom, Esther packed her schoolbag and set it by the front door, ready for the morning. She wished she didn't have to go to school tomorrow.

As she stood at the top of the steps, she suddenly heard a crash downstairs and glass breaking. Then Mr. Mendel let out a heartrending cry. The sound quivered through Esther like an electrical current, pinning her in place. Another crash followed.

Esther dropped her bag and ran down to the foyer to knock on Mr. Mendel's door. "Mr. Mendel . . . ? Mr. Mendel, are you okay?"

No answer. She could hear his radio playing inside. She knocked harder. Panic swelled inside her, filling her chest.

"Mr. Mendel!"

She tried the knob, but his door was locked. Esther threw herself against it with all her might, calling his name over and over. It wouldn't budge. Why didn't he answer? As her fear spiraled out of control, she remembered that Mrs. Mendel had once shown Mama where she hid an extra key.

Please let it be there . . . please let it be there, Esther pleaded as she felt along the edge of the stair risers for the key.

She found it! Her fingers shook so badly she could barely fumble the key into the lock, but the door finally flew open.

Mr. Mendel lay in a heap on the floor with his eyes closed, his face as pale as a ghost's. Shattered glass, crushed cookies, and a toppled lamp lay all around him. Esther ran out to the foyer and yelled with all her strength, "Penny! Penny come down here! Hurry!"

Penny thundered down the stairs, followed by Peter in his pajamas. Penny took one look at Mr. Mendel and grabbed for his telephone. "I'm calling an ambulance."

Esther sank down beside him, ignoring the shards of glass that lay scattered everywhere, and lifted his head into her lap. Peter knelt to hold one of his hands. All of them were crying, including Penny.

"Mr. Mendel . . . please wake up . . . please," Esther begged, stroking his face. The little skullcap he always wore had fallen off, and she tried to put it back on his head. *Please, God, please!* she silently prayed. *Don't let him die!*

At last, Mr. Mendel groaned softly. His eyes fluttered open. Esther could tell that he didn't know where he was or what had happened. His face still looked as white as paper.

"Are you okay, Mr. Mendel? I think you fell. Are you hurt anywhere?"

"My chest . . ." He drew a gasping breath. "Hard . . . to breathe."

"An ambulance is on the way," Penny said. "Don't try to move."

He looked from one of them to the next and whispered, "No tears . . . I will be fine." Esther wished she could believe him.

"Is there anyone else we should call?" Penny asked.

"Rebbe Grunfeld . . . his number . . . is on my desk."

Esther heard Penny calling him, asking him to come over right away. By the time she hung up, a siren had begun to wail in the distance. Peter heard it, too, and he scrambled to his feet as if he wanted to run away from it. He pressed his hands over his ears. He hated the sound of ambulances. Esther did, too. Penny pulled Peter into her arms, hugging him tightly, comforting him.

The siren screamed louder, closer. A flashing red light shone through the front window. Penny ran to open the door for the medics, and a moment later Esther heard footsteps and men's voices. They hurried inside and crouched down to examine Mr. Mendel, talking to him, listening to his heart. Esther closed her eyes and prayed. When she opened them again, she saw that the man with the stethoscope looked worried.

"We need to take him to the hospital," he said. The other medic went outside to retrieve the stretcher. As they lifted Mr. Mendel onto it, the rabbi arrived. Esther recognized the white-bearded man from the night of the fire.

"How is he?" the rabbi asked. "What happened?"

"I think he fell," Esther said. "I heard a crash and I came downstairs and found him here."

"The radio . . ." Mr. Mendel murmured, pointing to it. Music still played from it in the background, and Esther thought he wanted her to turn it off. But as the medics hoisted the stretcher, Mr. Mendel gripped the rabbi's wrist and said, "Nazis . . . in Hungary."

Esther didn't understand what he was trying to say. "I want to go to the hospital with him," she said.

"It's very late," the rabbi told her. "I think it would be better if you stayed here. I will ride with him to the hospital and call as soon as I have news. I promise." Esther grabbed a piece of paper from the memo pad on the desk and wrote down her telephone number to give to him.

"Promise you'll call right away?"

"Yes, I promise."

The front door opened and cold air rushed inside. Then the men were gone. The flashing light and wailing siren grew fainter and fainter. "You kids go on upstairs," Penny said. "I'll clean up this mess and take care of the dishes."

Esther shook her head. "I want to help you. Mr. Mendel keeps his dishes separated and I already know how to do it." She bent to straighten the lamp, not waiting for Penny's reply. Together, the three of them cleaned up the broken glass and washed all the dishes. They had just finished putting everything away, and Esther was about to turn off Mr. Mendel's radio and go upstairs when the nightly news aired once again:

"Nazi occupation forces marched into Hungary earlier today, invading that nation. As the Nazi troops stormed into Budapest and the surrounding countryside . . ."

"Hungary!" Esther shouted. "That's where Mr. Mendel's son is! That's what he was trying to tell us."

"That must have been what upset him," Penny said.

"Hitler is just like Haman. He hates the Jewish people. But who will be Queen Esther? Who will stop him this time?"

She saw Peter writing something. He held it up for her to see: *Daddy will.*

Esther covered her face. She couldn't stop her tears. For the first time she understood why her father needed to go to war and what was at stake. She felt Penny's arms around her, pulling her close, rubbing her back, letting her cry.

"Come on," Penny said when Esther finished crying. "Let's go upstairs and wait so we can hear the telephone."

They all got ready for bed, then settled on the couch to wait, wrapped up in one of Grandma Shaffer's crocheted afghans. Esther couldn't imagine what it would be like to lose Mr. Mendel. He had become like a grandfather to her. She felt a little of the fear he must face every day at the thought of losing his family to the Nazis.

Peter began to doze after a while, but Esther couldn't sleep. When the telephone finally rang, she leaped up to answer it. "Mr. Mendel is doing much better," the rabbi told her. "The doctors don't believe he had a heart attack, but his heart did get out of rhythm. He has suffered a terrible shock and—"

"We heard the news on the radio. The Nazis invaded Hungary."

"Yes. He was able to tell us. His doctor would like to keep him in the hospital overnight, and if all goes well, he will be allowed to come home tomorrow or the next day."

Esther felt very tired the next morning. She didn't want to go to school, but Penny said that she had to. "I have to go to work, and I don't think you should stay here all alone all day."

"Can we visit Mr. Mendel in the hospital if he doesn't come home?"

"Yes. We'll all go together, I promise."

Esther knocked on Mr. Mendel's door the moment she arrived home from school and was relieved when he answered it. She wanted to hug him, but he looked so frail she feared he might fall over if she did. "I need rest, that is all," he said. "I am so sorry for frightening you last night." He held the door open only a small crack, not inviting her and Peter to come inside.

"Would you like me to cook for you or something?"

"Thank you, but the women from my congregation have been showering me with food once again. I will eat like a prince."

"We heard the news about the Nazis in Hungary," she said softly. "The announcers keep talking about it on the radio and it's in all the newspapers."

Mr. Mendel reached for Esther's hand. She saw tears in his eyes. "I cannot talk about it just now. I am sorry."

"Is there anything we can do?"

He thought for a moment. She wondered if he would tell her to pray, but instead he said, "Will you play the piano for me, upstairs? I would like to hear it. Then I am going to rest again. We will talk tomorrow."

"I'm glad you're okay, Mr. Mendel."

"Thank you."

Esther took the stairs two at a time and went straight to the piano bench to get out her practice books. She would play every piece she knew for him. She sat down on the bench, propped the music on the stand, and played through her entire repertoire, hoping Mr. Mendel would enjoy it and that it would make him well.

When she was too tired to play another note, she closed the lid and sat on the bench for a long, long time, thinking about her mother. Mama would be proud of her, she thought. Mama's music had made everyone happy, too, whenever she'd played.

Thinking about her mother made Esther happy and sad at the

same time. She wished she knew more about her and why she had decided to get married instead of studying music. And why Mama's parents had gotten angry with her for that.

"I will search the world to find the people I love," Mr. Mendel had told them last night. *"I will never give up."* But with the Nazis in Hungary, she wondered if he ever would find them again.

Now more than ever, Esther longed to find her mother's family.

CHAPTER 29

Budapest, Hungary
March 1944

Dear Mother and Father Mendel,
    I am standing at the very edge of despair. The Nazis have
invaded Budapest. All hope is gone, and my heart is as empty
as our cupboards. The Hungarian government is no more.
Our leaders have been ousted. The Nazis control us now—the
very thing we feared the most. Their troops have seized all of
the railroads and taken over the government buildings. We no
longer know what is happening in the rest of the world, because
the Nazis control the radio broadcasts, the post office, the
telegraph.
    Before the invasion, it seemed from all the news we heard
that Hungary might stop fighting in this war and make peace
with the Allies. We learned that American troops were in Italy
and that the German army had surrendered to the Soviets in
Stalingrad. With so many other battles to fight, why would Hit-
ler bother to invade Hungary now and deport the Jews?

But that is exactly what he has begun to do. As soon as the Nazis arrived they began to persecute us the way that they persecuted Jews in Germany and Poland. A man named Adolph Eichmann is in charge of us. He has ordered all Jewish businesses to close and all Jews must register and wear a yellow star. Here in Budapest, we have been rounded up and forced to move to a ghetto. A Jewish council has been set up to assign living quarters to everyone and to ration our food and water. The council members are Jewish but they must take their instructions from the Nazis. Anyone who disobeys is arrested.

We still live in Uncle Baruch's apartment in the ghetto, but nearly two dozen people now crowd into it along with us. Aunt Hannah, her two cousins, and other relatives have been separated from us and forced to live in another apartment, but I am still with my mother and Fredeleh. Aunt Hannah is very sick with coughing and a fever, but there is no medicine or doctors, and we are banned from the hospitals.

We all know what is coming next. The Jews who escaped into Hungary from Poland told us what the Nazis did to them there. The Nazis have condemned us to death, like our enemy Haman of old. What we don't understand is why they hate us so much. And why the world stands by and allows it. Why doesn't someone come to our rescue? And the biggest question of all is why does Hashem allow it?

A few people who have fled to Budapest from the countryside have told us that the Nazis have rounded up all the Jews in the provinces and small villages like the one we came from. Long trains of boxcars are arriving in Hungary every day, but they aren't bringing the food and supplies we so desperately need. *They are arriving empty. They have come to deport us all to labor camps in Poland.*

If the reports are true, our families back home in the village may already be gone. My sister and three brothers and their families, my aunts and uncles, Avi's relatives, your relatives, all of them gone. I cannot stop weeping for them. If only they had come to Budapest with us when Avi begged them to. We have heard terrible rumors from those who have escaped, saying that these are not labor camps at all but extermination camps. I don't want to believe that it's true. And so I worry and pray and wonder what has become of my family and my Avraham and if I will ever see them again. If help doesn't arrive soon, we fear that when the Nazis finish deporting everyone from the provinces, they will come for us here in the city. The horror and fear are too much for me, as they are for everyone. No one knows what will happen tomorrow.

If only I had hidden little Fredeleh in the Christian orphanage months ago. I should have brought her there right after Avraham was taken from us. Now it has become too dangerous to go out into the streets with so many Nazi soldiers. We are not supposed to leave the ghetto. The Nazis can stop us and ask where we are going and demand to see our identification papers. And so I am begging Hashem to forgive me for not hiding her there sooner and pleading with Him for a way to take her there now. I can't bear the thought of the Nazis coming for her.

I know you are praying for us back home in America, and that Avraham is praying, too, wherever he is. I find it harder and harder to pray when my prayers seem to go unanswered. Once again, the book of Tehillim is my only comfort:

"Hear my prayer, O Hashem; let my cry for help come to you. Do not hide your face from me when I am in distress . . ."

May He deliver us from our enemies and bring all of us together soon.

With love,

Sarah Rivkah and Fredeleh

CHAPTER 30

ESTHER'S OVERNIGHT VISIT to her grandmother's house had seemed to last forever. She had tried to learn more information about her mother from Grandma Shaffer, but she hadn't been helpful, insisting that she didn't know anything else. Esther wished her father had never arranged for her and Peter to stay there on the weekends. She told him so in her letters, but Daddy said Penny deserved to have some time off. Now, as she boarded the bus to return home, Esther decided to sit beside Penny instead of riding in the back where she and Peter usually rode.

"Penny, do you remember my mother?" she asked.

"I remember when your parents got married," Penny said. "Your grandmother gave a little party for them out in her backyard. She invited me and my parents."

"So you knew Mama?"

"Not really. Just as a neighbor, watching from a distance." It seemed like an odd reply to Esther. And Penny's voice sounded sad. "I remember how pretty your mother looked the day they got married," Penny said. "And how happy she was. Your mother couldn't stop smiling—and neither could your dad." Esther wondered why Penny seemed so sad about Mama if she never knew her.

Esther gazed out the bus window, watching the storefronts and office buildings and tenements go slowly by. The city looked dreary in these weeks of waiting before spring arrived. The snow had melted but the trees were still bare, the grass brown. Everything reminded her of death, and she didn't want to be reminded. First Mama had been killed. Now Daddy was in danger. Mr. Mendel had collapsed and nearly died. And Esther worried that if Grandma Shaffer got sick and died, there would be no one left to take care of her and Peter. Esther had thought about it a lot lately, which was why she was determined to find Mama's family. Finding her grandparents would be a way to hang on to a little piece of her mother's memory, too.

She turned to Penny again. "Mama was pretty, wasn't she?"

Penny nodded. "I remember what a tiny little waist she had. Your father could have wrapped his hands right around it with his fingers touching."

"Remember you said you would help me find out more about her family? Can we start today? When we get home?"

"We can try."

Esther had wondered if she would feel like a traitor asking Penny for help. She had resented Penny's interference in her life at first and had fought against Penny's efforts to get close to her. But something had begun to change at Christmastime when they went to Times Square together and later when they decorated the tree. Esther's attitude had changed even more on the night that Mr. Mendel had gone to the hospital and Penny had comforted Esther and wept with her. Or maybe it had happened earlier that same evening as they had celebrated Purim. Ever since Daddy left, Esther had been angry with God for leaving her all alone—but she wasn't alone. He had sent Penny.

"Mr. Mendel said we could start by looking for your mother's birth certificate and marriage license, remember?" Penny said. "That way, we can find out what your mother's maiden name was and maybe the names of her parents. Do you know where your daddy keeps important papers like that?"

"I don't know. Maybe in the storage closet upstairs where the Christmas decorations were?"

When they arrived at the apartment, Esther and Penny spent more than an hour dragging everything out of the upstairs closet, searching through boxes of baby clothes and old toys and outgrown clothing. They didn't find any papers. Esther surveyed the mess they had made in disappointment. "The only other place I can think of is in Daddy's closet," Esther said.

Penny winced. "I would feel funny snooping through his things."

"Please? I'll look in there myself if you don't want to. I need to find Mama's family. It's important. Remember what Mr. Mendel said? We should search the whole world to find them."

"I don't know, Esther. You said your mother's family didn't want anything to do with her. Maybe it's not such a good idea to look for them. They might turn their backs on you, too, and I would hate to see you and Peter get hurt."

Esther hadn't considered that. She had imagined herself running into their open arms, happy to be reunited at last. But by rejecting Mama, her grandparents had rejected her and Peter, as well. Even so, Esther wanted to know why.

"Wouldn't you want to talk to your real mother and father if you could?" she asked Penny. "Even though they gave you away? Don't you want to know why?"

Penny gazed into the distance, looking thoughtful. "Yeah, I guess I would," she finally said. "But let's put all this stuff away before we go rooting through any more closets."

Esther closed the flaps on one of the boxes and shoved it back into the closet. When they had put the boxes away again, Esther led Penny into Daddy's bedroom. Penny's clothes took up a very small space in the closet, as if she knew that this room didn't really belong to her and that she wasn't staying forever. Or maybe Penny didn't have very many things. Esther wondered where Mama's clothes had gone. She couldn't remember Daddy packing them up and taking them away, but he must have.

"Before we start," Penny said, "let's try to remember how everything looks so we can leave it the way we found it, okay? I don't want to mess up any of your daddy's things."

"Okay. But I don't think he'll notice. He isn't very neat."

They moved his shoes and slippers out of the way and found a dust-covered box buried in the back of the closet. Esther pulled it out and yanked open the flaps, hoping to find what they were looking for—and found something even better.

"These things belonged to Mama!" Esther remembered seeing them on her mother's dressing table. She pulled them out and examined them, one by one: her silver vanity set with the mirror, comb and brush, her perfume bottles and talcum powder.

"Daddy cleared off her dressing table after she died," Esther said. "It was too hard to look at them every day and be reminded of her, he said. I'm glad he didn't throw them away, though." She lifted a perfume bottle to her nose and sniffed. Her mother's scent brought tears to her eyes.

"You should have these, Esther. It's not too hard to look at them now, is it? Wouldn't your mother want you to have them?"

"I don't know. I wouldn't want to make Daddy sad again." She remembered his reaction when she'd played Mama's piano for him when he was home on leave. But Esther longed to have these small tokens of her mother.

Penny laid her hand on Esther's shoulder. Her eyes looked soft in the dim light of the closet's single light bulb. "You're becoming a young woman now, you know. We should think about rearranging a few things."

"What do you mean?"

"Well, for starters, you and I could share this bedroom. Two girls together, you know? You would have more privacy than sharing a room with your brother."

"Won't he be lonely all by himself?"

"We could ask him. Let Peter decide. You're not going to be a little girl forever. You're growing into a woman. You and your friends will want privacy to talk about girly things."

Esther didn't have any friends. Only Jacky Hoffman and Mr. Mendel. Jacky kept inviting her to go to the movies with him, again and again, but she and Peter always had to go to their grandmother's house on Saturday.

She returned to the contents of the carton and found a collection of Mama's scarves and gloves and purses. Beneath one of Mama's Sunday hats, Esther found the jewelry box that Daddy had given Mama for Christmas one year.

Esther glanced up at Penny before opening it. Ever since they'd found the carton of Mama's things Penny had been sitting back, allowing Esther to look through it by herself. "Go ahead." Penny nodded. "Open it."

Inside were necklaces and bracelets that Esther remembered her mother wearing. Mama had never worn a lot of flashy jewelry like bangles and rings—just her wedding band and a pearl necklace and a few other simple pieces. The rest of her jewelry was for special occasions.

At the bottom of the jewelry box were three old black-and-white photographs. "This is Mama!" she said, examining the first one. "She looks a lot younger. I don't know who these people are with her." There was an older woman with snowy hair and two young men. Esther peered closely. It was hard to see their faces. Were they Mama's boyfriends? Or did they look a little bit like Mama—her brothers, maybe?

In the second photograph, one of the young men from the first picture posed by himself. The third photo was a portrait of a stern-faced couple and three small children, two boys and a girl. Could the little girl in dark ringlets be Mama?

"This is so frustrating," Esther said with a sigh. "I want to know who these people are and why Mama kept the pictures."

"You should show them to your father when he comes home. He might know."

There was one more item in the jewelry box, a small, black velvet bag with a drawstring. Esther untied the string and let the item drop into her palm. It was a small brass box with strange lettering on it.

"Let me see that," Penny said, reaching for it. "This looks like the little box that Mr. Mendel has on his door, only smaller."

"I wonder why Mama has it?"

"Mr. Mendel owns this apartment, right? Maybe it was on the door when your parents moved in, and your mother removed it."

"I guess so," Esther said with a shrug. She began putting her mother's things back in the box, disappointed that they hadn't found her birth certificate.

Suddenly Penny struck her forehead. "I'm such a scatterbrain! I just remembered seeing a drawer full of papers in the dining room. I was looking in the buffet for napkins and a tablecloth and saw a bunch of papers in the bottom drawer. I thought it was a funny place to keep papers."

They left the contents of the closet strewn on the floor and hurried downstairs. Penny pulled the drawer all the way out of the buffet and set it on the dining room table. "See?" she said. "This looks like a copy of the lease for this apartment . . . and here are your old report cards . . . and look, Esther! Your birth certificate!"

She took it from Penny's hand and sank onto a dining room chair to read it. *Father's name: Edward James Shaffer. Mother's name: Rachel Rose Shaffer. Maiden name: Fischer.*

Esther stared and stared at it while Penny continued searching through the drawer. "Here's their marriage license," she said. Esther scanned the page with her. Rachel Rose Fischer had married Edward James Shaffer on June 10, 1930. Mama's parents' names were David Fischer and Esther Fischer.

Esther gaped in surprise. "Mama named me after her mother! She couldn't have stayed mad at them or she never would have given me the same name, would she?" Seeing the names neatly typed on the official-looking document made Mama's family seem real to Esther. She imagined them looking just like the couple in Mama's photograph, only older. David and Esther Fischer. Her grandparents.

"Well, we know their names," Penny said. "Now what? Fischer seems like a pretty common name."

"We could ask Mr. Mendel what he thinks we should do." Esther stood, ready to race downstairs to ask him.

"You should wait until tomorrow. Don't bother him now. He might be resting."

Esther sank back onto the chair with a sigh. Now that she was one step closer to finding her family, she didn't want to wait.

"Hey, you have a birthday coming in another month," Penny said, studying her birth certificate. "You'll be how old? . . . Thirteen? How do you want to celebrate?"

"I don't know."

"How do you usually celebrate birthdays? Dinner at your grand-mother's house? A party with some of your friends?"

Mama had made birthdays fun when she had been alive, but nobody had celebrated them since. Esther didn't have any close friends from school. She used to play hopscotch and skip rope with a group of neighborhood girls, but everything had changed after Mama died. Esther had been sad for such a long time that no one wanted to play with her anymore—and she had wanted to be left alone. Besides, the girls all acted as if their mothers might die, too, if they got too close to Esther.

"Mama used to bake birthday cakes for us," Esther finally said. "But I don't want to eat it at Grandma's house. It's so cluttered in there that I can't breathe. If I could have my wish, I'd like to have cake with Mr. Mendel."

"I don't think he can eat our food. He said it has to come from special Jewish stores, remember?"

"There's a Jewish bakery across the street from the fruit stand where . . ." Esther paused. It was across from where her mother and Mrs. Mendel had died. Esther had always avoided that block and the bad memories of that day. But she would gladly make an exception for Mr. Mendel's sake. "I'll bet he could eat the cake if we bought it at the Jewish bakery."

"Are you sure that's all you want? Just to have cake here at home?"

"Well . . ." She thought of Jacky Hoffman. "Instead of staying overnight at Grandma's that weekend, could I please go to the Sat-urday matinee with my friends? I know that means you won't get the weekend off, but—"

"That's okay. I don't have any place special to go. Your birthday is much more important. You can go to the movies with your friends that Saturday and come back here for cake with Mr. Mendel. How would that be?"

"Could I go to the movies without Peter?" she asked in a whisper. "Just my friends? I don't want him to feel bad, but . . ."

"I understand. I'll get him to help me with something here in the apartment."

"Thanks, Penny."

As the time for her birthday approached, Esther grew more and more excited about her trip to the movies alone with Jacky. It would almost seem like a grown-up date. She was thirteen years old after all, and she had seen kids from school holding hands as they stood in line for their tickets. She might even agree to sit upstairs in the balcony this time. Only the little kids like Peter sat downstairs.

When the day finally arrived, Esther nearly danced with happiness as she walked to the movies alone with Jacky. "Are you going to let me pay for your ticket this time?" he asked, flashing his roguish grin.

"If you want to . . . It's my birthday, after all. I'm thirteen now."

She was a little disappointed when Jacky didn't hold her hand as they waited in line. But he led the way upstairs to the balcony and put his arm around her shoulder when the lights went low. His arm was really around her shoulder, too, not just on the back of the chair. She saw the couple in front of them smooching during the newsreel, but she was relieved that Jacky didn't try to kiss her. Their hands brushed as they shared the popcorn and candy, and it was so exciting to sit close to Jacky and feel grown up that Esther could barely follow the plot of the film they watched.

Afterward, Jacky finally reached for her hand outside the theater and held it all the way home. He even took the long way home so they could be together longer. "Can I give you a birthday kiss?" he asked when they halted in the alley behind Esther's apartment building. She hesitated, then shook her head. She didn't have quite enough courage for a first kiss, especially in broad daylight where the neighbors might see them. Her heart already pounded harder than it ever had in her life.

"Come on, just a little peck?" he coaxed.

"Okay, but here . . ." She pointed to her cheek. Jacky put his hands on her shoulders and moved very close. When he bent his head down and pressed his lips to her cheek, Esther thought her heart might explode. He smelled good up close—like Daddy did when he got dressed up.

"Happy birthday, Esther," Jacky murmured before he pulled away again. The place on her cheek where his lips had touched felt like it was on fire. This had been one of the best birthdays in her life. It felt great to be thirteen.

"Would you like to come in and have some birthday cake with us?" she asked.

"You having a big party or something?"

"No, just my brother and Penny and me. And our landlord, Mr. Mendel."

He turned away. "No, thanks. Maybe another time. I should get home."

In a way, Esther was relieved. She didn't want anyone to know how she felt about Jacky. And Penny didn't know that the "friend" Esther had gone to the matinee with was a boy. Besides, Peter didn't like Jacky, and he might spoil the afternoon for them.

"Hi, I'm back," she called as she came in the kitchen door. "Peter . . . ? Where is everyone?"

"Come upstairs for a minute," Penny called down to her. "Peter and I want to show you something."

Esther still felt like she was floating as she went up to the third floor. When she reached her bedroom, she saw that Peter and Penny had moved the furniture around while she'd been gone. Esther would still sleep in the same room with Peter, but they had rearranged the beds so they weren't side by side anymore. The toy box had been moved, and Mama's dressing table and mirror stood in its place with a wrapped birthday present for Esther on top. She couldn't stop smiling as she gazed at the transformed room. Was the dainty little dressing table really hers now?

Peter held up his slate. He had written *Happy Birthday Esther* in colored chalk. "Thanks, Pete," she said. "And thanks for changing everything around. The room looks . . . it looks wonderful!"

Peter pulled out the stool to the dressing table and gestured for

Esther to sit down and open her present. There was no tag on the gift. "Who is this from?" she asked as she tore off the paper. "Is it from you, Peter?" He shook his head.

"You'll see when you open it," Penny said.

Esther tore off the last of the wrappings and pulled the lid off the carton. Inside were Mama's silver comb and mirror set, and her jewelry box.

"I wrote to your father," Penny said, "and asked if I could give them to you for your birthday. He said yes! I wrote to him the same day we found your mother's things, and I was so afraid that the letters wouldn't get all the way over to England and back in time for your birthday. But they did. Your daddy's letter arrived yesterday."

Esther couldn't believe her eyes. It was as if Mama herself were here, smiling at Esther, telling her she was no longer a child but a young woman.

Esther stood and threw her arms around Penny, hugging her tightly.

CHAPTER 31

MAY 1944

PENNY BOARDED THE BUS for work on a beautiful spring morning and saw her friend Roy Fuller saving a seat for her. It struck her all of a sudden that he was a very nice-looking man, clean-cut and wholesome-looking. He was the kind of all-American guy that every mother wanted her daughter to marry.

"Hey, stranger," she said as she sat down beside him. "I haven't seen you around in more than a week. I was wondering what happened to you."

"I know. I've missed talking with you. I've been working odd hours and longer shifts because we're training our replacements at the Navy Yard. I'm finally being shipped out."

"Oh, Roy. That's what you've been hoping for, isn't it?" She could see that he was thrilled, but Penny hated to think about losing her friend. "I'm sure going to miss you."

"I'll miss you, too, Penny. And Sally is going to miss all the romantic things I've been writing to her—or that you've been writing to her, I should say."

Penny laughed. She still gave Roy a sentence or two every now and then to help him express his love, and he was always grateful. "No, you don't need me anymore, Roy. I think you're getting the hang of it. When are you leaving Brooklyn?"

"In about ten days."

"Ten days!" The news devastated her.

"I'll be going home to say good-bye to Sally and my family first, then it's off to war at last."

"Oh, Roy." Tears filled Penny's eyes. "I want to be happy for you because this is what you've wanted for so long, but . . . but I'm going to miss you so much." She reached for his hand and squeezed it.

"Yeah. I'll miss you, too. You've been a great friend." He cleared his throat. He might be a tough marine, but she could see him swallowing hard. She remembered the first time she ever talked to him on this very same bus, how cheerful and generous he'd been as he'd given up his seat for her. Roy had been a good friend to her all these months, encouraging her, cheering for her, giving her advice with Eddie, helping her with the children last Christmas. She hated to see him go overseas, yet she knew he had wanted this deployment ever since he'd enlisted.

"They won't tell us exactly where we're going," he continued. "But they said we'll be taking a train to San Diego, then getting shipped out from there."

"Will you have to start fighting right away? Just like that?"

"No, not right away. First they'll take us somewhere to train for amphibious landings. We have to finish winning back all those little Pacific islands from the Japanese. We're working our way closer and closer to Japan every day."

"But the Japs aren't giving up without a fight. It says in the news that most Japanese soldiers would rather die fighting than surrender alive."

"That's true. They're putting up a terrible fight. But once we land on the island of Okinawa, we'll have a foothold on real Japanese territory for the first time. From there, we can establish an air base for bombing runs on Tokyo."

He talked bravely, but Penny felt afraid for him. His job would be much more dangerous than Eddie's was, and she worried about Eddie constantly. "The Marines always do the hardest fighting," she said.

"Seems that way. But we get a lot of help. First come the air strikes from carrier-based planes. Then the navy bombards the enemy with all they've got. Once they've softened up the place, the Marines can go ashore and do the land-based fighting. That's how we're taking back the Solomon Islands and Tarawa and all those other places."

Penny shuddered, remembering the fearsome casualties from all those battles. "I would be so worried about you if I were Sally. You're her fiancé!"

"She doesn't know yet that I'm being deployed. I want to tell her in person. Maybe she'll finally be proud of me for what I'm doing."

"It's not fair to talk like that, Roy. Everybody has a part to play in fighting this war, whether it's making sure the jeeps and ambulances keep running like Eddie does, or fighting the Japanese in the Pacific, or guarding an important shipyard so the navy will have new boats to use. You should be proud of what you've done."

"Thanks." But Penny could see that he wasn't convinced.

She said good-bye and got off at the bus station to begin her day. It had become a smooth routine—punching the time clock, climbing behind the wheel, driving her daily bus route. She could hardly remember what her life had been like before she'd started driving. Penny enjoyed her work and liked getting to know some of the regular passengers on her route. But all day long she couldn't stop thinking about Roy and how he would head off to fight soon. He was a good man. He had become a good friend, all because she had put aside her fear and talked to a stranger. Now she wondered if she would ever see him again. This war had disrupted everyone's life, in good ways and in sad ways. Would it ever end?

At the end of her shift, Penny steered the bus around the last corner and into the parking lot behind the bus station. "End of the line, folks," she announced. "Have a nice evening." Friday at last. She had the weekend off from work.

She saw Sheila inside the station and felt a little sad that her friend had acted cool ever since the night of the USO dance, not saying much more than hello and good-bye as they passed each other at the time clock. It had been nice having a girlfriend, even if they didn't have much in common. And now her friend Roy was going away, too.

Penny had just punched the time clock and was heading toward the door when she saw her father. He sat in the hallway between the public part of the station and the employees' back rooms, perched on a chair that wasn't usually there. His cane lay across his lap as he stared out toward the ticket booth where she used to work. Both he and the chair looked so out of place that she had to walk a little closer to make sure it was really him. In all the years that she had worked for the bus company, he had never come to the station before. What was he doing here?

Suddenly it hit her—*Eddie!* Something terrible must have happened to Eddie. Her body went limp with fear.

"Dad!" she yelled. He turned and saw her for the first time. She stumbled toward him, her legs as shaky as a newborn calf's. "Dad, what's wrong? What are you doing here?"

"Penny?" He tried to stand and sank onto the chair again. He looked her up and down, and she saw his shock as he stared at her uniform pants. His mouth opened and closed but he couldn't speak. Penny gripped his shoulders, wanting to shake him.

"Dad, what is it? What's wrong?"

"What's wrong?" He found his voice as anger took control. "I came to the bus station where my daughter sells tickets because I needed to talk to her—but the man tells me that she no longer works here. She hasn't worked here since last fall, he says. She's a bus driver, of all things. A bus driver! I argued with him. He must be thinking of a different person. My daughter doesn't know how to drive a bus. . . . But here you are. And look at you! In men's clothes!"

Penny's stomach churned with dread and guilt. "I'm sorry. I should have told you sooner, but—"

"How could you lie to us all this time?"

"I'm sorry but—" She stopped. Why should she feel guilty for not mentioning her new job when her father had been lying her entire life? She wanted to accuse him in return and shout, *How could you lie to me all this time?* And she realized that the real reason why she hadn't told her parents about her job was because of her outrage at learning she'd been adopted. She was furious with them for never telling her. She nearly blurted out the truth, but stopped in time.

"I didn't know how to tell you," she said instead. "I knew you would worry."

"I have to learn what my daughter does for a living from a perfect stranger?"

Penny listened to him rant on and on as he aired his grievances for everyone in the bus station to hear, and again she felt the urge to shake him. She needed to know why he was here.

"Did something happen, Dad? Tell me why you came here."

"Mrs. Shaffer from next door needs you."

Penny pressed her fist to her mouth to keep from crying out. For a moment she thought she might be sick. Eddie had told her that if anything happened to him, the army would contact his mother. And Mrs. Shaffer would go next door to tell Penny's parents.

"Why does she need me?"

Her father didn't offer any more information, probably to punish her. He was furious with her. She took his arm and pulled him to his feet. They needed to go home right now. She was desperate to start walking. Her father hobbled so slowly with his cane that Penny longed to leave him behind and run all the way home. She gripped his arm to steady him, wishing she could carry him piggyback the way Roy had carried Peter.

She needed to know what had happened, but she feared finding out. Eddie would remain alive in her mind until the moment someone spoke the terrible words aloud. With every slow, agonizing step Penny prayed, *Oh, God, no. Please, no. Not Eddie,* until she couldn't stand waiting any longer.

"Why does Mrs. Shaffer need me?" she asked again, trying to keep her voice steady. "Tell me what happened, Dad."

"I looked out the front window for the mailman, and I saw the boy coming with a telegram. I know what that means. Everybody knows what it means. So I went to the kitchen and got your mother, and we both went next door."

Penny couldn't breathe. "Who was it, Dad? Who got killed?"

"The youngest son, Joe."

Penny nearly sank to the sidewalk with relief. She knew she shouldn't feel relieved when Joey Shaffer lay dead on a battlefield somewhere, but she couldn't help it. God forgive her, but Eddie was still alive.

Joe, the youngest of the three Shaffer boys, was dead. He had always been so lively, tearing up and down the street on his bicycle, hitting a baseball through the Pattersons' front window, shooting pebbles at stop signs with his slingshot.

"That poor woman," Penny finally managed to say. "Mrs. Shaffer has been so worried about all three of her sons, and now this."

"Your mother stayed with her for a while. She helped her call everyone and tell them the news. There is a sister in Queens who is coming to stay with her. . . . But she wants you to tell the children the news."

"Me?"

He nodded, too winded to speak. He had to stop every few yards and catch his breath. It seemed as though they waited forever for the traffic light to change, then it took another eternity to limp across the street.

How could she tell the children? They worried constantly about their father. To learn that their uncle had been killed would only deepen their fear.

When Penny and her father finally reached the duplex, she went inside Mrs. Shaffer's house alone. Penny's mother had gone home to start supper, leaving Penny to talk to Mrs. Shaffer. The poor woman looked devastated, sitting in her cramped living room in a daze. She was no longer crying, but she looked as though she had been. Penny knelt down in front of her and took her hands.

"I'm so, so sorry, Mrs. Shaffer . . . so sorry."

"I keep thinking that it must be a mistake," she said. "Maybe they'll come back with another telegram and say that it was somebody else's son who died, not mine."

"I can't imagine how you must feel." Penny felt at a loss. She had never been through anything like this before. "What can I do? How can I help?"

"I'll have to get another banner for the window. I'll have to hang a gold star . . ." She covered her face with her hands and started weeping. Did she really want Penny to go out and purchase a gold star? Grief caused the mind to think of the strangest things.

"Can I call someone to stay with you until your family gets here, Mrs. Shaffer?"

"I should tell the people at my church."

"Your church? Which one is that?" She had never known Mrs. Shaffer to go anywhere on Sunday, not even at Christmastime.

"The church where Eddie and the kids go. I used to belong before my rheumatism got so bad that I couldn't manage it anymore. I still have friends there from years ago."

Penny looked up the number and called the pastor. He would know what to do and what to say to comfort her. Sadly, there had been other young men from the congregation who had died before Joey Shaffer. "I'll come right over," he said when Penny told him the news.

"He's on his way, Mrs. Shaffer."

She stared vacantly into space, gripping the arms of her chair as if the room spun like a carnival ride. "I want you to tell the children for me," she said. "Esther and Peter need to be told."

"Of course." But Penny had no idea how she was going to do it.

After the pastor and one of the church deacons arrived, Penny said good-bye and walked to the bus stop, worrying all the way about how the children would react. When the bus she was waiting for pulled up, she was relieved to see Roy on board. Running into him twice in one day seemed like a miracle.

"What's wrong?" he asked as she sank down beside him. "Have you been crying?"

"Something awful has happened. We just found out that Eddie's youngest brother, Joe, has been killed in action over in Italy."

"That's terrible." He put his arm around her to comfort her, gently squeezing her shoulder.

"I'm on my way home to tell the kids that their uncle died, and I have no idea what to say. They had a terrible scare two months ago when Mr. Mendel was rushed to the hospital—and now this, on top of all the other sorrows they've faced. Peter already shuts himself off from everybody. Esther worries all the time about her father, obsessing about every news report, and I'm afraid that this will make her worry more than ever. I don't want to tell them, but they have to know. How do you tell children something like this?"

"There's no easy way. It's going to be hard on them no matter what you say." He pulled a handkerchief from his pocket and handed it to her. "How did you find out that he'd been killed?"

"My parents live next door to Eddie's mother—and to make everything worse, my father is mad at me now. I never told him that I drive a bus. He thought I still sold tickets. He found out today when he came to the station to tell me the news, and he's furious with me. My mother will have a conniption fit when he tells her."

"Why would they be angry? They should be proud of you."

"You don't know what they're like, Roy. They've worried about every little thing I've done, all my life. They never wanted me to go out into the big bad world with so many *strangers*. And to make matters worse, my father saw me wearing slacks today. He's barely speaking to me."

"Talk about a rotten day."

"It's going to get worse. I still have to tell Esther and Peter about their uncle."

"Do you want me to come with you to tell the kids?"

"I couldn't ask that of you. You've worked hard all day."

"I don't mind. I like Esther and Peter. And you're my friend. I'd be happy to help you out. This will be a tough job to do alone."

"Well . . . I could really use your help . . . if you don't mind."

He got off the bus with Penny and they headed toward the apartment. "I've known Eddie's family all of my life," she said as they walked. "I lived next door to them, grew up with them. Joey Shaffer is only a few years older than I am. It's such a tragedy. How do you get through something like this?"

"One day at a time. And make no mistake, it's going to be really hard at first. Each time you celebrate a holiday or a birthday, there's an empty place at the table. For the first year or so, you think you'll never be happy again, that you shouldn't be happy. But little by little, the grief starts to ease and you can remember all the good times you had together and not feel quite so sad. You have to take it day by day. That's all you can do."

"You sound like you know firsthand."

"My mother died when I was fifteen."

"Oh, Roy. No wonder you're so good with Peter and Esther. Do they know?"

"I told Peter about my mother. I told him that I understood how he felt. And I do."

"We've been friends all this time, and I've never asked you about your family or what you did for a living before the war. Where did you work?"

"I taught history at the high school in Moosic. Sally was a senior the first year I taught there. I could see that she had a crush on me, but I never let on that I noticed, never treated her any differently. Even after she graduated I probably never would have gotten up the nerve to ask her out if we hadn't met at a picnic at a friend's house and hit it off."

"Wow. So do you think you'll teach again after the war?"

"I would like to. I enjoyed my job. My parents were both teachers. My dad is the principal of the elementary school now."

They reached the front porch of the apartment building. Penny took a deep breath. "You're so good at distracting me from my fears. Thanks for doing this, Roy."

"No problem. You know it might be best if you just tell them the news right away. Don't drag it out. They'll know from your expression that something is different."

"I knew as soon as I saw my father in the bus station that something was wrong. It took him forever to tell me. I was terrified that it was Eddie who had died." She took another breath and exhaled. "They're probably in Mr. Mendel's apartment."

"Why don't you tell them while they're with him, so he can help out? I know they think the world of him."

"You're right. Maybe he can help answer their questions. He's a very wise man." She knocked on his door and waited for him to open it.

"Good evening, Penny."

"Hi, Mr. Mendel. This is a friend of mine, Roy Fuller. Are the kids here?"

"Yes. They are doing homework in the kitchen. Would you like to come in?"

"Thank you." He led the way to his kitchen, and Penny saw Esther's surprise when she looked up and saw that Roy was with her.

"Hey, it's Roy! What are you doing here?"

"There's something we need to tell you," he said, "and it isn't about your father, so don't worry. He's fine." But the look of dread in the children's eyes nearly broke Penny's heart.

"Your grandmother received a telegram today," she said. "Your Uncle Joe has been killed over in Italy."

Peter folded his arms on the table and lowered his head onto them. Roy went to his side to comfort him.

Esther sprang to her feet. "See?" she shouted. "I told you that praying didn't do any good! I told you! We've prayed and prayed and asked God to keep everyone safe and He didn't listen! He didn't do it!" Her hands balled into fists, and she looked as if she wanted to punch someone. She pushed past Penny as she tried to run from the kitchen, but Mr. Mendel stopped her before she could get very far.

"Just a minute, Esther. Slow down and listen to me. How can Hashem answer such a prayer in the middle of a war? We are the ones who started this war, not Him. People are not puppets that Hashem controls, making us do whatever He wants. Nor can He be manipulated to do whatever we ask of Him. Human beings chose to start this war, and that means we are responsible for putting the people we love in danger, not Him. But Hashem can bring good from this, even if we cannot see it."

"How? How can there be any good from this? Uncle Joe is dead!"

"Your uncle was in Italy, right?" Roy asked. "Think of the people in that country who had no freedom, living under the thumb of that crazy man, Mussolini. Thanks to your uncle, they're free again."

Penny listened to Roy and Mr. Mendel as they offered comfort and was grateful for their help. Both men had been strangers a few months ago, but now she realized how rich she was for knowing them. She thought of how much she would have missed if she had stayed sheltered in her parents' duplex, living with the same fears and prejudices that they did. Penny knew she could no longer go back and live there with them again when the war ended.

An hour later, the conversation ended. Roy sighed. "I have to go, Penny." She walked out to the front porch with him. "Listen, I'd hoped I would have a chance to say good-bye to Esther and Peter before I went overseas," he said, "but under the circumstances, I don't think it's a good idea to tell them I'm leaving. At least not today."

"You're right. They would be as sad to see you go as I am."

She gazed at the synagogue across the street, remembering how it had looked the first time she saw it the morning after the fire. Now the tan brick building was almost fully restored. She saw signs of life all around her on this balmy spring evening: emerging leaves and new green grass and dandelions the color of school buses. Yet all Penny could think about were death and change. She wondered if the police still thought Mr. Mendel had started the fire. Five months had passed since he'd last mentioned it, and he'd been so worried at the time. What in the world would the kids do—what would she do—if they lost their friend Mr. Mendel, too?

"The trouble with getting close to people," she told Roy, "is that it makes it so much harder when you have to say good-bye to them."

"Can I ask you something, Penny? You can say no if you want to and I won't feel bad—but would you mind sending me a letter every now and then when I'm overseas? I know I made a fuss when Sally told me she was writing to other soldiers, but I understand it now. So if you want to . . . and if your boyfriend doesn't mind . . . I'd really like to hear how you and the kids are doing. I would hate to lose touch with you after all this time."

"I would be happy to write to you. I'll be thinking about you all the time, anyway. I hope you'll write back once in a while when you're not too busy fighting the Japanese, and let me know that you're okay."

"You bet I will."

"And I hope I get an invitation to your wedding when you marry Sally after the war."

"I guarantee it. And I want to be there when you marry Eddie, too."

"We're a long way from getting married, Roy. At least you and Sally are engaged." Penny wrote her address on a scrap of paper from her purse and handed it to him. "Here's my address. Make sure you send me yours as soon as you know it so I can write back."

"I will. Thanks, Penny." He folded it and placed it in his shirt pocket. "You've been a great friend. I hope I see you again before I leave, but who knows?"

Tears filled Penny's eyes. They moved toward each other at the same time, clinging to each other as they hugged. She was tired of saying good-bye to people she cared about, tired of watching them leave. Would this war never end?

"Take care of yourself, soldier."

"You too."

He released her, and she watched him until he was out of sight. Penny didn't think that her heart could contain any more grief, but here was another load of it. On top of Joey Shaffer's death, losing her friend Roy was a hard blow. She would worry about him.

When she took the children to their grandmother's house the next day, it seemed as though she should see Roy sitting in his usual seat behind the driver. But the spot where he always sat was empty.

An assortment of cars was parked in front of the duplex when they arrived. Penny could see through the front window that the house was filled with people. How did they fit inside with all that clutter? "You two kids go on in," she told them. "I'll come back for you in an hour or so."

Esther gripped Penny's sleeve in panic. "Wait! Aren't you coming in?"

"I don't think there's room inside for one more person. Besides, I don't want to intrude. I'm just a neighbor, not part of your family." She felt embarrassed when she remembered how she used to hang around uninvited, making a nuisance of herself as Mother used to say, just to get a glimpse of Eddie.

"But Peter and I don't know what to do or what to say."

"Just give your grandmother a big hug. Sit beside her. That will be comfort enough. You don't have to say anything. And maybe this will give you a chance to meet some of your other relatives, right? Isn't that what you wanted?"

"But everyone will be so sad. Like they were when Mama died."

"I know. It's hard. But you'll both be fine. Make your daddy proud." Penny squeezed Esther's shoulder and stroked Peter's hair. Then she left and went next door to see her parents.

"Hi, it's me. I'm home," she called as she came in through the back door.

She had dreaded this moment ever since she had walked her father home yesterday. She knew they would still be furious with her. Her parents held on to grudges as if they were nuggets of gold. She felt the strength of their anger the moment she walked into the living room. Neither of them greeted her or even looked up at her. Father's raised newspaper shielded his face. Mother never took her eyes off the hat she was knitting to send to the soldiers overseas, her needles poking and stabbing furiously at the yarn. Penny walked over to the blaring radio and turned it down so they could talk.

"You have a lot of nerve coming in here as if you've done nothing wrong," her father said from behind his newspaper.

Penny couldn't reply. Didn't he understand that there was genuine hardship in this world? That families were being torn apart by greater tragedies than this? How could their hurt and anger compare with the terrible grief of their neighbors next door?

"The children are with their grandmother," Penny said quietly. "Are you going to talk to me or do you want me to leave?"

"I want to know why you've been sneaking around behind our backs," Mother said, needles clacking. "Why did you try to hide what you're doing from us?"

"Because you always worry about me. I didn't want you to have even more to worry about."

"Why shouldn't we be worried?" Her father's newspaper rustled as he lowered it and folded it. "Driving a public bus through the streets of Brooklyn? Are you out of your mind?"

"It turns out I'm a very good driver. The instructor said I was the best driver in my class."

"Don't take that tone of voice with me! I know a thing or two about how dangerous those streets are!"

Mother gave up trying to knit and stuffed the balled-up project into her knitting bag. "Why would you expose yourself to so many strangers that way?"

"I'm getting to know some of the people on my route. I ask how they're doing, tell them I hope they have a nice day . . . It's so much better than sitting in a cramped ticket booth all day." Or sitting in this dreary house, she wanted to add, cut off from people, from life. "Besides, I make more money now than I did with the other job."

Her father shook his head. She could tell he wasn't listening. "You're so naive. You never did have a lick of common sense. You don't know the dangers in this world and what could happen to a girl like you."

"Nothing is going to happen." But as soon as Penny spoke the words she knew they weren't true. Things did happen, whether you were careful or not. Rachel Shaffer and Miriam Mendel had been killed by a runaway car. Joey Shaffer lay dead on a battlefield in Italy. But living captive to worry and fear meant not living at all.

"I should have known you were up to no good when you started dressing like a floozy," Mother said. "I should have made you come back home right then and there."

"Mother, listen—"

"We've been so careful with you all your life, trying to keep you safe—and then you go and do something like this behind our back. Lying to us!"

"I didn't lie. Tell me how I lied?"

"You're going to go straight to your boss on Monday morning," Father said, "and tell him that you're quitting. And then you're going to pack your belongings and move out of that Jewish man's apartment. It's time you came back home where you belong."

"I can't leave the children now. How can Mrs. Shaffer possibly take care of them? You saw how much grief she's suffering, didn't you?"

"I also saw that she has other relatives—sisters and brothers and cousins," Mother said. "I called some of them for her, remember? We're ordering you to quit, Penny—the apartment and the job."

Penny's own anger swelled dangerously out of control. Her parents treated her like an ignorant child who needed to be protected. Until Eddie had enlisted and had needed her help, she had believed them. Now she had proven them wrong. She had learned how to drive a bus. She was the best driver in the class. She knew how to run a household on her own and take care of two children. She had made a life for herself with new friends, like Roy and Mr. Mendel.

"I'm not quitting and I'm not coming home," she said. Her voice shook as she stood up to them for the first time. "I'm not a child anymore. You can't tell me what to do."

Her mother couldn't speak, as if shocked that Penny would defy her this way. Her father wagged his finger at her. "Someone has had a very bad influence on you, and I want to know who it is. We didn't raise you to lie to us and deceive us."

His accusation was the last straw. "No?" Penny shouted. "No? Then why have you been lying to me all my life?"

"What are you talking about?" her father said. "How dare you speak to us that way?"

"I know that I'm adopted."

It was as though a bomb had gone off in the apartment, leaving her parents stunned. They stared at Penny, eyes wide with shock.

"I needed my birth certificate to apply for my new job, remember? And when you wouldn't give it to me I went out and ordered a new one." Her father's face turned so red she feared he might have a stroke, but Penny was too angry to stop. "I found out that you aren't my parents at all. You adopted me. You've been lying to me all this time. Why didn't you tell me the truth?"

"We did it for your own good," her mother said.

"My own good? I don't understand why you ever adopted me in the first place. All my life, you've acted as if I'm a huge inconvenience to you, like I have no common sense. You're always telling me that I'm dumber than everyone else is. Why did you adopt me if you didn't want me?"

"You want to know why?" her father asked. His face resembled simmering coals that were about to burst into flames. "I'll tell you why."

"Albert, no! Be quiet!"

"She needs to know, Gwendolyn. She needs to hear the truth before she turns out to be just like her. This is how it all started with Penny's mother, too. Remember?"

"Albert! Shut up!"

"First, Hazel started lying to us, telling us she was going one place when she was really going someplace else. And that's exactly what Penny is doing—telling us she works at the bus station when she doesn't work there at all. Running all over Brooklyn with no thought to the danger she's in. You want the same thing to happen to Penny that happened to Hazel? You want to go through this all over again?"

"Stop it, Albert!"

"Like mother like daughter! That's just how she's turning out!"

Penny groped for a chair as she realized what her father was saying. She had been standing all this time, but now she had to sit down, too stunned to remain on her feet. "Hazel is my mother, isn't she?" she murmured. *Her sister was really her mother.* Everything made sense now. Why hadn't she seen the truth before?

Mother began to weep. "See what you've done, Albert?"

"How else was I supposed to keep her safe at home where she belongs? You want her to end up getting raped like your other daughter?"

Penny stopped breathing. Raped? Her sister had been *raped*? No wonder Hazel hadn't wanted her. Penny was a reminder of an unthinkable act. No wonder her parents had always been so protective of her, so fearful of strangers.

Penny couldn't take it in—didn't want to take it in. Her real father was a *rapist*? Mother had always said that she wasn't like other girls and now she knew why. Her father was a criminal. A rapist.

"You've had a good life here with us up until now," her father said. "Why couldn't you leave well enough alone?"

Penny wished that she had. Everything that she had believed about herself had been wrong. She had been conceived from an act of violence. Even if Eddie did fall in love with her, she didn't deserve a good man like him. She couldn't be a good mother to his children.

Not with a criminal's blood flowing through her veins. Not with a rapist for a father.

Without saying another word, Penny stood and walked out of the house.

CHAPTER 32

MORNING PRAYERS AT the newly rebuilt shul had come to an end. Jacob removed the tefillin from his forehead and arm and waited for Rebbe Grunfeld to finish his duties. He stood by the window of the study room, watching as a steady spring rain made puddles on the sidewalk and turned the steely gray city green. His friend Meir Wolf came to stand beside him. "Are you taking care of yourself, Yaacov, my friend? Your heart is fine now?"

No. Jacob's heart was breaking. The Nazis were in Hungary.

Not a day went by that Jacob wasn't aware of that horrific reality. He tried in vain not to imagine what might be happening to his family, his homeland, but his work with the War Refugee Board had made him all too aware of what the Nazis were doing to the Hungarian Jews.

"I am fine, yes. The doctors say that I did not have a heart attack. They called it a heart arrhythmia." He did not tell Meir, but they also said that the shock he had received probably had caused it. He should rest, the doctor said. Let younger men be involved with fund raising for the Refugee Board. Don't put himself under such stress. But how could Jacob sit and do nothing?

"I am happy to hear that you are well," Meir said, patting Jacob's shoulder. "And so pleased that you are praying with us again. We have missed you."

"Thank you." He did not tell Meir that he still questioned his decision to return to the shul. Meir and Rebbe Grunfeld had brought him home from the hospital after his collapse and had visited him every day. The congregation had showered him with food.

"We are able to have daily prayers at the shul once again," the rebbe had told him. *"The building is not completely finished, but there is now a room where we can pray. Please come back and join us, Yaacov. Prayer is more important than ever before with the Nazis in Hungary, yes?"*

Jacob had agreed, reluctantly. Praying was the very least he could do.

"What's more," the rebbe had said, *"I believe I have finally convinced the police that you could not possibly have started the fire. But it would be good if you came back to pray with us, to show them that we are united."*

Jacob still saw the two detectives roaming the neighborhood from time to time. He knew they had not given up on finding the arsonist. And they had seemed so certain that it was him. But maybe if the rebbe had convinced them, Jacob would have one less thing to worry about.

And so he had crossed the street every day to pray with the others, putting on his tefillin for the first time since Miriam Shoshanna had died. At times he silently raged at Hashem for allowing a man like Adolf Hitler to live, questioning Him, arguing with Him. Sometimes when Jacob's faith was at its lowest ebb, he knew he was simply going through the motions of prayer. Today had been one of those days.

Rebbe Grunfeld finished storing the Torah scroll inside the ark. "So you are ready to leave for our meeting in Manhattan, Yaacov?"

"Yes, Rebbe." Jacob unfurled his umbrella and stepped out into the rain. After a long subway ride on an overcrowded train, they arrived, damp and rumpled, at the synagogue where the meeting was being held.

The moment Jacob walked through the door, he felt the now-familiar tightness in his chest, the knot in his stomach. The weekly mixture of good news and bad, the journey from hope to dread and back to hope again always took a toll. At a previous meeting the State Department had confirmed that Hungary had been close to negotiating a peace agreement with the Allies—it was what had prompted the Nazi invasion.

On May 10, a *New York Times* article had said that the Nazis were "now preparing for the annihilation of Hungarian Jews." Jacob had read those words, and for a moment he hadn't been able to breathe. The world should be horrified. This should be front-page news, not just a small, insignificant article lost among all the others. Why wasn't it in the headlines? No one seemed to be paying attention. Americans were focused on winning the war, not on the fate of the Jews. Especially when they had loved ones of their own engaged in combat.

"At least the fate of Hungary's Jews is before the entire world," the State Department spokesman had said. *"Whatever the Nazis do, it will not be done in secret."* President Roosevelt had broadcast statements around the world, promising that those responsible for genocide would be punished. Leaders from Protestant and Catholic churches in America had publicly pleaded with Hungarian Christians to protect their Jewish neighbors. But would all of these efforts save Jacob's family?

At last week's meeting he had learned that the United States, working through neutral nations, had agreed to accept Jewish immigrants from Germany and Hungary if the Nazis would allow them to leave. Thousands of visas would be authorized for Jewish children and for Hungarian relatives of American citizens. The news had seemed miraculous, an answer to Jacob's prayers. The visas that Avraham had tried so hard to procure for his family would finally be issued.

Today Jacob had brought with him a three-page list of names and addresses of relatives who still lived in Hungary. He was filled with hope, eager to begin filling out the visa applications. But his hope began to sink when he glimpsed the somber faces of the government officials.

"I am afraid I have bad news," one of them began. "The Nazis have refused our offer to allow the Jews to emigrate." A fist squeezed

Jacob's heart. "Nevertheless, we will accept your visa applications in the hope that the Nazis will change their minds in the near future."

Jacob sat in a daze of disappointment as the rabbis and Jewish leaders debated the other items on the agenda. He wished he could go home. The strenuous emotions and angry tempers exhausted him. But he would remain until the very end in order to fill out every last visa application, just in case Hashem decided to answer his prayers.

The roomful of tightly packed tables and chairs, the rows of over-stuffed bookshelves all faded into the background as Jacob listened to one of the leaders talk about the possibility of Allied bombing raids on Hungary. "Why not send American planes to destroy the railway junctions used for deporting Hungarian Jews to Poland?" the man asked.

"American bombers have been flying missions from a Soviet air base at Poltava," the spokesman confirmed. "But they are concentrating on military targets. Besides, the railway junctions could easily be repaired, causing only temporary delays in the deportations." Judging by his bland expression, he might have been discussing transports of cattle, not human beings.

"Yes," the rabbi replied, "but every day that the trains are delayed, lives would be saved."

Jacob rested his elbows on the table and put his head in his hands as he listened in despair to a proposal to bomb the Nazi deportation camp at Auschwitz.

"But thousands of Jews are being held there," a rabbi protested. "They would all be killed!"

"The plan is to put the camp out of business. True, some Jews might be killed—but if they are doomed anyway . . ."

"Then the Germans could accuse us of atrocities. We would be the ones massacring Jews."

Jacob listened until he could no longer remain silent. He stood, requesting permission to say something. "I speak for those of us who may have loved ones in those camps, and I beg you not to risk killing a single innocent person. Let the Nazis be accountable before Hashem for their deeds, not us."

When the debate ended, the Jewish leaders and rabbis unanimously opposed the plan to bomb Auschwitz.

The final topic of discussion was a "blood for goods" deal offered to the Allies by the Nazis. "The lives of one million Jews would be exchanged for ten thousand trucks and other military supplies that the Nazis need," the State Department spokesman said. "The British have refused to discuss this proposal, but President Roosevelt has ordered the negotiators to keep talking to the Germans."

"Why should we give food and army supplies to the Nazis?" someone asked.

"Because as long as we continue to talk about it, those one million Jews may continue to live."

Once again, Jacob asked to speak. "Food . . . trucks . . . wouldn't you willingly pay any ransom they demanded if it might spare the life of your child?"

When the meeting ended, Jacob filled out visa applications for all his family members and wearily left for home. "You shouldn't put yourself through this, Yaacov," the rebbe said as they stood on the subway platform. "It is too hard on your health." The underground air smelled of hot steel and too many people. The afternoon rush hour had begun, but Jacob and the rebbe managed to find empty seats in the overcrowded subway car. Commuters crammed the aisle beside them, gripping the leather straps, swaying with the train's movement as if in prayer.

"No, it is much worse to be at home doing nothing," Jacob replied, "wondering what is going on. As difficult as it is to know all these things, it is much harder not to know them. I find the silence unbearable."

At last they reached the final stop and climbed the steep cement stairs, emerging from underground for the short walk home. "What about those names I gave you?" Jacob asked the rebbe. "Has there been any progress in finding those people?"

"You mean David and Esther Fischer? I have sent inquiries to rabbis in other shuls in Brooklyn. Some I have heard from, some I have not."

Weeks had passed since Esther and Peter had shown Jacob their birth certificates and the Shaffers' marriage license. "We found out that Mama's maiden name was Fischer," Esther had told him. "Now what do we do? How do we find our grandparents?"

Jacob had realized the truth the moment he saw the names. Their mother, Rachel Fischer, was Jewish. How could he have forgotten? Miriam Shoshanna had told him about it shortly before she died. At the time, Jacob had been outraged to learn that Rachel had abandoned her faith to marry a gentile. He didn't want Miriam to have anything to do with her or her children. He had been so unbending back then—just as Rachel's parents no doubt were. They had disowned her, considered her dead to them, and Jacob would have done the same thing. Now he saw it differently. Why allow anything to separate a family? His son, his daughter-in-law, his grandchild might all very well be dead, but the Fischers' grandchildren were not.

"Fischer is a common name," he had told Esther and Peter as he had stalled for time. "I will have to think about it. I will let you know if I have any ideas."

He had asked Rebbe Grunfeld to help him. If the Fischers belonged to a Jewish congregation in Brooklyn, Jacob would find them through the network of synagogues who worked with the War Refugee Board.

Now the two men halted on the sidewalk in front of Jacob's apartment building. The rain had finally stopped, and the rebbe shook the water from his umbrella before folding it. "These children who live upstairs from you," he said. "They mean a lot to you, yes?"

Jacob nodded. "They do not know that their mother was Jewish, or that they are considered Jewish, as well. Their mother died alongside my Miriam. Their father is fighting the war in Europe. They deserve to meet their mother's family. I never realized how important a family was until Hashem chose to separate me from my own."

"Please don't blame Hashem," the rebbe said gently. "What you feel for your son, your longing to find him, to hear from him, to be reunited with him—imagine how much more Hashem longs for us, His children."

The words haunted Jacob as he said good-bye to the rebbe and went up the porch steps to his apartment. He had just turned on the lights and the radio when someone knocked on his door. He opened it, expecting to see the children, but found Penny Goodrich. She wore her work uniform and carried her lunch box and umbrella.

"I saw you come home ahead of me," she said, "so I knew the kids weren't here with you yet, and I wondered . . . could I talk to you alone for a minute?"

"Certainly. Come in."

She stepped across the threshold just far enough for him to shut the door, but she remained standing. "I have been thinking, Mr. Mendel. I know you told Esther and Peter that you would help them look for their grandparents, but I'm worried the children are going to get hurt. I mean . . . what if they find out something really terrible about them and . . . ?" She couldn't finish.

"Please, come in, Penny. Sit down." He led her to the sofa, and she slumped down on it, her body hunched over as if she expected to be beaten.

"Sorry . . . I'm sorry," she mumbled as she tried to compose herself.

"You do not need to apologize. . . . If you want to tell me what is wrong, I will gladly listen. But if not, then I will not pry."

She pulled a handkerchief from her sleeve and blew her nose, then took several deep breaths as if about to plunge into icy water. "I found out who my real parents are and now I wish I never had. The truth is so much worse that not knowing. I'm afraid the kids will find out something horrible, too, and they'll be so hurt—"

He waited while Penny blew her nose again and wiped her eyes. "What could they learn that would be so hurtful?" he finally asked. But even as he spoke the words, he wondered how they would feel to learn that their mother was Jewish.

"My mother gave me up because she didn't love me," Penny said. "She couldn't love me. She was raped."

Her words struck Jacob with brute force. What could he possibly say? He sat down beside Penny and rested his hand on her shoulder. "My poor, dear girl."

"I haven't told anyone except you. I can't tell anyone. I'm so ashamed."

"Why in the world should you be ashamed? You are innocent of any wrongdoing. You are not responsible for the misdeeds of your father." But he could tell she wasn't listening to him.

"It turns out my older sister, Hazel, is really my mother. My parents—the people I always thought were my parents—are my grandparents."

"Ah. I see." Jacob had suspected as much on the night they had celebrated Purim, after Penny mentioned a much-older sister and elderly parents. He had kept his suspicions to himself. But he had never imagined a rape.

"Eddie would never want to marry a wife who had a criminal for a father or let her be the mother to his children. No man would."

"Now, listen. Any man who would blame you for something you could not control is not worthy of you. Besides, I see no reason at all why you should even mention your father to Mr. Shaffer or to anyone else."

"Eddie deserves to know there's a criminal in my background. My father's traits are in my blood."

"Nonsense. Every single one of us is capable of sin, not just your father. This war has revealed mankind at our very worst, yes? Even the Scriptures show us some very revered men who have sinned. Moses and King David committed murder, yet Hashem used them in His work. Do not carry a burden of sin that is not yours. Hold your head up high, Penny. Scripture says that we must not blame children for the sins of their parents."

Penny nodded, but Jacob could see that she would need time to think about what he had said. The wound she had received was still much too raw.

"Have you talked to your birth mother since learning the truth?" he asked.

"She wouldn't want to see me, and who could blame her? I'm a reminder of a horrible tragedy. No wonder she never comes home to visit us."

"Perhaps. But I encourage you to see her, just the same. What is the worst thing that she might do? Tell you to go away? She cannot change the past by refusing to see you. It still happened. And you deserve to meet your real mother. Tell me, does she know that you have learned the truth?"

"I don't think so. I haven't spoken to her, and I don't think my parents will tell her."

"Then why not go to visit her as a sister? As if you never learned the truth? You can judge by her reaction how she feels about you. You strike me as sensible enough to understand why she might have bad feelings."

"Thank you, Mr. Mendel. Maybe I will." She heaved an enormous sigh and said, "Anyway, I'm telling you this because I'm worried about how the kids might react if they learned some awful truth about their mother."

"That is very thoughtful of you." Jacob considered for a moment, then decided to tell Penny what he'd been doing. "The children do not know it, but I have been searching for their family. I have already decided not to say anything to Esther and Peter until I learn more about their grandparents and their reasons for rejecting Rachel. I agree with you—I do not want them to be hurt in any way. I assure you that I will do my best to protect them."

"Thank you." She looked greatly relieved, as if she might want to hug him. "I guess I should go," she said, rising from the sofa.

"Before you do, may I talk with you about a concern that I have?"

"Of course! I'm sorry—"

"I am worried about Esther and the boy she has been seeing so often."

Penny appeared shocked. "A *boy* . . . ? What boy?"

"He lives in the building next door, and everyone in the neighborhood has heard quarreling in that family over the years. The boy is a little older than Esther, I believe, and I fear that he is also more worldly-wise. I have seen the two of them holding hands as they walk home from school."

"What?"

"I am sorry for shocking you. But they often stand out back in the alley for a while while he smokes a cigarette or two."

"I feel terrible! I had no idea! I should have been more careful and asked more questions—"

"It is not your fault." He rested his hand on her arm to calm her. "You have never raised children before. Besides, young people like Esther often want to act grown-up. They seldom tell their parents everything they are doing."

"My sister, Hazel—I mean, my mother. I mean . . ." She exhaled. "My parents said that Hazel started sneaking around behind their backs and that's how she got into trouble."

"I do not think it is nearly that serious. Esther has a good head on her shoulders. I only meant to say that school will soon close for the summer, and I think she should be supervised while you are at work. I may not be home every day to watch over her now that my work takes me away so often."

"You're right, Mr. Mendel. Thanks so much for telling me. I'll make sure the kids stay with their grandmother while I'm at work."

"I think that would be a good idea. And please think about what I said, yes? About visiting your mother?"

"I will." She edged toward the door. "I'd better get upstairs or they'll wonder what happened to me. Thanks for your help, Mr. Mendel."

"You are very welcome."

CHAPTER 33

JUNE 1944

ESTHER DUMPED CORNFLAKES into a bowl and poured milk over them. She could hear Penny bustling around upstairs, making the beds, collecting laundry—who knew what else? Esther wished she would hurry up and leave for work. Penny never allowed them to listen to the radio in the morning, saying she didn't want them to get distracted by it and be late for school. But Esther couldn't stand to wait all day to hear the latest news about the war.

At last Penny rushed into the kitchen and grabbed her lunch box from the tabletop. "Bye. I'm off to work. See you kids later."

Peter looked up from his cereal and waved to her.

"Bye," Esther said. She listened for the front door to close, and the moment it did, she leaped up from the kitchen table and hurried into the living room to turn on the radio, carrying her bowl of cereal with her. The downstairs door thumped shut just as the radio finished warming up.

"The long-awaited Allied invasion of Nazi-held territory in France began early this morning, Tuesday, June 6. According to reports, the assault began with the saturation bombing of coastal batteries by over one thousand RAF heavy bombers, followed by the nighttime airborne invasion by the U.S. 82nd and 101st Airborne Divisions, along with the British 6th Airborne Division . . ."

"Peter!" Esther shouted. "Peter, come here and listen to this!" He ran barefoot into the living room, wiping his mouth on his pajama sleeve. "They did it, Peter, they did it! You know the big invasion everyone's been waiting for? It's happening, right now over in France. It's finally D-Day!" He perched on the arm of the sofa, his mouth open in surprise as they listened together.

". . . At dawn, fifty convoys began landing five divisions of Allied troops on the beaches of northern France. Meanwhile, naval escort carriers and destroyer squadrons patrolled the English Channel for Nazi U-boats. According to early reports, the Allied Expeditionary Force met with stiff resistance on at least one of the landing sites, suffering severe losses . . ."

Before Esther could stop him, Peter jumped to his feet and switched off the radio. "What are you doing? Turn it on. I want to hear it." He blocked Esther's attempts to reach the dial, butting against her with his shoulders and elbows, furiously shaking his head. But she was bigger than he was, and stronger. She dodged his flailing arms and shoved him out of the way. "Move, Peter!"

He staggered to one side and fell to his hands and knees, and at first Esther feared she might have hurt him. But just as she heard the announcer say, "Late in the day, Nazi Panzer divisions began a counterattack against Allied forces," Peter yanked the plug out of the socket. The radio died.

"What did you do that for? Plug it in! I need to hear it." He continued to shake his head, his jaw thrust out in anger. He crouched in the corner with the plug in his fist, ready to fight back if she tried to approach him. "What is the matter with you? Daddy might be fighting in that invasion. Don't you want to hear it?"

Peter put his hands over his ears, shaking his head. She wanted to kick him in frustration. "Well, I want to hear it! Plug it back in!" He refused. He pointed to himself, then to her, then to the front door. Esther understood his sign language well enough to know what he was saying. They needed to get dressed and go to school or they would be late. And he was right.

"You make me so mad sometimes!" She stomped her foot. "This is one of the biggest battles in the whole war, and we're going to miss it, thanks to you!"

She ran from the living room and hurried upstairs, determined to get dressed before Peter did and beat him downstairs to the radio. They had moved Esther's bureau into Penny's room, and Esther had begun changing her clothes in there for privacy after Penny had taken her shopping for new undergarments. Esther had needed her first brassiere. She had been embarrassed at first, but several other girls in her class wore them, too.

Esther dressed as quickly as she could, but when she came out, Peter stood waiting for her by the bedroom door. He handed her the little chalkboard. He had written her a message: *I'm too scared to listen if Daddy might be there.*

Her anger melted away. Peter had witnessed the crash that had killed their mother, and now he didn't want to hear about a battle that might claim their father. Esther sighed. "Okay, I'll keep the radio off." They finished getting ready, grabbed their lunch boxes and book bags, and left the apartment together without saying another word.

The news vendor on the corner hawked his papers, shouting "Extra! Extra! D-Day invasion! Read all about it!" Esther longed to buy a copy, but there wasn't time.

At school, her teachers and fellow students talked about the Allied landing all morning. Her social studies teacher pulled down the roller map of Europe and showed them the narrow sliver of blue water called the English Channel and the Normandy coast where the invasion was taking place. Esther couldn't stop thinking about the war, wondering where her father was and what he was doing. She made up her mind to listen to the radio when she got home, whether Peter liked it or not.

She bounded up the porch steps after school and found two V-mail letters from Daddy in the mailbox—one for her and Peter, and the other for Penny. Roy Fuller had sent Penny a V-mail letter, as well. Esther read their father's letter first before giving it to Peter. Daddy had written it before the invasion while he was still somewhere in

England. He said that the Allies expected to cross the channel any day, as soon as the rain let up and the weather cleared.

She handed Daddy's letter to Peter, but he looked so frightened as he sat slumped on the sofa reading it that she didn't dare turn on the radio, afraid they would get into another argument like the one they'd had this morning. She left him alone and went downstairs to see if Mr. Mendel was home. He would listen to the news and talk about it with her. But he wasn't home. She trudged back upstairs and sat down at the dining room table with Peter to do her homework, then she practiced the piano. Finally Penny arrived home. Esther raced into the hallway to meet her.

"Did you get today's newspaper? Did you read it?" She had talked Penny into buying a newspaper at the bus station every afternoon on her way home from work, and Esther had begun cutting out articles and pictures the way Mr. Mendel used to do. She had used some of her allowance to buy a big scrapbook and a bottle of glue at the five-and-dime store and had already filled more than half of the scrapbook's pages with clippings.

"I bought two newspapers," Penny said. "This is a really big day, isn't it?"

"Everyone at school said it's the biggest day since Pearl Harbor."

"Here. Take both papers. I need to start supper."

Esther didn't ask Penny if she needed help. Instead, she carried the newspapers into the dining room, reading the front page as she walked. As soon as she sat down at the table with them, Peter closed his arithmetic book and disappeared up the stairs. Esther didn't care. She spread out the first paper and began to read, too excited to sit still. She cut out several articles about D-Day, as well as a big map that showed where the Allies had landed. She hadn't even finished cutting the first paper when Penny called her and Peter to dinner. Penny had heated up last night's leftover casserole along with a can of peas, opening a can of pears for dessert. They ate at the kitchen table.

"How's Roy?" Esther asked, remembering the letter.

Penny smiled and it seemed like a light bulb had switched on, lighting up her face. "He's doing good—same old Roy, always making corny jokes. He can't say where he is, of course, but he says the weather is hotter than a burnt biscuit. He feels like his skin is going to melt right off. He says they eat so much rice, day after day after day, that he never wants to eat another spoonful of it as long as he lives. Oh, and he said to be sure and say hi to you kids."

Esther scooped up a forkful of peas. She gobbled down her food like a starving person, eager to return to her newspapers. "I like Roy," she said. "I wish they hadn't sent him overseas. He said he might take us to Coney Island this summer and we'd go on all the rides at Luna Park."

"I know. Maybe we can find someone else to take us."

"Who?" Esther said with a huff. "There is nobody else."

"Roy added a note to you, Peter," Penny said. "He wants you to write and tell him how the Dodgers are doing this season. And he said he's sorry he won't be able to take you to a game like he had hoped."

Peter nodded without looking up.

After she and Penny washed and dried the dishes, Esther cut up the second newspaper. "Can we listen to a news program?" she asked when Penny turned on the radio. Peter tugged on Penny's sleeve, shaking his head in protest. Penny looked from one of them to the other.

"I think we should listen to a regular program, Esther. Isn't *The Lone Ranger* on tonight? You like that show, don't you?"

"But I want to hear the news!"

"There's plenty of news in the papers."

"But I want to hear more."

Penny put her arm around Peter's shoulder and pulled him close. "Not tonight," she said quietly.

Esther stomped her foot. "Why not?"

"You're becoming more and more obsessed with the news, Esther, and it isn't good for you. I think you should put the papers away for tonight and come listen to a program with us. Stop torturing yourself."

"I need to know what's happening!"

"Why? You can't change anything or control it."

Esther knew she was right. The battles raging over in France were as out of her control as the car that had killed her mother. She couldn't do anything to keep her father safe, either. "I want to know because I'm scared," she finally said.

"Peter, find us a program to listen to," Penny told him. While he knelt to tune the radio, she went to Esther.

Esther quickly crossed her arms and turned away, fearing that Penny would try to hug her. "Listen," Penny said gently. "Remember when we read Queen Esther's story with Mr. Mendel? Remember what he said? God was there with Esther all the time. He didn't say anything, but He was there, controlling all the details."

"But it's so hard to wait and not know what's happening."

"I know. It's hard for everyone who has loved ones fighting in the war. But as far as today's battle is concerned, your father probably didn't go ashore with all those other soldiers. The army won't need trucks and jeeps right away. They'll wait a few days until they can move away from the beaches and go farther inland, like the newspaper said they would do. He'll be okay."

"Just because Peter doesn't want to listen to the news doesn't mean I should have to wait. Why does he get his own way?"

"Because this time he's right. Hearing it would frighten all of us. We need to stay calm until we get another letter from your father. Then we'll know where he is and what he's doing. In the meantime, we have to stay strong. Think of poor Mr. Mendel. He hasn't received any news about his son in more than two years."

"I hate waiting to hear."

"I do, too. But we shouldn't let our imaginations run wild in the meantime. Worrying too much about your father isn't good for any of us."

"Why are you worried about Daddy?"

For a moment, Penny looked flustered. Her cheeks turned bright pink, as if the apartment were very warm. "Because he's my friend," she finally said. "Listen, as long as we're talking about your father, I want to read you part of the letter I got from him today." She pulled the V-mail from her apron pocket and unfolded it. "You listen, too, Peter. Your father said, 'I know the kids will be out of school for the summer soon, and I don't want them to stay home alone all day while you're at work, Penny.' "

"What? That's not fair! I'm old enough to stay home by myself. I don't need a baby-sitter."

Penny held up her hand for silence. "Don't stomp your foot like that, Esther. Poor Mr. Mendel will think the ceiling is coming down. This is what your father wrote: 'Last summer, the kids stayed with their grandmother during the day, and I think it would be a good idea if they stayed there this summer, too. Especially after what you told me about—' " Penny stopped reading and quickly refolded the letter. "Never mind. I read you the important part."

"Especially after what?" Esther asked. "I want to know what else Daddy said."

"It's private." Penny slid the letter into her pocket. "I know you're growing up, Esther, but with Mr. Mendel away so much of the time, we all agreed that it isn't a good idea for you to be here by yourselves. You can ride the bus with me when I leave for work in the morning and spend the day with your grandmother, then—"

"No, I don't want to. It's not fair! I won't get to spend any time with my friends!"

Jacky had promised Esther that they would hang around together this summer when he wasn't working at the grocery store. She had been looking forward to it.

"In exchange," Penny continued, "you and Peter get to stay home on the weekends instead of sleeping overnight at your grandmother's house. You'll have all day Saturday to be with your friends."

It was a small consolation. "Can I go to the movies with them?"

"Sure. And maybe the three of us can go other places together, like to the zoo or the beach."

"I'm still going to write to Daddy and tell him I'm old enough to stay home."

"You can try, but I don't think he'll change his mind," Penny said. "Your father also said that he doesn't think your grandma should be alone all day. She has too much time to feel sad about your uncle Joe. She's lonely without her family, Esther, just like Mr. Mendel is. You two kids have cheered him this past year and helped him not to miss his family so much. Now you need to spend some time with your grandma and cheer her up, too."

Esther wanted to scream in frustration. Then she thought of something else. "How am I supposed to practice the piano at Grandma's house? She doesn't have one."

"Well . . . I guess you'll have to wait until we get home every day—"

"That stinks! I was looking forward to summer and now it's ruined!" Esther stormed out of the dining room and just kept going, slamming the front door and thundering down the steps. She thought about telling her troubles to Mr. Mendel, but she knew that he probably would agree that they should spend time with their grandmother.

Esther unlocked the front door and stomped outside onto the porch just as Jacky Hoffman walked past the apartment. "Hey, hey, beautiful . . . What's wrong? Where are you running off to?"

Esther didn't want to tell him that she was angry for being treated like a baby—especially when she was pouting like one. She took a breath to calm down and shrugged her shoulders. "No place . . . Did you hear the news about the invasion?"

"Sure, everybody has."

"Yeah . . . well . . . I'm worried about my father."

He tilted his head to one side in sympathy. "You poor girl . . . Come here . . ." He reached out his hand to her in invitation, and she went down the porch steps to him. "Come with me, Esther." Jacky took her hand in his and led her around the corner of the house and down the narrow walkway between his apartment building and hers. When they reached his back courtyard, Jacky ducked into a cubbyhole beneath the stairs and pulled Esther down beside him. "This is my own special hangout," he said.

The dark space smelled musty, and there wasn't very much room. The ground was cold and damp beneath her skirt. But Esther's heart felt like it might jump right out of her rib cage as Jacky wrapped his arms around her and held her close. "There," he murmured. "Feel better now?"

"Yeah. Thanks." She hadn't felt this frightened and excited and breathless since Daddy took her on the roller coaster at Luna Park.

She wasn't sure if she should be alone with Jacky this way, but it felt so good to be held and comforted that she decided to stay. Esther missed her father's hugs.

"Where is your father stationed?" he asked.

"He's over in England. I'm worried that he might be in the D-Day invasion." Jacky listened patiently while Esther unloaded her fears, describing details from the news articles she had read. She talked until long after the sun had set and the first star began to shine in the evening sky. And all that time, Jacky kept his arms wrapped tightly around her, his cheek resting against her hair. Her cheek was pressed against his chest as they sat squished together in the tiny space.

She stopped talking when she heard footsteps shuffling up the walkway between the two buildings. Jacky put his finger over her lips to shush her. A figure emerged from the shadows, and Esther recognized her brother's silhouette in the dim light.

"That's Peter," she whispered. "He's looking for me."

"He can't see us. He'll go away."

"I should go home. They'll be worried."

"Stay just a little longer." Jacky began to caress her shoulder.

Esther didn't think her heart could beat any faster, but then it sped up, not from excitement but from unease. It no longer felt comfortable to be alone with him, sitting so close to him. She was afraid that he might try to kiss her, and she didn't want him to. Kissing was something that grown-ups did, and Esther didn't think she was ready to be a grown-up.

"I can't stay." She squirmed away from him and crawled out of the cubbyhole, brushing dirt from her damp, wrinkled clothes.

"Hey, don't go yet."

"I have to. Thanks for talking with me, Jacky." She ran back to her apartment as if someone was chasing her, her footsteps echoing in the narrow space between the buildings.

Chapter 34

Jacob sat at his desk late one afternoon, composing a fund-raising letter for the War Refugee Board, when he heard a knock on his door. He opened it to find Peter holding up his little slate with a message on it: *Can I use your radio?*

"My radio? Is something wrong with yours?"

He shook his head as he erased the words and wrote, *Esther likes the news and I don't.*

"Ah. I see. Yes, certainly, come in. Which program did you want to hear?" Peter held an imaginary bat in his hands and pantomimed hitting a baseball. "The baseball game. Of course, I should have guessed. Well, there is my radio. Help yourself to it."

Jacob returned to his work while Peter twirled the tuning dial, eventually finding the baseball game. He flopped down on his stomach on Jacob's rug, his chin propped on his fists. Several times in the past few weeks, Peter had complained to him about how often Esther listened to the news. Jacob knew she was worried about their father. The children still hadn't received a letter from him since the D-Day invasion, and to make matters worse, the Nazis had begun to fire their new, deadly V-1 missiles at military bases and civilian targets in England—where Ed Shaffer was stationed.

"Either way, Daddy is in danger," Esther had told Jacob, "whether he's fighting on the mainland or staying behind in England."

"If your father is in England," Jacob had told her, "I am sure he will find safety inside a bomb shelter when the V-1 missiles strike." His assurances hadn't helped. Esther continued her obsession with the news, which was why Peter came to his apartment every day.

Jacob could no longer concentrate on his letter. He laid down his pen and turned to Peter. "Have you ever watched your team play at the ball park?"

Peter nodded, then sat up and wrote, *Daddy used to take me.*

"I see. And is it different to watch a game in person?"

He nodded again and wrote, *Much better! I want to catch a fly ball.* Peter pointed to Jacob, silently asking if Jacob had ever seen a game.

"No, I have never been to a ball game. It is not something I would think to do."

The telephone rang and Jacob reached to answer it, recognizing Rebbe Grunfeld's voice greeting him. "I have good news, for you, Yaacov. I believe we have found David and Esther Fischer." Jacob stopped breathing. "They belong to a congregation in Crown Heights—Reform, not Orthodox. They're not observant. Their rebbe said they have two sons and a daughter named Rachel, who died. Does this sound like the people you are searching for?"

"Yes! Yes, it does!" Jacob couldn't stay seated. He paced in a small circle, as far as the telephone cord would reach.

"David Fischer is a medical doctor," the rebbe continued. "His wife does charity work, primarily with fine arts organizations."

"Is there a way I can contact them?" Jacob nearly dropped the telephone receiver as he shifted it to his other ear, searching his desktop for his pen and a blank piece of paper. "Did you get an address for me or . . . or a telephone number?"

Rebbe Grunfeld gave him both. By the time Jacob thanked him and hung up, he could have danced a little jig. He saw Peter sitting cross-legged, looking up at him, and he realized his voice had been raised in excitement.

"Sorry, Peter. Sorry. I did not mean to interrupt your game." Jacob longed to tell him the good news but knew that he'd better wait until after he'd met these grandparents. Penny Goodrich had been right to suggest caution in order to avoid hurting the children.

But Jacob could no longer concentrate on the work he'd been doing. Instead, he listened to the announcer's droning voice as he narrated the game, talking about RBIs and batting averages and something called a "full count." This baseball game was in an entirely new language. Avraham had shown some interest in baseball, playing back-lot games with his friends after school. But when Avi had been Peter's age, Jacob's work and all his meetings at the shul had kept him much too busy to attend a sporting event.

"Peter?" he asked suddenly. "Would you like to go to the ball field sometime and watch your team play?"

Peter scrambled to his feet, grinning and nodding his head so hard it looked as though it might come loose. Jacob rested his hand on his hair. "After school is out in a few weeks, I will purchase tickets for us. Perhaps Esther would like to come with us. And Penny, too." Peter wrapped his arms around Jacob in a fervent hug.

Jacob hugged him in return. He had found the children's family. A grandfather and grandmother. A miracle. David and Esther Fischer had two sons—two new uncles for the children. He felt so excited it was as if the Fischers were his own family. But now what to do? How should he approach them? Should he telephone first?

Jacob thought about it for the rest of the day before deciding that he would pay them a visit in person, unannounced. He would bring information to them about the War Refugee Board and begin by talking about the need for funds. The prospect made him too excited and nervous to sit still.

On a warm June afternoon, Jacob took a bus to Crown Heights and got off within walking distance of the Fischers' apartment—a stately limestone building on a quiet, tree-lined street. He had planned to go directly to their door and ring the bell, but a uniformed doorman stopped him in the spacious lobby. "May I help you, sir?"

Jacob hadn't counted on a doorman. He cleared his throat. "I am here to see David and Esther Fischer in apartment 612."

"Are they expecting you, sir?" Jacob shook his head. The doorman picked up a telephone receiver. "May I tell them your name, please?"

"Jacob Mendel. I work with the War Refugee Board." He held his breath as the doorman talked on the telephone for a moment. When the man hung up, he nodded and led Jacob to the elevator.

"Turn left on the sixth floor."

Esther Fischer was waiting for Jacob with her apartment door open. "Mr. Mendel? Hello, I'm Esther Fischer." She was an attractive woman in her late fifties with dark glossy hair and manicured nails. Jacob remembered how lovely Rachel Shaffer had been, as well. "Come in, please."

"Thank you." He touched the mezuzah on the doorpost before going inside.

"My sister and I were just having coffee in the living room. Would you care to join us?"

"Yes. Thank you."

Mrs. Fischer summoned her maid. "Kindly fetch another cup and some more coffee for my guest," she said, then led Jacob into a spacious living room with a fireplace and several seating areas. A baby grand piano filled one corner of the room and stunning artwork covered the walls. He glimpsed the East River in the distance through a set of tall windows.

"Mr. Mendel, this is my sister, Dinah Goldman." She gestured to an elegantly dressed woman seated on the sofa. "We know all about President Roosevelt's War Refugee Board and the work they are doing. It is a very worthy cause, and my husband has contributed generously."

"Yes . . . good, good." He felt tongue-tied and a bit guilty for coming here with hidden motives. He sat down in an armchair, and when the maid appeared with his cup of coffee, he took his time adding cream and sugar from a sterling silver tray on the table. "I see you have sons in the service?" he said, nodding to the flag in the window with two stars.

"Yes. One is an army surgeon stationed in England, and the other is with the Army Corps of Engineers in the Pacific. He rebuilds roads and bridges after they've been destroyed in the war. It seems like such a waste, don't you think? Blowing things up and then building them all over again?"

"Yes. War is a great tragedy for everyone." He spent a few minutes talking about his work and the need for more money for displaced refugees, then asked, "Have you heard about the president's plan to create an emergency refugee shelter here in the United States? It has just been approved, and I believe that plans are under way for the first shelter to be built in upstate New York, in a town called Oswego. The first Jewish refugees will come from areas that have already been liberated, such as southern Italy."

Mrs. Fischer set down her cup, shaking her head. "The president is going to encounter a great deal of opposition to any plan that allows more Jews into this country."

"I understand he had to promise that they would all leave the country again after the war. But at least they will be safe, for now."

"I don't understand such prejudice and hatred," Mrs. Goldman said. "Do you, Mr. Mendel?"

"No. But I have seen it firsthand. I left Hungary as a young man, thinking I would be free from it here in America. But hatred is everywhere, I believe." He paused while the maid poured more coffee into his cup, then he nervously cleared his throat. "Mrs. Fischer, I hope you will forgive me. I do raise funds for the War Refugee Board, but that is not the only reason that I came to see you. I-I knew your daughter, Rachel."

Her posture stiffened as she looked away. "I don't wish to talk about her," she said in a tight voice. "My daughter is dead."

"I know. I know she is. Rachel lived in the apartment upstairs from me. She was with my wife, Miriam Shoshanna, when the car went out of control. They died together."

Mrs. Fischer remained tight-lipped, struggling to stay in control.

She stared into the distance, not at him. Mrs. Goldman slid closer to her sister and took her hand.

"I'm very sorry for your loss," Mrs. Goldman said. "But surely you can understand why my sister doesn't want to talk about it."

Jacob set down his cup and continued talking. "For a long time I felt that the accident was my fault. It was my habit to shop at the market for Miriam on the eve of Shabbat. But I was too busy to go that day. And so your Rachel went with her instead."

"She is not my Rachel," Mrs. Fischer said softly. "My husband says she is no longer our daughter. She died to us several years before the accident."

"I understand. In the past I would have felt the same way as your husband does if my child had married a gentile. But not anymore. Not since this war began." Mrs. Fischer finally looked at him, waiting for him to explain. "I have only one child, Mrs. Fischer—a son named Avraham. Before the war, he went overseas to Hungary to study Torah. He got married and had a little daughter, Fredeleh. I have not heard from him in two and a half years."

Mrs. Fischer's expression softened. "Please accept my sympathies—for the loss of your wife and for your missing son."

"I would give everything I have—my own life, even—if I could bring Miriam back, or bring Avi and his family home. I have never met little Fredeleh, my only granddaughter. But I have met your grandchildren, Mrs. Fischer. They live upstairs from me. And I have grown to love them very much."

A tear slipped down Mrs. Fischer's cheek. He couldn't know why. She drew her sweater tightly around her body and crossed her arms as if she felt a chill. But she didn't reply.

"You do know that Rachel had two children, yes? And that she named her daughter after you?"

She closed her eyes. "Please stop," she whispered.

But Jacob would not. "Esther just turned thirteen. She plays the piano beautifully—"

Mrs. Fischer sprang to her feet, bumping the coffee table, spilling the coffee from Jacob's cup onto the saucer. "You need to leave now. I'm sorry."

He braced his hands on the armrests and slowly stood. "The children asked if I would help them find their grandparents. I did not tell them that I had found you—or that you are Jewish. They are wondering why you want nothing to do with them."

"My daughter converted and became a Christian. A *Christian*, Mr. Mendel! My husband did everything he could think of to discourage her and bring her back to us. He offered to send her to the finest music conservatory or let her take a trip abroad—anything she wanted. We have never been religious people, but . . . but this was unacceptable to us. David thought that if we disowned her, pronounced her dead to us, that she would change her mind and come home. Instead, she fell in love. She met a Christian man and married him."

"Yes, Edward Shaffer. And your daughter has two beautiful children. Did I tell you about Peter?"

"I don't want to hear—"

"Peter's hair is the same color that his mother's was—and as yours is. He recently turned ten, and he is a very smart little boy. He loves baseball, the Brooklyn Dodgers. I have promised to take him to a game this summer because he has no one else to take him. His father is stationed overseas in England. He has been away for ten months now."

Mrs. Fischer covered her face. Her shoulders shook as she wept. Her sister rose to comfort her. Jacob talked louder, faster, aware that he might never have a chance to speak to her again.

"The day the children's father went away to war, Peter stopped talking. It was not a conscious choice on his part, but a result of the trauma of losing his mother and then his father. He needs the love of a family to help him heal. He needs you, Mrs. Fischer."

"Why are you doing this to me?"

"Do you read the newspapers? Are you aware of what Hitler is doing to the Jewish population of Europe? So many, many people have already lost their families, myself included. Our loved ones have been taken from us by force, and we had no choice in the matter. But you do have a choice, Mrs. Fischer. You still have a family. They live in the apartment upstairs from me. And they need you."

"My husband will never allow it."

"You may lay the blame on him if that helps ease your conscience. But it seems to me that it is your decision as much as his. No matter where those children worship or who their father is, they are still Jewish by birth, through your daughter. You did not lose these beautiful grandchildren of yours. They are found."

"I wouldn't know what to say to them."

"If you would like, you may come to my home and meet them. I will not tell them who you are unless you give me permission."

"My husband would never allow it," she said again.

"Would you like me to talk to him?"

"I-I don't know . . . I need some time . . ."

"It seems to me that too much time already has been lost. I would give everything I have for more time with my wife, my son." Jacob pulled a note from his pocket and gave it to her. "Here is my address and telephone number. Please call me when you decide."

One week later, after Jacob had given up all hope that he would hear from her, Mrs. Fischer called. They arranged for her to come to Jacob's apartment that afternoon, just before the children arrived home from school. "They always visit me as soon as they get home," he assured her.

Mrs. Fischer brought along her sister, and as the time approached, the two women sat on Jacob's sofa as if it were stuffed with rocks. He feared that Mrs. Fischer might change her mind at any moment and leap up to run from the apartment.

At last he heard children's footsteps tromping up the porch steps. The lid to the mailbox squeaked as they checked for letters. Esther's key rattled in the front door lock. The children knocked on his door as soon as they came inside. Jacob hurried to open it, as nervous as Mrs. Fischer was.

"Hi, Mr. Mendel. Guess what happened in school today—" Esther stopped short when she saw the two women. Peter nearly bumped into her as he walked into the apartment behind her. "Oh, you have company. I'm sorry."

"No, no. Come in, please. Have a piece of cake with my friends and me." It felt awkward not to introduce the two women by name, but Jacob had no choice. "Ladies, these are my friends, Esther and Peter Shaffer. They live in the apartment upstairs from me."

The children sat on the floor in front of the coffee table to eat the cake he'd sliced for them while Jacob nervously tried to make conversation. "So . . . only three more days of school, yes? Then summer vacation?"

"Yes. Finally! I can't wait for school to get out." For the next few minutes, Esther filled in all the awkward spaces with small talk, describing the last few days of her school year. When Mrs. Fischer finally joined in, her voice sounded hoarse.

"What grade are you in, Esther?"

"I'm finishing seventh and Peter is in fourth."

"Do you have a favorite subject?"

"Mine is music. I play the piano. Peter likes science, right?" He nodded shyly. Esther paused to finish eating her cake, then said, "Our father is stationed over in England. Yesterday we finally got a letter from him, the first one since the D-Day landing. I was getting so worried about him, but he's safe."

"I have a son serving in the army over in England. He is a doctor. I haven't heard from him since D-Day, either, but I know he's probably very busy, taking care of all the wounded soldiers."

"Hey! Maybe he knows our father. Daddy sometimes repairs ambulances when they break down."

They talked until the cake was gone and the conversation began to lag. Esther rose to her feet, pulling Peter to his feet, too. "Come on, Peter. We should go. I'm sure Mr. Mendel wants to visit with his guests now. Besides, I need to practice. I have a piano lesson tomorrow—the last one before summer starts. I wish I didn't have to stop lessons, but my teacher is going away on vacation. Thanks for the cake, Mr. Mendel. And it was very nice meeting you."

"It was nice meeting you, too."

Jacob walked the children to the door and said good-bye. When he turned back to face their grandmother and great aunt, the women had stood, preparing to leave. Mrs. Fischer's hand trembled as she held it over her mouth. Tears filled her eyes.

"You're right," she said. "The children are lovely. . . . We need to go now."

"No, wait a moment longer please," Jacob said. "I would like you to hear something." They all stood in awkward silence for a few moments until Esther began to practice the piano upstairs, starting with the exercises she always played to limber up her fingers.

Her grandmother covered her face and wept.

Jacob waited, not wanting to rush past her tears with words. He had spent too many years hurrying past tears, afraid of emotion. When the music stopped, he finally spoke, his voice hushed. "You are welcome to come back and visit any time," he said.

CHAPTER 35

PENNY SET THE TWO GROCERY SACKS down on her parents' kitchen table. "How long are you going to stay mad at me?" she asked her mother. The question had festered inside Penny as she had walked up and down the grocery aisles with her silent mother, then traipsed home from the store in the sullen June heat.

"How long are you going to go against our wishes?" Mother's eyes looked as cold and hard as coal.

Penny took out a handkerchief and wiped perspiration from her forehead. "What about my own wishes?" she asked. Mother grunted in reply, her lips pressed together in a tight line. Penny hated the boulder of ice that stood between them but didn't know how to melt it.

"There is no reason in the world why you can't quit all this nonsense and come home," Mother said. "Those children are with their grandmother all day now that school is out. They can just as easily spend the night, too. It's time to stop all this traipsing back and forth. Time to get rid of those hideous, unladylike trousers and start acting like our daughter again."

Penny looked down at her uniform and sighed. She hadn't changed her clothes after her shift at the bus station, in a hurry to take her mother on this errand. Besides, all of her clothes were at Eddie's apartment. She started to defend herself, then stopped. It was useless to argue with her parents, and even more useless to hold a grudge against them for not telling her she was adopted. Grudges did no one any good. The past could never be changed.

None of them had mentioned the argument they'd had a month ago or the fact that Penny's parents were really her grandparents. She still called them Mother and Dad. But Penny knew that she was not the same person, the same daughter, who had left home to take care of Eddie's children last fall.

"Is there anything else I can help you with before the kids and I go home?"

"Oh, so that apartment is your home now? Not here with us?"

"It's the children's home. I'm sure you can see that their grand-mother's house isn't a proper home for them."

Mother turned away without replying. Penny wished she knew how to make things right between them so they could talk to each other without fighting. She wished that, just once, her mother would look at her with love in her eyes instead of disappointment and stern disapproval. She had wished for it all of her life, carrying the longing like a burden that grew heavier each year. But wishes seldom came true.

Penny finished emptying the grocery bags, putting the cans away in the cupboard and storing the eggs in the refrigerator. How had they come to this terrible impasse? She paused to gaze out the kitchen window, and as she watched Peter romping around the yard with Woofer, Penny remembered how it had started. She had fallen in love with Eddie Shaffer and had leaped at the chance to become part of his life. It had started with the hope that he would love her, too, and maybe marry her someday. But that seed of hope had grown out of control into a sprawling, tangled vine, uprooting secrets and changing her life completely. So much upheaval—and in the end, Eddie probably wouldn't marry her after all. Mr. Mendel had said that the crime her real father had committed wasn't her fault, but even if Eddie did fall in love with her after the war, he deserved to know the truth about her.

Penny finished stowing the groceries. She wanted to go home. Yes, she did think of the apartment as her home now. Maybe there would be a letter from Eddie or Roy today. Roy's letters always made her smile as he described his clumsy attempts to express his love to Sally. He still counted on Penny for advice, even though his love life was already much more successful than Penny's was. She wrote to both men nearly every day, trying to boost their morale by reminding them of the life they would return to one day. Meanwhile, Penny's life had fallen into an enjoyable routine after ten months—but it would all turn upside down again when the war ended. And the war would end soon. The news from Europe was good. The Allies were making progress.

"If there's nothing else you need help with," Penny told her mother, "I guess I'll take the kids home."

"Your father might need something. He can't get around like he used to, you know. There are a lot of things he can't do anymore."

"I'll ask him." Penny could see how much her parents had aged in the past year, and her guilt mushroomed every time they reminded her of it. But had they really imagined that she would stay here and live with them forever?

She found her father napping in his chair in the living room. The cigar he held between his fingers had burned out. She hesitated, wondering if she should wake him, and as she looked around the room for a chore that might need to be done, she saw her parents' address book lying open on top of the desk. The book would have her sister Hazel's address in it.

Penny tiptoed to the desk and picked it up. She couldn't remember Hazel's married name, so she started leafing through all of the pages, searching for *Hazel*. All the while, she watched the kitchen door for her mother and stole glances at her father to make sure he stayed asleep.

Halfway through the names she found it: *Hazel and Barry Jeffries*. They lived in Trenton, New Jersey, not even a hundred miles away. But it may as well be a thousand miles as far as her parents were concerned. Penny tore off a slip of paper and quickly copied down the address, then put the book back where she'd found it. Now all she had to do was summon the courage to go to New Jersey and talk to her sister—her mother.

Penny's father stirred in his sleep and opened his eyes. "Dad? I'm leaving in a minute," she told him. "Is there anything you want me to do before I go?"

He shifted and sat up straight. "Can't think of anything."

Penny started to leave, then had another thought. "Say, Dad— Peter wants to plant a victory garden next door."

"Who does?"

"Peter Shaffer, the little boy I'm taking care of. I know how much you enjoy looking after your tomatoes and rhubarb plants every summer—do you think you could help him with it?"

Her father studied his dead cigar, frowning before placing it in the ashtray. "I can barely manage my own garden anymore. Wasn't sure I'd even have one this year."

"I know. But you wouldn't have to do any work. Just look over Peter's shoulder once in a while and encourage him. Maybe give him a few pointers."

"What does he want to grow?"

"Some tomatoes and beans and things. He started the seedlings at school, and the teacher gave the kids a little booklet that tells all about growing a victory garden. He's been keeping the plants in his bedroom, but shouldn't they go into the ground soon?"

"Of course. It's June already."

"Could you help us pick a good spot on Mrs. Shaffer's side of the yard to plant them? The kids and I will do all the digging. The backyard at our apartment is so shady I don't think anything can grow there, even grass. The ground is as hard as cement."

"I suppose I could have a look. But he'll have to tell me what he wants to grow."

"Thanks, Dad. We'll start bringing the plants over here tomorrow. It'll give Peter something to do all summer." It would give her father something to do, as well. And maybe if he made friends with Peter and Esther, he would begin to understand why she had volunteered to take care of them in the first place, and why they needed her so badly.

"I'll see you tomorrow."

Penny went out to the kitchen to get her pocketbook, and was about to tell her mother good-bye when someone pounded on the front door, ringing the bell like a five-alarm fire. She ran through the living room to open it and found Esther on the doorstep, crying and wringing her hands.

"Penny! Penny, come quick! You gotta help us!"

"What's wrong? Is somebody hurt?" Penny's heart raced out of control, as it always did when she was reminded of her heavy responsibility for these children.

"Woofer got out of the house and she ran away! Hurry, we have to catch her!" Esther jogged in place as if ready to take off running. Penny dropped her purse on the floor and hurried after her.

"What happened? How did she get out of the yard?"

"Peter held the front door open too long and she ran out between his legs. You know how Grandma is always hollering at us to shut the door so the dog won't get out and now . . . now she's furious with Peter!"

Woofer was nowhere in sight when Penny reached the street. Grandma Shaffer stood on her front step, calling to the dog in a tremulous voice. Peter stood watching helplessly, unable to call to the dog he loved. Penny ran to him and pulled him into her arms.

"It's okay, Peter. It's going to be okay. We'll find her. Do you know which way she went?" He pointed in the direction of the bus stop and the busy boulevard. Penny's heart sank with dread. "Come on," she said. She took off jogging up the street, with Esther and Peter right behind her, calling the dog's name, whistling for her.

"Woofer has never been out of the backyard before, except on a leash." Esther said, breathing hard. "What if she gets hit by a car?"

"Don't talk like that, Esther. We'll find her. She can't be far." They ran until they were out of breath, then walked up and down the streets, around and around the block, calling Woofer's name, asking neighbors and passersby if they had seen her. No one had.

An hour passed and the sun moved lower in the sky. Suppertime had come and gone. All three of them were hungry and exhausted. "We need to go home," Penny said.

"You're giving up? We can't give up!"

"I'm not giving up, Esther, but it'll soon be too dark to see. We'll need to come back with flashlights. Besides, we need to eat something. Woofer must be getting hungry, too. Maybe she'll come home for dinner on her own."

Penny rounded the corner toward home and saw Grandma Shaffer still standing on the front step, calling Woofer's name. When she saw the three of them dragging home without the dog, she went inside to her bedroom and shut the door, inconsolable. Penny opened a can of soup and made sandwiches, but no one felt much like eating. Peter got his grandmother's flashlight from the kitchen drawer and stood by the door with it, waiting to resume the search. They combed the neighborhood for another hour with no luck.

"We need to head home," Penny finally told them.

"No, I want to stay at Grandma's house tonight," Esther said, "so we can search some more in the morning." Peter nodded in agreement.

"Well . . . I guess we could do that." Penny would have to sleep in her old bedroom at her parents' house. She wondered if she would be welcome. She could wear the same uniform tomorrow, and maybe there would be time to resume the search before work. "Let's leave the porch lights on all night and the back gate open in case Woofer decides to come home during the night."

"She's never been outside all night before," Esther said. "She'll be so scared. What if she gets hit by a car or somebody kidnaps her?"

Penny didn't reply. What could she say? She couldn't reassure them that everything would be okay. Peter looked so dejected and guilt-ridden that all Penny could do was hold him in her arms and let him cry. "It isn't your fault, Peter. Woofer is the one who decided to be a bad dog and run away. She could have escaped when any one of us opened the door, even your grandmother."

"Can we pray for Woofer to be safe?" Esther asked. "Is it okay to pray for a dog?"

Once again, Penny didn't know the answer. She said good-night to everyone and went next door to sleep at her parents' house. As she lay in her old bed, staring at the ceiling, she wished she could do something more—but what? She didn't have the good sense that God gave a green bean.

CHAPTER 36

Budapest, Hungary

Dear Mother and Father Mendel,

The thing we have long feared has finally happened. The Nazis have come for us.

They surrounded our ghetto shortly before dawn, hundreds of soldiers with guns and dogs. They awakened us with gunfire and loudspeakers, shouting, "All out! All out! Anyone who does not come out will be shot." They gave us only moments to pack a few of our things before herding us outside into the street. Mama and Fredeleh and I quickly did as we were told. We had been sound asleep only moments before, so we could barely think, let alone decide what we might need or what we should take with us.

When we got outside we heard screaming and gunshots and weeping as the Nazis went from house to house, searching. They shot anyone who tried to hide. All of the elderly people and those who were too sick to get out of bed were killed on the spot.

We stood huddled in the courtyard while all of this went on, shivering with fear. As the sky slowly grew light, I could hardly bear to look into our neighbors' faces. We all knew what was coming next. We have all heard enough stories by now to suspect that the rumors are true.

When everyone in the ghetto had been evacuated or killed, the Nazis marched us through the streets as fast as we could go, shouting at us to hurry, hurry! They didn't take us to Budapest's train station, but to the freight yard on the edge of town. There we saw a long line of empty boxcars standing with their doors open. The soldiers pointed guns at us and herded us inside the freight cars like animals.

All I could think of was that I should have done what Avi said. I should have saved Fredeleh a long time ago while I still had the chance. I couldn't stop weeping, from regret as much as from fear, as I prayed to Hashem and pleaded with Him for help.

Hundreds of us were stuffed into a single train car—the few men who were left and all the women together with no privacy. There was not even enough room for everyone to sit down. We were given one bucket with drinking water and another empty bucket for necessity. When there were so many of us jammed inside that we could barely breathe, they rolled the door closed and locked it. All around me, people were weeping, cursing, praying. Some lost their minds with fear. I huddled close to Mama, clutching Fredeleh in my arms, praying for a miracle— and for forgiveness. How could Avraham ever forgive me for not taking Fredeleh to safety at the Christian orphanage?

Mama did her best to soothe me, trying to keep me calm for Fredeleh's sake. "I love you, Sarah Rivkah," she said as she held me close. "You have been a wonderful daughter to me. I want

*you to know, no matter what happens, how much I love you
and Fredeleh."*

*"Please don't talk like that, Mama. We'll be okay. They're
just taking us to a work camp."*

"I know. I know."

But we both knew the truth.

*The train stood on the side rail with the doors sealed shut
for a very long time. The summer sun grew hot, the boxcar
stifling. The train still had not begun to move when we heard
a commotion outside. The people who were close to the door
and were able to see between the wooden slats told us that a big
black car had pulled up outside. It was the kind that important
officials drove and had blue and yellow flags flying from it.
Swedish flags, someone said.*

*While the German authorities spoke to the man in the car,
a group of men began moving along the tracks behind the line
of railcars, stuffing papers between the wooden slats to those of
us inside. My mother managed to grab one of them. We stared
at it, not sure what it was, before deciding that it was some sort
of identification paper. It bore the blue and yellow colors of the
Swedish flag, and an insignia with three crowns on it, along
with a lot of important-looking stamps and seals.*

*"The German soldiers are coming back to the railcars,"
those nearest the door informed us. We could hear the doors
to the other boxcars up the line from ours sliding open. A few
minutes later, our door rolled open, too. Fresh air and blinding
sunlight poured inside.*

*One of the soldiers called out to us: "If there are any
Swedish nationals on board, come out and show your papers."
People began pushing toward the open door, jumping down from
the cars, waving the papers that had just been passed to us. But*

we had only one paper for the three of us. Mama pushed it into my hands.

"Take it, Sarah Rivkah. You and Fredeleh, go! Hurry!"

"No. I won't leave you, Mama."

"You need to save yourself and Fredeleh. Go!" I clung to my mother, unwilling to leave her behind, but Mama shoved me as hard as she could toward the door. Fredeleh clung to me, screaming in all the confusion.

I wanted to save my daughter. I would do anything for her. And I knew that Mama wanted the same thing for me. But how could I leave my mother behind in a car meant for animals—to go who knows where?

I felt hands pushing me. I looked over my shoulder, but Mama wasn't there. She had disappeared in the overcrowded car, shrinking back among the others so I could no longer see her. I knew she wanted to make it easier for me, and also that she didn't want to watch Fredeleh and me leave. The other people in the car continued to push me forward, saying, "Hurry, girl! Go! You have a paper."

Just as I was about to step off the train with Fredeleh, a young mother pushed her way to the open door and shoved her baby toward me. Terror filled her eyes. "Take him, please," she begged. "Have mercy and take my child so he will live!" I saw her desperation and her love. "His name is Yankel Weisner. He is four months old. I am Dina Weisner, his mother."

The baby and his mother were both crying. I was, too. I shifted Fredeleh to my hip and propped the baby against my shoulder. His mother gave him one last kiss.

My legs felt so weak I could barely walk as I stepped off the train. I went forward, clutching the two children, and showed the German soldier my paper. My heart pounded with fear. Would he believe me?

He looked over the document for a very long time, glancing up at the two children and me. At last he handed it back to me. "You may go."

We were free. Fredeleh and I and baby Yankel were all free.

I set Fredeleh down and we hurried toward the black car with the Swedish flags on it. A group of people from the trains had gathered around it, and they beckoned to the others and me, calling us to come, to follow them. When everyone who had Swedish papers had gotten off the trains, the soldiers turned back to the boxcars, walking down the line, closing the doors again and sealing them shut. The sound of those doors slamming and locking shivered through me. I couldn't watch.

I turned and followed the black car as it drove slowly away from the freight yard, clutching Fredeleh's hand in mine, holding the baby tightly against my chest. Some of the Swedish men walked with us, leading the way back into Budapest. No one spoke a word. I felt as though I were sleepwalking.

When we had walked about a quarter of a mile, the shriek of a train whistle sounded in the distance behind us. Then iron wheels began rumbling along the tracks as the long line of freight cars moved away from us, leaving Budapest. The whistle shrieked again. I will hear the sound of that train for as long as I live.

CHAPTER 37

A WEEK HAD PASSED since Mrs. Fischer came to Jacob's apartment to meet her grandchildren, and he had not heard a single word from her. He paced the floor in his living room, glancing at the telephone from time to time, debating whether or not to call Mr. and Mrs. Fischer and tell them that he did not understand such hardheartedness. But that wasn't entirely true. He did understand it. He used to be every bit as inflexible as they were.

He stopped pacing and turned away from the telephone. He needed to stop thinking about the Fischers and find something to do. He headed toward the kitchen to fix something to eat when he heard footsteps thumping across the porch, then a key in the lock. Penny and the children must be home. They hadn't come home at all yesterday—on a weeknight, no less—and he had been concerned about them. He met them at his front door and saw three very sad faces.

"Something terrible has happened!" Esther said. "Grandma Shaffer's dog ran away yesterday. We looked and looked for her, but we can't find her!"

"I am so sorry to hear that." These children already had suffered so much loss—why another one? Esther had told Jacob how much Peter loved that dog, how he wished that the dog was his.

"Is it okay to pray for a dog, Mr. Mendel? Grandma misses Woofer so much, and she was already sad because Uncle Joe died."

Jacob paused, searching for the right words to say. "I think you know by now that prayer is not a magic spell that we say so Hashem will give us what we wish for. But you can pray that Hashem will comfort your grandmother when she grieves. And we can—" Jacob stopped. He felt like a hypocrite. How had Hashem comforted him when he had grieved all these months for Miriam and Avraham? Then he saw Peter and Esther standing in front of him, looking to him for help, and he knew that Hashem had sent these children into his life. Their love had indeed comforted him. He could do the same for them.

Jacob opened his arms to them and drew them close. "We must trust Hashem," he murmured, "even when we cannot see Him working." He spoke the words to himself as much as to the children. He remembered the words he recited every year on *Tisha B'Av* when his people mourned the destruction of their temple, and now he offered them as comfort: " 'Though He brings grief, He will show compassion, so great is His unfailing love. For He does not willingly bring affliction or grief to the children of men.' " And as he held the children in his arms, Jacob felt Hashem's comfort, as well.

Shortly after the children went upstairs to eat their dinner, the telephone rang. He recognized Mrs. Fischer's voice and his pulse sped up.

"I have a proposal for you, Mr. Mendel. Well, it's really a proposal for the children. I would like to arrange for Esther to study at the Brooklyn Conservatory of Music this summer. Could you help me do that? Do you think she would like to study there?"

He couldn't speak for a moment. "Yes! Yes, I'm sure it would be possible. I would first need to speak with the young woman who takes care of the children, and I would need to ask Esther, of course."

"This must all be done anonymously, Mr. Mendel. She cannot know that the scholarship is coming from me, or that I am her grandmother."

He opened his mouth to chide Mrs. Fischer for not stepping forward and becoming part of the children's lives, but then changed his mind. "Tell me more about this school."

"The conservatory has been around since the 1890s, and it's in a lovely old mansion in Park Slope. They teach students of all ages. I have friends on the board of directors there. Esther can take private piano lessons, music history, theory classes—anything she would like. And she may continue her lessons in the fall, if she wishes. Just bring her over to the conservatory's admissions office, and she can sign up for whatever she wants to. I'll make arrangements to pay all of her expenses."

"That is very generous of you, Mrs. Fischer. I am sure she will be delighted." What a relief to know that Esther would have something to keep her occupied this summer besides the unsavory neighbor boy and her obsession with the news reports.

"I would like to do something for Peter, as well," Mrs. Fischer continued. "It could be music lessons if you think he would enjoy them, or whatever else you suggest."

"Peter has been taking piano lessons, but he does not have the same interest or ability that his sister has. What he does love is baseball. I have been wondering myself if there might be a team for him to join, but under the circumstances . . . the fact that he does not talk . . . I have not been able to come up with a solution. He never plays outside with the other boys because they make fun of him."

Mrs. Fischer's silence lasted so long that Jacob wondered if the telephone had gone dead. At last she spoke. "I have an idea, but I'm not sure if . . . well, let me tell you what it is and you can decide. Our synagogue sponsors a baseball team for our youth during the summer months to help keep the kids occupied. They practice a couple of times a week and sometimes play against teams from other yeshivas. I know the man who coaches the boys. I could speak with him and explain about Peter . . . that is, if you think his family would allow it. They might not want him to be part of a Jewish team since they are Christians."

"I think Peter might enjoy it, but again, I will have to talk to the family."

"Good. Good. Our shul isn't far from the music conservatory and it would give him something to do while Esther takes lessons. If she decides to study there, that is."

Jacob could hear the excitement in Mrs. Fischer's voice. He longed to encourage her to announce the news to the children herself and accept their thanks firsthand, but he remained quiet for now. At least their grandmother had stepped into their lives for the first time—and it was a momentous first step.

Jacob waited until he thought the children might be in bed that evening, then went upstairs to talk to Penny about Mrs. Fischer's offer. She looked very surprised to find him at her door. "Mr. Mendel, come in. I hope nothing's wrong . . ."

"No, everything is fine. In fact, I have good news. Could you come downstairs, please, so we can talk? I do not want the children to hear what I have to say."

Penny closed her door and followed Jacob down to his apartment. "I have found the children's grandparents," he said as soon as they were inside.

Her eyes went wide. "Really? That's wonderful!"

"Well, yes and no. I have also learned the reason for the estrangement—and the separation is likely to continue, I'm afraid."

"But why? What could be so terrible that it could keep a family apart this way?"

"Please sit down, Penny." She sat down on the sofa and he pulled out his desk chair to sit across from her. "This may come as a shock to you . . . but the children's mother was Jewish. Their grandparents are Jewish. The estrangement between them began when Rachel left the Jewish faith to become a Christian. When she married Ed Shaffer, a gentile, it was the final straw."

"Oh my! I had no idea. . . ."

"The fact that Rachel was Jewish was one of the reasons why I think she and my wife became so close. Miriam Shoshanna was like a mother to her in many ways. But you must understand that the Jewish people have been able to endure in exile for thousands of years precisely because we have always discouraged mixed marriages—to the point of expulsion from our family when a child marries outside of the faith. I know that seems harsh, but . . ." His voice trailed off. He didn't know how to finish. He saw the confusion and astonishment on Penny's face as she tried to digest his words.

"However," Jacob continued, "even though Mrs. Fischer is not ready or able to publicly accept Esther and Peter as her grandchildren—"

"You met their grandmother? You talked to her?"

"Yes. I went to her apartment, then invited her to come here to meet the children. They did not know who she was when they visited with her, only that she and her sister were my guests. Mrs. Fischer also had the opportunity to hear Esther play the piano. Now she has offered to pay for music lessons for Esther this summer—but she wants to do so anonymously. She says there is an excellent school here in Brooklyn where Esther can take classes. A music conservatory."

"That would be a dream come true for her. I know she's frustrated because her piano teacher will be away for most of the summer."

"All you need to do is take Esther to the school and sign up for the lessons. Mrs. Fischer will pay for the classes."

"I can take her this Saturday on my day off. Can you come with us, Mr. Mendel?"

"I would love to, but I cannot. Saturday is Shabbat—our Sabbath day." Jacob surprised himself even as he spoke the words. Slowly, without even realizing that he'd done so, Jacob had returned to Hashem's Torah and the routine of prayers and holy days and rules of kashrut. Most of the time it seemed completely natural to him.

He still had many, many unanswered questions, but he knew that Hashem revealed His will through His Word. The way to find answers was through obedience to that Word.

"I am sure you will be able to handle everything just fine by yourself," he told Penny. "Their grandmother has made all of the arrangements."

"I can't wait to tell Esther. She'll be so excited."

"Mrs. Fischer also asked if Peter would enjoy piano lessons, but we decided that he would much rather play on a baseball team this summer."

"I think he would like that, but the neighborhood kids make fun of him."

329

"Yes, so he has said. The team that Mrs. Fisher has in mind is the one from her synagogue. I do not know how Peter's father would feel about that."

"I don't know, either. And by the time we write and ask him and he writes back, the summer will be half over. Do you think Peter would fit in with the boys on that team? And that they'd be nice to him?"

"Mrs. Fischer's shul is different from mine across the street. The boys will all look and dress the same as Peter does. He will be accepted as Jewish because his mother is Jewish. And Mrs. Fischer will explain to the coach that Peter cannot talk. Better he should play with nice yeshiva boys than with the ruffians in this neighborhood."

"Yes, I agree. Let's ask Peter and see what he thinks. Wow, this really is good news. The kids were so disappointed that they had to spend the summer at their grandmother's house, and then the dog ran away and everything . . . I can't wait to tell them about this!"

"I believe it also will be good for Esther if she does not spend so much time with the young man who has been pursuing her."

"I have no idea how to talk to Esther about boys, Mr. Mendel. My parents never allowed me to go anywhere by myself or have any boyfriends."

"I cannot be much help to you, either," he said, smiling. "One final thing: I have promised to take Peter to see one of his baseball games. I planned to invite you, as well, but on second thought, perhaps you could use that day to visit your sister—or your mother, I should say."

Penny stared at her lap for a moment before looking up at him. "I'm too scared to go see her, Mr. Mendel."

"Would you like the children and me to come with you?"

"I would like that . . . and I'm grateful that you would offer. But I would hate for Esther and Peter to find out about my real father."

"I am certain that they would not think any less of you."

Penny stared at her shoes, shaking her head. "I have no idea how my sister will react when she sees me. I would hate for the children to see her slam the door in my face. . . . No, if I ever do go to see her, I think I need to go by myself. But thanks for offering."

"I do not want to interfere in your life, Penny—but do you recall your own words a few minutes ago when we were talking about the children's grandparents? You said, 'What could be so terrible that could keep a family apart this way?' I believe the answer is 'nothing.' Nothing should keep families apart. I urge you to go see your mother. I think her reaction might surprise you. If you do not go, you may spend the rest of your life wondering what might have been."

Penny nodded and rose to leave, smoothing the wrinkles from her skirt. "I promise to think about it. And I'll tell Esther and Peter the good news about the music lessons and the baseball team tomorrow."

Jacob didn't know what to do with himself after Penny left. He felt too excited and restless to sit and read a book, but it was too early to go to bed. He would never be able to sleep. He turned on the radio and found a station that broadcast the news.

"On the eastern front, the Germans have suffered enormous losses at the hands of the Soviets along an eight-hundred-mile battlefront in White Russia. The Nazis have been driven back nearly four hundred miles . . ."

Jacob closed his eyes, astonished by the news—yet afraid to hope. If the Soviets continued to defeat the Nazis this way, pushing them westward, Hungary might soon be liberated, too. He quickly switched off the radio again. He did not want to hear any news that might dim his hope.

Could Hashem truly be working behind the scenes to free his family?

CHAPTER 38

JULY 1944

ON THE DAY that Mr. Mendel took the children to the baseball game, Penny boarded a bus to Trenton, New Jersey. She had made up her mind to go at the very last minute, and she would arrive at Hazel's home unannounced. Penny knew that she was taking a risk—Hazel might not even be home. But as badly as Penny wanted to see her real mother and find out how she felt about her, it would also be a relief if Hazel wasn't home. Penny could simply turn around and take the bus back to Brooklyn.

As she traveled southwest across the state of New Jersey, through the cities of Elizabeth and Rahweh, stopping in New Brunswick, Monmouth, and Princeton, Penny tried to calculate how old Hazel would be now. If she had been seventeen when Penny was born, and Penny was now twenty-five, Hazel would be forty-two. It didn't seem possible. Penny knew from reading Hazel's Christmas cards every year that she and her husband Barry had two sons. How old were they? Younger than Penny, of course, but they would no longer be the little boys that Penny always pictured in her mind.

She watched people getting on and off the bus at each station, watched the tearful reunions and partings. More than half of the passengers were servicemen. She thought of Eddie and Roy and the welcome they would receive when they finally came home again.

At last she arrived in Trenton, every nerve in her body jittering. Penny hired a taxicab to go from the train station to Hazel's house. Long before Penny was ready to face her mother, the cab halted in front of a neat brick bungalow, one in a long row of identical homes. Her fingers felt clumsy as she paid the fare. She climbed out of the car and slowly walked up the sidewalk to her mother's house. Her real mother's house.

The July day was hot and Penny's dress drenched with sweat from the cramped bus ride. Her hair was curling out of control, her dress sticking to her. She should have used the ladies' room at the bus station to comb her hair and refresh her lipstick. She was not going to make a very good first impression after all these years.

As Penny walked up the steps to the front door, she spotted a mother's flag with two stars on it hanging in the bay window. Could Hazel's sons—Penny's half-brothers—be old enough to be serving in the military? It didn't seem possible.

She knew someone must be home because the outer door was open and she could hear a radio playing inside the house through the screen door. Penny felt limp with fear. She wanted to turn back, but the taxi had driven away. It was too late to change her mind.

She drew a deep breath and rang the doorbell. A moment later, Hazel stood in the doorway. She didn't look much different from the photograph their parents kept on their bookshelf, taken when Hazel was twenty years old. She wore an apron over her housedress, and her curly brown hair stuck out from beneath a kerchief. But even in work clothes, Hazel looked pretty.

"Hi, Hazel. It's me . . . your sister, Penny."

Her eyes went wide with surprise. "Penny! My goodness! . . . Oh my! . . . Is-is it really you?" She flung open the screen door and enveloped Penny in her arms. They stood that way for a long moment, locked in an embrace.

Hazel finally released Penny and held her at arms' length, studying her from head to toe. "I'm so happy to see you. My goodness! How did you . . . what are you doing here?"

"I had the day off from work, so I decided to visit you."

"Come in, come in. I was just washing the dishes and listening to the radio." She led Penny by the hand through the tiny living room and dining area and into the kitchen, where a Frank Sinatra tune played on the radio. "You should have warned me you were coming . . . my house is a mess and so am I. Why didn't you tell me you were coming?"

"I-I don't know . . . I just made up my mind at the last minute."

An ironing board stood in one corner of the kitchen with a basketful of clothes waiting beneath it. The half-finished dishes were piled around the sink. Hazel had an electric fan blowing, but it didn't do much to cool the room. She pulled the kerchief from her head and untied her apron.

"Sorry about the mess."

"I don't care about the house," Penny said. "I came to see you." She couldn't stop smiling. Hazel had greeted her so warmly. The sight of Penny hadn't repulsed her or reminded her of the rape. Mr. Mendel had been right—her mother's reaction had surprised her.

"Let's sit out back," Hazel said. "I think it's a little cooler on the porch. Would you like something cold to drink? I have iced tea."

"Sure. That sounds good."

But Hazel made no move to fetch the tea. Instead, she reached out to stroke Penny's hair in a tender gesture. "You're so pretty! Gosh, I can't stop staring at you! I feel tongue-tied. . . . I can't wait for you to tell me all about yourself."

"Sure." Penny could barely reply through her tears. Hazel finally pulled her gaze away and took two glasses from the cupboard and a pitcher of tea from the refrigerator. She cracked open an aluminum tray of ice cubes and dropped some into each glass. Penny saw Hazel's hands shaking.

"Mother says you sell tickets at the bus station?"

Penny cleared the lump from her throat. "I used to. Last fall, my boss asked me if I wanted to learn how to drive a city bus and so I did. I have my own bus route now. The pay is real good, and I get to meet all kinds of interesting people."

"My baby . . . sister," Hazel murmured, hesitating slightly between the two words. "Good for you, Penny!"

She led the way through the back door to a small covered porch and two wicker rocking chairs. Penny felt sweat trickling down the back of her neck, but whether it was from the warm July day or her nerves, she couldn't tell. Maybe both.

"I admire you for taking on a job like that," Hazel said as she sat down beside Penny. "I kept to a more traditional job as a secretary, but I guess you're like one of those Rosie the Riveters they're always talking about in the magazines, tackling a man's job so they can go fight the war."

"Yeah, I guess . . . Tell me about your life, Hazel. I can't even remember the last time I saw you. I wasn't even old enough for school yet."

"There's not much to tell. I'm an ordinary housewife. Barry is in sales; his company has a government contract, so he travels a lot. He won't be home until next week—" Hazel stopped, and Penny could see her struggling to control her emotions. "Sorry . . . I'm sorry . . . it's just that seeing you again is so . . . I always dreamed we would be together one day, but I never thought . . . and here you are, so pretty . . ." She smiled through the tears that rolled down her face.

Penny no longer wanted to pretend that Hazel was her sister. "I know the truth," she said. "About you and me." As soon as the words were out, Penny wanted to take them back. What if Hazel got angry or upset?

But Hazel sprang from her chair and bent over Penny, pulling her into her arms, hugging her tightly. "My baby . . . my dear little girl . . . At last, at last! Oh, Penny! Can you ever forgive me?"

"What for? There's nothing to forgive. I don't blame you for what happened."

Hazel pulled back to face her. "I didn't abandon you, Penny, honest I didn't. I never wanted to give you up at all! I've thought about you every day for the past twenty-five years."

"I wish I had known sooner," Penny murmured. "I just found

out about us." At last they released each other and Hazel sank down on her chair again, wiping her eyes and blowing her nose on a handkerchief.

"You have to understand that I was only seventeen when you were born. Our parents were furious, of course. They sent me to a home for unwed mothers until you were born, then they moved to where they live now so that none of the old neighbors would find out. I lived there with them and raised you until you were two and a half."

"You did?"

Hazel nodded. "I changed all of your diapers and bathed you and read stories to you and rocked you to sleep at night. I watched you take your first steps. Then Father and Mother decided that I should go to secretarial school. They saw how close we were becoming and that you thought of me as your mother, and they were afraid that I wouldn't let you go. And believe me, I didn't want to let you go."

She paused to take a deep breath and wipe her tears. "I thought about running away with you, but I had signed all the adoption papers. You were officially their daughter and always would be. They made me give you up, Penny. Single girls don't have babies. They told me that you and I would always live in shame if I kept you." She reached to take Penny's hand as if pleading with her. "I loved you and wanted the very best for you, and so they convinced me that giving you up was the best thing to do. You could grow up with two parents and have a normal life. No one would ever know the truth. They wanted me to have a normal life, too, without the scandal of a baby. I didn't care, but they said the truth would hurt you—and I would rather die than let that happen."

"Why didn't you come to see me? You never visited us."

"They didn't want me to. They knew how close we were, how attached you were to me, and I think they were afraid I would tell you the truth. Those months after I left, I was so lonesome for you. I just wanted to hold you again and see you smile and hear you laugh. . . . They sent me pictures once in a while when I begged them to. But they insisted that this was the best thing for everyone. They said you were happy and that I shouldn't rock the boat. You were happy, weren't you?"

Penny nodded. She had been, for the most part. "They weren't like other parents, but I did have a good life. They always told me that I wasn't like other girls, but I never knew why. They said I had to be more careful, and they were very protective of me, afraid to let me do anything. But everyone thought I was their daughter—and so did I until I needed my birth certificate. That's how I found out I was adopted."

"If I could do it all over again, I would never give you up."

"Why didn't you write to me?"

"I did! I sent letters and birthday cards and birthday presents every year. And Christmas presents. And each time you got a year older I would cry because I missed watching you grow up. Didn't you get my presents?"

"They may have given them to me, but they never said they were from you." Penny swallowed her anger at the injustice. "Why did they do this to us?"

"They thought it was for the best."

"Well, they were wrong! I wish I could stay here and live with you."

"I wish you could, too. But I have a husband and two sons now. They don't know about you, Penny."

"Oh . . . I don't blame you for being ashamed of me."

Hazel gripped Penny's hands in hers and squeezed. "Never! Never in a million years am I ashamed of you. But I never told my husband that I had you, and I don't know how he'll react. I need to talk to him first. I can't just spring it on him. But, oh! It will be so good to have you back in my life, Penny!"

"I thought you might hate me because I would remind you of . . . of what my real father did to you."

Hazel looked away for the first time, and Penny immediately regretted mentioning her father. She wished she could take back her words. When Hazel finally looked at her again, she seemed embarrassed. "I'm so sorry, Penny. But what I told them about your father isn't true. I lied because I couldn't face my own guilt. I loved your real father. Or at least I thought I did at the time."

"So you weren't raped?"

Hazel shook her head. "Lies have a way of multiplying and making matters worse. I made up that story about being raped because I was ashamed to admit the truth. They didn't know about my boyfriend—and they were so strict! I was ashamed that I had let Mark have his way, so when I realized that I was pregnant I made up a story about being raped. I'm so sorry."

Penny leaned back in her chair, stunned. The lie had affected Penny all of her life. It was the reason her parents had treated her the way they did, the reason they'd been so protective, the reason they could never quite love her. But at last she was free from the lie. "It doesn't matter," she said. "At least I know the truth now."

"Don't hate Mother and Father. It wasn't their fault. I was rebellious and made a mess of things, and they did the best they could to fix my mistakes."

"Who's my real father? You said his name is Mark?"

Hazel gave a sad little smile. "He was a boy from high school. I thought I loved him and that he loved me. It's funny how your opinion of love changes when you're finally old enough to understand what love is all about. He disappeared from my life when he found out I was pregnant, but I don't really blame him. He came from a good family and was hoping for an appointment to West Point after we graduated. He's probably a general in the war by now. He always was very smart. But we were both young, and we let ourselves get carried away."

"So he knew about me?"

"He knew I was pregnant but not what happened to us. After I graduated from secretarial school I got a good job in an office and met my husband, Barry. I'm sorry for the mistakes I made, but I was never sorry that I had you. You have Mark's smile, you know—that dimple in just one cheek that's only there when you smile."

"Could we find my father? I want to know what happened to him."

"Let it go, Penny. After all this time, why turn his life upside down? He probably has a family, too."

"I would still like to know his name and find out more about him. I promise I won't show up on his doorstep or write to him or anything."

"I'll have to think about it." Hazel picked up her glass of iced tea and took a sip, then set the sweating glass down again. "You're so pretty, Penny. I can't stop looking at you."

Tears filled Penny's eyes. For the first time in her life, someone was looking at her with eyes of love, the way she had always wished her mother would.

And that was enough, for now. It was more than enough.

CHAPTER 39

THE STICKY SUMMER AFTERNOON made Esther as limp and damp as melted ice cream. As she and Peter walked from the bus stop, she knew it would be even hotter inside Grandma Shaffer's tiny, crammed house. She never opened her windows and had only one puny fan to stir the hot air.

"Grandma, we're here," Esther called as she opened the back screen door.

"I'm in here." Grandma sat in a living room chair, fanning herself with a Chinese paper fan. She had taken off her shoes and propped her feet on a footstool, and her pale ankles looked as huge as cabbages. "There you are," she said when she saw Esther and Peter. "I've been worried about you two. According to the radio, the baseball game ended an hour ago."

"The ball park was full of people, Grandma, so it took a long time to empty out. But once we got to the street, the bus brought us straight here, just like Penny said it would. We're fine."

In fact, they were more than fine. As Peter had sat in the stands with Mr. Mendel, watching his beloved Dodgers play, he looked happier than Esther had seen him in a long, long time. He still looked happy, his cheeks and nose freckled from the sun. Esther wished they could have gone home to their own apartment with Mr. Mendel so Peter wouldn't be reminded that Grandma's dog was still missing. Maybe he would stay happy for a little while longer. But Penny had gone to New Jersey for the day and wouldn't be home until late. They would have to spend another night here.

"Oh my, look at your faces!" Grandma said. "You both got too much sun. You should put some witch hazel on your skin to cool it off."

Esther's arms and face did feel very hot, but she didn't care. "The Dodgers won, Grandma, six to nothing. They even hit a home run with two runners on base."

"Did you eat anything? Are you hungry?"

"Mr. Mendel bought roasted peanuts for us. And hot dogs."

"The Jewish man bought them? Didn't Penny give you any money to spend?"

"He wanted to treat us. He couldn't eat any of the food, but there's no law against buying it for us."

"If you're hungry, you'll have to fix yourself something. I can't do a thing in this heat."

Peter tapped Grandma's shoulder and pointed toward the backyard, then made a pouring motion. "He wants to know if you checked on his garden, Grandma. Do you think it needs watering?"

"I saw Penny's father out there with a watering can. You would think they were his plants the way he hovers over them. He checks on them three or four times a day when you're not here." But Peter disappeared out the back door to check on his garden, just the same.

Grandma stopped fanning herself and sighed. Her face looked as pink as a peony. "Is Penny going to be back in time to go to work Monday?"

"She said she would be." Esther found a piece of cardboard on top of one of the piles and used it to fan herself, making sure the limp breeze reached her grandmother's face, too. "Are you coming to church with us again sometime, Grandma?" She had gone with them this morning in Penny's place, and Esther thought it had cheered her up. Ever since reading Queen Esther's story with Mr. Mendel, Esther had enjoyed going to church again. As her Sunday school teacher and minister prayed for all of the men who were fighting in the war, she could more easily imagine how God might be working behind the scenes.

"We'll see. Who knows how long my ankles will stay swollen."

Esther hopped off the arm of the chair where she had been sitting, too excited to remain seated. "I have a piano lesson on Monday. I can't wait! Penny already showed me which bus to take to my music school. I'll go straight there in the morning, but I'll be back in time for lunch."

She had felt scared the first time she'd walked up the steps of the music conservatory. The beautiful old mansion looked like something from a Hollywood movie. But once she'd stepped inside and heard music pouring from all of the rooms, filling the building with glorious sounds, Esther had felt as though she had come home.

"Are you sure your father would approve of you riding buses all over Brooklyn by yourself?"

"I'm thirteen, Grandma. Besides, Penny knows all the drivers. She made them promise to watch out for Peter and me. And Mr. Mendel says he knows of a baseball team for Peter to join. Penny is going to take him there and see if he likes it. It'll give him something to do while I'm in music classes."

"Who's paying for all of this? That's what I want to know."

"I don't know," Esther said with a shrug, although she felt pretty certain that Mr. Mendel was, even though he denied it. It didn't matter. She had gone to her first lesson and had loved it.

Peter still wasn't enthusiastic about joining the baseball team and had refused to even consider it until Mr. Mendel had coaxed him. *"Go for one time, Peter. If you do not like it, you do not have to continue. But who knows? You might have a good time."* Peter would try it for the first time on Wednesday.

Esther remembered thinking that this would be a terrible summer, but maybe it wouldn't be so bad after all, even if she couldn't spend much time with Jacky. The only sad part had been when Woofer ran away. Peter looked a hundred years old every time he walked past the empty dog dish in the kitchen. Esther wished Grandma would put the dish away so it wouldn't remind them that Woofer was gone. Penny was the only one who had refused to give up. Every afternoon when she arrived from work to take them home, she would walk through the neighborhood one more time calling Woofer's name. They had made "lost dog" posters and given them to all of their neighbors. So far no one had seen Woofer. Good news and bad news always seemed to happen together.

Once again, Esther remembered her piano lesson and gathered up her courage to ask something very important. She fanned her grandmother a little harder with the cardboard as she did so, drying the wisps of white hair that had stuck to her forehead.

"Um . . . Grandma? I'm going to need to practice the piano during the day this summer, and since I'll be here, not at home . . . well, Penny talked to her parents about borrowing their piano. She says it's just gathering dust next door in their living room. They got it years and years ago for Penny's sister, Hazel, to play."

Grandma gave a little frown, as if she didn't understand what Esther was leading up to. "Anyway, they're willing to let me use it for practice, but they don't want me to play it over there and disturb their peace and quiet. Could we please, please bring it over here to your house? Peter and I will help you make room for it. Please?"

"A piano? In here? . . . Where in the world would we put it?"

"I'll go through the stuff in your boxes with you and help you decide if you really need everything or not."

"Of course I need everything."

Esther saw the fear in her grandmother's eyes and knew that physically moving the boxes would be easy compared to coaxing Grandma to change her habits after all these years. She was obsessed with this junk, even though half of it consisted of stacks of old newspapers. Then Esther remembered her own obsession with newspapers and winced. She had filled three large scrapbooks with clippings about the war before her lessons at the conservatory began occupying her mind.

"If we just got rid of a few things, Grandma, I know we could make enough room for the piano. It's a very small upright." She stopped fanning and went to the pile closest to Grandma's chair. "We could start with these old newspapers. You're done with them, aren't you?" They were yellow with age and at least five years old, judging by the date on the top one.

"I need those. I always line the bottom of the birdcage with newspapers."

Esther looked at the size of pile compared to the size of the birdcage and wanted to laugh out loud. Grandma kept enough papers to bury the poor bird beneath a pile six feet deep. But Esther didn't laugh. She felt sorry for Grandma. And even if she hadn't needed a piano to practice on, she still wanted to help her. She put her arm around her grandmother's sweaty shoulders.

"You get a newspaper every week, right? How about if I count out enough pages to change the birdcage for a week? Then the rest of these could all go for the war effort. They need newspapers very badly, you know."

"They do?"

"Yes. They have special drives for all sorts of things that they need—scrap metal, cans, rubber . . . If you donated some of your things, it might help us win the war."

"I wouldn't know how to go about it."

"It's easy. They have a place to drop things off over at the bus station where Penny works. She could help us bring stuff there."

Grandma kneaded her forehead as if it hurt to think. "Well . . . I suppose if they need it for the war . . ."

Esther bent to give her a hug. She might be different than other grandmothers, but Esther loved her, junk and all. "Thanks, Grandma. I can help you get started right now, since I have nothing else to do."

Peter came inside a few minutes later and helped Esther bind the papers and magazines with twine so they could carry them to the collection center. When they found a box of old school notebooks and homework assignments and report cards that had belonged to her father and uncles, Esther coaxed Grandma to tell stories about Daddy when he was a little boy. It brought tears to Grandma's eyes to talk about Uncle Joe, but Esther knew that it felt good to remember him, too. She had long been afraid that Mama would be forgotten entirely if no one ever talked about her.

Later, they found two boxes filled with random pieces of cardboard. It looked years and years old. "Do you still need this, Grandma?" She was careful to ask gently, not in a challenging way.

"I-I might . . . I'll have to think about it." The process would be slow. Esther would have to be patient. She couldn't expect Grandma to change overnight.

By bedtime they had cleared away a very small space. It might only be big enough for the piano stool, but it was a start. Eventually there would be room for a piano. Grandma turned off the radio and covered up the cage so the bird would stop chirping. She said goodnight and went to her room, taking the fan with her. Esther and Peter lay down on their makeshift beds. The house was quiet.

Esther was almost asleep when she thought she heard a scraping noise by the front door. She sat up. "Peter? Did you hear that? Listen . . ." She heard it again, something scratching against the front door. Then she heard a sound that she definitely recognized—a dog barking.

Peter heard it, too, and he scrambled up from his bed on the floor and ran to yank open the front door. Woofer raced inside, her tail wagging so hard she could barely stand up. Esther couldn't believe her eyes.

"Where have you been, you naughty dog? Grandma! Grandma, come quick!" she shouted. "Woofer's home! She came home!"

Grandma limped into the room in her nightdress, hair askew, groggy and flustered without her eyeglasses. "What's wrong?" Then she saw the dog and smiled—a real smile. The first one Esther had seen since Uncle Joe died. "Oh my. I don't believe it."

Peter was delirious with joy. Esther watched as he rolled on the floor, letting Woofer cover his face with sticky kisses. The dog's return seemed like a tiny sign of hope to Esther, like the Hanukkah candles or the Christmas tree shining in the window. Woofer was home, safe and sound. And maybe Daddy and Uncle Steve and Penny's friend Roy and Mr. Mendel's family would soon be home, too.

CHAPTER 40

Budapest, Hungary

Dear Mother and Father Mendel,

*We followed the Swedish diplomat's car from the freight
yard to a "safe house" in Budapest. There are more than thirty
of these houses, all flying a blue and yellow Swedish flag in
front. They have been declared a safe zone from the Nazis,
protected by International Law. Thousands of Jews already
lived in this protected district, but when I arrived with the other
refugees from the evacuation trains, they quickly made space for
more of us, sharing their food and giving milk to Fredeleh and
baby Yankel. He cries and cries for his mother—and when I am
alone, I cry for mine.*

*I've learned that the man who saved us is a young Swedish
diplomat named Raoul Wallenberg. He came to Hungary for
the sole purpose of saving as many Jews as he possibly could.
At first he set aside a special section for Jews in the Swedish
embassy, but after more than seven hundred people fled there
for protection, he began renting safe houses and claiming them*

as Swedish property. He also buys food and medicine for us with money from America. He said that Jewish people in America are raising money to help us, and that the United States sends this aid to us through neutral nations, such as his.

Mr. Wallenberg knows that the Nazis respect official documents and identity cards, so he designed the Swedish identity papers that his men passed to us on the train. He bluffs the Nazis with seals and stamps and signatures, claiming that those of us who hold these papers are Swedish nationals. He has saved countless lives this way. His staff works around the clock to print the documents and distribute them to us. Meanwhile, I'm told that Mr. Wallenberg never sleeps. He surfaces everywhere in Budapest—the way he did at the freight yard—doing everything he can to rescue more Jews. He somehow finds food and medicine in a city plagued with shortages. He operates soup kitchens and clinics, since Jews are banned from all of the hospitals, working with the Swiss embassy and the Swedish Red Cross. When the wife of one of Wallenberg's Jewish workers was about to give birth, he took her to his own apartment and brought a doctor there to deliver her baby.

No one knows how much longer our Swedish friends will be able to bluff the Nazis this way, and so I knew it was time to hide Fredeleh in the Christian orphanage where she will be safe. My mother said good-bye to me so that I could go free, and Dina Weisner said good-bye to little Yankel. Now I had to say good-bye to my daughter so she will live.

Before I had time to change my mind, I asked one of the men from the Swedish embassy to help me take Fredeleh and baby Yankel to the Catholic convent. The Swedish man agreed to go with me, pretending to be my husband, showing his identification papers to any soldiers who stopped us. It was the longest journey of my life.

An elderly Christian woman who runs the orphanage met us at the door. I told her about the evacuation train. "My husband said that you would hide my daughter here. Please, can you take Fredeleh? And this little boy, as well? The Nazis took his mother away."

I gave Fredeleh's papers and your address in America to the Christians. I told them Yankel's name and his mother's name. Then I hugged Fredeleh and kissed her good-bye. She clung to my neck crying, "Mama! Mama!" She didn't want to let go of me, but I pried her away against both of our wills. I knew how she felt, not wanting to leave her mother. I also knew how my own mother felt, wanting her daughter to be safe. And so I pushed Fredeleh away and turned my back on her, just as my own mother had turned away from me.

I don't know why I have survived this long when so many, many others have not. Here at the Swedish safe house we ask each other that question every day, wondering how it can be that we are here when all of the others were taken away on the trains.

Today we learned that the deportations have stopped for now. The Nazis need the trains to transport soldiers as the Soviet army marches closer and closer to us.

I live day by day, trying not to think about the past or the future. I have no idea what has become of Avraham or if I will ever see him again.

But if Hashem is willing, Fredeleh will survive. And for that I am grateful.

Love,
Sarah Rivkah

CHAPTER 41

AUGUST 1944

PENNY SAT IN THE BLEACHERS on a stifling August afternoon, cheering as Peter's baseball team tagged out another player. Peter hadn't made the play—in fact he made very few winning plays. But his team was winning by a score of seven to three.

Penny nudged Esther, seated beside her. "He looks a little lonely out there, doesn't he?"

"He's guarding left field. He's supposed to stand way out there in case the other team hits a fly ball." Esther had smiled as she'd said it, and Penny realized how far they had come since she had begun taking care of Esther and Peter nearly a year ago. In those first few months after Eddie went away, Esther had barely spoken a civil word to Penny. Now they sat side by side, content with each other's company.

"I hope Peter stops looking up at the clouds," Penny said as she watched him, "or he's likely to miss one of those fly balls."

"But he's happy," Esther said. "I'm so glad Mr. Mendel talked him into playing."

"Me too." And she was relieved that he was finally out of the isolation of his room and away from the fantasy world of his comic books.

"Mr. Mendel is paying for this, isn't he?" Esther said. "And he's paying for me to go to the music conservatory, too. He won't admit it, but I know it has to be him."

Penny simply shrugged. She hated secrets and longed to tell Esther that it was her grandmother who had arranged everything. Secrets had caused so much damage in Penny's own family. "Mr. Mendel loves you two kids, you know," she said instead.

"I know. We love him, too."

Penny looked around at the other families in the crowd. Some of the men wore beards and little beanies like Mr. Mendel did. She couldn't help smiling to herself. Here she was, watching a baseball game with Jewish people, at a school for Jewish children. Her parents would have a conniption fit if they knew about it. But Peter had blossomed this summer. He was no longer such a thin, spindly-looking boy but had grown strong and tan from the sunshine and fresh air and exercise. And best of all, he was happy. Maybe he would even start talking again, one of these days.

"Do you think Mr. Mendel will ever see his son, Avraham, again?" Esther asked suddenly. Penny couldn't reply. "Tell me the truth," Esther added.

Penny sighed. "I wish I knew. I think we have to keep hoping . . . And I know we have to keep praying. Like Mr. Mendel says, we have to trust God, even when things don't turn out the way we want them to."

"So you think they might be dead? Like Mama and Mrs. Mendel and Uncle Joe?"

Penny had read the accounts of the deportation camps in the newspapers. She held only a slender thread of hope for Mr. Mendel's family. And after attending so many meetings with government officials, Mr. Mendel surely knew the chances of their survival even better than she did. She struggled to form an answer for Esther. "Remember how we were all ready to give up hope with Woofer? But she came home safe and sound, didn't she?"

Esther looked up at her and smiled, nodding silently.

Peter's team won the game by two runs. He looked hot and sweaty and exhilarated as he and his teammates thumped each other on the back. "Good job, Peter," the coach said. Peter needed a bath and a change of clothes, but Penny didn't want to go straight home to the apartment. "We need to go to the duplex first," Penny told them. "I need to check on my parents. And your grandmother. They really suffer in this hot weather."

"Can we buy a newspaper on the way home?" Esther asked.

Penny hesitated. Esther hadn't seemed as obsessed with the news now that she spent so much time with her music. But deadly battles still raged all around the world, and Penny always feared news of a catastrophe. "I guess so," she finally replied.

They bought one at a corner store, and the three of them divided up the various sections to read on the bus ride. Peter asked for the sports section, of course. Penny ended up with the front page and nearly missed their stop, engrossed in the news that the Allies had liberated Paris. She read every article and studied every picture, trying to imagine Eddie over there, taking part in this drama. She did the same thing when she read an article about the Marines fighting in the Pacific, picturing Roy fighting bravely alongside his comrades. In the battle for Saipan, twenty-five thousand Japanese soldiers had been killed. Penny couldn't imagine that many people dying. She folded the paper closed and climbed off the bus, thinking of Mr. Mendel's family and Esther's question as they walked to Grandma Shaffer's house.

The moment Peter opened the back door, Woofer rushed forward to meet him. Penny had to smile. "I think you're feeding Woofer too much," she said. "She's getting so fat! Look at her, waddling around like a penguin."

Penny went inside to see if Mrs. Shaffer needed anything, then went home to check on her parents. Her mother began to scold Penny as soon as she walked through the door.

"Look at your face! You got too much sun today. You should wear a hat. Your father should, too. Every day he stands out there, fussing over that ridiculous garden you coaxed him to plant—in the hot sun!"

Penny went to the kitchen window and watched her father putter around outside. "He looks content, Mother." The garden had been a big success. Peter's plants had blossomed and flourished just as he and Esther had this summer.

"And all these tomatoes," Mother grumbled. "I don't know what he thinks we're going to do with all of them."

"I'll take some to work with me. The other drivers loved the last batch I brought to the station. Do you want a salad for supper? I'll cut everything up for you."

"Somebody has to start eating all of these vegetables."

Penny got out a chopping board and a knife and began to work. A year ago she hadn't understood her mother's bitterness or why she hid inside the house like a hermit, terrified of strangers. But the secrets that had grown beneath the surface all these years had been unearthed like a crop of potatoes, giving Penny a new understanding of her parents.

They had never mentioned Hazel again. Nor did they know that Penny had visited her or that Hazel hadn't been raped after all. Perhaps that truth would come to light in the future, but for now Penny was content. She and Hazel wrote letters to each other, sharing all their news. But Hazel mailed them to Eddie's apartment to avoid more arguments.

Penny saw her parents differently now. She would help them and be kind to them, but they no longer held her hostage with guilt. She had broken free from all the things that they feared: She drove a public bus and talked to strangers—and Jews. Penny smiled again as she remembered sitting in the bleachers at Peter's baseball game.

"What's so amusing about cutting up tomatoes?" Mother asked.

"Nothing. I was just thinking of something else."

Her parents had raised her the best that they could. Rearing children was a daunting task—as Penny had discovered with Esther and Peter. Penny hadn't had any idea what she had volunteered for nearly a year ago when she'd naively told Eddie she would take care of his children while he was away. She never could have done it alone. Mr. Mendel, Grandma Shaffer, even her father had helped Penny raise them. And now the children's Jewish grandmother. Penny smiled again, thinking of how God was always at work behind the scenes.

Mrs. Shaffer's screen door slammed shut with a *bang*, jarring Penny from her thoughts. Mother clucked her tongue. "I wish those kids wouldn't slam that door all the time. They never listen."

A moment later, Esther pounded on the kitchen door. "Penny, come quick! Something's wrong with Woofer. I think she's dying!"

Penny dropped the knife and wiped her hands on her apron. Her father came up the porch steps behind Esther with two green peppers in his hands. "What's wrong?" he asked before Penny had a chance to.

"Woofer is just laying on the kitchen floor, panting! She won't get up."

"She's probably overheated," Father said. "All dogs pant when they get hot."

"No, something's really wrong, I can tell! She's whimpering, too."

Penny didn't know what to do. The children didn't need any more sorrow in their lives, especially now that they were finally happy. "Will you come with us, Dad?" she asked.

"I don't know anything about dogs." But he set down the peppers and followed them into Mrs. Shaffer's kitchen. Woofer lay in the corner on one of Mrs. Shaffer's old rugs. Her tongue lolled from her mouth like a long, pink sock, and her sides heaved up and down like a bellows. She did, indeed, look as though she was dying. Penny knelt down and stroked the dog's head.

"What's wrong with her?" Esther asked. "Should we call a doctor?"

Penny looked up at her father for advice and saw his shoulders shake as he began to chuckle. He tried to cover his mouth to hold it inside, but his laughter grew louder and louder until he was laughing out loud. She couldn't recall the last time he had laughed this way. "Dad? What is it?"

He wiped his eye with the heel of his hand, grinning. "There's nothing wrong with that dog. She's having puppies!"

And much to everyone's surprise, she did—four of them, sleek and squirming and beautiful.

CHAPTER 42

SEPTEMBER 1944

JACOB TURNED OFF HIS RADIO, too disheartened to listen to any more news. He gazed out his living room window, staring at the trees that lined the street. Summer had ended, the children had returned to school, and now the trees were changing with the seasons. Today the vivid orange and scarlet leaves reminded Jacob of flames. Flames rising from American ships in the Pacific after Japanese Kamikaze pilots smashed into them. Flames in the cities of Europe as the Americans battled to liberate them. Smoke and flames rising from Nazi death camps.

A year had passed since the shul across the street had burned, a year since Ed Shaffer went away. And more than two years since Miriam Shoshanna died. The shul had now been restored. They would hold services there for Yom Kippur soon. How could time pass so quickly yet seem to stand still?

Jacob glanced at the clock. Soon the children would arrive home from school. And sure enough, a moment later he saw Peter hurrying up the street, walking alone with his head down, his hands in his pockets. He ran up the porch steps and through the front door and up the stairs to his apartment. Why the rush? A moment later, Jacob understood why when he saw Esther walking with the boy from next door.

He closed his eyes in dismay. Not again. He had hoped that Esther's continuing lessons at the conservatory would leave no time for that boy. He watched as they approached the porch, hand in hand. He could see by the way Esther laughed, the shy way she looked up at him, that she was enamored with him, flattered by his attention. With her father so far away, she must hunger for a strong arm around her shoulders, someone to hold and protect her. She was vulnerable to the boy's advances, and her father wasn't here to protect her from them. Should Jacob step forward and protect her?

He put on his jacket and hat and left the apartment for a walk just as Esther waved good-bye to the boy and came up the porch stairs. "Hi, Mr. Mendel."

"Hello, Esther. Who is your young friend?" Although he knew very well who the Hoffman boy was. Everyone in the neighborhood knew. He remembered how Esther's mother had once referred to him as a hooligan or a ruffian or some such word. Should he remind Esther of her mother's opinion?

"That's Jacky Hoffman. He offered to walk me home from school."

"Hoffman? . . . His family lives in the building next door, yes? Was he one of the boys who got into trouble a few years ago for vandalizing some garages in the neighborhood?"

Esther looked away, embarrassed. "He's changed a lot since then, Mr. Mendel. Jacky has a job now. He delivers groceries for the A&P on the next block. People should give him a chance."

He could see that she was becoming defensive, unwilling to listen to what a nosy old man like Jacob had to say. But he cared enough to continue, just the same. "I have seen you with him on several occasions, but why is it that I never see you with any other friends?"

"I don't know," she said with a loose shrug. "Jacky's my best friend now."

"You must be careful not to let him monopolize all of your time. You are too young to limit your friendship to only one person, especially a boy. What do you suppose your father would say if he saw you with him?"

"We're just walking home together, that's all. And he's been protecting Peter. Jacky won't let any of the other kids make fun of him."

"Peter does not seem very grateful. I have noticed that he does not seem to like him."

"That's Peter's problem. Jacky is always nice to him." She looked angry and uneasy, shifting from one foot to the other as if in a hurry to leave. "I have to practice piano now. See you later, Mr. Mendel."

"Good-bye, Esther."

Maybe he was wrong, he thought as he continued on his walk. Esther had a good head on her shoulders, didn't she? And maybe the boy really had changed since the war began, becoming more responsible. Jacob walked to the end of the block, then crossed the street and walked another block, trying to shake off the uneasy feeling he got whenever he thought of them holding hands.

The smell of fall filled the air—decaying leaves and bonfires, the scent of change. As he neared the A&P, he decided to go inside and talk to the store manager, just to ease his mind. Jacob knew the man slightly. They both attended Congregation Ohel Moshe.

"Good afternoon, Mr. Shapiro," he said, extending his hand. "Jacob Mendel. I am wondering if I could ask you about one of your delivery boys. I would like to know something about his character. His name is Jack Hoffman."

Shapiro's pleasant smile faded. "He no longer works for us."

"I am surprised to hear that. I was told very recently that he delivered groceries for your store."

"I had to fire him about two weeks ago. To be honest with you, we suspected him of stealing from some of our customers. We had been getting complaints all summer of stolen money and missing ration books, and everything pointed to him."

"Are the police involved?"

"They said we didn't have enough evidence. It was all circumstantial. But we let Jacky go, just to be sure."

"Thank you for your time."

Jacob strode from the store as if it were on fire, furious that such an unsavory boy would come near an innocent, vulnerable child like Esther. He needed to do something, but what? As he walked home, deep in thought, he saw Jacky leaning against a car that was parked along the street in front of his apartment, smoking a cigarette. "Excuse me—Jack Hoffman? I would like to have a word with you, please."

"I don't talk to kikes." He tossed his cigarette butt at Jacob. It bounced off his chest and landed, smoldering, at his feet.

The action startled Jacob, but he didn't retreat. He took another step forward, snuffing out the flame beneath his shoe. He wondered what the boy would say if he knew that Esther's mother was Jewish. Jacky stood up and folded his arms across his chest, meeting Jacob's gaze with a look of defiance. "What do you want, old man?"

"I want to talk to you about Esther Shaffer."

"I'm her boyfriend."

"No. You are not. She is much too young to have a boyfriend."

"What business is it of yours?"

"I am looking out for her while her father is away. Protecting her."

"You're making that up. Esther would have told me if she had a dirty Jew for a bodyguard."

Jacob pressed on, determined to remain calm. "I just talked to your former employer and have learned that you have been fired. He says that you are not a very trustworthy person. I plan to tell Esther this fact, as well. So from now on, I do not want you to walk home from school with her or to have anything to do with her. Stay away from her. I will be watching to make certain that you do not come near her."

Jacky's arms dropped to his sides. His hands tightened into fists. "Who do you think you are, telling me what to do?"

"And if you ever do anything to hurt that girl or take advantage of her, I will make certain that you regret it."

For a moment Jacky looked as though he might take a swing at Jacob, but there was too much traffic on the street. Instead, he unleashed such a nasty string of curses and ethnic slurs that Jacob turned his back and walked away. Such hatred, especially in one so young. Jacob had been right to intervene.

"You'll be sorry you ever interfered, old man!" Jacky called after him. "You hear me?"

The confrontation, though necessary, left Jacob shaken. Now more than ever, he would need to convince Esther to stay far away from the boy. He remembered his faltering attempts to talk to her a few minutes ago and knew that this was not something he could do alone. Esther needed a woman's guidance. Penny did the best she could, but she was naive and inexperienced herself. Perhaps if Jacob explained the situation to Esther's grandmother, he could convince Mrs. Fischer to step forward and help raise her young granddaughter. He would call Mrs. Fischer right away, he decided. He would plead with her to become part of Esther's life.

Jacob kept walking, disturbed by the venom in young Jacky's heart, and as he passed the synagogue again, Jacob knew he must examine his own heart in preparation for Yom Kippur. This was the time to settle accounts with those he had wronged. To confess his sins and turn away from them. To forgive those who had wronged him before daring to ask Hashem for forgiveness. Jacob knew he had sinned many times during the past two years. He had been angry with the heartless government officials for not allowing Avi and his family to come home. Angry about the car accident that had taken Miriam Shoshanna's life. Most of all, he had been angry with Hashem.

He turned the corner, and as he neared the market where Miriam died, Jacob saw the owner stacking apples in a pyramid in front of his store. The grocer had been his friend, but Jacob hadn't returned to the shop or spoken to Chaim since the accident. Now, before Jacob faced Hashem on the Day of Atonement, he knew he must reconcile with the man. He crossed the street and went to his old friend, extending his hand.

"Hello, Chaim."

"Jacob! My friend!" A huge smile spread across his face as he engulfed Jacob's hand between both of his. "I haven't seen you in . . . how long? I thought surely you must have moved away."

"It has been too long, and I am sorry. I remember that you tried to speak with me at Miriam Shoshanna's funeral, but I turned my back, and for that I apologize. Please forgive me."

"I understand, Jacob. I understand. I only wanted to tell you that I was the one who was sorry. I know you must blame me for what happened. My stand was too close to the street. But see? I have moved it back."

"I do not blame you. The accident was not your fault. That car could have smashed into any one of the stores on this street."

"But it smashed into my store, and I will never be able to forget it. I will always blame myself."

Jacob shook his head, sorry that he had waited so long to reassure his friend that he held no grudges. "I should have come and talked to you much sooner. I should have told you that I never blamed you. I have been angry with Hashem, not you. All this time I have been asking why He would allow such a senseless thing to happen. Asking why He did not warn Miriam to move out of the way."

The grocer got a funny look on his face as if confused by Jacob's confession. "What is it, Chaim? Why do you look at me like that?"

"I thought you knew what happened . . . I thought the police must have told you."

"Told me what?"

"About the accident. I saw everything, Jacob. I heard the car and the racing engine. I looked up and saw that little boy standing right in the car's path. Your wife saw him, too. We had only a split second to act, it happened so fast . . . like this," he said, snapping his fingers. "I don't know how your Miriam reacted so quickly, but she did. She ran forward and pushed that child out of the way. She saved his life, Jacob. Miriam died so that the little boy who was with her could live."

Jacob stumbled over to a discarded packing crate and sank down on it. Tears filled his eyes. He tried to stop them but couldn't.

"The little boy is okay, isn't he?" Chaim asked.

"Yes. Yes, he is okay." All of a sudden Jacob was sobbing. How like Miriam Shoshanna. How fitting that she would do something like that.

"It happened so fast," Chaim said, "but that much I did see.

Don't the rabbis say that if you save one life it's as if you saved the whole world?"

Yes. The whole world. Peter Shaffer would grow up and have a family, children and grandchildren, and a future. Hashem hadn't taken Miriam from him without a reason. Her death had served a purpose.

Would Jacob sacrifice his own life for Peter Shaffer? Yes, now he most certainly would. But that wouldn't have been true before the war. Back then, he had been too wrapped up in books and laws to notice people who might be standing in harm's way. Too blind to see that Hashem cares for people most of all.

"Thank you," Jacob said when he could speak. "Thank you for telling me." At last he stood. His knees still felt weak, but they would hold him now.

"You will come again, Jacob? Please don't be a stranger anymore. I have missed you."

"I will be back on Friday, Chaim, to buy vegetables for Shabbat."

Chaim squeezed Jacob's shoulder. "I'll look forward to your visit."

Jacob stared down at the sidewalk as he retraced his steps toward home. The car may have been out of control, but Hashem hadn't been. How much easier it was to trust Hashem knowing that a tragedy served a purpose.

But would Jacob still trust Him if Avi and his family were among the dead? He didn't know the answer. He thought of the man named Job from Scripture, and the battle behind the scenes that Job had not been able to see. In the end, Hashem restored everything Job had lost and even gave him a new family. It had always bothered Jacob that Hashem would heartlessly take Job's children and then offer a replacement family. How could there be a replacement family?

Then he thought of Esther and Peter. Maybe he did understand.

Jacob wanted to believe that what his enemies meant for harm, Hashem could turn into good, even if he couldn't see it. He was slowly learning that walking in faith meant leaving a way of life in which he was in control and willingly walking in uncertainty, trusting that God was in control.

On Yom Kippur, Jacob would ask Hashem to forgive his lack of faith. And he would ask for help in trusting His goodness, even when he couldn't see it.

CHAPTER 43

ESTHER LEAPED UP from Mr. Mendel's sofa, shaking with fury. "You have no right to tell me what to do! You aren't my parents!" She couldn't believe what she was hearing. Penny and Mr. Mendel had ganged up on her. They had sat her down in his living room to tell her that she could no longer have anything to do with Jacky Hoffman. Who did they think they were? She wouldn't stay seated for this.

"We are two people who love you," Mr. Mendel said. "And when you see someone you love heading toward danger, it is natural to try to protect them."

"Why won't you believe me that Jacky is nice now? He's changed?"

"Because the evidence shows that he has not changed. I wish I did not have to tell you this, Esther, but he was fired from his job at the supermarket. The manager told me that he suspected Jacky of stealing from his customers."

"That's not true! Why does everyone hate him?"

"To you he seems charming and flattering. But others who know him say that he cannot be trusted."

Esther didn't want to cry. She wanted to stand up to Penny and Mr. Mendel and make them see that she was right and that they were wrong about Jacky. Her tears were from anger, she told herself. They weren't childish tears. "He's my friend!" she shouted.

"You are much too young to have a boy for a close friend," Mr. Mendel said, "and to be holding his hand."

"Were you spying on us?"

"I know that you do not understand, and that you may not understand until you are much older. But Penny and I have made this decision for your own good because we care about you. We want to spare you suffering of a much harsher kind."

"I don't want to hear any more." She put her hands over her ears and turned to leave.

Penny stopped her. "Wait. You can leave in a minute, but I want to tell you a story first."

Esther crossed her arms and looked away. She didn't want to hear anything that Penny Goodrich had to say, but since they probably wouldn't leave her alone unless she listened, she may as well get it over with.

"When I took that trip to New Jersey last summer it was to meet my real mother. I found out that she was only seventeen years old when I was born. That's not much older than you are, Esther. She had a boyfriend when she was in high school, and she thought they really loved each other. Some boys will tell a girl anything she wants to hear, just so he can take advantage of her. . . . D-do you know what I mean?"

Yes, Esther knew what Penny was fumbling to say, and she felt her cheeks grow warm. She gave a curt nod.

"My mother thought it was love, but it wasn't. And when she told her boyfriend that she was pregnant with me, he took off. He had other plans for his life, and they didn't include a wife and baby. My mother had to give me up for adoption. Her life was turned upside down by her mistake . . . and so was mine."

For a brief moment, Esther felt sorry for Penny, stuck with two old people for parents instead of a real mother. But her sympathy lasted only a moment before she remembered that Penny had forbidden her to see Jacky. She got mad all over again.

"Are you finished?"

"Listen, Esther. I wish you could meet my mother and talk to her yourself. I think I know what she would tell you. Don't give your heart away to the first cute fellow that comes along. Wait for a good man. And as Mr. Mendel found out, Jacky isn't a good man."

"May I go?" Esther asked, tapping her foot. Penny nodded. But before Esther could leave, Mr. Mendel laid his hand on her shoulder.

"I am so sorry to hurt you this way. But please trust us. We believe your father would make the same decision that we made, if he were here."

Esther bolted all the way upstairs to her room on the third floor and flung herself facedown on her bed, sobbing over yet another loss in her life. As badly as she wanted to be a grown-up, she felt like a very small girl—and she wanted her mama. Other girls had mothers to hold them and soothe them and give them advice, to help them heal from a broken heart. Esther longed to have her own mother back again, if only for a moment.

But Mama was gone.

By the time Esther's anger and grief were spent, night had fallen. Her bedroom was dark, her pillow soaked with her tears. She rolled onto her back and thought about Jacky Hoffman. It had been flattering and exciting to receive so much attention from an older boy, especially one who was as cute as a movie idol. But Esther had to admit—if only to herself—that along with the thrill there had been an icy sliver of fear. She remembered feeling uncomfortable with him the time they had hidden beneath his back stairs, as if part of her had known that she wasn't ready to be a grown-up yet. Once or twice she had seen a side of him that she hadn't liked but had tried to ignore, such as the time he had called Mr. Mendel names and said he wished they would tear down the synagogue. If she were really honest, she would admit that she would much rather go to Grandma Shaffer's house on Saturday afternoons and play with Woofer's puppies than sit in the balcony at the movie theater with Jacky's sweaty arm around her shoulder and stale popcorn crunching beneath her feet.

But for now, Esther couldn't move beyond her outrage that Penny and Mr. Mendel had interfered in her life. They had forbidden her to see him. They had no right! No right at all!

The next day when Jacky offered to walk home from school with her, Esther had to tell him that she couldn't be friends with him anymore. She expected him to be as outraged as she had been, but he simply shrugged and walked away. By the end of the week he was already holding hands with another girl from Esther's class. She felt humiliated and angry all over again. And lonely. She didn't have any other friends.

"I wish you could talk to me, Peter," she said as she trudged home from school with him.

He nodded sadly and pointed to himself. She knew he was saying, *Me too.*

They walked up the steps to the porch and checked the mailbox. No letters today. They got as far as the foyer when Mr. Mendel's door opened. "Could you both please come inside for a moment? There is someone here who would like to talk to you."

Esther had met the woman in Mr. Mendel's apartment once before. They had eaten cake together. Esther couldn't recall her name.

"Let me take your coats," Mr. Mendel said. "Sit down, please." He acted so polite and formal that he made Esther nervous. The woman looked uneasy, too, standing in the middle of the room. Was she going to tell them that something terrible had happened to Daddy? Esther glanced at Peter as they sat down on Mr. Mendel's sofa. She moved closer to her brother, just in case.

The woman drew a deep breath as if to steady herself, then exhaled. "The last time we met I asked Mr. Mendel not to tell you my name. It's Esther Fischer. I'm . . . I'm your grandmother."

Esther's mouth opened, but nothing came out. The room seemed to spin. She didn't know what she would say even if she could speak. Was it really true? Was this tall, elegant woman really their grandmother?

As she stared in shock at the woman, Esther began to see the resemblance. Her hair was the same color as Mama's hair and Peter's, but with gray strands woven through it. And her hands. They were slender and graceful like Mama's.

"I'm sorry . . ." Mrs. Fischer began. She couldn't finish.

Warring emotions pulled Esther in two directions again. She wanted to leap up and hug this woman. She wanted to explode in anger and accuse her.

"Where have you been?" Esther finally asked. The words came out angrier than she intended them to.

"I've . . . I've been right here. In Brooklyn. It's a long story, Esther, and I . . . I hope you'll let me explain it to you."

"Why didn't you come to Mama's funeral?"

Mrs. Fischer put her hand over her eyes. She had been standing all this time but now she sank onto a chair.

"Give her a chance, Esther," Mr. Mendel said quietly. "Try to understand."

"Are you the one who found her for us?" she asked him.

He nodded. "Your grandmother arranged for your music lessons at the conservatory. And for Peter to play with the baseball team last summer."

"Why did you keep it a secret? Don't you like us? And why did you get mad at Mama?"

Mrs. Fischer uncovered her eyes and sat up straight, composing herself. "Would it upset you to learn that I'm Jewish, like your friend Mr. Mendel? And that your mother was Jewish?"

"No, she wasn't! She used to go to church with us on Sunday."

"But her father and I are Jewish, Esther. Your mother was raised in a Jewish home, like this one. When she became a Christian, it divided us."

Again, Esther couldn't speak. She reached for her brother's hand as she tried to take it all in.

"I no longer want anything to divide us," Mrs. Fischer said. "I would like to get to know both of you . . . if-if you will let me. I would like to be a family."

Tears filled Esther's eyes. She had found Mama's family—her

family. She had longed for this, hadn't she? It had been her greatest wish, besides having Daddy come home safely. But fear and mistrust pinned her in place like two giant hands. She couldn't move.

Mrs. Fischer picked up a photograph album from Mr. Mendel's coffee table. "I brought some pictures of your mother to show you. Would you like to see them? She has two brothers, David and Samuel. They're your uncles."

Peter rose from the sofa first and went to Mrs. Fischer's side. He studied her face for a long moment as if searching for traces of their mother, then he looked down at the photos. He leaned against her, and Grandmother Fischer put her arm around his shoulders.

After a moment, Esther rose, too. She went to stand on the other side of her grandmother to look at the album, seeing pictures of her mother's family for the very first time.

CHAPTER 44

November 1944

Dear Mother and Father Mendel,

This may be the last letter I will be able to write to you, but I need to let you know what is happening here. Just when the war seemed close to an end, we once again despair for our lives.

In October, the Hungarian government tried to sign a truce with the Allies again. The Nazis found out about it and sent their SS troops here to arrest Hungary's leader. They have taken him to Berlin as their prisoner and have replaced him with the leader of the Hungarian Nazi Party, the Arrow Cross. These vicious men control our country now, with help from the SS.

The Nazis' angel of death, Adolph Eichmann, has returned to finish deporting the remainder of Budapest's Jews. The Arrow Cross does not respect the Swedish safe houses or our documents. Our angel, Raoul Wallenberg, fights for us day and night and tries to protect us, but Arrow Cross members come boldly into the safe houses to brutalize people, killing them or hauling them away to be killed. Mr. Wallenberg has tried to organize the Jewish men who are left into an armed force so they can protect us and bring in needed food and medicine. Many of our friends have already been arrested or have disappeared. We fear they are dead.

We know that the Russians are moving closer and closer, but this only makes the Nazis more determined to be rid of us before time runs out for them. Adolph Eichmann has been unable to get the railroad cars he needs to deport us, so we have learned that he plans to march us to deportation camps on foot. We don't know if our Swedish savior can rescue us from these death marches or not.

I have decided to leave this letter and the others I have written here in the Swedish house, hoping that—if the very worst happens—they will be found someday and sent to you in America. Please know that even though my faith is very weak and I don't understand why we are made to suffer this way, I still believe in Hashem's goodness and in a better life in the world to come.

> With love,
> Your daughter-in-law,
> Sarah Rivkah Mendel

CHAPTER 45

DECEMBER 1944

ON A COLD AFTERNOON in early December, Jacob returned to his apartment after his daily walk and turned on the radio to listen to the news. He wished he hadn't. The Nazis had launched a massive surprise counterattack against the Allies near the border between Germany and Belgium. They had penetrated the Allied front with troops and Panzer divisions and artillery pieces, supported by V-1 and V-2 rockets. The Americans had sustained heavy casualties in the nearly round-the-clock fighting. Fresh, inexperienced troops were under heavy enemy gunfire, many for the first time. Bitterly cold temperatures, dwindling ammunition supplies, and knee-deep snow added to their misery. Ed Shaffer was likely in the middle of it all. The children would be terrified for his safety—and with good reason.

Jacob hauled himself to his feet when the doorbell rang. When he saw who it was, his heart stood still. The two police detectives with the Irish names had returned. Beyond them, a police car waited at the curb with the motor running.

"Yes?" Jacob asked.

"We need you to come to the police station with us, Mr. Mendel."

"For what reason?"

"You are under arrest for arson."

Jacob could only stare in disbelief. He felt a weight on his chest as if the two men were sitting on it. While he had seen them canvassing the streets from time to time, talking to his neighbors, Jacob thought that the rebbe had convinced them of his innocence.

"Why are you harassing me this way?" he asked.

"We've known all along you were guilty," one of them said, "and now we have the evidence to prove it."

"It was only a matter of time before you were caught," the other detective added.

"But I had nothing to do with the fire."

"Well, we have two witnesses who say that you did. They'll testify that they saw you enter the synagogue through the back door carrying a paper bag, shortly before the fire started."

"They are mistaken. Or else they are lying."

"That's up to a court to decide. The district attorney is filing charges against you. It will save everyone a lot of trouble, Mr. Mendel, if you simply confess."

Jacob shook his head. "Confess to something that I did not do? I am telling you I did not start the fire."

"In that case, you better hire a lawyer."

Jacob had no money for a lawyer. He had given away nearly every cent he had to the War Refugee Board. His monthly pension check and this apartment building were all he had left. Would he have to mortgage it to clear his name?

"Let's go," one detective said, motioning to the car.

Jacob's chest ached. "May I go inside first and get my overcoat? And there are some pills that I should bring with me."

"Make it quick."

The two men followed him inside, waiting impatiently while he called Rebbe Grunfeld. Jacob knew that he could not go through this ordeal alone. Now more than ever he needed a friend to stand alongside him. He quickly told the rebbe about the detectives.

"They say that I will need a lawyer, but I do not know of one."

"I'll call Abraham Stein from our congregation right away. We'll meet you at the police station. Don't worry, Yaacov. It isn't good for you to worry."

But how could he help worrying? Jacob fetched his pills and his overcoat. He locked the doors to his apartment and rode with the detectives to the station. Jacob had never been inside a police station in his life, and he found the noisy, confusing place intimidating. The two detectives made him sit down in a tiny gray room without any windows and began to interrogate him. One of the men stank of perspiration.

The next hour reminded Jacob of a scene from Hungary in the old days. One after the other the men badgered him with accusations and questions, telling him what he supposedly had done and demanding that he confess. It was the way that Jews had been treated for centuries. He might as well have remained in Hungary.

"I cannot confess because I am innocent," Jacob repeated. "I did not start the fire."

"Our two witnesses say you did. We've been talking to your neighbors all along, you know, keeping the crime fresh in people's minds. And it finally paid off."

"Whoever they are, they are not telling the truth."

The room seemed to be running out of air as the men continued to attack him, trying to wear him down. The pain in Jacob's chest grew worse. Finally he became so weary that he simply stopped talking. They weren't listening to him anyway.

"Okay, if you refuse to cooperate, Mr. Mendel, then here's what's going to happen. We're taking you downstairs to be fingerprinted, and then you'll go into a holding cell until your arraignment. You're entitled to have your lawyer with you for that."

"Will I be spending the night in jail?"

"The judge will decide that when you are arraigned—but I wouldn't count on going home, if I were you. Arson is a felony."

By the time a policeman finished taking Jacob's fingerprints, Rebbe Grunfeld had arrived with Abraham Stein. The lawyer listened to Jacob's story and agreed that they would plead "innocent" at the arraignment. When it was their turn to stand before the judge, Mr. Stein asked that Jacob be released from custody due to his age and health considerations—and to the undue hardship that eating non-kosher food would create.

"The rabbi of the synagogue in question is willing to vouch for Mr. Mendel's character, Your Honor. The defendant has no prior criminal history and strong ties to the community."

The judge set bail at a moderate amount. Within a matter of minutes, Jacob's arraignment was over. Once he posted bond, he would be free to go home. Somehow Rebbe Grunfeld managed to scrape up enough money for the bond. By the time Jacob stepped outside into a freezing December night, it had become dark.

"What happens now?" Jacob asked Mr. Stein.

"I'll ask the district attorney for time to research your case and see how credible these two witnesses are. I'll also need to find out what other evidence they have against you. Once I have all that information, you and I will meet to prepare your defense."

"How much time until the case goes to trial?"

"The courts are short-staffed due to the war. And they usually recess for the holidays, too. We're probably looking at sometime early next spring for a court date. Unless you want me to petition to have your case tried sooner? You have a right to a speedy trial with felony charges."

"No, there is no hurry. I will need time to raise money, somehow. I need to pay you back, Rebbe, for posting bond."

"Don't worry about that for now, Yaacov."

"And I must also pay you, Mr. Stein."

"I won't push for a speedy trial, then. In the meantime, Mr. Mendel, take care of yourself."

Jacob took a taxi home. He didn't sleep at all that night. Would the final years of his life be spent in jail? He had lost his wife and his son; now he might lose his home and his freedom. He thought about the story of Joseph, and how he also had been sent to prison for a crime he did not commit. Eventually, Hashem had turned Joseph's trials into something good. But how could Hashem possibly bring anything good from this?

Chapter 46

February 1945

Penny hunched her shoulders against the bitter cold as she picked her way down the snowy sidewalk to the apartment. The streets were dark when she left for work in the morning and nearly dark when she returned home, but not only from the setting sun or the overcast skies. The government had ordered a national dim-out all across the country to conserve fuel from January 15 until May 8.

And now it was snowing again. The steadily falling flakes dusted the shoulders of her overcoat as she walked and made the sidewalks treacherous. Tomorrow she would have to drive the bus through the fresh snowfall. This was her second winter as a bus driver, but she still dreaded driving on slippery, snow-covered streets.

This winter had seemed especially long to her, and it was only February. Christmas had come and gone ages ago. Last year Roy had made the holiday fun and memorable for Penny and the children, and it had been lonely without him this year. Still, Penny had bought a small Christmas tree and the children helped decorate it. They opened presents on Christmas Day and ate dinner at the duplex. She and the kids had made care packages to send to Eddie and Roy.

January had brought more cold, snowy weather. On New Year's Eve, Penny remembered going to the USO dance a year ago with Sheila. How could an entire year have passed, and still the war dragged on? This year, she and the children spent New Year's Eve in the apartment, listening to the radio and playing Parcheesi.

Penny climbed the slippery front steps and stopped on the porch to check the mailbox, hoping and praying that there would be a letter from Roy today. Her shoulders sagged when she saw that there wasn't. How long had it been? More than two and a half months! Roy's last letter had arrived right after Thanksgiving, and he had been reminiscing about celebrating Christmas with her and the children last year.

Penny no longer felt mere disappointment each time she saw the empty mailbox, but real fear. She hadn't told the children how long it had been. As much as she needed to talk to someone about her concern for Roy's safety, she hadn't wanted to upset the kids. They loved Roy, too.

As Penny stepped into the warm foyer, wiping her boots, Mr. Mendel's apartment door opened. A man in a dark suit and carrying a briefcase was just leaving. "They're going to set a trial date for sometime in April," the man was saying. "But we'll be in touch before then."

"Thank you again, Mr. Stein."

"Please, Jacob. Call me Abraham."

Mr. Mendel had been away so much lately, Penny hadn't spoken with him very much. She had seen him coming and going with the white-bearded rabbi and this man with the briefcase and knew they had important business to conduct. She looked at her friend now, and he seemed worn and worried.

She waited for Mr. Stein to leave and asked, "Is everything okay, Mr. Mendel? You haven't been sick, have you?"

"No, Penny. Just busy."

"We haven't seen you in a long time. We've missed you."

"Would you like to come in? I just made tea."

"That would be wonderful." She left her boots outside his door and followed him into his kitchen, slipping her coat over the back of her chair. He had indeed just made tea, and he poured a cup for her. "I read in the newspaper that Russian troops have arrived in Hungary," she said as she waited for it to cool.

"Yes. We are all wondering if mail service might be restored once the country is liberated. But it is still much too soon to hope. The battles are still raging in Budapest. Anything can happen."

Again, Penny thought of Roy as she pondered Mr. Mendel's words: *Anything can happen.* "The children got a letter from their father yesterday," she said, blowing on her tea. "He says it's been a cold winter over in Europe, too."

"Are the children well? It seems I am always away when they arrive home from school."

"They're fine. Their Grandmother Fischer picked them up from school today to take them shopping for clothes. That's why they aren't home. They're both growing so fast that nothing fits them anymore."

"And you are well, Penny?"

She nodded, but it wasn't true. Her eyes filled with tears. He reached across the table and laid his hand on top of hers, saying nothing.

"Sorry. I know you're worried about your family, too, Mr. Mendel. . . . It's just that I haven't gotten a letter from my friend Roy Fuller in a long time now, and I'm really worried about him. He usually writes to me at least once or twice a week."

"Where is he stationed?"

"Over in the Pacific somewhere. He's fighting the Japanese. I'm trying not to worry, but the Japanese have these suicide bombers who crash their airplanes into American ships, making them explode and catch on fire. And I read that the Marines are fighting a terrible battle right now in a place called Iwo Jima, and . . . and it's so hard."

"I understand."

They were simple words, but Penny knew that Mr. Mendel, of all people, did understand. She had waited only two and a half months to hear from Roy, while Mr. Mendel had been waiting years for news of his family. He knew the frustration of having loved ones in danger far away and what it was like to be out of touch with no way to reach them. He must have experienced the helpless anger she felt, knowing there was nothing you could do as you waited for news that never came.

"If something has happened to Roy," she said, "I don't know how I will ever find out about it. He has a fiancée and a family back home in Pennsylvania who would be notified, but I don't think they would write and tell me. I mean, Roy and I are good friends, but he may not have mentioned to anyone that he was writing to me. I . . . I just don't know what to do."

"I think you already know what my advice will be," he said quietly. "We should never stop searching for the people we love."

Penny bit her lip, holding back tears. "I know. And I'm so thankful that you talked me into visiting my real mother. I just wish . . ." She paused to pull a handkerchief from her purse along with one of Hazel's letters. "I want to show you this, Mr. Mendel. It's a newspaper clipping that my mother sent me." She slid it across the table and waited while he unfolded it.

"An obituary?"

"The soldier who died was my real father. He was a career army officer, killed in action in Belgium last December."

"I am so sorry."

"I feel sad about him dying, even though I never knew him, because now we never will meet." Mr. Mendel studied the clipping, but Penny knew every word of it by heart. "It says he had a wife and three children, but that's not right. He had four children. I guess I'll never know if he ever thought about me or wanted to meet me. . . ."

Mr. Mendel folded the paper and slid it back to her. "This missing friend of yours—Roy. Where was he from?"

It took Penny a moment to react to the change of topic. "He's from Moosic, Pennsylvania. I always remembered the name of the town because I thought he said *music* the first time he told me."

"Is it far from here?"

"It's near Scranton, I think. He used to take a bus home whenever he had a weekend off, so it can't be too far."

"The regret that you feel for having never met your father is understandable. And regrets are very hard things to live with over a lifetime. You should not pile on more regrets, Penny. You need to search for your friend and find out why he stopped writing to you."

"But . . . the only way to do that would be to go ask his fiancée or his family."

"Well, then . . . ?" he asked, spreading his hands.

"I can't just show up on their doorstep . . . can I?"

"That is what you did when you visited your mother, yes?" Penny nodded. "I believe it would ease your heart if you went and spoke with Roy's family. And if something has happened to your friend, you could offer your condolences and share your grief with them. One thing I have learned during these past few terrible years is that our grief and sorrow should be shared, not carried alone."

Penny knew it was true. She had seen how other people had helped Mrs. Shaffer grieve after her son Joe died. And Penny had felt better after sharing the news about her real father with Mr. Mendel just now.

"More tea, Penny?" he asked. She shook her head as she studied her friend. Mr. Mendel had more gray hairs mixed through his hair and beard than he used to have. And he seemed different to her, not merely sad but . . . defeated.

"Won't you share with me why you're so sad, Mr. Mendel?"

He stared at the tabletop, not at her. "When the time is right, Penny." He rose to clear away the tea things and put them in the sink. "Mrs. Fischer told me she is taking the children to a concert on Saturday, yes? I think you should go and visit your friend's family that day. The truth may be difficult to hear, but believe me, if I could end the suspense of waiting I would gladly do it, no matter how painful the truth may be."

The following day, Penny checked the bus schedule to Moosic, Pennsylvania. Mr. Mendel had been right when he'd advised her to visit her mother in New Jersey. Now she would take a bus to Moosic and find out about Roy. She had no address for either his family or Sally, and couldn't even recall Sally's last name. But she trusted that Moosic was still the small town Roy had described to her, where everyone knew his neighbor. Someone would certainly know Roy's father, who was the principal of the elementary school.

Penny left very early Saturday morning and rode the bus from Grand Central Station to Scranton. The journey over the steep, snowy mountains of eastern Pennsylvania was beautiful, the forests and the views breathtaking. A year ago, she never would have had the courage to ride so far all alone, especially to visit the home of strangers. Yet here she was, on her way to find out what had become of her friend. Her best friend.

Every time she read one of Roy's long, chatty letters, it had seemed as though he were sitting right beside her on the bus again, talking to her. She wished Eddie would write letters like that. Eddie's letters were short and to the point, as if she was his employee instead of his friend. But Roy never failed to make Penny smile, even though he also shared news about the war and about losing friends in battle. And he always asked Penny how she was doing, making it seem as if her boring life really interested him.

She arrived in Scranton at noontime and changed to a local bus for the short trip to Moosic. The little town was nestled among the mountains in coal-mining country. She was starved by the time she got there and stopped to eat a quick lunch at the diner that also served as the village bus station. She wondered if the friendly teenaged waitress had once been one of Roy's students at the high school. Penny was about to ask, then realized the girl would have been too young for high school when the war began three years ago. Instead, Penny asked the waitress if she knew Mr. Fuller, the elementary school principal.

"Oh, sure. Everyone in town knows Principal Fuller."

"Do you know where he lives? I'm a friend of his son Roy. I know that Roy is stationed overseas, but I need to talk to his father." The girl directed Penny to the house, which wasn't far away. It would take her ten or fifteen minutes to walk there, the waitress said.

As Penny followed the directions, she wondered what it would be like to live in a nice little town like this, far away from the noisy city. It must be wonderful to know all of your neighbors by name and stand outside in your yard and talk to them instead of barricading yourself behind locked doors all your life like her parents had done.

If Eddie ever did fall in love with her and asked Penny to marry him, she wondered if he would like to move to a pretty little place like Moosic. She had no idea. She didn't know what Eddie liked and didn't like, or what his hopes and dreams were for the future.

She found the house without a problem and walked up the neatly shoveled sidewalk to knock on the door. The man who answered it seemed as wholesome and friendly as Roy was.

"Hi, Mr. Fuller? You don't know me, but my name is Penny Goodrich. I'm a friend of your son Roy."

"Come in, Miss Goodrich. It's much too cold to stand out here."

"Thank you. I promise I won't take up too much of your time."

She stomped the snow off her feet and stepped inside, reminding herself not to babble. She always went on and on whenever she was nervous and never gave the other person a chance to get a word in edgewise. And she was nervous now, no doubt about it.

The house was a little shabby and old-fashioned, but wonderfully warm. Penny unbuttoned her coat but left it on as Mr. Fuller led her into a well-worn living room. "Can I get you some coffee or a cold drink?" he asked.

"No, thanks. I just had lunch at the diner."

Mr. Fuller gestured to a chair and sat down across from her. "You say you're a friend of Roy's?"

Penny nodded. She drew a deep breath, steeling herself for bad news. "I met Roy when he was stationed in Brooklyn at the Navy Yard. That's where I live. In Brooklyn, I mean, not the Navy Yard. Anyway, Roy and I got to be friends, and he helped me out so many times that I lost count of them all. He told me all about his fiancée, Sally, and I told him all about Eddie, my . . ." She paused, stumbling over the word. "M-my boyfriend."

"Yes, I remember him talking about a good friend he met in Brooklyn. You two rode the same bus every day, right?"

"Yes, that's right." She smiled, surprised that Roy had mentioned her to his father. "Roy and I have been writing to each other ever since he went overseas, but I haven't gotten a letter from him in more than two months now, and I've been very worried. And so . . . and so I came to . . . to find out . . ."

"All the way from Brooklyn." He said it as a statement, not a question, smiling faintly when he said it. "You must be a very good friend, Miss Goodrich." Mr. Fuller paused, and Penny realized she was holding her breath as she waited. "Roy was injured in the Battle of Leyte in the Philippines. The Marines sent me a telegram with the news."

Penny swallowed. "Is he going to be okay?"

"Too soon to tell. He's in a field hospital somewhere in the Pacific, too sick to be moved home for now. He was severely burned following an explosion. They're not sure if he will recover his sight."

"That's terrible!" But she was relieved to know that he was still alive. "He's going to live . . . isn't he? He has to live!"

"The doctors aren't making any promises. With burns that severe, there is always the risk of infection—and he's in such a primitive part of the world."

But Penny felt relieved to know that Roy was alive. The trip had been worth it just to find out that much. She longed to do something more for him so he wouldn't lose hope. "If I keep writing letters to him, do you think he'll get them?" she asked.

"I'm sure he will. I can give you his new address." He got up to copy it for her.

"How is Sally doing?" Penny asked. "She must be so worried about him."

"I imagine so." It seemed like an odd thing to say, and Mr. Fuller had looked away when he said it. "She works in the hair salon near the bus station if you'd like to stop by and see her."

"Thanks. Maybe I will." Penny stood. She had found out about her friend, and now she faced another long bus ride home. "I'll be praying for him, Mr. Fuller. And for you, too," she added when she remembered that he was a widower. "If you don't mind, I'd like to give you my address, too, so you can let me know if there's any more news about Roy—or if there's anything I can do to help."

"I'd be happy to do that."

"I should go," she said after giving it to him.

"So soon? You just got here."

"I know. But it's a long ride home again." She walked with him to the door. "Roy is a good man, Mr. Fuller. You must be very proud of your son."

"Thank you. I am."

"And Sally is a very lucky girl."

Penny retraced her steps to the bus station and easily found the beauty parlor where Sally worked. The salon had a large glass window in front, and Penny could see the beauticians working inside, cutting and styling and shampooing hair. She had her hand on the knob, ready to go inside when she recognized Sally, laughing and smiling as she combed an older woman's hair. Sally was even prettier in real life than in her pictures.

Suddenly, meeting Sally seemed like a dumb idea. What if Roy hadn't told her about his good friend in Brooklyn who happened to be a girl? What if Sally didn't know that the two of them had been writing to each other all these months? Penny would never forgive herself if she did something stupid to break them up, especially after all the trouble Roy had gone through to woo her. Penny knew how much Roy loved Sally.

Don't be a green bean, she told herself. She turned away from the salon and hurried to the bus station for the long, cold ride home to Brooklyn.

CHAPTER 47

APRIL 1945

ESTHER LAID THE NEWSPAPER she had just purchased on the dining room table and went into the living room to turn on the radio. Spring had finally arrived, and events in the world were happening so rapidly that she had fallen into her old pattern of listening to news broadcasts every morning and night and reading every newspaper she could get her hands on.

Two weeks ago it had been Easter Sunday, and she and Peter had eaten the dinner Penny had prepared at the Goodrich house. Grandma Shaffer had come to church with them and even came next door for Easter dinner, too. The Sunday newspaper had carried huge headlines that day: *American Troops on Okinawa*. Mr. Goodrich explained that the tiny island was part of Japan, which meant the war was one step closer to being over.

Ten days after Easter, on April 11, Allied soldiers had liberated a Nazi death camp called Buchenwald. Eyewitness descriptions of the horrors they had found appeared in all the newspapers. Esther had gone downstairs to console Mr. Mendel.

"Thank you for thinking of me, Esther," he had said. "But you must promise me that you will stop reading about these atrocities. If you look at these images, you will never be able to erase them from your mind."

The very next day, news of President Roosevelt's sudden death from a brain hemorrhage shocked and stunned the nation. He had seemed like a beloved grandfather to Esther throughout the war, coming into her living room each week to encourage everyone with his fireside chats. And now, just when victory was within sight, the president wouldn't be here to celebrate it with them.

Esther spread out her latest newspaper on the dining room table. She was scanning the headings, searching for new articles to clip, when a photograph of a burned-out building caught her eye. She had stared at the ruins of the synagogue across the street for so many months before they rebuilt it that she recognized the photograph immediately.

"Hey, Peter, come look! There's a story in the paper about the fire across the street. The caption says, 'Trial Set for Man Charged in Synagogue Fire.' " Peter and Penny both hurried into the dining room to peer at the picture over Esther's shoulder. "Did you see this article, Penny? I didn't know they had arrested someone, did you?"

"No, I haven't heard anything about it," Penny said. "I'm surprised Mr. Mendel didn't mention it."

Esther read the article out loud to them: " 'The trial is set to begin on Monday, April 23, for the man charged with arson in the fire that left a Brooklyn synagogue severely damaged eighteen months ago. Police arrested a former member of Congregation Ohel Moshe last December after two witnesses to the crime came forward. The accused man, Jacob Mendel—" Esther halted, staring at the name in shock.

Jacob Mendel.

She couldn't move, couldn't utter a sound. It couldn't be true. Someone had made a terrible mistake. As she stared at her friend's name in disbelief, Esther heard a strangled cry behind her, in her ear.

"Noooo!"

She whirled around. The cry had come from Peter.

"Noooo!" he said again. The harsh sound squeezed from his throat as if ripped out by force. His entire body writhed as if in terrible pain as he tried to squeeze out more words. "He d-d-d-didn't . . . !"

It took Esther a moment to realize what she'd just heard—Peter was talking! He was talking again after all this time!

"We know he didn't do it," Penny said, trying to soothe him. "They'll find out that he didn't do it."

Esther could only stare at her brother. Finally, after all these months, he was no longer silent. But it had taken a terrible catastrophe to bring it about. *Mr. Mendel had been arrested!*

Peter flailed wildly as he squirmed out of Penny's arms. He staggered to the front door and thundered down the stairs. Esther heard him pounding on Mr. Mendel's door as she and Penny hurried after him.

"I s-s-saw . . . !" Peter stammered when Mr. Mendel opened his door. "I-I know!"

"He's talking," Esther said in wonder. "Peter's talking!"

Mr. Mendel held Peter's shoulders to steady him. "What are you trying to say, son?"

"The f-f-fire . . ."

"We just read about it in the newspaper," Esther said. "Is it true? Did the police really arrest you?"

Mr. Mendel nodded. "The trial begins on Monday."

"Why didn't you tell us?" Esther cried out. "This is awful!"

"I have been hoping that it could be avoided. My lawyer has been working to get the charges dismissed, but—"

Peter gripped the front of Mr. Mendel's shirt. His face turned red with effort as he struggled to say more. "What is it, Peter?" Mr. Mendel asked. "Take your time. It's okay."

"You didn't do it! . . . I know! . . . The f-fire . . . I was there! Jacky did it."

"Jack Hoffman? He is one of the witnesses who is accusing me."

Esther recalled Jacky saying that they should tear down the ruined synagogue and make a ball park. And she remembered how he and his brother, Gary, had laughed and splashed in the puddles as they'd watched the building burn. "Why would he accuse you?" she asked Mr. Mendel. "Why would he lie?"

"Because he knows that I was the one who made you stop seeing him."

"Oh no!" Esther felt sick to her stomach. Mr. Mendel was in terrible trouble, and she was to blame. She never should have trusted Jacky Hoffman. "Did Jacky really set the fire?" she asked her brother.

"Y-yes," Peter said. "Yes. Him and Gary . . . and . . . and me."

"You?" Esther breathed.

Peter began to sob, making it hard to understand what he was saying. "I found the kerosene . . . I went inside with them because I was mad at Daddy for going away. . . ."

"No," Esther murmured. "Oh, Peter . . . no."

"And . . . and when it started to burn, they . . . they told me to keep my mouth shut or . . . or else . . ."

"That's why you couldn't talk all this time?" Esther remembered how Peter had run into the bedroom as Daddy was packing to leave. Peter had clung to him, whimpering, just as the fire sirens began wailing in the distance. Peter hadn't said another word since.

"I didn't mean to . . ." he wept. "I'm sorry!"

"Shh . . . shh . . ." Mr. Mendel soothed. He held Peter tightly, consoling him. "I know, I know, Peter. It will be all right."

"No it won't! . . . T-tell them it wasn't you!"

"You poor child, holding on to such a terrible secret all this time. No wonder . . . no wonder . . ."

"Will Peter be in trouble with the police?" Esther asked.

"He is just a child. Surely the older boy will be held responsible."

"What should we do now?" Penny asked.

"Let him grieve. And then, when Peter is ready, I will call my lawyer and let him hear what Peter has to say."

They all sat down in Mr. Mendel's apartment, and by the time the lawyer, Mr. Stein, arrived, Peter had calmed down. Esther listened in disbelief as Peter explained how he had found the can of kerosene in the basement by the washtubs. He had been angry with Daddy and had wanted to do something drastic to convince him to stay home. The two Hoffman brothers had come along just then. The three of them had crept into the synagogue while the back door was unlocked and hidden in a stairwell until after the men finished their prayers and went home.

When the boys came out of hiding, Jacky found a room filled with books, and they'd emptied the shelves, ripping out pages and making a huge pile in the middle of the room. Gary poured the kerosene over them while Jacky handed Peter a box of matches. "You want to light it?"

Peter had been afraid. All of a sudden it hadn't been fun anymore, and he wanted to go home. They called him a chicken, then tried to force him to light it. Peter had tried to run away, but Jacky caught him and held on to him and made him watch while Gary lit the match and tossed it onto the pile. The paper ignited with a *whoosh.*

"You're guilty now," Jacky had told him as the books began to smoke and burn. *"You better keep your mouth shut, because if you tell anyone, we'll set you and your house on fire next."*

Jacky had held Peter's arms behind his back and made him watch as the flames grew higher and higher, the smoke thicker. Peter had been terrified. He tried to scream but nothing came out. When the fire spread to the curtains, Jacky pushed Peter to the ground and ran. Peter scrambled to his feet and ran out of the synagogue, not stopping until he reached home.

Esther stared at her brother when he finished his story. He was guilty of arson. She was astounded, grief-stricken. Everything was falling apart. She had wanted to get Mr. Mendel out of trouble, but not this way. "Are they going to arrest my brother?" she asked the lawyer.

"I already looked into the backgrounds of the two so-called witnesses in preparation for the trial," he replied. "Jack and Gary Hoffman have a record of vandalism and other delinquent acts. Your brother doesn't, does he?"

"No, he's a good kid," Esther said. "He didn't mean to do it."

Mr. Stein had been taking notes on a tablet, which he now stowed in his briefcase, snapping the latches shut. "I'll need a few days to file some motions and bring this new evidence to the police. I don't want to get everyone's hopes up prematurely, but I think we can get this case closed and the charges against Mr. Mendel dropped."

"What about Peter?" Esther asked.

"He is a minor. I will do my best to ensure that he isn't charged."

Mr. Stein left a few minutes later. Mr. Mendel, Penny, and Peter sat looking at each other as if numb with shock. Esther couldn't move, either. "I wish I had never trusted Jacky," she said.

"I'm sorry," Peter murmured. "I didn't mean it . . . I'm sorry."

"Listen to me, both of you," Mr. Mendel said. "We all make mistakes, every one of us. But we Jews believe—and I think you Christians do, too—that if we confess our sins to Hashem, if we repent of our wrongdoings and promise to turn away from them and go in a new direction, then He will forgive us. We should make restitution for what we have done whenever possible. And sometimes there are natural consequences from our actions that must be faced. But the Scriptures say that as high as the heavens are above the earth, so great is Hashem's mercy toward us. As far as the east is from the west, so far has Hashem removed our sins from us. We can be forgiven. And then we can begin to live new lives from that day forward."

Esther knew he was right. She had just listened to the Easter message in church earlier this month. Her sins were forgiven because of Jesus' death. Peter's would be, too.

CHAPTER 48

JUNE 1945

JACOB HAD JUST STEPPED onto his porch to check his box for mail when he saw Esther skipping up the sidewalk. "They're calling this 'V-E Day,' Mr. Mendel," she said. "Victory in Europe Day." She held up the newspaper she had just purchased to show him the headline: *IT'S V-E DAY! Last German Units Yield.*

A week ago, Hitler had committed suicide. Yesterday, Germany had officially surrendered. Today, everyone celebrated. Well, nearly everyone. The Jewish community looked on in stunned horror as the secrets of the extermination camps became fully known, the death trains and gas chambers and crematoriums. The news was worse than anyone could have imagined. The battle-hardened soldiers who had liberated the camps were unable to hide their tears when they glimpsed the shriveled corpses and emaciated survivors. Jacob had made Esther promise not to look at the pictures.

Now that the Russians occupied Hungary, news slowly trickled in. Jacob had learned that Jews from the villages and provinces had been among the first to be transported to the death camps—towns such as the ones where Avraham and Jacob's brother Yehuda and most of their extended family lived. The Jews in Budapest, where his brother Baruch lived, had been deported last. Jacob tried desperately to find out about his loved ones, waiting in suspense while organizations like the Red Cross tried to locate missing people and reunite families and send word to relatives in America. These past few weeks of waiting seemed like a lifetime as Jacob braced himself for the worst.

"I guess this means your father will be coming home soon, yes?" he asked Esther.

"Yes! We'll have our daddy back again!" She opened her mailbox and removed two letters. "I was mad at him for going away and leaving us, but now I understand why he had to fight."

And poor little Peter had been angry, too. Angry enough to commit a terrible act. Jacob had learned two days ago that all charges against himself—and Peter—had been dropped. He thought it fitting that Miriam Shoshanna had saved Peter Shaffer, and now Peter Shaffer had saved him.

"When Daddy comes home I'm going to tell him that I'm proud of him," Esther said. "See you later, Mr. Mendel." She waved and ran up the stairs to her apartment. Jacob waved, then turned and opened his own mailbox.

He found a letter inside addressed to Jacob and Miriam Mendel. He recognized the handwriting immediately. It was Avraham's handwriting.

Jacob staggered and nearly fell. He leaned against the porch wall, his heart lurching with joy and hope. He turned the letter over to rip it open and saw a note in Hungarian scrawled on the back of the envelope in someone else's writing: *Our village is now in Russian hands. I am mailing this to you as I promised your son, Avraham Mendel, and trusting God that it will reach you safely.*

Jacob made his way to his apartment, holding on to the walls and doorframes for support. He sank onto the nearest chair to read the letter, written nineteen months ago.

October 1943

Dear Mama and Abba,

It has been so long since I've received a letter from you, and I know the silence must be just as hard for you to bear in America as it is for me here in Hungary. Every time I look at my little daughter and I try to imagine being separated from her, not knowing if she is well or if she is suffering, I understand how you must feel. And so after much prayer, I have decided that I must write this letter to you and trust that Hashem will allow you to receive it in America someday.

I have made friends with the minister of the Christian church here in our village. He is a very kind man, and I plan to give him this letter and ask him to mail it to you after the war ends . . .

Jacob read through the rest of the letter quickly to learn what had happened to Avraham, hungry to hear his son's voice after all this time. He would read it again when he finished, more slowly the second time.

Avi had known what Hitler was doing to the Jews, even when the rest of the world hadn't believed it. But his son hadn't lost faith in Hashem.

As the prophet Habakkuk has written: "Though the fig tree does not bud and there are no grapes on the vines, though the olive crop fails and the fields produce no food, though there are no sheep in the pen and no cattle in the stalls, yet I will rejoice in the Lord, I will be joyful in Hashem my Savior."

Avraham described how he had narrowly escaped being conscripted to work in a labor gang when all the other men in the village were taken. Afterward, Avi had decided to flee with his little family to Budapest to stay with Jacob's brother Baruch.

*I love you, Mama and Abba. And I am hoping that even
if the worst happens to us, you will receive this letter, someday.
I place all of my trust in Hashem, who is able to keep us in His
care.*

Love always,

Avraham

Two things in the letter gave Jacob hope: Avraham and his family
had been in Budapest all this time, where some Jews had managed
to survive. And his son had clung to his faith in Hashem, in spite of
everything.

Jacob hovered near his mailbox for the remainder of June, waiting
for more news from Hungary. June turned to July, and he knew from
newspaper reports that several organizations were working with the
displaced refugees in liberated Europe, trying to reunite families with
their loved ones. With millions of people unaccounted for, it was a
daunting task. In August, America dropped two atomic bombs and
Japan surrendered. The war was over at last.

Jacob had just returned from prayer at the shul on a hot August
afternoon when he found a thick envelope in his mailbox. According
to the return address, it was from the Swedish Red Cross in Hungary.
His heart pounded so hard with dread and hope and fear that he
could scarcely breathe. He hurried across the street again with the
parcel clutched to his chest and found Rebbe Grunfeld still in the
study room.

"Yaacov, what's wrong? You look as white as a ghost."

"This came in the mail for me, from Hungary. I have waited for
such a long time for news but now . . . I cannot do this alone."

"You're right, Jacob. The very worst thing you could do is read
something like that alone. We need one another. And on the day
when my letter comes, I know you will stand with me."

Jacob handed him the envelope. "Here. Read it to me, please." The
contents would be in Hungarian, a language that the rebbe also spoke.

Jacob sat down and waited for him to open it. He couldn't stop shaking, as if he were standing outside naked in a bitter winter wind.

"These look like letters, Yaacov. There are several of them."

Jacob quickly glanced at the pages. "They are not in Avi's handwriting, though. That much I can see."

"The first one begins, 'Dear Mother and Father Mendel. This is your daughter-in-law, Sarah Rivkah, writing this letter to you. Avraham asked me to keep writing to you the way he used to do so that after the war you will know what has become of us.'"

The rebbe stopped and thumbed through the packet. "There are several letters from her in here, all with different dates on them, like a diary."

"Then she and Fredeleh are alive?"

"I will read the last one for you and see."

"No, Rebbe! Wait!"

Now that news had finally come, Jacob wasn't prepared for it. He wanted to postpone his grief for a little while longer. Hearing the truth would make everything final. "Read the letters in order, Rebbe. I need to hear Sarah Rivkah's story unfold slowly, so it will be easier to bear when I learn how it ends." Jacob sat down to listen while Sarah Rivkah told her story, his heart beating as slowly and ponderously as a tolling bell.

She described how they had settled in Budapest with Jacob's brother, but eventually Avraham had been taken away to work in a forced labor gang. Before leaving, he had found a Christian orphanage that had agreed to take Fredeleh and hide her there along with other Jewish children.

"Then I can find my granddaughter there?" Jacob interrupted. "In this orphanage?"

The rebbe read a little further. "I'm sorry, Yaacov. Sarah writes that she cannot bear to be separated from both Fredeleh and Avraham. She did not take Fredeleh there."

Jacob couldn't blame her. He leaned back in the chair again to listen to the second letter, dated March of 1944, five months ago. The Nazis and Adolph Eichmann had arrived in Hungary. Sarah and the other Jews in Budapest had been rounded up and confined to the ghetto. Meanwhile, Sarah's family and Jacob's family—all of the Jews in the provinces—had been deported by train to the death camps.

The rebbe paused. "Are you all right, Yaacov? Do you need a moment?"

"I think I already knew the truth," he said quietly. "We all knew, yes? Even so, it is hard to hear."

The news in Sarah's next letter was even worse. The Nazis had come to liquidate the ghetto in Budapest. They had awakened Sarah, her mother, and Fredeleh at dawn and loaded them onto the deportation trains. But then a miracle, like the one Jacob had prayed for as he and the children had lit candles at Hanukkah: A group of Swedish men had arrived to rescue them, providing false identification papers, which the Nazis had accepted. Sarah, Fredeleh, and a little baby boy were among those who had been spared—but Sarah Rivkah's mother was taken.

The rebbe moved immediately to the next letter, which told how a Swedish diplomat named Raoul Wallenberg had used funds sent by the War Refugee Board to save as many of Budapest's Jews as he possibly could. Sarah Rivkah had found refuge in a Swedish safe house. The rebbe paused, and he and Jacob stared at each other for a moment. All the fund-raising they had done, all the prayers . . . Hashem had been at work behind the scenes.

Jacob could hear Sarah's despair on the next page as she finally took Fredeleh to the convent and surrendered her to the Christians for safekeeping. It meant that one of Jacob's family members might have survived. His little granddaughter might still be alive, even if Sarah and Avi were not. Sarah then explained that the Nazis and Adolph Eichmann had returned in November, and even the safe houses were no longer safe.

The rebbe drew a deep breath as he prepared to read the last few letters.

" 'Dear Mother and Father Mendel,

The few Jewish men who were left in Budapest—some as young as sixteen, some as old as sixty—were taken to

the outskirts of Budapest to dig earthworks to stop the
advancing Russians. We heard that the Soviet army is
moving closer and closer. Meanwhile, the Nazis have never
wavered from their plan to deport every last one of us to
the camps. But since there are no more trains, Adolph
Eichmann decided to round us up and force us to walk to
the German border, more than one hundred miles away.

They came for us on a day when the weather was bitterly cold, and we were not dressed for it. Many of us were
already weak from illness and malnutrition. The Nazis
didn't care. Anyone who collapsed with exhaustion along
the way was shot. Those who couldn't keep up were beaten
to death. Some who fell down were later found frozen to
the ground. I thought of Avraham and Fredeleh and made
myself keep walking. I don't even know how long or how
far we walked.

When I feared that I couldn't go another step, Raoul
Wallenberg arrived in his big black car like an angel from
Hashem. "Does anyone here have a Swedish passport?" he
asked. About three hundred of us were allowed to return
with him to Budapest.

I prayed that this nightmare would soon be over. We
could hear the battles raging around us in Budapest. But
once again, just as the Russians were about to set us free,
the Nazis decided to blow up the Jewish ghetto and kill
everyone in it who still remained. They took us from the
safe houses and marched us to the ghetto to die with all
the others. Again, Mr. Wallenberg intervened, warning the
Nazis that if they did this horrific deed, he would make certain that they would be charged with murder and genocide
after the war. Once again, he saved our lives.' "

Rebbe Grunfeld paused as he struggled to clear the emotion from his throat.

"So Sarah Rivkah is alive," Jacob murmured. "I owe this man, Raoul Wallenberg, a great debt. But how do you repay a man for such a thing as this that he did?"

The rebbe shook his head and turned to the next letter.

" 'Dear Mother and Father Mendel,

The war is over. The Nazis have been defeated. When I was certain that it was safe, I went to the convent to find Fredeleh. They had kept her safe and well fed, and she was overjoyed to see me. I took her home with me to the safe house and now she won't let me out of her sight. That is fine because I cannot take my eyes off of her, either. I wanted to take the baby, Yankel Weisner, home with me, too. His mother entrusted him to my care, and I fear that he may have no family left in this world. But there is barely enough food to feed Fredeleh and myself, and so for now he will be better off with the Christians.

I still don't understand why I survived when so many others did not. I cannot think about it. I must live day to day, feeding my daughter and myself, and searching for Avraham and the rest of my family.

We've learned that the Allied forces are searching for all of the Hungarians who survived the concentration camps, and when they are able to be moved they will be brought to a building here in Budapest. Fredeleh and I and the rest of us from the safe houses travel by tram to that huge old building every day to search for our families as the survivors trickle in. We hold photographs in our hands, showing them to strangers and asking, "Which camp were you in? Did you see this person or that person?" We study each other's faces, searching for a familiar one.

When relatives or friends find each other there is much rejoicing and weeping, and everyone stops to weep along with them, our hope renewed. Perhaps we will be the next lucky one to find our missing families.

We also post notices on a board with the names and descriptions and former addresses of our loved ones, asking if anyone has seen them or knows what has become of them. The returning survivors often scribble notes on these signs, saying, "We were in such-and-such a camp together," or "I saw him alive after we were liberated." And sometimes they sadly tell us that they saw our loved one being sent to the left during the selection process—to the gas chamber. But I will spend the rest of my life searching, if I have to, and never, ever give up.

All our love,
Sarah Rivkah and Fredeleh' "

Jacob drew a deep breath as the rebbe paused to turn to the next letter. He could see that the pages had dwindled down to the final few. "Are you all right, Yaacov?" the rebbe asked. Jacob nodded and asked him to continue reading.

" 'Dear Mother and Father Mendel,

Today a miracle! I found Dina Weisner, the stranger on the train who entrusted me with her son, Yankel. I had posted a notice for her on the board, and we found each other. She told me that by giving up Yankel, she unknowingly saved her own life, as well. All of the women from her train who had little children with them were sent to the left, to the gas chambers. But because Dina was young and strong and alone, she survived in a work camp. When I asked her if she knew about my mother, she nodded sadly. Mama was gone.

She is gone.

I still cannot accept the truth. I remember our last moments together on the train, and I don't understand why I survived. I am grateful to Dina for telling me about Mama. At least I am not left to wonder. But I don't know how I will go on if I learn that Avraham is gone, too.

I took Dina to the orphanage to find Yankel. She wept for joy when she finally held her baby in her arms again. We have seen so much sorrow and suffering, and now a moment of rejoicing and hope. The four of us returned to the Swedish house to live while we await word of our husbands. Every day I hope. Every day I despair. I know that you are praying along with me in America. I believe that it is your prayers that have sustained me so far.

> With love,
> Sarah Rivkah and Fredeleh' "

"Thank you for reading the letters to me," Jacob said when the rebbe finished. "I could not have faced them alone. Sarah Rivkah and Fredeleh are alive. Hashem be praised."

He stood and reached for the packet, needing to feel the letters in his hands and hold them close to his heart. He would read them again and again.

"Wait, Yaacov. There is one more . . .

" 'Dear Mother and Father Mendel,
I have found Avraham! He is alive!' "

Jacob sank to the floor and wept.

CHAPTER 49

THE WAR WAS FINALLY OVER. Every day the mail brought more good news. Penny had received a letter from Roy's father saying that Roy had been evacuated on a hospital ship to San Diego. His burns were healing, but since he still couldn't use his hands, the nurses had to write letters for him. Penny stopped to thank God when she read that his sight had recovered fully and he was able to see. The next letter said that Roy was being discharged from the hospital and from the Marine Corps, and was returning home to Sally. Penny hoped Roy would remember to send her an invitation to his wedding.

Hazel wrote to say that her two sons—Penny's half-brothers— would soon be discharged, too. She wanted Penny to meet them. It seemed like a miracle to suddenly have a family. It was something she had never imagined. Penny promised Hazel that she would visit her again after Eddie came home and Esther and Peter were back in his care. But the visit might have to wait until all of the returning servicemen had returned home. The buses and trains were so jammed with men you could hardly get a ticket.

To Penny, the best news of all was that Mr. Mendel's son had been found, emaciated but alive. The U.S. Third Army had rescued him and thirty thousand other inmates from the prison camp at Dachau, and he was recovering in a Red Cross hospital. Mr. Mendel worked night and day as he tried to process the paper work to bring his family home.

The war had turned everyone's life upside down and now victory was turning things right side up again. Penny knew that there would be a lot of changes in her life, too, in the coming months. Her boss at work had already warned the women drivers that their jobs would be given back to the men who'd had them before the war. Penny felt sad as she returned to her old ticket booth, but she understood. At least she had learned how to drive and had discovered that she really wasn't as dumb as a green bean after all.

On a beautiful September afternoon, two years after he enlisted, Eddie returned home. Once again, Penny put on her new gray suit and shoes and went with Esther and Peter to welcome their father home. This time they waited at a pier in Manhattan for his troop ship to dock. The ship overflowed with soldiers, hanging over the rails and waving ecstatically to the mob of loved ones on the pier. Penny thought there was enough joy aboard that huge ship to float it to the moon.

And here came Eddie, hurrying down the gangplank, running toward them. He might be dressed like all the other soldiers, but Penny could have spotted him anywhere. He looked as handsome as always, his curly blond hair finally growing back in preparation for civilian life. The children ran to him, and he swept them into his arms. Everyone was in tears, reunited at last.

"Welcome home, Daddy!" Peter said it loudly and clearly.

"It's so good to hear your voice, Peter. It's the best welcome home present ever. And look at you, Esther—you're so grown-up. You were a little girl when I went away and now you're a beautiful young lady."

Eddie saved a hug for Penny, and it felt good to hold on to him— alive and happy again. Then they went back to the apartment to eat the welcome-home dinner she had prepared. But as everyone sat around the table, laughing and eating and enjoying each other, Penny looked at Eddie Shaffer and saw a stranger.

It was more than simply the fact that he had been away for so long. His physical appearance, his voice, his gestures were all the same. But Penny realized that she knew nothing about him—not his favorite color or his favorite foods, not his hopes or dreams or plans for the future. Nor did he know any of hers. Her love for Eddie Shaffer hadn't been love at all, but just a foolish crush on the boy next door. For a girl who had been as sheltered and stifled and as fearful of strangers as Penny had been, the boy next door had been a safe fantasy.

They finished dessert, and Penny washed the dishes. She knew that it was time for her to leave. "You don't have to go yet, do you?" Eddie asked. "Can't you stay and visit with us for a while?"

"No, I really do need to go. You should spend time alone with your family. They deserve to have you all to yourself." She remembered how she used to make a nuisance of herself, hanging around Grandma Shaffer's house whenever Eddie and the children visited, and the memory embarrassed her. She had been a nosy, pathetic neighbor who hadn't belonged there.

The children were sad to see her go. "Thank you for taking care of us," Esther said.

Peter gave her a hug. "I wish you could stay."

"Don't worry," she said, hugging him in return. "We'll still see each other. I'll be right here in Brooklyn, a phone call away, whenever you want to talk to me."

Penny had her suitcase packed and waiting near the door. She had bought a brand-new one to carry her belongings home. Maybe she would use it to visit Hazel someday. Who knows, she might even go someplace new like Niagara Falls or Atlantic City. Penny gazed out the bus window on the way home but didn't see a thing.

"Hi, Mother. I'm home," she said as she came through the back door.

"To stay for good, I hope," Mother said with a frown. "It's high time you stopped running all around and stayed home where you belong."

Penny chose to believe that in spite of her mother's angry tone, her comments were said out of love, that she had missed Penny and was happy to have her home. One day soon she would have to explain to her mother that she didn't belong here anymore, and that she was looking for an apartment of her own. But Penny couldn't afford one yet, and finding a roommate wasn't easy. Most of the single girls from work were expecting marriage proposals now that their boyfriends had returned home from the war.

Penny gave her mother a quick hug and carried her suitcase full of belongings into her old bedroom. She would stay, for now. Until she could decide what to do next.

Three weeks later, Penny walked out of the bus station after her shift ended and saw Roy Fuller standing on the sidewalk, just ten feet away from her. She almost didn't recognize him. He had on a suit and tie instead of his marine uniform and wore his hat pulled low, half covering his face. He held one hand curled awkwardly against his side and the skin on his face looked shiny from scars, but to Penny he looked exactly the same—and she was overjoyed to see him.

"Roy!" She ran to him, throwing her arms around him, hugging him tightly. "What are you doing here?" she asked when they finally pulled apart.

"I went by the apartment and Esther told me you still worked at the bus station. She said you would be getting off work right about now."

"Oh, it's so good to see you! You look wonderful!"

"So do you."

They stood in the parking lot with buses pulling in and out and people rushing around, but Penny was only dimly aware of the activity around her. Roy gazed at her in a way that he never had before, looking right into her eyes, and it made her heart race in a way it never had before, too. She searched for something to say.

"So . . . how's everything with Sally? I'll bet she's happy to have you home again."

"I guess so." He paused, and she waited for him to continue. "People change, Penny. War changes everyone. I'm not the same person I was before the war—and neither is Sally. She says she still loves me, but I can tell she has a hard time looking at me, seeing past the scars."

"Don't talk like that, Roy. I'm sure it's you she cares about. And you're the same wonderful guy you always were. I can see that, plain as day." Again, he didn't reply. "What brings you to Brooklyn?" she finally asked.

"You do, Penny. I came to see you. Even though I was finally home with Sally, I kept thinking about you. And so I decided to come and see how you and Eddie were doing. Are you two getting together one of these days?"

Penny shook her head. "We were never together except in my imagination. All those years when I thought I loved him, I had no idea what love really was. It isn't love when it's one-sided. And that's all it ever was. Eddie didn't know I existed until I offered to take care of his kids. He's still in love with his wife, still trying to get over her."

"He said that?"

"No, but it's true. He's been very nice to me since he's been back. We've even gone a few places together with the kids, and it seems like he's finally starting to notice me after all these years. But we're starting from scratch. We still have to get to know each other and see if we have anything in common besides loving his kids. I'm not sure if we will ever fall in love . . . or if I even want to."

The conversation made Penny sad, and she didn't want to ruin their time together by feeling sorry for herself. "It's good to see you. You gave us all a scare, you know, wondering if you would recover or not."

"You know who I kept thinking about all the time I was in the hospital? You. And you know whose letters I made the nurses read to me over and over? Yours. That's when I realized how much I care about you, Penny."

Her heart beat so fast she felt dizzy. She wondered if she might faint. Had she really heard him right?

"Me? . . . But what about Sally?"

"She had a schoolgirl's crush on her teacher—me. She was thrilled when she finally got me to notice her. That's not love. I had been awkward around girls all my life, so I was thrilled to think I had won such a beautiful girl as Sally."

"She is beautiful, Roy. I saw her when I went to see your father—did

404

he tell you I came? But I didn't talk to her. I didn't want to mess things up for you."

"My father said that you showed more concern for me than Sally ever did, traveling all that way just to find out what happened to me. Sally and I never talked about things the way you and I used to do. I knew you better after only a few months than I ever knew her. Every time I went home on leave to see Sally, we had nothing to say to each other."

Penny couldn't believe what she was hearing. She must be dreaming because it was much too wonderful to be true. She pressed her hand to her chest, afraid that her heart might burst.

"But you and Sally are engaged, aren't you? You gave her a ring."

Roy gave a short laugh. "You know why she accepted my proposal? She told me it was because of my letters. She thought they were so romantic. I think you know who really wrote all of those romantic things." He laughed again. "I finally realized why I always had so much trouble telling Sally how I felt. It was because what I felt wasn't love. A man in love should have no trouble at all. Even if he's tongue-tied, he should overflow with ways to express how he feels. I never felt any of that. I was dazzled by her beauty and by the fact that she would even look twice at a guy like me."

"You're a wonderful man, Roy. Who wouldn't look twice?"

Roy didn't seem to hear her. "Sally is still so young. She has never been out of Pennsylvania, and I've been to hell and back. When I finally got home we were strangers. I think we both realized that there was nothing there. But we're both afraid to break it off and let the other person down. Especially now that I'm all scarred up this way. It's not honorable to reject your fiancé when he comes home from the war wounded."

"Honest, Roy, the scars aren't even noticeable."

"And so I decided to come and see you. You always gave me good advice where Sally was concerned. I wanted to find out if you and Eddie were making out any better than we were." He paused, ducking his head shyly. "To tell you the truth, I've been hoping that maybe things haven't been so good with Eddie."

"There's nothing there yet. And even if there was . . . I used to want to be Rachel's replacement. But now . . ."

"You shouldn't be anyone's replacement. He'd be a lucky man to have you."

"All this time I thought I was in love with Eddie, but I think I was in love with the idea of love. I guess I watched too many movies and read too many books. Now I know that love has to go both ways. It isn't love if only one person feels it."

"You know what I wish?" he asked softly. To Penny's astonishment, he began to repeat the words she had written for him so long ago. "'I wish I could put time in a bottle and throw it into the ocean. Then I would have forever to spend with you. I wouldn't need air to breathe or food to eat. Holding you in my arms would be all the food I would need. Having your love would be the only air I would need to breathe.'"

"You remembered that? After all these months?"

He nodded. "I would love to go back in time because this time I would be smart enough to see that I was falling in love with you on the crosstown bus." He held her gaze for a long moment. "What do you think, Penny?"

"I love you, too, Roy." She had never been more certain of anything in her life. She threw her arms around him and hugged him tightly, never wanting to let him go.

Then he kissed her, right there in the parking lot at the bus station, and it was her very first kiss—the one that Penny Goodrich had dreamed of her entire life. Except it wasn't Eddie Shaffer she was kissing, it was Roy.

And it was every bit as wonderful as she had imagined a kiss would be.

EPILOGUE

NOVEMBER 29, 1947

JACOB LEANED TOWARD THE RADIO, listening intently, hanging on to the announcer's every word. Avraham, Sarah Rivkah, and Fredeleh sat on the sofa together, listening along with him as the United Nations voted on a resolution to create a Jewish state in Palestine. The broadcast was live, and they listened in suspense as each nation cast its vote. Avraham kept a written tally, waiting to see if two-thirds of the U.N.'s members would decide in their favor.

And suddenly the suspense ended. It was over. The thirty-third nation voted yes to Resolution 181. The Jewish people would once again have their own nation and homeland, after nearly two thousand years of exile.

"Abba! We have seen prophecy fulfilled before our eyes," Avraham said as they laughed and wept and hugged each other. "Remember what Isaiah wrote? 'Who has ever seen such a thing? Can a country be born in a day or a nation be brought forth in a moment? Yet no sooner is Zion in labor than she gives birth to her children.' That's what just happened before our eyes. A nation—our own Jewish nation—born today."

"Out of the ashes," Jacob murmured.

It was what the prophet Ezekiel had written, as well: *"The Sovereign Lord says: O my people, I am going to open your graves and bring you up from them; I will bring you back to the land of Israel. Then you, my people, will know that I am the Lord, when I open your graves and bring you up from them."*

Hashem had shown Ezekiel a valley filled with dry bones. *"Son of man, can these bones live?"* Hashem had asked. The prophet's reply would be Jacob's reply from now on, whenever he had difficult questions for Hashem, questions that seemed to have no answers: *"O Sovereign Lord, you alone know."*

Author's Note

RAOUL WALLENBERG, A THIRTY-TWO-YEAR-OLD Swedish business-man, volunteered to go to Nazi-controlled Hungary during World War II as a diplomat in order to help rescue Jews. When he arrived in Budapest in June of 1944 he learned that the Nazis had already deported four hundred thousand Jewish men, women, and children to the death camps. With daring, courage, and ingenuity, Wallenberg tirelessly dogged the Nazis, pressuring them to accept the Swedish identification papers he created, snatching Jews from deportation trains and death marches, and providing food and shelter in "safe houses" under the protection of the Swedish flag. He is thought to have saved as many as one hundred thousand Jews who remained in Budapest.

When the Soviet army arrived to liberate Hungary, Wallenberg and his driver left Budapest on January 17, 1945, to visit the Soviet military headquarters, telling friends he planned to return in about a week. He and his driver have been missing ever since.

According to the Russians, Raoul Wallenberg died of a heart attack in a Soviet prison on July 17, 1947. But to his family and to the thousands of Jews who consider him a hero, a satisfactory explanation for his arrest and disappearance has never been given. The government of Israel designated Raoul Wallenberg as one of the "Righteous Among the Nations."

DISCUSSION QUESTIONS

WHILE WE'RE FAR APART

1) Which character did you identify with the most? Why?

2) How were the concerns for family different for each of the characters: Penny Goodrich? Esther and Peter Shaffer? Jacob Mendel? Avraham and Sarah Rivkah?

3) In what ways did various characters find their family or become part of a new "family"?

4) What similarities were portrayed between the Jewish and Christian faiths? What differences were obvious? Did your view of Judaism change in any way?

5) How did Penny's view of love change throughout the story? What contributed to that change?

6) Compare the way Penny's parents raised her with the way that the Shaffers raised Esther and Peter.

7) Why do you think Esther was drawn to the neighbor boy, Jacky

Hoffman? What drew Penny to Eddie Shaffer? Why do you think Penny and Roy Fuller became such good friends?

8) How was the theme of silence developed throughout the story? How was the theme of waiting developed? The dilemma of unanswered prayer?

9) What importance did letter-writing play in the story?

10) Did you pick up on any clues that Rachel Shaffer was Jewish? Any clues about the identity of Penny's real mother?

For additional book club resources, visit *www.bethanyhouse.com/ anopenbook*.